The Memory Keeper

By
Lisa Stowe

Published by Storyriver
Copyright © 2011 by Lisa Stowe

Cover design by youngerbookdesign.com

Chapter 1

Cody Marsh breathed through her mouth in the funeral parlor's back room, trying to avoid underlying odors that the heavily perfumed potpourri could not disguise. Instead she tasted death, scents transferring to her tongue, adhering to her throat, and forming an aching lump. Something inside had been keening for two days now, but that sound of terrified abandonment could not quite drown out the question.

What would happen if she reached out a finger and closed his mouth?

The mortician should have done something. After all, he had combed her grandfather's fine gray hair neatly, and washed away all the bodily fluids that seeped out during death. If only the man had shut Charles's mouth, her grandfather would have been able to retain some dignity. But not now.

Decorated in basic generic, the small rectangular room held a sand colored armchair that faded into thin carpet of the same non-color. Next to the chair was a glass end table with a strategically placed box of tissue. And along the back wall was the high gurney holding the body. Standing inside the doorway Cody waited for movement, for some sign that the grandfather she barely knew and greatly loved hadn't abandoned her. Instead she saw how his feet stuck out beyond the end of the stretcher. There was no dignity in that, either. Didn't the funeral parlor have a rolling bed long enough for an old man? He'd told her once he'd been well over six feet, but his back had curved with years of crawling on his hands and knees putting in carpet and linoleum and hardwood.

A fine trembling moved through her, waking up loneliness so deep she could not retreat from the abyss.

Did she want to touch him, to say something that would send the silence fleeing? What was she here for, if not to connect with him somehow, to deny this end? Why had she insisted on seeing him before he was cremated? There was nothing left to forge more history with, to hang on to. Her grandfather was gone.

The trembling deepened until her breath shuddered out. She stepped back against the door, fumbled behind her for the knob, and left what might have been.

Carpet muffled Cody's dragging footsteps as she reluctantly followed an umbilical cord of a hallway toward her mother. The dry air charged her cropped red hair with electricity and she could feel the curls she tried to kill with scissors tightening and cringing like her emotions. She headed toward what was left of her life and what had always been.

Her mother overflowed the boundaries of a chair next to the mortician's desk, arms folded and resting on the round shelf of belly. Wadded tissue peeked between thick fingers that were growing around rings, but no tears were visible in the folds of May Marsh's plain face. Her white hair failed to mute the bright pink and green flowered caftan she wore.

"All done then?"

"Except for the bill," Cody said, testing, waiting to see what her mother would do.

"Of course," May said. "If you could hand me my purse, Cody?"

Cody crossed the room and picked up the large handbag from where it rested next to her mother's swollen feet. She placed the purse in May's lap and retreated to the doorway again, distancing herself. If she signed nothing, had no part in paperwork, then maybe none of this would be real. She waited, craving solitude, while her mother and the mortician moved through the formalities.

"Could you help me up, Cody?" asked May as the leather portfolio closed, the business of death concluded.

Obediently, Cody took her mother's hand and heaved her up, feeling the warmth she knew would have been missing from her grandfather's fingers. If she'd had the courage to touch him, that is. Maybe she should have. Maybe reality would have sunk in with the feel of his chilled flesh.

Outside, the rain fell in slanting sheets blown by a cold wind, as if fall had arrived with death. Zipping her dark green fleece, Cody ran for her old Subaru and drove it to the entrance where her mother waited, sheltered from the late afternoon storm.

"Since we're in town, do you mind going by the grocery store so I can pick up a few things?" May asked, wheezing as she extended the seatbelt as far as it would go and buckled it. "And I thought maybe we could go to McDonald's. And I wanted to rent some movies, since we'll be right by the store. I'm in the mood to watch a romance."

"I need to get home," Cody said in rare defiance. "But I'll run you through a drive-up."

"There's nothing you need to get home for," May said. "It's Friday night. I know you don't have plans."

"I want to go through my grandfather's things."

"Grandfather. It's not like you knew Charles or anything. I've spent twenty three years doing more for you than he ever did." Embedded lines of disappointment bracketed May's mouth. Now her lips crimped down deeper into those old cracks. "If he wanted to be your grandfather he should have been around all your life. Just like his son should have stuck around. I'd be a lot better off right now if I'd never even met your father."

"I'm sorry dad abandoned you." Cody's hands ached from strangling the steering wheel, saying the familiar words she had repeated over many years, well trained in what her mother needed to hear. "My grandfather would have come sooner if he could have found us. It says a lot that he was looking."

The words resonated in heart-pain. Her grandfather. Hers, so briefly.

"So he says. Personally I doubt he spent all that time looking for you. I'm just glad this business is over." May poked Cody's shoulder with a thick finger. "There's McDonalds. After that the grocery store won't take long."

Cody bit her tongue, tasting the familiar futility. Underneath, guilt tried to suffocate the growing dissatisfaction. After all, she did love her mother. But she loved her grandfather as well, and how could she tell him when he was dead? Yes, she'd only known him a couple months, but she'd treasured the evenings when he had shared stories of his childhood, his steady voice bringing a world to life she had never known. How could she show him she had listened, had absorbed, had swallowed his words as his life opened up what lacked in hers? There had to be ways she could cling to him. There had to be more stories somewhere, people who had known him. Cheated out of time with him, she craved more.

His stories about growing up in the mining town of Wallace, Idaho echoed in her memory. How long before she forgot the sound of his voice? If that happened he would truly be gone. How could she prevent more loss? Would the town he grew up in hold anything of him still, after all these years? If she found his history, maybe she'd find a way to build her future.

"I'm going to take some time off," Cody said softly, under the rustle of paper bags and the snick of her mother's jaw as she bit into her first burger, filling the car with the scents of onions and grease.

"Don't be silly." May had always had excellent hearing.

"I am, Mom." Cody might pay for the disobedience later, but right now the words felt right. As did the decision.

"I'm going to Wallace."

Chapter 2

Cody was at the end of her seven-hour drive from western Washington. There was a tiny bubble of excitement deep inside, almost too ephemeral to acknowledge. She climbed out of the car and stretched, surveying the town. The mountains crowded in, bending to watch Wallace and she doubted anyone with claustrophobia could live here. To the west, tall columns supported a surprisingly graceful arc of highway, coursing over a town refusing to join the present. She had never seen a road that so physically dominated a place, with cars flying overhead like migrating birds. Wallace itself looked like it had stopped moving some time in the 1800's, bypassed by the modern world above the gorge it rested in.

She locked the car and shoved the keys into her jeans pocket, along with her wallet. The buildings were snugged up to the very edge of the sidewalk where she stood, their false fronts adding to the image of rough frontier days. As did the man walking toward her, with his too long hair, well used hat, and heavy coat. Cody stepped back against the side of her car but he touched the brim of his hat with two fingers as he passed. The old world gesture was comforting, as if she'd just been granted permission to be there.

A cool breeze, scented with coming rain, eddied around Cody. On the canyon walls above town, swathes of brilliant fall gold swept through the trees. They looked like evergreens but she had never heard of ones that changed color. Whatever the trees were, they glowed through the gray day like welcoming candlelight.

Cody stood on the curb, overwhelmed by her reasons for being there. She was twenty three. It wasn't like she was a teenager running away from home. Yet she couldn't stifle the guilt. When May combined silence with a profound sadness in her eyes, Cody knew she had once again broken her mother's heart. And May had been very silent when Cody left, using her most powerful tool, perfected over the years. Still, after braving all that to get here, Cody had no idea what to do first, as if she still needed May to make decisions for her.

Now that Wallace had become a place of reality and not a goal, she feared she'd made a mistake. Had she been stupid to think she could come to a town and find the history of one man, now dead? What could she do, stop people to ask if they'd known a man named Charles? If it had taken him years to find her, how could she learn more about him in her allotted two week vacation? Her earlier ideas evaporated as she stood in the street by her car. What was it she had planned so easily while driving? She rubbed her thumb across her fingernails, struggling to recall the mental list she'd made. Dusk dropped rapidly down the sides of the mountains and the air grew chilly. Her stomach rumbled loudly.

She ran her hands through her hair to make sure no curls were exposing themselves, and crossed the street to a glass fronted deli. Tomorrow would be a better time to start her search anyway. The decision to postpone talking to strangers relieved her, since she didn't know what she hoped to find. She'd planned to look for people with stories to tell, but maybe she could simply figure out where her grandfather had lived and take pictures of the places he had been. Maybe that would be enough.

Cody pushed through the glass deli door and took her place in line behind a dark haired man in khakis and denim shirt and the most exotic woman Cody had ever seen. Tall, lean, and graceful, with long, shining black hair and high cheekbones that etched her cultural history on her face, she should have been gracing a magazine cover. Instead, she was a ragbag mixture of layered tie-dyed handkerchief skirts and a man's plaid coat several sizes too big.

"Oh you and your logic. You see this?" The woman held up her necklace, a leather thong supporting what appeared to be a hooked piece of claw, three or four inches long. The man did not pull back or even look at the necklace, but watched the woman calmly. Even so Cody backed away from potential conflict.

The woman held the menacing piece of jewelry across her palm as if a sacrifice as she continued. "This is a claw from a grizzly bear. It's been in my family for generations. When there were still grizzlies here. Before all your mining destroyed their habitat."

"Oh come on, Rivers," the man said. "Mining can't be blamed for the scarcity of grizzlies. Talk to hunters and loggers."

The woman lowered the thong with its claw and shoved her hair back, exposing a long black feather hanging from a silver post in one ear. "No matter. I still want you to promise to never open another mine."

"Right," the man said, lifting the claw and inspecting it before lowering it back to her chest and touching it lightly with his fingertips. "Look at this from my point of view."

"Why should I?" she asked, untying a leather bag that hung around her slender waist.

"I'm buying," the man said, pushing away the money she pulled out. "Look at my point of view so you won't be as narrow minded as you accuse me of being."

"Oh, I don't think you're narrow minded," she said, patting his cheek. "Stubborn maybe. But surely you realize what a Judas job you have? You're a mine engineer. You've seen what an environmental ghost town Burke is. And now you're helping to open another mine."

"Pay me more than I'm making now."

"I'm serious Jim. You need to listen to me."

"I know," he said. "That's why I'm having dinner with you."

"Here's your order, Rivers," said a waif-like, multi-pierced young woman behind the deli counter.

The man took the bag, and the pair left, with the girl behind the counter sighing heavily as the door shut.

"She's, like, so smart. She helped me write an essay on the impacts of environmentalists chaining themselves to trees to prevent logging."

"Oh?" Cody said, clueless about what a proper response should be.

"Oh yeah. She's chained herself to, like, lots of stuff. So what can I get for you?"

Cody placed an order for turkey and Havarti on sourdough, and picked up a bag of chips to go with it, knowing her mother would make a comment about plump people eating chips. She ignored the guilt and waited, standing stiffly, unsure how to be still and fit in a strange place.

The door was pushed open and a young man in the gray-green uniform of a forest ranger came in with the freshness of cold, damp air. His curly red hair and freckles rivaled hers and she cringed. Had he been told when he was little that freckles were the result of walking too close behind cows, like her mother had told her? Had boys sat behind him on the school bus spitting in his hair and snickering that people with red hair came from the Land of the Weird? Her shoulders bowed slightly under the weight of past humiliation.

"Hey gorgeous," he said to the girl behind the counter. "I've got a huge order here." He handed over a piece of paper torn from a green stenographer's notebook.

The girl looked at the paper and laughed. "Geez, Kelly. You guys, like, starving or what?"

"We've been helping Search and Rescue rappel a climber off Desolation since this morning." He winked at the girl. "We've worked up an appetite."

"I've got an order ahead of you but it won't take long. Do you, like, want to hang around or you want me to call the station when your stuff's ready?"

"I'll hang around."

He turned back to Cody and she resisted the urge to step away, managing a tentative smile. She was more used to casual dismissal than eye contact or conversation.

"Haven't seen you here before. Visiting?" His hazel eyes were framed by deep laugh lines.

Nodding, a blush heated Cody's cheeks and she hoped her limited response would end the polite conversation. But then she remembered her grandfather's weathered face and her goal. If she wanted to find out about him, she'd have to talk.

"My grandfather grew up here." She rubbed her fingernails. "I want to see a few of the places he told me stories about, maybe find someone who knew him."

"Yeah? What was his name?" He leaned against the deli counter and put his hands in his pockets, as if settling in for a long visit.

"Charles Mogen."

"Doesn't ring a bell," he said. "But I've never been good with names. You should try the museum. Or maybe talk to my sister. She knows a lot about the history of this place. She's the mayor."

"There have been, like, Naylor's here for generations, right Kelly?" The girl behind the counter gestured toward the windows with a spatula and mayonnaise splatted to the counter.

"From the beginning," he said. "My grandfather thought I should be mayor, but I can't get into politics. Kendra, my sister, loves it though. Tell you what. Give me your name and where you're staying and I'll see if she has time to meet with you. She's kind of a pain, but she'd be a good resource."

He pulled a battered steno pad from a back pocket and flipped through pages covered in sprawling handwriting until he found an empty space. Next came an obviously chewed on pencil from the same pocket.

"Cody Marsh," she blurted out, flustered by his friendliness. "I'm not sure what room I'm in yet, but I'm staying at the Maggie's Rest Motel."

"Here's your order, Cody." A white paper bag appeared on the top of the deli counter.

Kelly reached it down, handing it to Cody. "I'll tell my sister. Good luck on that whole grandfather thing."

Cody thanked him and his attention returned to the girl behind the counter leaving her relieved as his cheerful energy found a new focus.

"Did you hear about that wild man, like, living up above town somewhere?" the girl asked.

"Yeah, hikers have reported seeing someone," Kelly said as Cody opened the door, moving toward escape. "Who knows, maybe it's Bigfoot."

Outside, Cody sat in the Subaru staring at her tightly clasped fingers. Why was it always so hard to be around people? She always messed it up. Through all her school years, she had followed others and failed the social skills. And here she was failing again.

The familiarity of her car and the security its enclosed space offered soothed her. Kelly had smiled at her hadn't he? He'd even offered assistance. Maybe she'd done okay after all. Her knuckles cracked as worry eased from her hands, and she picked up the directions to the motel, scanning them before pulling out onto Bank Street. Many of the businesses she passed were either closed for good, or closed for the non-tourist season. The town seemed half-alive or hibernating, as if waiting for the next silver boom to open mines and bring people back. Whatever the reason, Cody needed the tranquility.

The motel was a single story rambling building that had the look of something forgotten and left out in the rain. The roof sprouted growths of moss, and algae dusted the weathered boards of the siding. Cody wondered if she'd made a mistake, until she saw the inside was neat and clean, though the carpet was wearing thin between the door and the desk. The furniture had that settled, comfortable look of pieces that hadn't moved in generations and the walls were rough cut boards decorated with old sepia photos.

The older woman at the desk told her the place was practically empty, and blamed the time of year, with dampness and chill coming. She continued on the theme of bad weather as Cody signed in, and then settled back into an armchair with a tabloid paper. Cody picked up the key and escaped to what would be her sanctuary for two weeks, a room with a name on the door rather than a number. The Maggie's Rest clung to its origins as a brothel, and she unlocked the door to 'Sparrow's' room.

The bed sagged noticeably as Cody sat on it. She leaned against the pile of pillows and looked out the window at the parking lot. Beyond it, she could see the mountains climbing in steep folds up and away, disappearing into thick gray clouds. The first day at home that she had spent with her grandfather, he had gazed up into the heights of the Cascade Mountains as they walked an old logging road together.

"This reminds me of where I grew up," he had said. "The way this place sits right down in the ravines. Bet there was lots of mines here in the old days."

"All over," Cody said, taking personal pride in his recognition of the surrounding beauty. "Mainly silver and copper, some garnets."

"Just like Wallace. Some copper, a little gold, but mostly silver and zinc. Hard living, mining. Mind you, my father, your great grandfather, was a railroad man, not a miner. Probably rode the rails when he left us."

Tears pricked at the corners of Cody's hazel eyes. He tossed out words about family and history as if they were unimportant, and she caught them in the air, grabbing them as the precious gems they were. Family. Blood and generations and connections she hadn't known she had. A foundation, a place to be from, people of her own.

"He left? Your dad?" Cody asked, trying to palm wetness from her cheeks without his noticing. "Like mine did, just taking off?"

"I suppose it was like that. He and my mother were always scrapping. Of course, she wasn't an easy woman to live with. My son…well, he wasn't easy to live with, either. Maybe I can make up for you not having a father around. I know what that was like."

Cody turned from the memories as she watched darkness seep down between trees to cover Wallace with night. There had been a sameness there binding them with more than just words. Her grandfather had been her connection to family, but with him gone, that tenuous link seemed stretched too thin to hold her. He died before she had been able to meet any of the relatives he had talked about, and she didn't think she would be able to seek out strangers without him as a buffer.

After eating her sandwich and relishing each chip, Cody ran hot water into the bath and took the new Dana Stabenow mystery with her, reading while she soaked away the grime of travel and stress of being alone in a strange place. Steam rose around her and putting the book aside, she sank to her chin glad to be short enough to submerge. She thought of the red haired forest ranger and the deli girl, and realized she envied their easy camaraderie. It was something she had never experienced, being, as her mother often explained in kinder moments, invisible to men.

She had two full weeks of solitude away from the demands of May. There was guilty pleasure in that and she closed her eyes, letting warm water soothe away all the little cuts and digs her mother's words had created over the past few days. May's silent treatment the last day had made it clear she felt Cody should stay at home. But rare defiance had helped Cody down the road. Her grandfather would have been proud of her. And on top of that, she'd managed to talk to the forest ranger without mangling it up too badly.

Maybe she could do this after all.

Chapter 3

It was late morning but little was open as Cody walked along Bank Street, the gray misty weather contributing to empty streets. At the end of one, a rundown gas station sat against the canyon wall. It was a throwback to a generation long gone, with its individual rounded-top pumps and lack of anything computerized or digital. Seeing lights on, Cody went in, squeezing through narrow aisles and past displays of postcards to reach the counter.

"Help you?" A young man with long wispy black hair and black eyeliner flipped shut a cell phone with a finger circled by a tiny piece of studded black leather.

"Please. Do you happen to know if this gas station was owned by an Italian back in the 1940's?" Cody unzipped her fleece as the warmth of the room seeped in, put her hands in her jeans pockets, and then shifted to interlacing her fingers behind her back.

"That's what my boss told me when I got this job a few weeks ago. I just moved from Bozeman so I'm still learning the area. Cool rock climbing routes." The cell phone vibrated with a high pitched sound like an insane mosquito.

"Rock climbing?" Cody asked, shoulders slumping. She couldn't climb rocks. She wasn't sure she could hike without a heart attack. She was more of a walking, picnicking sort.

"Oh yeah, man. There's some real challenging routes, like Tempitchuous. Get it? Tempitchuous?"

"No." The conversation had become an errant child and Cody had no idea how to rein it back in.

"Oh. Well, it's a 5.10 climb with bitchin' pitches. The Climb Naked guys named it. Play on words."

"Climb Naked?" Cody asked.

"Oh man, I don't walk naked, let along climb. These guys are a club of nudist climbers."

"Sounds…uncomfortable." Warmth started creeping across her cheekbones.

"No shit, man. Oh, sorry, hope that didn't offend you. But think about it. Climbing a cliff with no gear and your…well, your, uh, manly parts hanging out there all vulnerable."

Cody's warm cheeks ignited and heat spread rapidly, as if her face had become a neon sign shouting embarrassment.

"Anyway, if you're looking for the Italian that used to own this place he's probably dead. He'd be an old guy now."

"I was looking for a hiking trail that's supposed to be behind his gas station."

"It's here. Pretty steep though," he said, as his cell phone vibrated again and he flipped it open to study the screen.

Cody ignored the apparent doubt in his voice that she could handle a steep hike. She had long ago resigned herself to the fact that her weight would spread out better if she was five foot five instead of five foot none. Her mother had told her many times that weight was genetic and Cody was destined to be just like May. She had accepted that as gospel for so many years it didn't hurt anymore. Either that or she'd developed pretty thick scar tissue.

"Is the trail head obvious if I go back there?" she asked. "Do I need a trail pass or anything?"

"Yep and nope. But I wouldn't go up there if I were you."

"Why is that?" Cody asked, edging for the door.

"Dude, some wild man's living up there. They're saying he's some nut but lots of people have seen him, or heard him, or something."

"Is he supposed to be violent?" asked Cody, remembering the conversation at the deli. The ranger had said something about a guy living in the woods.

"Who knows?" He shrugged, thumbs busy texting on the cell. "But I sure wouldn't take no chance."

"Well, thanks for the advice but I think I'll go anyway. My grandfather hunted a cougar up that trail once when he was a boy."

Cody hoped she didn't sound like she was bragging, but at the same time she wanted to claim the connection, to prove she had a right to be there.

"Yeah? Cool. Not that I'm into hunting. I'm vegan. Except when I go home. Mom makes this killer beef teriyaki. All homemade and man, there's nothing better. She gave me the recipe but I can't buy the meat."

"Really?" Cody said, then paused at the door. "Say, do you know what the gold trees are? The ones that look like they have evergreen needles but are changing color?"

"Sure. Tamaracks, though some call them larches," he said, lifting his chin in farewell as the insane mosquito in his cell phone diverted him again.

Cody left the man to his call, reaching to pull open the door, but as she did so someone outside propelled it inward. The door slammed against her hand, flexing it backward.

"Ouch!" She pulled her hand to her chest.

The man barely glanced at her as he pushed past a display of baseball hats, knocking it over. Cody backed up against a cooler of bottled water. She recognized him as the same one she'd seen when she first arrived. The one who had touched his hat and made her feel welcome.

"What the hell's going on, Cell?" he said, slamming his hands down on the counter.

"Uh…it's raining?"

Cody reached for the door. She didn't want to be inside and near this stranger's rage.

"I thought you were supposed to be doing something."

"I am, man, really." The clerk looked over the man's shoulder at Cody. "It's cool. Nothing to worry about."

Cody had the door open and stood in the empty space. "No police?"

"Police? What the hell for?" the man asked. "What have you done now, Cell?"

"Nothing! She doesn't know you. She probably thinks you're going to rob the place or something."

"I'm not going to rob anything. But I am going to get some answers. Aren't I?"

"Oh man, come on."

Cody slipped outside and went around the end of the building where she leaned against the stucco wall under the eaves, waiting for her thudding heart to ease. The gas station was run down from the front, and even more so from the back, signs of age and hard use obvious in the piles of rusting metal and bins of crushed aluminum cans. The mist thickened to a soft rain and she watched it fall, listening for sounds from inside. If it got loud in there she would find a phone. But when the quiet continued she left the shelter, heading for the trailhead a few feet away. The cell phone man had been right that it was easy to spot. He'd also been right about the steepness and she was out of breath within moments of entering the twilight of forest shadows.

And her grandfather, nine years old, had tracked a cougar here through deep snow.

"The bounty for a cougar back then was fifty dollars." His voice echoed in her memory. "And that was a lot of money. So I went out every day, tracking that big cat, up behind this old gas station owned by an Italian. But I kept losing the tracks in this clearing. What I didn't know was that old cat tracked me back out every time. And the Italian saw the cougar come out at the trailhead a few minutes after me. So one day he waits, and when I come back out, he ups and shoots the cougar and collects the bounty."

"Did he split it with you?" Cody asked.

"Nope."

"So you never got your money?" Indignation on the part of a little boy now long grown, over an event now long over, surfaced in Cody's voice.

"Well," her grandfather said, chuckling low, "I'm not saying I never saw no money out of the deal. Somehow there was a rockslide that broke out all the windows in back of the station. And replacing windows just happened to be my job. Though mainly for one local bordello."

"What?"

"A house of ill repute. The madam, Ethel, owned this classy place called the Silver Haven. She was one special lady. Watched out for me when I was growing up."

"Weren't you kind of young for hauling windows around?"

"No, Ethel's windows were Bavarian, lots of tiny squares. Anyway, that rockslide, like I said, broke out the Italian's windows, and he hired me to replace them. So I made some money out of it. Though not the fifty I'd dreamed of."

Looking down the steep trail now, Cody could make out the gas station through the thick evergreens. Everything matched her grandfather's words, and story became truth as she stood there in the rain. Oral tradition cemented her to a history she had only dreamed of as she turned back to climb. She would see how far she could get. Charles had said he always lost the cougar in a clearing. Would the place still be there?

Cody pushed upward, climbing the rocky ground until she was breathless and sweaty in spite of the cool day. Her coat sleeve was wet with rain, but she swiped it across her forehead anyway. And heard voices. Her tenuous connection to Charles dissipated with the intrusion of other hikers. She stood watching movement on the trail above her coalesce into two men, trespassers in her memories.

The ranger from the deli led the way, his hair glowing in the mist like the autumn leaves falling around them. Behind him a short muscular man with dreadlocks, jeans, and camouflage jacket scanned the trees along the trail.

"I'll talk to the other rangers." Kelly massaged his jaw with the knuckles of one hand as if he had a toothache. "You know the gossips in town are saying some wild man is living up here in the woods."

"No problem. Keeps people out of my way."

"True, but we don't want people scared off, either. Or locals deciding to go hunting a lunatic."

The man with Kelly caught sight of Cody and stopped, simply watching her. When Kelly noticed, he followed his companion's gaze and his easy grin spread out over the previous seriousness.

"Hey, Cody, right? Looking for our local wild man here?"

"No," she said, overwhelmed again by Kelly's good will. "My grandfather told me about hiking this trail so I wanted to see it."

"Grandfather?" the stranger said, stepping around Kelly. "When was he here?"

"The 1940's."

"Too early to have anything to do with what I'm looking for." He waved her off with a dirt engrained hand.

"So what are you looking for then?" Cody asked, feeling a tiny flash of irritation.

He was silent long enough that Cody thought he would ignore her, but finally he shrugged as if shedding her question. "My father spent time up here, too."

As he moved downhill past Cody she caught a whiff of dirt, pine needles and male sweat and she looked to Kelly, raising an eyebrow.

"I know," Kelly said, rubbing his jaw again. "He's different. On a quest, kind of like you. Seems one of those types who just doesn't like being around people. He's not breaking any laws, so I guess he'll be here a while."

"That won't bother me," Cody replied.

Kelly squeezed her shoulder lightly. "Good girl," he said, his easy grin resurfacing. "Never let ghost stories or wild men keep you out of the woods."

He headed down the trail after the stranger, and Cody watched until they were out of sight. She brushed her shoulder briefly with cold fingertips, feeling where his hand had been, before walking deeper into the woods. Kelly had touched her casually as if the merest gesture between friends and Cody realized she had been touched by a man who had shown only a relaxed friendliness and no judgment. Twenty three years old and she couldn't remember if she'd ever had a man do that before. He probably had no idea his trivial gesture had thrown her completely off balance. She didn't know whether to laugh or cry, to be thrilled or ashamed.

The trail climbed through tamarack, cedar, and pine, the gold and green needles catching misty rain and releasing plopping drops as Cody pushed to put distance between the two men and her confusion. A creek next to the path rushed downhill effortlessly as she struggled uphill next to it, gasping for air. To distract herself she tried to imagine what it must have been like for a boy, carrying his absent father's rifle, breaching waves of deep snow under these same trees. And Charles had done that for over a mile. While Cody, whose struggles were with cold and rain and her body's rebellion against upward movement, only wanted the mile to be over.

She passed through the small clearing before realizing what had happened. It was the subtle change in light that penetrated her self-centered haze of hiking misery. Here evergreens gave way to a stand of tamarack, bright and gold as if she stood in sunshine instead of misty grayness. This grove had obviously been more open in an earlier time, but years were slowly allowing the forest to reclaim what was its own. Here, her grandfather had lost cougar tracks. It was easy to recreate the scene, imagining it as if she had been there.

Her breathing slowed as she waited for something to happen. She didn't know if she sought some sort of inherited recognition of place, or simply confirmation. The memory of Charles's story needed something physical to go with it though, so Cody pulled out a small digital camera, snapping a few pictures. She tried to imagine a small boy in snow, tried to find something that would bring her grandfather to this place with her. The rain tap danced on leaves, soaking into ground both she and her grandfather had stood on. And yet she could feel nothing beyond the moment. She realized she had been half hoping for some mystical connection to pop into existence, pointing the way to Charles. Embarrassed by her fanciful weakness, she pocketed the camera.

The quiet cirque was peaceful as Cody crossed it and entered the denser tree line, starting back. In some ways, she could understand what kept Kelly's wild man up here in his hermit existence. Her social skills were totally inept, too, unless she was at work and could hide within the scripted role of a receptionist. But she longed too much for acceptance to be a hermit. And there was another reason why she could never be one. Who would take care of her mother?

A few feet from the grove, Cody heard a faint snap. She paused, straining to hear over her own breathing but the sound wasn't repeated. Maybe it had been some wild animal out in the trees. She continued down the trail, wondering if it had been wise to not carry bear spray or something similar, and the vision of stalking cougars pushed her downhill faster.

Quiet descended with her. The breeze remained behind in the high places, and the stillness was as unnatural as her presence in the forest. She had overstayed her welcome, and fought the urge to run.

Cody rounded the corner of a switchback and stumbled, her hand going to the rough bark of a tamarack for the balance and security its substance offered. She was being silly letting an unfamiliar place make her feel like an interloper. Catching her breath, she reluctantly stepped out from the tree.

Coming up the trail was the wild man. Cody, caught short by his appearance, jumped when he fell to one knee. Fully expecting him to stand back up embarrassed, she waited awkwardly for him to laugh his clumsiness off. Instead, he crumpled to the ground.

"Hey!" Cody ran forward. "Are you okay?"

Struggling, he managed to partially rise before collapsing again. Scared now, Cody bent over him.

"What's wrong?" she asked, words leaving her mouth seconds before her brain registered what she saw. "Oh god," she said, hands shaking violently. "You're bleeding!"

It wasn't just that he was bleeding. It was more like he was emptying. A large fist sized hole opened up his back, with a smaller hole in his chest where blood pulsed through, soaking his clothes, seeping thickly down to mix with earth and rain. His voice was heavy liquid.

"Get..."

"Get help," Cody said for him, standing. She'd have to run for the gas station. Why hadn't she purchased a cell phone before leaving, like she had debated doing?

"No," he said, grasping her ankle with red fingers. "Get...away."

"Don't talk," Cody said, not sure why. It seemed to be what people always said in emergencies.

She stripped off her coat, jerked it off her hands where the damp material clung, and draped it over him, as much to keep him warm as to hide the obscenity his chest had become. "I'm going for help. Hang on." More clichés and she realized the phrases slipped in when there was nothing else one could do.

Cody sprinted down hill, rounded a corner, and stopped so abruptly her momentum carried her to the ground next to Kelly. He was face down in the middle of the path, his outstretched hand inches from her knee.

"Kelly?"

He wasn't covered in blood. Maybe he'd just knocked himself out or something. Maybe he'd wake up and know what to do, would tell her he'd take care of everything. But when she reached for him, she saw the small hole in the center of his back.

Terror flooded through her, wiping out all emotion, until she was as silent and empty as the woods around her, a wild animal gone into hiding. No, not completely gone. Some thoughts were still present. She knew with a heightened certainty, that someone stood in the green light of the woods, watching her through the mist. Had someone tracked these two just like the long dead cougar had hunted her grandfather?

Shaking, afraid to look over her shoulder, she reached for Kelly, feeling for a pulse in his neck, even though she wasn't sure she was in the right spot. The odd flaccid feel of his skin, the stillness of the hand stretched out, told her she wouldn't find any sign of life. She fumbled around his uniform belt until she located the radio. Never having used one before, she turned what looked like the appropriate knob.

"Hello?" she said into plastic and electronics, with no real belief her voice would carry across distance to help. "If anyone can hear this, two people have been shot. One is still alive, but I think..." her insides were waking up, coming back to life, reacting with nausea and uncontrollable tremors. "Oh god, I think Kelly's dead. Please come quickly. Please help me. I don't know what to do." Dropping the radio, she gagged, cold hands pressed against colder lips.

"State your position," a female voice crackled loudly over the radio.

Grabbing it up with fumbling fingers, she hit the same button as before. "A trail behind an old gas station at the end of town. We can't be too far up the path." She paused, thoughts plummeting around in her brain, screaming for her to do something. "Should I come down and lead you in?"

"Are you in a safe position? Is the shooter visible?"

"I think it's safe. I don't see anyone else." She felt someone near, but knew the words would sound crazy.

"Then stay where you are," said the woman. "Stay with the radio. We'll be there in minutes."

Minutes. Help. People to take over, to save the stranger, to take control. Cody sat, wrapping arms around her knees, hugging them to contain the quaking. She dropped her head, eyes closed against death, and never heard help arrive, until a hand touched her hair and a voice spoke.

"Are you hurt?"

Jumping violently at the sudden contact, she looked up, catching a brief glance of a ranger uniform and blond hair, before focusing on the man's green eyes.

"Are you hurt?" he asked again.

Trembling so hard she bit her tongue, she simply shook her head.

"The one still alive?"

"Up the trail," she managed to shudder out. "Not far."

He straightened, leaving her at a run, and someone else dropped a wool blanket over her shoulders. The previously silent woods were full of sounds as people swarmed, radios crackled, voices overlapped. Help had arrived. But as Cody watched the tall ranger come back down the trail, shaking his head and gesturing, she knew it had come too late.

Chapter 4

Clutching a mug of tea, Cody struggled to remember details of something she wanted only to forget. She steadied herself with a hand on the back of a cold aluminum chair, and then sat down on it slowly. The metal bit into her and muddy water from her rain soaked jeans dripped onto the cracked linoleum floor of the small conference room in the ranger station. The tall ranger sat nearby, elbows on knees, fingers buried in his hair, not speaking. One of the shortest women Cody had ever seen bounced on her tiptoes where she stood near the man. Coiled blonde springs danced against her shoulders with each skip, and her constant motion made the cold room feel even smaller.

A Native American woman with a no-nonsense black braid as smooth as oil sat behind a battered metal desk. She watched the bouncing blonde with a deep calmness in her dark eyes, but she tapped her pen on the desk as if it was full of jumping beans rather than ink.

"Feeling better?" she asked.

Cody shook her head.

"Can you answer some questions?"

"Yes."

The woman stopped tapping the pen. "I'm Jess Hawking, detective with the Shoshone County Sheriff's Department. Ranger Matt Tanner, Ranger Hailey Cutler with the Wallace Ranger Station. Let's start with seeing if you remember touching anything."

"I touched Kelly's belt," Cody said. "To find his radio."

"What about Nate Johnson?" Jess asked, tapping the pen again.

"Who?"

"The man with Kelly."

"Oh. I never knew his name. I covered him with my coat, but I don't remember touching him."

"And tell me again what he said."

"I thought he was telling me to get help, but he said for me to get away." She twisted the mug back and forth between her hands.

"You never heard gunshots or saw anyone else?" Jess asked, taking notes instead of tapping.

Cody's response must have been too slow in coming, as Jess looked up.

"No, I never heard anything, or saw anyone. But...well, I thought someone was watching me. Through the trees, uphill."

"Wood jitters," Hailey said. "It happens to people inexperienced in the woods. Probably a squirrel."

"Or probably not," Jess said. "We have a team combing the area. If someone was there, we'll find something."

"I'm wasting my time here," Matt said, jerking his coat off the back of the chair so hard the chair rocked against the desk.

"Then go, Ranger Tanner," Jess said, tossing her pen down. "I'll continue from this end and we'll meet late this afternoon." She pinched the bridge of her nose and closed her eyes a moment. "I know this is hard Matt, but procedure will solve this not rage."

"Don't patronize me, Hawking. I'm not some newbie."

"I didn't say you were, and we've worked enough cases together that you should know by now I respect your strengths. You're better in the field. I'm better in the office. Besides, this happened on forest service land. You're the lead agency. So get out of here."

Matt's green eyes passed over Cody and their lack of expression was as chilling as his voice. This was more than the casual dismissal she was used to. This was blame. Shivering in the frost emanating from him, Cody watched the door shut behind the man.

There was a moment's silence as if the detective gave the air in the room time to warm up before she leaned back in her chair.

"He hired and trained Kelly."

"I'm sorry," Cody responded, feeling guilty without knowing why.

"Speaking of Matt," Hailey said, finally holding still. "You shouldn't have sent him out like that. You're basically putting him in charge of the forest service end of this investigation."

"Yes, Hailey. I am aware of that."

"Then I assume you're also aware of the mistake you're making in not taking proper advantage of the resources available."

Jess tilted her chair back, watching the ceiling. "No, Hailey."

"Look Detective Hawking, this is a serious mistake. Use your resources."

"No, Hailey."

"Ranger Tanner has been doing this job too long. You and I both know he hates it. I've just finished my forensic training."

Jess straightened and the chair thudded to the linoleum with a sharp exclamation. "I said no, Hailey. Matt's experienced. You're not. Plus, he's your supervisor. You want to work an investigation as a lead someday, you should shadow Matt now and learn from him instead of going behind his back."

Hailey bounced onto her toes again, hands on her hips. "Oh, I'll shadow Matt. And when he screws up I'll be there to fix it and solve this." She bounced, spun, and stormed out of the room.

"You do that," Jess said to the door that slammed behind Hailey.

The sudden stillness in the room was a relief. Cody stared hard at the scum forming over her cooling tea, wondering if she should ignore the conflict or try to come up with something to ease the fallout. Undecided and uncomfortable, she said nothing.

"God I get grumpy when shit like this happens." Jess sighed heavily, planting her elbows on the table. "Okay, so what brought you to Wallace?"

"My grandfather was from here," Cody said, realizing the deaths of two strangers had diminished her quest. "He died recently and I came here trying to find out more about him."

"How long are you planning on staying?"

"I'd thought two weeks."

"Fine. I'll need you to sign this report then you can go for now." Jess pushed a form across the desk to Cody. "We'll probably have more questions for you as things move along."

"What are the chances of you catching who did this?" Cody asked, rubbing her thumbs over her fingernails.

"If Matt can keep Hailey under control we'll have a better chance."

Cody, again, didn't know how to respond.

"Sorry," Jess said. "That was unprofessional. She gets under my skin. But we'll do our best to catch this person. Kelly was a great guy."

Jess stood and Cody did the same, leaving the mug of stale tasting tea on the desk.

"Does she always bounce so much?" Cody asked, pulling her damp coat off the back of the chair.

A deep laugh bubbled up as Jess pocketed her notebook. "I think she's trying to make herself taller. So what are your plans for the rest of the day?"

"I don't know," Cody said, distracted from thoughts of Hailey by the question. "I'd been thinking about going to the museum, but that doesn't seem right." Death had tilted her universe, and its touch had trivialized all her hopes.

"No, it's what you should do. Normal things. It helps, believe it or not."

Outside, the rain had eased to a fine lacy mist and Cody raised her face to the fresh coolness. Why was she alive? Why did she deserve to stand here looking up at shrouded mountains, when Kelly and Nate would never again do so? Looking for stories about her grandfather seemed frivolous, but she didn't know what else would fulfill the need to seek out connections with him. The unfairness of death was overwhelming and fueled an anger she didn't want and had never known what to do with. It was a loss of control, and she was better at burying emotion than dealing with it.

She could so clearly picture the three men in death. Her grandfather, who had meant so much, two who had so briefly touched her life, and all three become nothing. She could feel heat inside, flames that scorched a lump in her throat, that burned behind her eyes, that made her understand the iciness of the tall ranger.

The afternoon stretched out in normality that seemed somehow indecent. How could Cody go about her plans as if nothing had happened to shift the essence of the day? Life had ended, lives of those left behind had been shattered, and here she stood, shivering in the dampness. She shoved her hands deep in the pockets of her jacket, and the stiff material where Nate's blood had dried scraped her knuckles. She jerked her hands back and ripped off the coat, holding it by two fingers as mist collected on her gray tee shirt. She stared at the blood stains then gently touched them. It was all that remained of Nate. Slowly, she pulled the coat back on. She felt too disjointed and lost to forge on to the museum like she planned, so she walked to the old gas station, crossing the pocked pavement and going behind the building.

The trail was a green sentence marked with a broad yellow highlighter stripe of caution tape, the hue obscenely bright and cheery on a gray day. Matt stood next to an old Bronco with a Forest Service insignia on the side, listening to Hailey and making notes on a clipboard.

At a loss, Cody stood silently.

"Can we help you?" Hailey asked.

"I wondered if you'd found out anything yet, or if there was anything I could do," Cody said, flustered. "It's hard to go on with daily plans as if nothing has happened."

"This is an investigation in process," Hailey said. "We aren't able to tell you anything."

"Maybe you can answer a question for me," Matt said.

"If I can."

"I don't get the timing here," he said. "You say you met Kelly and Nate as they were going down the trail. You then had time to hike all the way up to the cirque, hang out for what, ten minutes? Yet you still managed to catch up with them before they made it to the trailhead."

"Yes?" Cody crossed her arms over her body, cupping her elbows.

"Don't you think two healthy guys should have been able to hike all the way out in the time it took you to go up and come back down?" Matt gripped the clipboard so tightly his knuckles became pale moons. "They died too quickly to have been shot right after you left them. So they weren't lying on the trail bleeding until you came back down."

"For all I know, they stopped to pick flowers," Cody said, cut by the accusation in his tone. "Or maybe they were talking to whoever shot them. How the hell should I know what delayed them?"

Profanity slipped out in anger, and it caught her breath away. Mad and swearing, it was as if her mother's voice blurted from her mouth and the similarity horrified her. She stepped back, as if distancing herself physically could somehow reduce her shame.

"I'm sorry, I shouldn't have said that." If only the apology could reach out, grab her words, and pull them back inside.

"Apology accepted," Matt said. "But not your answer. We're missing something and since you can't help us, we need to get on with our investigation."

He pulled a backpack out of the Bronco, and turned away from Cody, as if in dismissal, but Hailey blocked him.

"Ranger Tanner, I need you to see the mistakes you're making here. You're allowing emotion to interfere with doing the job."

"Which detective novel did you read that in?" Matt asked, stepping around Hailey and starting up the trail.

Hailey stared after him for several seconds, hands on hips, before pulling out a small journal covered in a tiny floral print. She wrote rapidly, filling a page before shoving it into a pocket and approaching Cody.

"Have you remembered anything more?" she asked.

"No, sorry."

"Call me if you do."

"The detective, Jess, wants me to call her."

"And you do that." A deep intensity cemented the blue eyes, the curls, and the soft features into hardness. And that hardness looked like it was going to be around awhile.

"I wish I could help more," Cody said.

"So do I," Hailey said. "It's too bad you don't have observation skills like I do. That's part of all the training I've had. But whatever. I'm pissed because Kelly didn't deserve this. And because I know what to do and Ranger Tanner won't listen." She pulled a pack similar to Matt's out of the Bronco and shouldered it on. "And now I'm going to have to follow him and take orders while he screws everything up. If you want to help solve this the right way, you'll call me first."

Silent, Cody watched the young woman duck under the caution tape. She was glad Hailey hadn't seemed to expect a reply because she didn't have a clue how to respond. How could words from a bouncing petite blonde feel like a threat? Cody returned to the street. Heavy clouds were sinking over mountain edges, filling gorges and obliterating trees from view. It wouldn't be long before the rain dropped twilight and created an early evening. Tomorrow she would start early with a trip to the mining museum, and use that as an attempt to refocus.

Cody knew there was no way she could put these deaths behind her, even though she had known Kelly and Nate so briefly they could not even be called acquaintances. Yet in some way the loss of these two strangers seemed to connect her to her grandfather. Maybe it was simply death binding them. Or maybe it was because Kelly had touched her, and that brief, casual gesture had shown him as someone she could have been friends with. With friendship a scarcity in her life, and male friends even more rare, a potential connection had been taken from her that would never be able to develop, but would forever remain an unresolved future. Just like with her grandfather.

That was the link, she realized, binding the three men together in her mind. The thought of what might have been, the amorphous idea of family and friends, now vanished before she could grasp it and hang on. Maybe it was selfishness to think of their deaths in terms of what she had lost, but if so, she would mark herself as selfish.

And then she would find out if there was a way to honor their lives and make sure she never forgot them.

Chapter 5

A motel brochure on historic walking tours of Wallace listed directions to the Idaho Mining Museum, a rectangular building of aged brick and grimy windows. Cody twisted the glass doorknob and when it didn't turn, pushed on it instead. A cowbell clanged loudly as she stepped into a small lobby but no one responded to the intrusion. She peered through floating dust motes at stapled packets of papers and flipped through one on the fire of 1910. In the weighted quiet she next read about the disaster of the Sunshine mine fire, but still no one appeared. Wondering if the place was closed after all, she tiptoed to a long display case. Inside were silver earrings, silver necklaces, silver dollars, and vials of silver flakes floating in mineral oil. A large doorway led down to a lower level where Cody could see displays of mining scenes, but no people. Maybe it was time to leave.

The gray morning light tried to penetrate the aged coating on the windows but succeeded only in laying long shadows over shelves of rusting equipment. More than likely they were related to mining, but for all Cody knew they could have been bits of medieval torture devices. Rubbing her fingernails with her thumbs, she walked softly back to the door. The place was too empty of people and too full of unknown memories to welcome a stranger. It was as if she had no right to stir the dust, to question what might be better off resting.

"Shit!"

The voice made Cody jump so violently she banged into a shelf near the door and toppled pieces of metal to the floor. She whirled around to see a young woman with bobbed brown hair standing in the large doorway, clutching her chest with one hand and the wood frame with the other. She had dramatic eyebrows a few shades darker than her hair, and eyes an even darker brown, and if it hadn't been for her fair skin and faint freckles, she would have looked as if she was made of earth.

"Oh god, I'm sorry," the woman said. "I didn't know anyone was here. That damn cowbell. I never hear it in the back room. I caught the shadow of someone moving and it scared the hell out of me."

"Sorry," Cody said, backed against the shelf and held there by her racing heart. "I thought the place was open. I didn't mean to trespass."

"It is open. I'm just not used to people coming in."

"I can always come back," Cody said, bending to retrieve the spilled pieces. She hefted up something that looked like a hoe had mated with a rusty axe, started to put it back on the shelf, and then paused to study the odd tool.

"That's a Pulaski head," the woman said. "Invented by a local guy after the 1910 fire to make fighting wild fires easier. So the story goes. I need to get a wood handle on it. I want it in a display I'm working on. Just drop it in that box there. Someday I'll get all this junk cleaned up. What can I do for you?"

Cody lowered the axe head into an already full wooden box. "I'm looking for information on my grandfather who grew up here in the 1940's."

"Great. I need an excuse to get away from the back room. I swear all the old papers around here breed at night. What's his name?"

"Charles Mogen." Cody cautiously moved back into the lobby as the woman slipped behind the display case.

"Not familiar with Charles. Any relation to Alice?" The woman pulled down thick journals and let them thud to the counter top. More dust rose in the air.

"I believe Alice was his mother."

"She was nuts. Unstable to begin with, worse after her husband dumped her. We have lots on her because she was always in jail for some scam or other. And getting in trouble for neglecting her son. He must be the grandfather you're looking for."

"I know he started working pretty young," Cody said, tentatively touching the counter. "I think he supported her."

"Well, she had a lot of mental health issues, as they say now. I've heard stories she used to lock herself up for days in her bedroom, and had this cat door thing installed so food could be shoved through to her. Oh yeah, I'm Rachel by the way. Rachel Blaine."

"Cody Marsh. Have you lived here all your life?"

"Not in Wallace. In Burke, down the road. You want to see a dying town, go there. It's an environmental disaster. The big wigs keep trying to buy out the few people still living there so they can close the place down, but no one will go in spite of the conditions." Rachel opened a journal and flipped coarse pages. Her hands were rough, calloused, and scarred, the fingernails cut so short there weren't even slivers of white left. Cody glanced at her own nails and saw the same eclipse.

"Let's see what I've got here," Rachel said.

"What are those books?"

"Lists of names, mostly. Pretty much everyone who's ever lived here. Compiled from birth and death certificates, old newspaper articles. Anywhere a name showed up it got added here. So why are you looking for Charles?"

"He died recently and I wanted to see where he grew up or if there were any stories about him."

"Cool. You know, my granny might be a good person to talk to. She was just a child, but I remember her telling me about how scared she was of Alice."

"I'd like to meet her then," Cody said.

Once again Cody wished she'd had more time with her grandfather. The idea of a child taking care of an unstable mother made her ache for a boy she would never know. Maybe they could have healed each other, given each the family the other had never had. She swallowed against the lump in her throat.

"This might take a while," Rachel said, licking her thumb and flipping more pages. "But it sure beats being grilled by forest rangers."

"Forest rangers?" Cody asked, knowing what was coming with a certainty that became a dull weight in her stomach.

"Oh yeah. Instead of good cop/bad cop it was pissed off ranger and bitchy ranger. Not much to choose between."

Cody placed her hands flat on the glass display case, letting the coolness leach away the flush of memory. "Matt and Hailey?"

"You know them?" Rachel asked. "Oh hell, you're the tourist who found them aren't you?"

Cody knew Rachel was no longer talking about Matt and Hailey, but didn't know how to respond. Saying even a simple 'yes' felt almost like boasting. Look at me, I saw people murdered. Explaining what happened would feel like telling a story not hers to speak of. But Rachel must have seen the answer on Cody's face because she stepped back, bumping up against a cash register on the counter.

"I'm going to barf."

Going around the display case, Cody saw an old piano stool and rolled it up to Rachel.

"Here, sit down. What are you supposed to do for throwing up? Put your head between your knees?"

"I think that's fainting," Rachel said, sinking onto the stool and dropping her head down anyway.

Cody pulled a waste basket over just in case, and sat on the floor next to Rachel, waiting quietly. After a few moments, Rachel sat back, leaning her head against the wall.

"Kelly was a great guy," she said. "We went to school together, though we didn't hang much afterwards. Too busy with life, you know? You never expect people your own age to die."

"If it helps any, I don't think Kelly suffered," Cody said. She saw a roll of paper towels and stood to get it in case Rachel needed it. Holding it in her arms like a baby, she leaned on the counter. "I think he died right away. It didn't look like he struggled or anything."

"And there was another guy?" Rachel asked.

"Some guy who's been staying up there. He didn't live long, either, though he tried to tell me to get away."

"From what?" Rachel reached for the paper towels, her eyes wide with the question.

Cody shrugged, wishing she could stop scenes replaying in her mind.

"You think the killer was still there?"

"No. I don't know. I didn't see anyone. But I didn't feel alone. If that makes sense."

"This is just the shits," Rachel stood and kicked the piano stool hard enough that it spun away from them and fell over. "Shouldn't happen to people like Kelly."

"Maybe he was in the wrong place at the wrong time," Cody said.

"What difference does that make? He's still dead isn't he?"

Cody recoiled in a step backward, fumbling her way out from behind the case. "I'm sorry. I just meant maybe it was because of Nate, that no one had a reason to kill Kelly."

"Hell," Rachel said, following Cody. "I'm pissed and taking it out on you. It's just so damn senseless."

"I understand. It's no big deal. You have the right to be angry and upset. You knew him, after all."

"Doesn't mean you have to be a floor mat and let me walk on you." Rachel fisted her hands on her hips. "You always so nice?"

"Well trained," Cody corrected, fighting another urge to apologize.

"Then we're going to end up best friends. No one but a saint could put up with me. Which is why I haven't been laid in months. Men in particular can't deal with me."

Cody laughed, half in surprise and half in embarrassment.

"Matt's smart," Rachel said, going back to the journal, with one hand on her flat stomach as if nausea still threatened. "He's taking this personal, which is why he's out talking to everyone. He'll figure it out. Especially if Jess is helping and keeps Hailey out of the way."

"The bouncing ranger?"

"That's her. The Bouncing Bitch. Come on, distract me with your grandfather."

"Well, he mentioned a woman who used to look out for him. An Ethel Stevenson."

"Ethel!" Rachel paused a moment, watching Cody. "Sure. She ran the Silver Haven. She was the madam of the place. The rumor mill at the time said she had a long running affair with the mayor Keith Naylor. Everyone knew it except his wife, from the sounds of it. Though some said she knew and wouldn't give him a divorce. I wouldn't either. I'd cut off his balls instead."

Cody had no idea how to respond to Rachel's bluntness. "The mayor allowed bordellos?"

"Wallace was famous for them. Still is. Some are hotels now, one's a museum dedicated to the fallen angels, as they were called. Back then though, police would close the front doors and town officials would open the back doors. As long as there's been bordellos that mayor and his descendants have been involved. Sometimes it's amazing how all the old families interconnect and stick around."

"I heard about the current mayor," Cody said. "Kelly's sister. He was going to give her my number."

"Yeah, she'd probably be a good resource for you, since her granddad's still alive, but he's one scary, mean bugger. I've always wondered if his family changed their name to have something to rhyme with 'mayor'."

Cody looked at the journals, thinking about history, and how easily names became real people when you learned their stories.

"Did you say your grandmother knew Charles?" she asked.

"Yeppers. And she's some story teller." Rachel's words dropped away and she studied her hands, rubbing calluses for a moment.

"Are you okay?" Cody asked.

"Granny is in the beginning stages of dementia," Rachel said finally. "I don't like talking about it. Not even to my therapist."

Cody felt like she had just opened the door on a dark family closet, and wondered how to back out gracefully without intruding. "I'm sure I can find others to talk to."

"No, that's okay. Tell you what. I'll keep digging through stuff here. You give me your phone number and when Granny's well enough I'll call you. She's strong and stubborn and this isn't going to beat her."

Cody wrote the number down and handed it to Rachel, wondering how much the confidence in her grandmother came from hope.

"Do you mind if I look around the museum before I go?"

"Knock yourself out," Rachel said. "There's an amazing history to this area. I never get tired of coming across old stories. Yell if you have any questions."

Cody stepped down into the main part of the museum. Moving to the right, she meandered along display cases, pausing in front of the little alcoves. Some had mannequins frozen in various mining poses, with hammers and jacks and trolleys. Some had displays of minerals, with old scales and weights. The whole thing had been done professionally at one time, but now waited under a thick coat of dust.

Oddly enough one display held mementos from a movie about a volcano that had been filmed in Wallace. She had expected a rather obscure mining town, but instead had found one rich in history and famous as well as infamous. And one that would now be forever linked in her mind with death.

How much of the town's history formed the man her grandfather became? Having an unstable mother had to have had a dramatic impact on the person he grew to be. Yet she wondered how the timelessness of land could work its way under someone's skin until a person could never really be separated from the place. With no answers, she realized she wasn't going to find her grandfather in this museum and she was no further ahead in learning about him. Discouraged, she went back to the lobby, but Rachel was no where in sight and so Cody left.

By now it was nearing noon, and the misty rain showed no sign of letting up. Cody knew if she went back to the motel she would end up brooding, or worse, calling her mother. She needed to come up with something that would keep her busy. On impulse she went into the Silver Capital Arts building and approached a man standing near the doorway.

"Excuse me, could you tell me where I might find a senior center or nursing home?"

"Certainly. Head west on Bank, turn north on Seventh, turn east on Cedar, and you'll find a senior center on the north side of Cedar."

"Thanks," Cody said, wondering why people couldn't simply say "turn right" or "turn left". She had a terrible sense of direction.

After a couple false starts she found the small senior center, and as she stood dripping in the foyer, a man came out of one of the rooms zipping up a camouflage jacket. He was as bulky as his coat, with little neck, dark stubble instead of hair, and a thick reddened nose that looked as if it had met a few fists in its lifetime.

"It's lunch time," he said. "Haven't seen you in here before."

Cody stepped back from his advance. "No, I'm just visiting."

"Yeah? Who?" He rooted around in his pockets, fingers groping and searching while his eyes never left Cody's face.

"No one in particular," Cody said, backing up again.

"Got any money on you?" he asked, as his hands came up empty. "I have to drink regular or I get real sick. I get the tremors bad."

"No, sorry, I didn't bring any money with me." A flutter of apprehension blew through to her fingertips and she hoped he wouldn't see her hands shaking.

"My great grandpa's usually good for a buck or two," the man said, gesturing over his shoulder. "But he lost it all in a poker game. Believe that shit? Who lets old people play poker? Now I got to go scrounge money somewhere."

"Well...good luck," Cody said.

"Yeah. Like I said, they're having lunch in the cafeteria but the nurses will let you talk to them."

The man pushed through the door, hunching his shoulders against the wet weather. Cody watched him head down the sidewalk, relieved he was gone. She exhaled a shaky breath, managed to draw in a slightly calmer one, and walked into a large and airy cafeteria.

Two and a half hours later, Cody was back out in the rain, starving. She had spent the time visiting with several retired and elderly locals, and while a few said the Mogen name was familiar, most had no recollection of her grandfather. Even so she'd enjoyed their reminiscing about Wallace and the old days.

Walking back toward the motel, Cody wondered if she should call Matt or Jess to see if anything new had been discovered. She had no claim to information like a family member would, but she wanted to know what was happening. What was disconcerting was how so many aspects of the sad event seemed to resurrect memories of her grandfather. Even something as simple as thinking about calling the ranger station.

"When I was in my early twenties," Charles had told her, "I worked one summer in the forest service. Those rangers were always playing jokes. Tourists would come in looking for fishing holes and these guys would give the fishermen directions to Fool's Lake. Nasty steep hike, back into the high country."

"And was the fishing good?"

"No, there wasn't any lake. Just a spring that made a kind of puddle. And next to it a rock cairn where you could sign this old journal that you'd been there. When those hikers came back off the mountain, if they were angry, them rangers just let them stew. But if the guy laughed it off and said he'd had a great time fishing, then the rangers would tell him some real fishing holes. Kind of a test I guess. The journal made some fun reading, seeing what angry fishermen wrote in it. Signed it myself once, not that long ago."

Cody turned the corner by her motel, wondering if rangers still sent fishermen there. Maybe she'd be able to find the logbook and see what her grandfather had written. She'd have to remember to ask Matt or Hailey.

The motel room smelled slightly musty. She opened the window and stretched out on the bed, staring at the ceiling. She had learned a little more about her grandfather, but it was nowhere near enough. He was still a ghost. Why was this so difficult? She was intelligent, held a steady job, lived the life her mother expected. Over the years she had learned to accept the cutting words her mother used, and how to keep her dreams private and her tears more so. She had let go of aspirations long ago and yet here she was, trying to catch the amorphous spirit of a man who had briefly touched her life and claimed her as family.

She wanted what her grandfather represented. A normal family. For two months her grandfather had allowed her to let go of being a failure, and his unquestioning acceptance had allowed her to believe she could change.

Now, with his death, she was worse off because she'd had a taste of what it was to be loved unconditionally. The hole left behind gaped raw and aching.

Chapter 6

The early morning was clearing, clouds the color of sheep scattered and stretched across mountaintops like airy threads. A brief shower raced across town, but the fine rain was there only long enough to give birth to an elusive rainbow. Cody watched it fade away as she walked down Cedar Street toward Seventh and the City Hall.

Last night she had been reclining on the motel bed reading a history of Wallace and Burke, her open window filling the room with fresh cool air and the sounds of pattering rain. The ringing of the phone had startled her with its strident tones and for a moment she could not answer it. The only person who would call would be her mother, and she had no desire to learn what new dramatic problem May wanted to blame her for. But after three rings, Cody remembered she had been giving out her number to people, and grabbed up the phone with hope blossoming.

"Am I speaking with Cody Marsh?" a woman asked.

"Yes."

"The Cody Marsh who is looking for information on Charles Mogen?"

"Yes." Did she sound too anxious?

"If you could be at City Hall tomorrow promptly at eight a.m. I will have time to meet with you."

"Okay, but who is this and where is City Hall?" Cody asked, perplexed.

"This is Mayor Naylor." The woman's sigh conveyed exasperation. "The City Hall is on Seventh and Cedar. Do you need directions?"

"No, I can find it."

"Good. Ms. Blaine from the museum asked me to contact you, and said you were friends with my brother. She also mentioned you were the one to find him. Because of that I'm willing to meet with you, although I'm not sure how I can help you. Can you tell me exactly what you are looking for?"

"I'm not really sure," Cody responded, flustered and flushing in the presence of the professional voice. "I met my grandfather Charles Mogen for the first time a few months ago but he died before I could get to know him. He grew up in this area so I'm trying to find people who might have known him or heard stories about him. I'd also like to learn more about his mother, Alice, and a madam named Ethel Stevenson, who used to look out for Charles." Cody added the last part on impulse, realizing she might learn about her grandfather from people who had shaped his life.

"Well," the mayor said, her voice as cool as the autumn evening. "I'm not sure how much I can help but I'm willing to give you an appointment. It will have to be brief though."

"I understand," Cody said. "I know this must be a hard time for you."

"My brother's death, as horrible as it is, can't impact my work responsibilities. Tomorrow at eight is the only opening I have for several days. As it is, I'm going to have to reschedule several important appointments once the memorial is arranged."

Cody bit down on the words she wanted to say. "I'm sorry for the inconvenience," she said instead.

"The brief time your appointment takes will hardly be an inconvenience."

Cody hadn't meant her appointment but it would be obviously pointless to clarify her comment. "Well, thanks for the time anyway."

"Until tomorrow then." And with that, the conversation ended, leaving Cody simmering as if Kelly had been slighted somehow by a sister not grieving.

Now, a few minutes before eight, Cody walked up a narrow boxed in staircase in a squat brick building, similar in construction to the museum, but missing the dust and cobwebs.

The large airy office on the second floor was tastefully decorated with framed historical prints of Wallace. Nothing gave away the personality of the woman behind a desk of cherry wood that complimented her deep auburn hair and fair skin. She was the epitome of what Cody's coloring might have been if her hair had been less flame bright and her freckles invisible.

"Ms. Marsh. Thank you for being prompt. I'm Kendra Naylor, mayor of Wallace. And this is my grandfather, Keith Naylor Jr., former mayor."

Cody hadn't seen the elderly man when she came in, and his sudden appearance from a corner of the room startled her. He smiled confidently as he used a cane to maneuver slowly forward, as if aware of her discomfiture. A hump bowed his back and shortened his height but not his stature. When he reached her, he held out a gnarled hand.

"Cody is it? I hear you are looking for stories about some of our past residents."

"Yes," Cody said, taking his hand, expecting a brief handshake.

"Kelly was a disappointment," he said, his thumb caressing her knuckles.

"Pardon me?" The abrupt topic, with no warning, confused Cody. She tried to pull her hand back but Keith held on, watching her intently.

"He let my son, his father, down when he decided against politics. He was unduly influenced by Ranger Matt Tanner, got caught up in the romantic ideal of saving people. The reality was Kelly had a job that allowed him to play more than work. If he'd done what the family expected of him, and taken the job of mayor, I'd still have a grandson and Kendra would still have a brother."

"But you have to admit," Kendra said. "He would never have been the mayor I am, right?" Cody saw her reach out almost tentatively toward the old man, but he never looked at Kendra, just continued to rub Cody's hand.

"Your talent as a mayor is related to your ability to listen to my guidance," Keith said. "Though a lady would be married and fully round with child. A woman's job is to bear the family name forward. You are mayor because we had no male heir to step up."

Pinkness stole over Kendra's cheekbones even as color leached away from around her glossy lips, as if she gritted her teeth. Or maybe bit back words. If allowed to escape, Cody wondered if they would be words of anger or humiliation.

Cody tugged her hand away and couldn't stop from wiping her palm down her thigh. Keith's smile broadened as if he enjoyed her discomfort.

The old man nodded his head to Kendra, as if tossing her a tidbit of appeasement. "Certainly Kelly would have needed more guidance than you, though. Nevertheless his disobedience to me was his failure.

"I doubt Kelly asked to be shot in the back," Cody said, sickened into defending Kelly.

"Ah, but Kelly is neither here nor there," Keith said, seemingly oblivious to the cruelty of his words. "You ask about Charles, Alice, and Ethel. An interesting combination.

Alice I understand, but why would you ask us about an old whore?"

"Rachel Blaine mentioned Ethel was more a mother to my grandfather than Alice. And I'm looking for all stories that might connect to Charles." Cody spoke fast, reciting, wanting to end the interview and leave the old man.

"Of course you are," Keith said. "I remember Charles clearly, although we weren't companions, his being from a poorer family as it were. I remember a boy that kept to himself, worked any odd job he could find, unlike me. My only job was learning and excelling in politics. Charles came from a railroad family. Transients. My family, on the other hand, is still here."

"And still politicians," Kendra said.

Keith patted her on the shoulder, as if bestowing approval and Kendra smiled, her face lighting up.

"Did Charles have any friends that might still be alive?" Cody asked.

"As I just said, he was a loner. I'm sure he had some friends, but to be honest I didn't pay that crowd much mind."

"What about Alice?"

"Alice was quite religious. She was adamant about the evils of drink, and pushed for the closing of bordellos and bars. And yet, many times, she was picked up for being publicly inebriated. She felt communion must be done with real wine, and the faithful had communion with every meal."

Cody cringed inwardly at the thought of a little boy living in such an environment. At least her mother didn't drink, having found hypochondria to be a more productive addiction.

"Do you know anything about Ethel?" Cody asked.

"And now, Ms. Marsh, your appointment time is up," Keith said, rheumy eyes intent as he continued to smile.

"Pardon me?"

"We are done reminiscing. No more trips down memory lane. So goodbye." He turned his back on Cody and limped to the desk, picking up some papers and thumbing through them.

Cody looked at Kendra, who, fidgeting with a pen, seemed unable to meet Cody's eyes.

"Well...thank you for your time then." Cody started for the door, feeling the same humiliation she got after spending time with her mother.

"Ms. Marsh," Kendra said, standing and coming around from behind the barricade of the desk. "You are asking about a time when things were more traditional, and families kept their personal lives private, which is as it should be in most cases. If there was a child today living as Charles did, I would have acted on it, involved Child Protective Services. However, back then, people did for their own."

"Kendra," Keith said, almost impatiently, as he sat down in the mayor's chair and adjusted the computer keyboard. "You are a credit to your position as mayor, and the protection of children should be used as a platform for the next election. Shall we talk now about the new mining venture Mr. Russell is contemplating?"

Cody had become invisible. She recognized the signs, having seen them many times growing up, though rarely so blatant. She left the office, found a public restroom, and scalded her hands clean.

Out on the street, a brisk wind had finished clearing the sky, and the air held a cleansing damp coolness. Cody turned onto Bank Street, not sure if the meeting had accomplished anything. The more she thought about it, the more she found it strange Charles had not talked about his early years. He had rarely mentioned his childhood, and even more rarely, his mother. Had Alice always been unbalanced, or did it become worse when she was left alone with a child to raise? How could a man leave a child with a woman who was clearly unstable?

Cody's fingernails bit into her palms. Why had her own father left her in the care of a mother just as unstable in her own way?

Without warning, she was overwhelmed by the memory of her last birthday. It had been a cold January day, and with no friends or party to distract her, she had started wondering about her father. A spur of the moment decision had pulled her into her mother's bedroom to look for mementos of a man she barely remembered. Instead, she had come across her mother's journal, lying open on the bed. She had not wanted to read it, but the words had jumped up, impaling themselves in her heart.

"...her twenty-third birthday tomorrow and I suppose I should do something to mark that, but I've just been so light headed and dizzy. It's so hard to believe I have been a single mother for so long. And what a long, hard road it has been, too. Not only dealing with supporting her and raising her and all the financial hardship that means, but having to deal with her being so ungrateful and unappreciative. I'm afraid she's going to turn out selfish. Just like her father, take, take, take."

The words still humiliated Cody, and she walked faster along the street, as if she could outpace the memories. A few cars drove by, and one or two pedestrians passed her, but she was unaware of any of it until she realized she was at the gas station. She continued past to the trailhead behind the building, where caution tape hung limply between trees. Impulsively, she ducked underneath, climbing up into the cool dappled light of the fall woods, escaping the town and people, but unable to leave bitter memories behind as easily.

What had hurt most when she read the diary was the thought that her mother considered her selfish. Outside of work, her mother demanded every moment, and Cody had rarely begrudged it. Cody had spent so much of her life doing what was expected of her that she was left without the time necessary to invest in developing many friendships. In school she had been horribly shy, hiding in corners so that over the years most kids forgot she was there. As an adult, she'd continued in the background of life, where she was comfortable and safe.

Brushing against huckleberry bushes, the bright berries long gone, Cody climbed upward. When she reached the spot in the trail where Kelly had died, now cordoned off with more caution tape, she sank down on an old log, still thinking about her life. All Cody had forfeited and left behind and never experienced, all she had given to her mother, and in return May thought so little of her only daughter. The words had been, in a very real sense, a betrayal of love and trust, and had planted the first tiny seeds of dissatisfaction with her life.

Weak sunlight filtered down, sparkling off dampness left from the earlier rain that had washed away Kelly's blood. If it wasn't for the yellow tape, she might not have been able to find the exact spot. The woods had a clean, new feel to them, the air a cold purity that ached as she pulled in a deep lungful. Angrily she wiped tears away with the back of her hand. Why did she allow her mother's words to still hurt? And why didn't she have the courage to defend herself against nasty old men like Keith Naylor? She palmed her cheeks again. All crying did was give her a headache, and tears were nothing but another symbol of lost control.

Pressing the palms of her hands tightly against her eyes, she willed unwanted memories away, shuddering as the damp wood she sat on leached cold through her jeans. Water dripped from leaves, a wind stirred high in the treetops, and small brown creepers sang their autumn songs in the underbrush as they flitted back and forth. The place was peaceful, but Cody kept thinking about the three men who had briefly touched her life and then died.

Well, she thought, dropping her hands, her mother was miles away, and that in itself was a relief. She was just going through a rough patch because of her grandfather. She would finish what she came for and then step back into her old controlled life, hopefully able to continue as things had been before her grandfather appeared. If, secretly, she wearied of servitude to her mother, she had to admit it was safe and predictable.

Standing up, she decided to leave memories of humiliation where they belonged, and to quit punishing herself with them. Heading back down the trail Cody smiled slightly as a rogue thought entered, making her feel guilty even as she knew how unrealistic it was.

It was too bad she couldn't find a way to leave her mother as well.

Chapter 7

Back out on Bank Street, Cody watched a police cruiser come around the corner and slow to a stop beside her.

"You'd be a lot easier to find if you carried a cell phone," Jess said, bending over a center console hidden under a laptop and crumpled wads of paper. A pad of paper and a couple pens rested on the passenger seat.

"I don't like them," Cody said. "Seems egotistical that a person's conversation is so important strangers have to hear it."

"How about a microchip?"

"Might work."

"Easier than cruising streets," Jess said. "Got time for a couple questions?"

"Of course. Where?" The guilt she always carried surged upward, that automatic assumption she'd done something wrong. She tried to shrug it off, hunching her shoulders.

"Right here." Jess lifted the paper and pens out of the way.

When Cody shut the door Jess pushed a button, raising the window, and the soft mechanical noise was a soundtrack to the feeling of isolation from the outside world. Cody relaxed back into the seat and reached for her seatbelt.

"You won't need that," Jess said, pulling the car to the curb and killing the engine. "You'd be surprised how often I use this for an office."

Cody looked out at the few cars passing and the even fewer people going in and out of stores. She entwined her fingers, folding the cup of her hands in her lap.

"There's more people when it's tourist season," Jess said, lifting her chin to indicate the streets. She sat with one wrist on the top arc of the steering wheel, long fingers dangling. Her uniform was neat, her braid smooth, and the cruiser filled with faint scents of laundry soap and starch.

Cody gave her attention to Jess's angular profile, watching her as she watched the town.

"You told me what happened on the trail, but I'd like to hear about before," Jess said. "Did you see anyone walking in the vicinity of the gas station or the trail?"

"No," Cody said. "But I was inside. Anyone could have gone by then."

"Inside? For how long?" Jess's dark eyes tightened as she turned toward Cody.

"I'm not sure. Ten minutes maybe?"

"Did you interrupt many cell conversations?"

Cody relaxed. "A few. And a few text messages."

"Cell is going to end up with a phone shaped brain tumor. What did you talk about?"

"The trail, the history of the gas station. Oh, and rock climbing."

"That figures," Jess said. "When you left, did Cell show you the trailhead? Could he have followed you up?"

"I don't know. He was too busy arguing with a man when I went out. I suppose after the guy left he could have, but I never heard anyone following me." Cody's fingers were growing numb from gripping them together and she took a deep breath, relaxing her hands. The thought that someone had followed her and she hadn't been aware of it, let the sense of responsibility loose again. Would Kelly and Nate be alive if she'd been more aware of her surroundings?

Jess reached out and covered Cody's hands briefly with her own. "You probably wouldn't have heard anyone coming up the trail unless they were right behind you." She flipped open one of the writing tablets and uncapped a pen, tapping it softly against the paper. "Tell me about this argument."

"A guy came in who was upset with Cell," Cody responded, not entirely reassured by Jess's kindness. "And Cell didn't seem too happy to see him, either. I thought at first they were going to get in a fight."

"What made you think that?"

"Because the other guy was so angry."

"What did he look like?"

"A younger version of Daniel Boone. Or Erwin Flowers. One of those mountain man types. Longish hair, a heavy work coat you see farmers wearing."

"Carhartts. Jake Conrad."

"Yes...I think Jake was the name Cell used, but I'm not sure."

"Jake lives up Thompson Pass, in a cabin that's been in his family for generations, before the area became forest service land. The place is grandfathered in but the forest service would love to find a way to get it back. That area's scheduled for logging, and Jake's fighting it, citing environmental impacts to his place." Jess sagged back in the seat, and the pen stilled in its dance against the paper. Her scribbled notes looked like tiny mouse tracks. "No love lost between Jake and any government agency. Excuse me a minute."

Jess flipped open a small cell phone and hit a button.

"Hey Tanner. Jake Conrad was at the station arguing with Cell shortly before Cody headed up the trail. Might want to talk to him." She paused, listening. "Who? Rivers? Ah shit Matt, you didn't. I'm going to get you for this."

Jess snapped shut the phone, and checked the mirrors before looking over her shoulder and scanning the road.

"Everything okay?" Cody asked. "Should I be ducking down or bailing for the sidewalk?"

Jess looked startled for a second and then released a deep husky laugh. "Nah. Matt just referred our local environmental hippie to me with some complaint about mining. As usual."

"Tall beautiful woman, very elegant?" Cody asked.

"Very. She in the gas station, too?"

"No, I was behind her in a deli line. She's hard to forget."

"Damn straight. So, no one else but Jake and Cell?"

"No, sorry."

"Don't apologize. That's more than I had before you got in, and it ties in with other information. Can I drop you anywhere?"

Cody considered. "No thanks. I think I'm going to go back to the motel. See if I can figure out where to check next for old stories."

"You tried the library yet?"

Cody stared.

"Sometimes the most obvious is what we don't see." Jess freed another laugh. "I'll run you over there. It's not too far from your motel. By the way, did you hear a memorial service is scheduled for tomorrow evening?"

"For Kelly and Nate? No. I just talked with Kendra and her grandfather and they didn't say anything."

"Just for Kelly. Guess the Naylors don't want to waste any time. They're having the memorial with no body." Jess started up the car and pulled out.

"No…"

"Autopsy. He won't be released by tomorrow. But they're having the memorial anyway. Going?"

"Oh, no," Cody said without thinking. "I didn't know him." She flashed back on Kelly's fingers touching her shoulder. His fingertips hadn't spoken of romance, but whispered of a friendship that might have been and was now lost. She felt cheated.

"You found them," Jess said as she pulled into the parking lot of a small library. "That gives you more of bond than anyone else. Call me if you change your mind and need a ride."

"Thanks," Cody said. She shut the door behind her and waved, but Jess was already talking on her radio, and pulling out onto the road.

The library might not have been very big, but inside it was crammed with books. Cody found the section on local history, pulled out several books, and sat at a long table with her choices, reading intently. She wasn't learning much about Charles, but she was finding out a lot about the area. She tried to concentrate on the words, but kept going back to the memorial service the next night. Maybe she should go. She hadn't known Kelly long enough to tell if her presence would have mattered to him, but maybe she could honor the gesture he had made.

She pulled a book toward her, hearing the spine creak as she opened it, as if no one had ever read it. The pristine pages listed mines in Wallace and Burke, both those that were inoperative as well as those being worked at the time of publication, which was only a year ago. The mine owner's names were shown along with a chapter devoted to the history of the mine. Cody didn't expect to find her grandfather's name here. He'd never been a miner. Yet she still idly scanned the contents, looking to learn a bit more about what the area had been like in the 1940's.

She missed the names at first, but then realized she'd seen something familiar. The Honey Do mine, owners Keith Naylor Sr., Patrick Cross, Wesley Smithwick, and Ethel Stevenson. Ethel, the woman who had watched out for her grandfather when he was a child. It gave Cody a gentle delight, to see in writing something Charles had told her, as if ink equaled truth.

No Charles Mogen was listed in the paragraph, but she bent over the pages. If she learned about the people that had surrounded him, maybe she would find who her grandfather had been. And maybe she'd be able to answer some of the questions he had never found solutions to. One in particular, about his parentage, seemed to haunt him more than others. She could remember only one brief conversation that had come up as a result of a disagreement she'd had with May. It had been the only time he'd alluded to his childhood.

"You sounded a bit short with your mother just now," Charles had remonstrated as they pulled out of the driveway on their way sightseeing.

"Well, you heard her," Cody said, feeling defensive. "She would be happy if I did nothing but sit by her side all day long."

"Granted May is difficult, but underneath she loves you, and you don't realize how lucky you are to know your parents."

"What do you mean?" Cody had asked. "Your mother raised you alone just like mine."

"Maybe," Charles had said, looking somehow wistful. "But I always wondered…well, perhaps it was nothing more than daydreams. You know how a child will develop a make believe world when their own is not the best?"

"Your childhood was difficult?"

"Oh, I'd say it was hard, but then those were hard times. Lonely times. There was a distance with my mother even though I think she loved me in her way. But my father told me once…"

"What?" Cody had asked when the silence dragged out.

"When I was just a tad, I remember him saying some day he would tell me about my true parentage. After he left us I used those words to create stories about him, reasons why he left. That he was the son of a pirate or a spy off saving the world." Charles shrugged. "The dreams of a child who can only escape through imaginings. I outgrew them, but never did find out what my father meant."

"I used to daydream about my dad. Until I got old enough to realize he was nothing to dream about." Cody caught her breath and raised a hand as if in supplication. "Oh, I'm sorry. I shouldn't have said that about your son."

"Not to worry," Charles said. "I loved my son, but I saw his faults."

"It used to make me angry that he left me but I don't think about it as much now." Cody felt the pride that blanketed her purposeful self-deception. She had perfected hiding her feelings about her father because May got so angry whenever the subject came up.

"But at least you had your mother to raise you," Charles said. "As difficult as she might be, she kept you from foster homes, or some other transient life."

Chastised, Cody had wished, for a moment, that her grandfather had taken her side rather than show a side of May she didn't want to see.

"We both were given mothers that did, or do, the best they can," Charles had said, resting a hand on her shoulder. "We both had fathers who left us with nothing but dreams and questions. I always wanted to know why my father left, and I realize I'll never know. Maybe some day you'll find out about yours."

"If he's ever found," Cody said.

"If he's ever found," Charles agreed.

Shaking her head at the memory, Cody looked back down at the book on mining and turned to the page that had caught her eye.

"The Honey Do Mine was a small silver venture operating from 1940 to 1942 and never producing enough to pay back what shareholders invested. Boasting a who's who of names in Wallace at the time, investors included the local sheriff, Wesley Smithwick, the mayor Keith Naylor Sr., a madam of a well-known bordello, Ethel Stevenson, and the pastor of the First Presbyterian Church, Patrick Cross.

"Sunk only two levels, the shallow surface mine was situated near Desolation, a notorious wall of granite lifting out of the north end of Diamond Gulch, that even today regularly claims the lives of climbers. The location made removal of ore difficult and, at times, dangerous, as it was impossible to bring in rail lines. The owners were forced to remove product the old fashioned way using mules to reach the nearest road. The cost incurred cut short the life of a mine never destined to fulfill the hopes of the stakeholders. It was closed without ceremony in September of 1942, and the owners moved on, as many miners did, the wiser for their monetary losses.

"At the time of this publication, papers have been filed to reopen the mine, but it is unclear if the new owner will be able to address all the environmental issues. As the mine was such a poor producer in the past, she may not be worth the costs of current environmental reviews."

Flipping back to the index, Cody looked in vain for Ethel's name elsewhere, but she obviously hadn't tried mining again. She picked up the book and walked over to the tiny information desk, waiting as a tall young man in a perpetual state of stoop helped a small girl asking where local dragons might live.

"Excuse me," Cody said when it was her turn. "Is there a copy machine here?"

"Of course, over by the checkout machines. Copies are fifteen cents."

"Thanks," Cody said. "Would you know if there are any other books that refer to Ethel Stevenson?"

"Let me just check for you," he said, turning to a computer monitor and touching the screen.

Cody felt a twinge of nostalgia for the Dewey Decimal cards of her school library, stacked in long thin drawers. Her school librarian had fought against admitting computers, and

Cody had inherited the woman's love of the old index cards as they had never failed to turn up treasures. She would be flipping through them looking for a specific book and the description or title of another would catch her eye and she'd be diverted into the wonderful world of an unread book. It just wasn't the same with computer screens.

A man came up behind her, and Cody glanced at him as she waited for the computer to do its job. The jet black hair and striking blue eyes looked familiar. It took her a moment to remember he had been in the deli with the environmentalist, Rivers.

"I have references to Ethel's Silver Haven business," the librarian said. "Though most of those are second hand, with the originals being held by the Oasis, a Wallace museum dedicated to the history of local bordellos. You could look through newspapers from that time period, too. Ethel was a prominent citizen so there's bound to be references to her."

Cody thanked him and as she stepped away, the newcomer moved to the counter.

"Hey Evan. I need some help finding an environmental report filed by Fish and Wildlife on Burke about five months ago."

"No problem."

Cody made her copies, returned the mining book, and left the library, deciding if any old newspaper articles existed, Rachel Blaine at the museum would probably find them faster than she could. Her stomach growled. It was mid-afternoon and clearly time to get her car and pick up something for lunch.

The local grocery store was easy to find and Cody stood in the checkout lane holding a deli Caesar salad, ignoring the rack of chips and feeling virtuous. At least until a tap on her shoulder made her jump and drop the salad. The lid came off and lettuce and croutons escaped the container.

"Sorry, didn't mean to startle you. I was about to ask if Ranger Tanner had spoken with you yet." Hailey once again stood with her hands on her hips.

Cody squatted down to gather up the salad, glancing up at Hailey standing over her. People were stacking up in line behind them and Cody felt embarrassment inflame her face. She scooped salad remains back into the box, pushed the useless plastic lid back on, and stood. "I'll pay for this and then go get another one," she told the checker.

"No worries," she said. "Like, accidents happen, right? I know you don't I?"

Cody looked at the young woman and managed a smile through the frustration. "You work at the deli."

"Oh yeah, but only part time. And weekends I'm down at the bar. The tips are, like, better than the wage. And I have a few other odd jobs, too."

Out of the corner of her eye Cody could see a couple people behind her switch to another checkout. One that seemed to be moving.

"Look," she said. "Let me leave this here while I go grab another one so I don't take up more time."

"That would work," Hailey said. "Since some of us are on a lunch break."

"Hey, not cool," the deli girl said. "You need to, like, try yoga or something."

Hailey responded by bouncing up on her tiptoes. As she opened her mouth, Cody fled for the salads. She took her time picking out a container, and then peeked at the checkout line before stepping up behind a woman with a full cart and three giddy children. Hailey was nowhere in sight.

When it was her turn again, Cody put the salad on the conveyor belt, stepped up to the register and saw tears in the deli girl's blue eyes.

"Oh, no," Cody said.

"That Hailey needs to chill," the girl said.

"I'm so sorry," Cody said. "She shouldn't have taken her frustration out on you."

"It's not your fault. She's, like, mean to everyone."

"Well, I'm sorry anyway. What's your name?"

The girl managed a smile and swiped tears away with a hand laden with silver rings. "Sue, but my friend Rivers says I got the wrong name at birth. She calls me Sunny. I like that better, don't you?"

Cody had to admit it seemed a fit for the girl. She pulled out money for her salad, Sunny insisting there would be no charge for the dropped one.

"Thanks. And I'm sorry again you had a rough time."

"Like, over and done with, no worries. Not worth wasting any more time on."

"Good attitude." Cody picked up her bag. "See you around."

The automatic doors gave out a pneumatic grunt, opening on the cool afternoon. Cody turned in the direction of her car and saw Hailey leaning against it, arms crossed over her chest.

"I never heard an answer to my question," Hailey said as Cody unlocked the door.

"I never heard a question."

Cody started to pull the door shut but Hailey caught it.

"Has Ranger Tanner talked to you yet?"

"No," Cody said, remembering the tears in Sunny's eyes. She tugged on the door again.

"We're on the same side here," Hailey said, releasing her grip. "You don't have to like me to realize that."

"I know," Cody said. "And I haven't spoken with the ranger."

"When you do I want to know about it. Right away."

"Then ask him," Cody said, giving in to the flare of irritation.

Cody could see Hailey in the rearview mirror as she pulled out. The petite ranger yanked out her floral journal, stared briefly at Cody's car, and started writing.

Cody gripped the steering wheel. She was so tired of feeling guilty.

Chapter 8

The memorial service was due to start in half an hour and Cody was still undecided about going. The motel room was quiet, rain sheeting down the windows and blurring the world outside. She watched the water, thinking about Kelly and Nate, then picked up her keys. She'd drive to the church and make up her mind there whether to go in or not.

The phone rang as she opened the door and she ran back for it, hoping for stories.

"Hello Cody," May said over distance that wasn't, after all, distant enough.

"Hi mom," Cody said, keys biting into the palm of her hand. "I'm about to head out the door…"

"This won't take long. I need you to come home earlier than you'd planned."

"What? I still have over a week."

"Yes, I know. But I'm having these serious dizzy spells, and last night I had such a hard time breathing I had to sit up in a chair all night."

"Well, why didn't you call 911?" Cody asked in impatient exasperation, knowing even as the words left her, that they were a mistake.

"Never mind. I'm sorry if my health is taking time away from a search for someone you only knew a few months. Don't worry about me, I'll manage just fine. Just like I always do." The curt words were followed by the click of the phone being disconnected.

Immediately Cody was flooded by equal parts anger at herself, anger at her mother, and guilt that she wasn't a better daughter. She grabbed up the phone but halfway through dialing the number, slammed the receiver back down. Instead she headed for her old Subaru. She would not call her mother back. Her mother had used those same lines over and over throughout the years. The words, and Cody's reaction to them, were all too familiar.

In the past, those phrases had always elicited the same response. Cody would swear her undying love for her mother, and appreciation for all May had sacrificed to raise Cody alone. Then, still full of shame that she wasn't good enough, she would atone by obeying May's requests. By making her tea, brushing her hair, and most demeaning of all, sitting on the floor beside May, scratching her mother's hairy legs, stroking from ankle to knee, watching the dry flakes of skin fall like snow, knowing they were collecting under her fingernails. Cody never let her fingernails grow, and the sight of long nails on others left her queasy.

Cody brushed away tears she didn't want, focusing instead on leaving the room, crossing the pavement, starting the car. Little steps took her further from the phone, further from the need to apologize. She wouldn't go running to May this time. She had family out there somewhere. She didn't need to cling to her mother, more fearful of being totally alone than humiliated by tasks her mother set before her. Yet guilt was a strong rubber band. She knew her mother still sat next to the telephone, fully expecting it to ring, and wondered briefly how long May would sit there.

The memorial service was at the First Presbyterian Church and Cody recognized the name from the book on mining at the library. She turned the Subaru off and sat, watching people stream inside. The building was plain but the stained glass windows were impressive, a contrast with the ending day. She rubbed the palms of her hands down her jeans. Everyone was dressed up. It was like watching a flock of ravens descend. Black suits. Black dresses. Black hats. Even black umbrellas. And here she sat in jeans, gray tee shirt, and green fleece. It had been either that or a white tee shirt. She hadn't packed intending to go someplace she had to dress up. Not that she dressed up normally anyway.

She was delaying. Letting her mind wander, watching rather than participating. Letting indecision be her decision. Yet with so many people, would anyone see her? She could slip in the back and maybe no one would know she was there. The alternative was returning to the motel, giving in to guilt and calling her mother.

The crowd thinned and only a few people still hurried to get inside. Cody thought again about May waiting for the phone to ring, and got out of the car. She ran her hands over her cropped hair, pocketed the keys, and tried to find something else that needed doing. When she came up empty, she reluctantly climbed the steep steps to the double doors, met by organ music and the low murmur of voices. The foyer was small and just inside the door was a stand with a pot of white lilies and a white cloth-bound book open to a page for signatures. It looked oddly like a guest book for a wedding, and Cody walked by without signing, averting her eyes from something that spoke of celebrations, or maybe boasting, rather than grief.

Inside the sanctuary the pews were packed with rows of black clad people visiting with each other. A minister stood behind a dais, hands on each side, nodding to people in the crowd. The front of the church was full of wreaths, of the overpowering scent of flowers that would soon die. The sickening sweetness pulled her thoughts back to the funeral home and her grandfather's body, and the memory became a deep ache she didn't know how to handle.

Cody scanned the benches closest to the door, wondering where she could find a seat. She had a sudden fear she would have to stand back here by the door, fully visible, looking like some sort of tithe collector or pew monitor. A flash of color caught her eye and she turned to see the exotic environmentalist from the deli coming through a side door. Between her height, her long glossy hair, and a flowing velveteen dress in patchwork squares of emerald, garnet, and sapphire, she was a pagan bird in a flock of black. Cody watched the woman scan the crowd, and felt her stomach curl up when the dark eyes found her and remained. Why had the woman singled her out? Did she recognize Cody as a stranger, and would she now ask Cody to leave?

"Thank the goddess, someone who's not in black," the woman said. "Though with that gorgeous hair you should wear bright colors. I'm Rivers Rainwater and you must be Cody. Jess has told me all about you. I'm very sorry for what you've had to go through."

"Oh, uh, thank you. I mean, I appreciate your concern." Cody ducked her chin, as if to hide the blush she could feel starting. Should she also thank the woman for the comment about her hair? Why would someone compliment that? Clueless how to handle the kind words, she dropped banalities into the conversational pause. "It's nice to meet you."

"Meeting new friends at a funeral of all places. Come on, let's find a place to sit. Preferably near the back because I know this is going to be a fiasco. If I'm near a door I can get out before my mouth gets me in trouble." Rivers tugged Cody's sleeve.

She followed Rivers to a pew and watched as Rivers simply squeezed in, shifting close to the next person, who moved away until there was room for Cody. Rivers was like a life preserver, something to hang onto that gave Cody's presence legitimacy. Now she looked like she knew people and had a right to be there.

"Have you been to fiascos before?" Rivers asked.

"I don't think so," Cody said. "How do you know it's going to be one?"

"Oh, of course it will. A room full of politicians? What else could it be?" She grimaced. "This isn't a memorial for Kelly. That's not even the regular minister up there. If you look around, there are very few of Kelly's friends here. Some of the rangers in that corner. The family will use this as a publicity stunt for Kendra's reelection. The mayor in mourning. The old spider has even invited the governor, and you know damn well he never met Kelly." Rivers sat forward, gripping the back of the pew in front of her.

"Spider?" Cody watched Rivers scan the crowd with a deep intensity clear in the tensed line of jaw and mouth.

"My name for Kendra's grandfather, the nasty old fart. Have you met him?"

"Yes," Cody said.

"He's a pervert," Rivers said, releasing her grip on the pew in front of her and settling back. "I abhor funerals. But Kelly was a wonderful person and he deserves to have people here who cared about him."

"I think he could have been a friend," Cody murmured. The sheer energy that came from Rivers overwhelmed Cody and made her feel like a small dark shadow, something insignificant.

"Oh, he would have. Great, great guy. I just wish you could have known him. He'd be glad you were here though. And he'd be worried about how you were doing. He always followed up on people who had been through some sort of trauma. He wanted closure, to make sure people put their lives back together, managed to survive. He wanted happy endings." Rivers laced her fingers and cupped them around a knee as she sat forward again. "Happy endings," she repeated, as sadness settled across her face like night sinking into mountain ravines.

Cody looked away from the vulnerability, not sure how to handle someone else's frailty. "How did you know Kelly?"

"Through the forest service. They are always wanting to log or build another access road, like the world needs one more logging road. I'm always trying to stop them, so I spend a lot of time at the ranger station. Kelly was very patient with me, and listened, rather than humoring me to get me out the door. So many people hear 'environmentalist' and immediately brand me as one of those extreme types."

"The kind who chain themselves to trees?" Cody asked, and was rewarded with a smile.

"Ah, you've met Sunny. She's put me on a pretty high pedestal. I dread the day when I fall off. But between us, I've never chained myself to anything and have no intention of doing so. I prefer using best available science."

"Ladies and gentlemen," the minister said, tapping the microphone. "We are gathered here today to honor the memory of one of our own."

"As if Kelly ever stepped foot in here," Rivers whispered.

"When a young man is taken in his prime, it is hard to understand why. Many of you will feel your faith challenged, and may even question a God who would allow such a thing to happen."

"If you believe in him to begin with," came more whispered commentary.

"But I say to you that this young man was such a good soul, the angels in heaven wanted him for themselves."

"I'm going to puke."

Cody stared hard at her folded hands, trying to force the highly inappropriate smile away.

"Yes, what I just said is a cliché," the minister continued. "But when we remember Kevin, what do we think of?

Someone always willing to help others, someone with a ready smile, someone loved by all who met him."

"Did he just say 'Kevin'?" Rivers asked, straightening. "Did he even know Kelly?"

"When a death like this happens, our first instinct is to demand justice. But I put to you, that we look to our loving Father who mourns with us. He will help us in our time of need if we have faith in him. And I know he will empower our mayor to find the killers of her brother and to bring those same killers to justice. Our own mayor, Kendra Naylor, will make sure violence is not rewarded, that killers will not be allowed, and that our town will remain a safe place to raise our children. She will do this by--"

"Is this a memorial to Kelly or a campaign for re-election?" Rivers asked, loud enough that a few people turned around.

Standing, Rivers eased past Cody and walked up the aisle, waving to the rangers. The sight of someone with so much courage and self-confidence caught Cody's breath. Walking past so many judging eyes was something she would never be able to do. A hand came down on her shoulder, and a whisper jarred.

"Scoot over."

Cody looked up to see Rachel Blaine from the museum standing at the edge of the pew. She slid into the spot Rivers had vacated, and Rachel sat next to her.

"Rivers has balls," Rachel said. "It's one of the things I like about her."

Cody shook her head in amazed agreement.

"I wasn't going to come, but Granny thought one of us should be here and she didn't feel up to it." Rachel continued. "But I'm glad now I did. This will be right."

The minister hung on to the dais with one hand and covered the microphone with the other as Rivers stepped up onto the small stage. She said something to him, and he shook his head. She moved in closer and the minister let go of the dais, using both hands to cover the microphone as he continued to shake his head. Even from the back of the church Cody could see Rivers sigh.

"Those of you who know me know I don't need a microphone to be heard," she said clearly. "Lots of experience with public speaking. Can you all hear me? Even in the back? Good. I am going to begin by telling you about Kelly. And then I'm going to encourage all of you who really knew him to do the same. He would have preferred to be sitting around a campfire out in the woods, swapping tales. But since we have to be here, let's make the best of it."

Cody watched the crowd as Rivers spoke. No one stood to argue with her. People fidgeted, looked at each other, looked at the floor. But no one told her to leave and let the minister continue.

"I first met Kelly when he arrested me," Rivers said. "Or rather, when he tried to. He was just too soft hearted. Ranger Tanner. I see you over there. Did Kelly ever manage to arrest anyone?"

Cody saw Matt, sitting with other rangers, shake his head.

"Of course not," Rivers continued. "He trusted every story, hoped for truth in every excuse, no matter how many times he heard it. He gave everyone second chances. And third, and fourth."

Over the next hour stories were told. Several by Rivers, several by the rangers. But none by the people in black. Cody sat through it all, feeling the thickness of tears in her throat, wishing she could join in. If only she'd known him long enough to be able to share, to partake in this long deep drink of grief. No one would have understood if she'd got up to tell them he had smiled at her, and then died, leaving like her grandfather.

Where were the stories about Charles? Where were the friends and family gathered to speak of him, to keep his memory alive?

The weight of tears made it hard to breathe. She stood, sidestepped in front of Rachel, and escaped.

Outside, the rain still fell, and the air was rich with the scents of wet cement and old brick. There was no wind coming down off the mountains with smells of earth. It was dark, but streetlights had kicked on, illuminating the church in a halo. Cody stood for a moment at the top of the steps, sorry she had come but proud of Rivers. And overwhelmed by the meaningless loss of Kelly.

The door opened and she heard the scuff of boots on concrete. She looked over her shoulder as Matt came up behind her.

"Kelly didn't like anything he had to dress up for," Matt said. He shifted, put his hands in his pockets, pulled them back out again and crossed his arms over his chest.

Intimidated by his height, Cody stepped back from the ranger, feeling irrational anger sweep through her.

"I wouldn't know," she said. "And what about Nate? Has everyone just forgotten him? I don't see any memorial service with fancy-dancy politicians scheduled for him, and yet he died the exact same way, in the exact same place. Both of them dead for no reason, and only one memorial."

Was she talking about Nate or Charles? She didn't know anymore and didn't care. It hurt either way and she palmed wetness from her eyes.

"He's not forgotten," Matt said, as rainwater cobwebbed and darkened his blond hair.

"Really? Then I have just one more question for you," Cody said, starting down the steps. "Wouldn't your time be better spent out looking for their killer then attending this?"

"Kelly was a friend," Matt said, following her. "And I have one question for you. What were you doing crossing crime scene barriers and going back up the trail yesterday? Interfering with an investigation, or revisiting the scene of your crime?"

Chapter 9

"Your crime scene barrier said 'caution', instead of 'do not enter'," Cody said sharply. "I was cautious when I entered. If you didn't want anyone up there you should have barricaded the trail differently."

Cody made for her car. Heat scorched her cheeks as a fine trembling that felt like tears spread from knees to heart. She had lost her temper. Something she rarely did. It seemed like her control had been unraveling since her grandfather had first appeared. Until his arrival, she was certain she had come to terms with her father's abandonment, her mother's domination, her own position in the society of family. But Cody's supervisor in the physician's office where she was support staff had brought her news that made her realize how insubstantial all her beliefs really were. Her self-delusion had been laid bare.

"Cody, there's a man out at the reception desk looking for you. He says he's family of yours."

"Family?" Cody had responded, turning away from her sack lunch of tuna and tomato slices. "A man?"

Years of convincing herself she didn't want or need a father were instantly swept away and she was shocked by the unexpected tidal wave of hope.

"Right," the woman responded. "Quite elderly."

The drop from wishful thinking to reality was made more painful because Cody hadn't known that seed of optimism even existed until it was just as quickly killed.

"Thanks," she had said, standing with something that resonated inside like anger. Or maybe it was fear.

In the lobby a man stood waiting patiently, shoulders stooped in an aged arc, thinning gray hair in an old fashioned flat top, work roughened hands with knuckles swollen and callused. He was a man carrying many years of hard toil.

"Cody," he said simply, the pale blue eyes lighting.

"Yes?"

"My name is Charles Mogen," he said. "I'm your grandfather. I've been looking for you a long time."

Cody's heart raced and an odd tingling feeling in her fingertips made her reach out for the back of a chair before she fainted.

"I'm sorry to just show up," he continued, "but May keeps hanging up on my calls. I've been afraid you would turn me away like your mother but I had to know one way or another, just for my own peace of mind. So I came by here...I know it's a shock...and...you look so much like my wife." He interrupted the flow of words to pull a huge white handkerchief from the front pocket of his bib overalls and dab unashamedly at tears.

Rather than looking comical, the handkerchief fluttered like a flag of surrender and Cody felt a sudden deep ache inside. Tapping into rarely used sick time, she quit work for the day, taking this stranger, this person of shared family, to a prosaic hamburger stop.

"After my wife died, I couldn't seem to move back into the same old routines," he had said. "She had cancer. Fought like the dickens, but it was too much for her. All her hair was gone there at the end, and she had beautiful glowing hair like a campfire on a cold mountain night. Hair your color."

Cody's breath had caught on the compliment, tasting the unfamiliar tang of it, not knowing whether to believe and swallow it whole to keep in her heart, or to protect herself by squashing it before it turned into a polite lie like so many others. She sat silently, feeling her life breaking loose.

"So there I was one day, going through her things, and I found an old picture of Will. Our son had let so many people down, but he was all I had left, so I sold up the old place, got me one of those little cab-over motor homes and decided to go looking for him."

"Did you find him?" Cody asked, not sure what answer she hoped for.

"Not yet. But I hired up a private eye and he found out Will had married and had a child. You can't imagine what that was like, realizing I had a grandchild."

"I think I can," Cody said. "I mean, finding out you have family."

"Well then, maybe you can," Charles said after a moment. "Looking for you took me so long because I looked for Mogens. But that private eye finally thought to see if May might be using her maiden name, and that's how we found you. I talked to your mother and explained who I was, but she wouldn't let me talk to you. So I parked out at that old Troublesome campground by your place. I didn't want to leave until I'd heard from you personally that you didn't want a grandfather hanging around."

They sat in silence, Cody fingering cold french-fries until Charles pushed back his coffee, and stood.

"So, you care to give an old man the time of day?"

She was enfolded in a hug, arms strong and safe, overalls rough against her cheek. A large callused hand patted the top of her head as if he had never done it before. And even though he was a stranger, she had cried there, held by her grandfather.

Cody's cheeks were now as wet as they had been then, and she self-consciously blinked them away. She leaned against her car, not caring that she was getting soaked. Matt was nowhere in sight, but Rachel came out of the church, looked around, and jogged over to the car.

"You okay?" Rachel asked as she pulled on a black leather jacket against the soft rain. "Matt just came back in looking pissed. He give you a bad time?"

"Not really," Cody said. "You're not staying for the rest of the service?"

Rachel leaned against the car next to Cody, wrapping her arms around herself. "Kelly's not there."

"Like Rivers said, I don't think he would have liked it anyway." Cody watched headlights of a car swing over them as it passed, simply to have something to look at rather than Rachel's sad eyes.

"No way he would have," Rachel said. "He'd have hated all that fuss. It makes me so mad. It's just a production for the mayor. You can bet that other guy, what's his name?"

"Nate," Cody said.

"Yeah. Nate. You can bet he's not getting some big hoo-haw. I think most people have forgotten two guys died out there."

"I wonder if Nate was the reason Kelly was killed," Cody said, fingering the metal tag of her fleece zipper. "Or if Nate was killed because of Kelly, or if they were both just in the wrong place when some psycho was hiking."

"Ah shit," Rachel said, boosting herself up onto the hood of the car. "I just keep going round and round about it. Matt says Nate was up there looking for his father. When I heard that, I thought about you looking for your grandfather, and how easily it could have been you. Shot I mean."

Cody stared at Rachel a long moment, not sure if she wanted to laugh at the words or shy away from them.

"I never thought about that," she said finally. "I mean, I was scared at the time, but I never thought about it like that I guess."

"Sorry. The whole thing just has me brooding on the randomness of life. You know what I mean? It's so, so sad, and there's no understanding it." Rachel slapped the palms of her hands on the car. "I'm going rock climbing tomorrow, see if I can get my head back on straight."

"That guy at the gas station climbs," Cody said. "Cell? He mentioned rock climbing routes. And some Climb Naked group."

"I've bouldered up a few routes with Cell, and he's an amazing climber," Rachel said. "But hey, you know what? Rivers goes with the Climb Naked group."

"You're kidding. She seems so..."

"Exotic? Eccentric? I'm sure she still is when she's naked." Rachel laughed. "But I'm not going to go along and find out. Hey, thanks."

"For?"

"Trying to distract me from all this heavy stuff. You're okay. Want to come climb?"

"Rachel, I can barely hike. There's no way I'm going to shinny up some rope."

"Fine, girl," Rachel said. "You stay grounded. For now."

People trickled outside and umbrellas opened against the drizzle, looking like round black thunderclouds in the light from the church. Matt's height and blond hair made him stand out, and Cody and Rachel watched him walk to the green Forest Service Bronco.

"Matt seems pretty angry." Cody, damp and chilled, suppressed a shiver. "I think he's mad at me for not being more help."

"Matt? He doesn't work that way. He'll be pissed at himself for not saving Kelly and taking it out on everyone else. I want to be there when he finds the guy. It won't be pretty." Rachel poked Cody's shoulder. "Hey, did you know Matt's dad was a ranger?"

"No. It's not like we've socialized or anything," Cody said. She slid her cold hands up her sleeves in an attempt to find warmth, watching the Bronco back out of the lot.

"Yeah," Rachel continued. "In his dad's day rangers did everything. Talks for kids, stories around campfires, nature walks, policing, restoration, preservation. Now they're all specialized. A ranger like Matt, who does the law enforcement, won't be the one teaching people about native plants. I sometimes think Matt would have been better off he'd gone with the flowers."

"Why?" Cody tried to picture the angry man surrounded by wild flowers, and failed.

Rachel shrugged. "In a small town, you know everyone. I think he gets tired of arresting people he grew up with. That shit would get old after a while."

"You said Matt asked questions about Nate, and his search for his father?"

"Yeppers." Rachel blew on her hands and slipped them into the pockets of her jacket.

"I suppose in investigations you get all the information you can and then decide what's important."

"I suppose," Rachel repeated.

"Do you know Hailey?"

"Some. Like I said, in small towns you know pretty much everyone. I've run into her a couple times climbing, but I don't know her well enough to call her a friend or anything."

"She's...focused." Cody couldn't come up with a more accurate word that wasn't unflattering. "Maybe she'll be able to solve this. I just wish there was something more I could do."

"Hey, you've done plenty. Not to sound too blunt, but we're all strangers to you. You came here looking for stories about your family. Hang on to that and don't get sucked into such a horrible event any more than you have to."

"You're probably right," Cody said, rubbing a thumb over fingernails. It was time to trim them down again. "I just feel some kind of connection to Nate and Kelly. Probably because everything lately seems tied to death."

Depression washed through her, leaving in its wake a profound sense of hopelessness.

"Oh, I don't know," she continued. "Why should I care about people I never had a chance to know? Even my own grandfather. I don't even know why I'm here."

"It's because of what might have been," Rachel said, not meeting Cody's eyes. "We dream about possibilities but end up left with this emptiness of not knowing. I think it makes us look for answers where we can, some way to hang on to those dreams. Or make them more of a reality. At least, that's what I tell my therapist," Rachel added with an attempt at a laugh that came out sounding more like trapped tears.

"I'll take the dreams," Cody said. "Reality sucks."

"Reality bites the big one," Rachel responded, rubbing her temples as her mouth relaxed into the slightest beginning of a tremulous smile.

"Reality's a dish best served cold."

"Reality's the shits," Rachel said. "I think that's supposed to be revenge. Served cold. Something like that."

"Oh?" asked Cody. "Revenge, reality, boils down to the same thing. Anger and abandonment."

"Hell, yeah." Rachel straightened. "I'm freezing my ass off. Think I'll go down to the bar and get plastered. Want to come?"

It had been surprisingly easy to talk to Rachel. But even so, Cody couldn't see herself walking inside a bar, let alone drinking to the point where she let go of self control.

"I think I'll pass," she said. "Stay grounded, like you said."

"Smart girl," Rachel said, sliding off the car hood. "No hangover tomorrow."

Cody watched Rachel head down the sidewalk, swallowed by a pool of darkness, haloed by a streetlight, and swallowed again. And wondered if she'd just let an opportunity for adventure and friendship walk away. Resigned to the familiar feeling of not knowing how to grasp life, Cody got in the car and started the engine, cranking up the defrost fan against the damp that fogged the windshield.

She swiped a clear spot with her hand so that she could see out. And shook her head. Too bad it wasn't as easy to find a way to see life more clearly.

Chapter 10

Collapsing on the bed, Cody closed her eyes. The day had dragged so many emotions out of her that she was empty. She listened to cars passing outside, to a door shutting somewhere, to the voices of an adult and child arguing. She was grateful for the quiet inside the room, and more grateful for the solitude.

The phone rang, jerking her up off the bed. She gasped, as if she'd just choked on her heart. May. No. It wouldn't be her mother after the last call. That would mean giving in and May never gave in, never shifted, never lost. Cody wiped the palm of her hand down her thigh, and picked up the hand set.

"Hello?"

Silence.

"Hello?" She repeated the word louder.

"You're a smart girl." The voice was soft, barely there, lifeless.

"What?" The fine hairs on Cody's neck stood up.

"You're a smart girl. You'll quit tattling. You'll go home."

There was no anger in the voice, no emotion of any kind. The click of the phone disconnecting was louder than the whisper.

Chapter 11

The phone rang again, and Cody threw the blankets back in the pearl light of morning. It didn't matter if the call was May or her prankster of the night before. Either way she wasn't going to give them what they wanted. A night disrupted by whispered dreams made her yank up the handset and wait in defiant silence.

"Hey!" came Rachel's cheery voice. "You just do heavy breathing in the morning?"

The pounding where her heart normally beat eased, the weight lifted and her breath came easier. "Sorry. Guess I'm still half asleep."

"Girl, it's nine. Time to rise and shine. Grab some clothes and breakfast and meet me outside in half an hour. Granny's having a clear day."

"Pardon?" Cody tossed blankets and stood, trying to get her brain to wake up.

"Granny. Remember I told you she has dementia? Well, she's pretty clear today and I thought it might be a good time for the two of you to talk about your grandfather. If you want that is."

"That would be great," Cody said, grabbing jeans with one hand.

"Perfect. Bring something to take notes with. She talks a lot and rambles all over. It can be hard to remember everything she says, so it helps to write down the gems. See you soon."

Normally self-conscious eating in front of people, Cody gave in to the time constraint and opted for the continental breakfast in the motel lobby, hiding behind a newspaper. She had only a few minutes to spare before Rachel was due. She stared at her plate with half a croissant still sitting there, hearing her mother's voice. You could never leave food on your plate, no matter how full you were. The plate had to be emptied. Food could not be wasted.

Cody looked out the front windows but there was no sign of Rachel yet. Instead, she saw her own reflection, and in that, she saw May. There were so many tiny irritations connected to her mother overflowing her blue chair, rocking minutes and years away, her demands and commands keeping cadence. Little things in themselves, in some ways almost petty, but adding up to a lifetime of bites out of Cody's psyche, until she was left with no idea who she was, only a map of who she was expected to be.

"I'm not my mother," Cody whispered to herself. "I'm not my mother." She stood, turned from her reflection, and left food behind, taking only guilt with her to the front door.

The morning air was chilly and damp, but the small window of sky between the mountains was clear, with the watered light of fall. Cody pulled on her fleece, eyes catching on the dark stain on the sleeve. She had to find a Laundromat. Nate's blood didn't look like blood anymore, instead like she had dragged her coat through mud. She didn't want to see the reminder, didn't want to touch it, yet didn't want to wash away the last of the man. She chose instead to ignore the morbid spot, tucking her hands in her pockets, and breathed deeply of the crisp air. She watched a battered and rusting yellow Jeep come down the street sounding like it was dying with the summer. She stepped back as it parked with two wheels up on the sidewalk. The side window rolled down and Rachel leaned over the passenger seat.

"Oops," she said. "Damn sidewalk. You ready?"

Cody pulled open the door, only to be met with a cascade of books and papers. She scrambled to catch the ones escaping, while Rachel shoved more into the backseat, adding to the layered collection already strewn across the cracked vinyl.

"This a car or a mobile library?"

"Granny calls it my purse on wheels," Rachel said, laughing. "Sorry."

"No problem." Cody pulled the passenger door shut behind her, trying to avoid stepping on more papers.

"Hope you didn't eat a huge breakfast," Rachel said as she bumped the Jeep back onto the street. "Granny's been baking like crazy. Of course, you never know if she's clear on what she's doing or not. One time she served up sautéed crayons. What a mess."

"Does she live here in Wallace?" Cody asked.

"No, she's north in Burke. She's lived in the same house all her life. Can you imagine that? My great-grandpa built the place and she grew up in it, and then after she married, her and grandpa continued living in it. I think those kinds of stories are what pulled me into history. She says she's leaving it to me in her will."

"What will you do with it?"

"Are you kidding? Wait until you see it. Great old place with lots of character. I'll leave my rental in seconds flat." Rachel was silent a moment, and when she spoke her voice was quieter. "Maybe someday I'll find the right guy. Keep the tradition going, you know? Kids and all that, more generations, adding to the story. Even though hardly anyone lives out in Burke anymore."

"Isn't that where Rivers lives?"

"Yeah. There's a few diehards that refuse to let go. Burke's a place you live in only if you have a history there."

The narrow road twisted back into even narrower canyons, and Rachel provided a mile by mile commentary, pointing out old mine sites. Barren, steep hillsides were covered in nothing but rocky mine tailings and the wooden remains of old cribbing, timber stacked to hold back hillsides. They passed wider spots in the road where tiny towns had once existed. Black Bear and Yellow Dog and Frisco, places with no people, no buildings, only the past and no future.

"Where does the road go?" Cody asked, watching a ribboned streamed that was like a silver net over the land.

"Into Burke, and then about half a mile past to the old power station," Rachel said. "The substation isn't used anymore, but there's an ATV road just past it that hunters use. Granny's right at the far edge of town so you'll get the grand tour. Burke's famous you know. The only town to have a main street so narrow you had to roll up awnings and move cars when the train came through. The tracks and the main street were the same. And you should see Nine Mile Cemetery. It runs up canyon walls so steep people are buried practically standing up."

"You're pulling my leg."

"Hell no."

When Rachel lapsed back into silence, Cody stared out her window, trying to picture the ghostly remains of life long gone. What had it been like during the days when mines were producing, when people huddled at the bottoms of these canyons hoping for the mother lode? Fall was just beginning, but already the sun didn't reach over the edge of the ravines. In the middle of winter the people here must have felt like they were living in a land of no light.

After a couple more quiet miles, Cody broke the stillness. "I got a prank phone call last night."

"Oh yeah? An offer for phone sex?"

"No," Cody said, blushing. She repeated what the caller had said.

"Girl, you need to call Jess."

"I don't want to cause extra work for anyone. I mean, it was just a phone call." Cody regretted bringing it up.

"This is shittin' serious. Call her now." Rachel tossed a cell phone into Cody's lap.

Cody dialed reluctantly and self-consciously, and was relieved to get voice mail. She left a message and shut the phone.

"Happy now?" she asked Rachel.

"Happy."

There wasn't much to Burke and the few homes showed their age, disintegrating but refusing to give up, gripping their bit of land between the steep rocky walls and the edge of the narrow street. The places were pieced and repaired, using scavenged bits of lumber and the ubiquitous duct tape and looked like they should have been closed up years ago. Two tiny places had been recently restored, but they were an anomaly. Most of the places didn't look stable enough to protect those who lived within, let alone provide shelter from the rocks the ravine seemed to be tossing at them. Burke was clearly a dying town, hanging on tenaciously in case better times came along.

Rachel was silent during the few minutes it took to drive the canyon floor. When they reached the end of town, she parked in a small, rocky wide spot at the road edge. She got out of the Jeep, slipping keys into the pocket of tight jeans.

There was no driveway to the old house. Instead, Cody saw a long narrow ladder of wooden steps leading up through slanting slabs of weathered rock, ending at a home with a steeply pitched roof, balanced precariously on the side of a canyon wall, like a tiny bird perched on a mountain.

"Defies gravity doesn't it?" Rachel asked. "I love it when people see it for the first time."

"How did it get up there?" Cody asked. "I mean, how did they build it?"

"Same way the old timers built most places in Burke and Wallace. Very carefully." Rachel laughed at what was obviously an old joke.

"Your granny can manage the steps?" Cody asked, climbing upward behind Rachel.

"For now," Rachel responded. "Her age shows up more in the mental problems than in physical difficulties. I hire Sunny to stay with her when I can afford it. I can get Granny out for her appointments, but I hate to think of when the stairs get to be too much. She'll probably have to live with me or I'll have to move in with her and she'll hate that, having a caretaker. But there's no way in hell I'll let her go into a nursing home."

"She's lucky to have you," Cody said. "I mean, you take care of her because you want to, not because you have to."

"She's my Granny," Rachel said simply, and then added words so quiet Cody almost missed them. "But it's damn hard sometimes."

At the first small landing, Cody stopped to catch her breath and admire the view of high hills reaching up into sky. With a strange sense of vertigo, Cody felt if she reached out her hand she could touch the snowfields breathing cold air down into the canyon.

"Some view, isn't it?" Rachel asked.

Cody could only nod before turning to follow Rachel the rest of the way.

Rachel pushed open the door, walking in without knocking, and Cody saw Rachel secure in her welcome, at home in a place where she knew she was loved. Following her inside was like entering some foreign land, scents of cinnamon and nutmeg mixing with the resin scent of burning wood in a cast iron wood stove. Doilies and antimacassars covered arms of horsehair chairs and created lacy surfaces for knick knacks and family pictures. Small rooms with large windows pulled Cody forward with the welcoming feel of a home that had known many generations of love. Pots of herbs and mason jars full of water and plant cuttings crowded together on deep windowsills made from roughly milled boards. Braided throw rugs decorated wide plank floors, and Cody felt as if she had stepped back into another century. No wonder Rachel had gone into the field of history. It was a job that must have spoken to her of good memories.

"Granny! We're here," Rachel called out. When there was no answer she crossed the creaking floor and poked her head into another doorway. "Granny?"

"There's my girl," a quavery voice answered. "Where's your friend then?"

"Right here. This is Cody Marsh. Cody, my granny, Florence Blaine."

"It's nice to meet you Mrs. Blaine," Cody said politely. Rachel's grandmother was a tiny woman with carefully curled and set gray hair, wearing an old flowered apron with a waistband that disappeared under large sagging breasts.

"Florence, dear. Or just Granny. That's what I'm used to answering to. I remember that when I don't remember much else some days. Do you drink coffee or tea? I've just taken cinnamon rolls out and they'll go down fine with something hot."

"Tea please," Cody responded, sitting down gingerly at an old schoolhouse table. She fell back on polite conversation, unsettled by feelings of being welcomed and treated like an old family friend.

"Rachel, put the kettle on, dear," Florence said, worming her ample bottom into a chair across from Cody. "Now then, I understand you want to hear old stories."

"Please."

"Well then, I think you've picked a good day for it. I think I'm doing all right. Who are you looking for again?"

"Charles Mogen."

"Charles," Florence said, folding her wrinkled hands in her lap. "Did I know a Charles?"

"Alice's boy, Granny."

"Alice. Strange, strange woman. She spanked her little boy one afternoon. I think he may have been trying to split kindling. She made him kneel on a piece of that firewood so his knees would hurt as much as his bottom. My parents were horrified. Papa was the sheriff back in those days, and I believe he tried mighty hard to come up with some way to get hold of her."

"She never lost custody though, did she Granny?" asked Rachel.

"Not that I ever knew. Did you know you're related to royalty, dear?" Florence asked Cody.

"No," Cody said, not sure how to respond. "Can't say as I did."

"Alice was convinced she was the long lost mother to the king of Sweden," Florence said, and giggled behind her hand as if she had to hide her mirth. "She got her little boy cuff links with crowns on them one year, so everyone would know he was half royalty."

"So she didn't neglect him completely then?" Cody asked, thinking of her grandfather wearing those cufflinks. Had he wished for his mother to give him attention instead? Or had he been glad she was in her own world and leaving him alone?

"I imagine the boy sold those cuff links," Florence said. "He probably made better use of the money. He was the sole support for his mother. He was a year or two older than me, but I remember him at school. Always by himself working on some project. One time he rewired the whole school sound system. He must have been fourteen or so then. And did you ever hear the story about his car?"

"Great grandpa," Rachel said softly.

"Car?" asked Cody, taking a pen out of the pocket of her jeans. Part of her wanted to write down what Florence said so nothing would be forgotten but she held the pen tightly, afraid of doing anything that would interrupt the flow of words.

"Well then, here was a boy needing a job, needing a way to support his mother, needing transportation, so he could work. There was this madam named Ethel. You heard of her?"

"Yes," Cody said. "Some anyway."

"Believe it or not, everyone liked her, even women in town. You couldn't not like her. She'd help anyone out." Florence picked up a coaster, set it back down carefully, studied it, and shifted it slightly to the right.

"Ethel, Granny?" Rachel prompted.

"Mama says Ethel has a real soft spot for that boy." Florence shifted the coaster again, and then looked up at Cody with eyes that were unfocused, shadowy, in the past.

Cody started to speak, but Rachel shook her head.

"I was going to school and it was snowing and so cold," Florence said. "Here was Charles standing on the sidewalk like he didn't know where to go. Flakes floating all around him, in the same jacket he wore in the summer. No cap, no gloves. And then out comes Ethel, arms full. She hands him this mug that's steaming. She starts swaddling him, wrapping a scarf around his neck, slipping mittens on. She even had a lunch pail for him. And after he's all wrapped up, she hugs him, just holds him so close." Florence paused, gazing over Cody's shoulder as if the snowy day was clearer than the kitchen.

Cody felt tears pricking, seeing in her mind the small shadowy boy in swirls of falling snow.

"I think to this day," Florence continued, "what meant most to that boy was her holding him. He stayed there like it was sanctuary."

"And great-grandpa and the car Granny?" Rachel asked after a moment of silence.

"Well, here was this boy needing a job so's he can get money to take care of his crazy mother. But he doesn't have any way of getting around. Papa said one day Ethel had a long talk with him. He was a tall drink of water, Papa. Always wore a fedora, tilted just so. And Mama was this tiny little thing that barely reached his belt buckle. Rachel!" Florence's voice became fast and vibrant. "Haven't you told your friend about Papa and Mama?"

"Wesley and Hazel Smithwick," responded Rachel. "They met when she was seven and he was ten, and she was crying because she'd lost a dime down the crack in the old boardwalk on her way to school. He got it out for her and said it was love at ten, and still love at ninety when he died."

"He used to chase children away from the mill," Florence said, and ducked her head as if to hide the slightly guilty smile that grew. "Including me. We'd crawl in under the milling area where wheat filtered through the floorboards and sneak cigarettes. Thought we were hiding but of course the smoke came up through the cracks."

"And the car Granny?" Rachel rested a hand on Florence's shoulder, gently stroking.

"Well, here was this boy needing a job. And Ethel talks to Papa, the sheriff, and what does Papa do? He takes that boy to a junkyard, and they tow home bits and pieces, and he teaches that boy how to work on cars and they build up one that the boy can drive. Then he teaches the boy how to drive, stands up for him as a sponsor so he can get his license. Months they spent together working on that old car. And all because Ethel put a bug in Papa's ear. Powerful woman."

"Did you know anything about Charles's father?" Cody asked. "I only know he was a railroad man."

"Lots of those around here. Always transient. No roots sunk into the ground like the miners." Florence reached up and patted Rachel's hand.

"Charles's father told him that one day he would explain Charles's parentage to him," Cody said. "So my grandfather always wondered where his dad came from, and what his dad's secret might have been."

Florence laughed, and the sound mingled with the whistle of the tea kettle boiling. "Catch that kettle, will you Rachel, dear? All I can say about parentage, is look at Wallace and its history. A place full of bordellos? I imagine there are many locals that aren't related to the parents they think they are."

Rachel handed Cody an obviously old and delicate saucer with a cup of tea balanced on its spider webbed surface.

"What do you mean?" asked Cody.

"Well dear, many babies were born from the wrong side of the blanket. If that boy had some mystery about his parentage, I'd wager the mother was the mystery, not the father."

Cody stared at Florence in silence, words swept away by the seeds the old woman had just planted.

"Granny," Rachel said, sitting back down at the table. "If his mother was the big secret, then how come his father left him with a woman who was not only crazy but also not his biological mother? And why would Alice have kept a boy that wasn't hers?"

"That's it dear," Florence said. "If she had no children of her own, and her husband leaving her, maybe she knew that little one was the only child she'd ever have."

"No," Cody said, thinking about her mother. "I bet she kept him so she'd have someone to take care of her."

"Could be, could be." Florence stood and moved to the counter, a knee ticking with each step. "How about some warm cinnamon rolls now the tea is ready?"

"You want to split one?" Rachel asked Cody.

"Sure," Cody responded. "How would I go about finding out who his biological parents were? I wouldn't even know where to start looking for something like that."

"With his birth certificate, I imagine," Florence said, coming back to the table with plates and forks. "But looking back over the years, I bet I can tell you who his mother was."

"Who?" asked Rachel.

"Why dear, the woman who loved that boy, kept an eye out for him, fed him, and who dressed him up warm when the snow fell."

Chapter 12

"I thought Ethel had some long running affair with the mayor," Rachel said, cutting a huge cinnamon role in half, releasing steam and scents of spices.

"She may have," Florence said. "But she was a madam wasn't she? Nothing to say she couldn't share her bed with whoever she wanted. Maybe some railroad man caught her fancy. You're the historian dear. See if there's something about Ethel going away for a vacation about the same time that boy was born."

"I'll do that," Rachel said.

"Do you remember any more stories about Charles?" Cody asked.

"Charles? Oh, he's a quiet boy. He takes care of his mother you know. He never gets to play with us." Florence pinched off a piece of cinnamon roll. "Of course, that was a hard time, what with the war and all."

Florence told rambling stories for two or three more hours, sometimes repeating ones she had already told, and sometimes forgetting what year she was in. But Cody and Rachel sat patiently through it all, listening to words of a time long past. There was nothing more about Charles, but Cody could have sat the day away, soaking in the warm acceptance of the old woman. But eventually Florence flagged.

"What was your name again dear?"

"Cody."

"That's right. And where was I, Carly?"

"About to head off for a nap," Rachel said, slipping a hand under her grandmother's elbow.

"Oh yes. It's been so nice having your friend here, dear. So nice to have company. What was her name again?"

Watching Rachel support her grandmother across the kitchen, head bent to catch Florence's rambling words, Cody saw with aching clarity what was missing with her mother. Rachel loved her grandmother. It was there in the patience, the respect, the kindness. Cody couldn't remember the last time she had done something for her mother without feeling anger or bitterness or frustration. She was sure she had loved her mother at one time, and maybe she still did, but if so it was buried beneath too many memories held onto for too long.

Cody never thought of herself as having any similarities to her mother, but maybe holding grudges past their due date was one of them. She had to admit she tugged out her mother's transgressions, chewing on them long after she should have tossed them away. Maybe, by hanging on to the hurtful words and demeaning actions, Cody had done nothing more than keep wounds open and bleeding.

"She's asleep," Rachel said, coming out of the back room and shutting the door behind her. "Want some more tea?"

"Sure," Cody responded, still thinking about May and the rocky road they traveled as mother and daughter. "Where are your parents?"

"Mine? Oh hell, I don't know. Traveling somewhere. You know, part of the 'retire and abandon their kid for the motor home' crowd. How about yours?"

"My dad's traveling as well," Cody said after a moment. "Well, sort of. He left when I was little and I've never heard from him since. My mother raised me alone, and I didn't know I had any other family until my grandfather showed up."

"I bet that made your mom and you close."

"Actually," Cody said, "Just the opposite. My mother is…what's a good word for her? A martyr. Know what I mean?"

"Not really. Give me an example."

"I take her grocery shopping, and we always park in the disabled slots. I don't know how she got a handicap permit. Her biggest health problem is her weight." Cody fidgeted with her plate, pushing crumbs around with her finger. "She gets out of the car just fine, but as soon as she sees someone, she'll put the back of her hand to her forehead, and get short of breath. She'll lean on me, and the person will go get her one of those motorized carts to ride around in, all the time looking at me like I'm a terrible daughter because I'm just standing there."

Rachel actually laughed and Cody had to think back over her words, looking for the humor she had missed.

"Shit, Cody. I can just picture it. Tell me another."

"I'll be at one end of the house and she'll call me into the room where she is sitting and ask me to bring something to her, and it will be something that is just out of her reach. So I'll have dropped whatever I'm doing, come from wherever I've been, to pick up something all she had to do was stand up to get."

Cody tried to smile, to add humor to the story, but it felt like a grimace on her face.

"And, god forbid if I complain, because then the martyr comes out with a big sigh, and she starts telling me to never mind, she'll get it herself, she's sorry she's such a hardship for me, and then she'll move into telling me all she had to give up to raise me, especially when…" Cody's words dried up. She had started out half joking, wanting to keep the conversation light, but the familiar phrases sank their teeth into her heart.

"When what?" Rachel asked, fingering back wisps of her hair.

Cody stared at the bobbed brown hair, at the way the light pooled gold in strands and wondered why someone with such beautiful hair would cut it so short. She would have grown it long, worn it as a badge of beauty. Unlike her own hair, ugly in its frizzy red wildness. It was why she kept it cropped, so she could ignore it. She had tried wearing it long and in a braid but it had still been too visible. Her eyes dropped to her hands, clenched in her lap, seeing freckles and mannish fingers that never seemed to hold a ring right.

"Cody?"

"Oh, sorry. I was just remembering."

"No you weren't. You were going to repeat what your mother said, and you clammed up."

"My mother can say things that hurt, and say them more times than you need to hear them. Sometimes it's like she doesn't think you realize her words are true, so she has to keep pounding them into your heart day after day long after you've given up telling her you don't need to hear them anymore. I end up mad, and then get angry because I'm mad."

"Let's go out to the living room," Rachel said, picking up her tea and another cinnamon roll.

Cody followed, hoping the weight of her words would slide off her heart and stay in the kitchen.

"I can tell you one thing anger does." Rachel sank onto an armchair and clumped her boots up on the coffee table. "It allows you to say things you might not have the balls to, and it helps you stand up for yourself. And damn, girl, that sounds like something you need to do."

The jarring notes of Rachel's cell phone invaded the room.

"What is that?" Cody asked, relieved to be saved from having to respond.

"Combiechrist," Rachel said, her boots clumping from the coffee table to the floor as she stretched her legs out so she could retrieve the phone from the pocket of her jeans. "Like heavy metal on acid. Love it." She flipped her phone open. "Hello? Yeppers Jess, she's right here."

Rachel tossed the phone to Cody, who managed to catch it before it hit the floor.

"I got your message about the prank phone call," Jess said. "You didn't say if it was male or female."

"It was a whisper. I couldn't tell."

"So nothing you could identify. Did you call the main switchboard to see if they transferred the call or if the person knew your room number?"

"I didn't think of that," Cody said. "I'm sorry. I guess I was rattled."

"No problem. I'll follow up on that with the motel. I'm also wondering if you've thought about what the call could mean."

"No," Cody said. "Unless by tattling they meant talking to you."

"I agree. Either that or they're worried about something more they think you might have to tell us."

Cody gripped the phone tighter. "I've told you everything."

"I believe you Cody. But I'm wondering if you might be willing to do something for me. Like go back up that trail. I'd like Matt to take you up there and see if anything jars your memory. You were in shock. Maybe you saw something you didn't realize the importance of."

"How does that help with the phone message?"

"It doesn't," Jess said. "It just gave me the idea. I'm working a couple angles with the phone thing. I don't want you worrying about that. If you get another call though I want you to call me or Matt immediately."

"I can do that." Cody relaxed. It was easier to agree to a phone call than going back up that trail.

"Great. So what about trying that trail?" Jess wasn't going to let her off the hook so easily. "Matt could meet you there in an hour."

"I'm at Florence's, but I guess Rachel could drop me off."

"Perfect. I'll let him know. Thanks Cody. And don't worry too much about the call. Like I said, I have a few ideas."

Cody closed the phone and handed it back to Rachel.

"So, we have time for another cinnamon half?"

The call had interrupted the confessional about May, and Cody was relieved when Rachel didn't bring her mother back up.

"How long have you worked at the museum?" she asked.

Rachel licked cinnamon off her fingers. "Oh, about five years I guess. I got the job right out of high school. The benefits are good and I love anything to do with history, but you saw granny. At some point I'm going to need to pay for a full time caregiver for her. My wages aren't going to cover that expense."

"How long before you have to do that?" Cody asked.

"No idea." Rachel stood. "Hell, she's strong. Come on, I'll run you down to town and then I'm going to come back and sit with Granny for a while."

Chapter 13

Back at the gas station Cody watched Rachel pull out, feeling like she had been abandoned. Matt locked the door to the forest service Bronco parked next to her.

"Shouldn't Jess be here, too?" Cody asked as they walked behind the station to the trailhead. "We could wait for her."

"Jess is a city girl," Matt said. "She doesn't hike. It's why she went into police work instead of the forest service."

"I don't think this is going to help any."

"You'd rather be hanging around Florence scarfing her baked stuff?" Matt asked as he held up the caution tape for Cody to bend under.

"We weren't scarfing," Cody said.

"Yeah, right. I've had Florence's cooking before. And I've watched how much Rachel can put away."

"So are you and Jess hoping I'll have some sort of epiphany when we get up there? Like I'll suddenly remember seeing someone standing in the trees holding a smoking gun?"

"Don't be obnoxious," Matt said, ducking under the tape. "Jess thought coming back up here might trigger a memory. Personally I think it's a waste of my time."

With no further words birthing between them, the woods filled the void with rustling breezes and leaves falling, foreshadowing the dance of snowflakes. Matt led the way up the now familiar trail, and Cody struggled to keep up, wishing she'd turned down the second cinnamon roll.

"What did you come up here for anyway?" Matt asked, holding back a golden tamarack branch until she caught it. "That first time. This isn't on the normal tourist routes."

"My grandfather hunted a cougar up here when he was a boy. He told me about it and I wanted to see it."

"He get the cougar?"

"No, some Italian did."

Matt stopped abruptly and swung around. "I know that story. Big bounty, small boy. Cougar tracking the boy back down the trail."

"Yes!" Cody said, flooded by so many confusing emotions they tangled around her heart. Here was a thread to tie together memories of her grandfather, to prove he had lived. Someone else to remember him besides herself.

"Don't you know the name of this trail?" Matt asked.

"No."

"Bounty Trail. Lots of people know that story. My grandfather was a boy then," Matt said. "He said it was why he went into the forest service when he grew up. He saw the cougar die and didn't want to let it happen again. He was a big softy for wild animals. More so than he was for people. Gramps thought the Italian should have paid the boy the fee though."

Cody touched a tree branch. Bounty Trail. Her grandfather's place, in a way. "Is your grandfather still alive?"

"No." The word was sudden in its curtness, and silence fell heavily.

Cody excused his brusqueness because he had unwittingly handed her an important connection to her grandfather. After several minutes of hiking steadily and silently, he stopped in the trail, not looking back at her.

"My grandfather and father died on Desolation. They were trying to help a climber. Gramps was too old to be there, and my dad had just retired from the forest service, but both of them were too damned stubborn to wait until I got there with gear and help. The fools thought they were immortal."

Anger split through the words, and Cody could think of nothing to say. What was it about family, that it created such twisted bonds of devotion and responsibility? She groped for words to fill the uncomfortable emptiness between them.

"My grandfather said an avalanche wiped out the Italian's windows," Cody said finally, her words sounding lame and worthless as she tried for something less emotional. "The Italian hired him to fix them."

"Gramps thought the boy started the rockslide. He'd laugh when he'd tell my dad and me the story." The anger was gone, Matt's voice deflated and as devoid of life as the leaves falling around them.

"Did you go into the forest service because of them?" Cody asked as Matt started back up the trail.

"Yeah," he responded, hunching his shoulders as if shielding against her words. "I have three uncles who were all miners, and when I was a kid, I wanted to be like them. But after the Sunshine fire, they never went back underground, and when I talked about it, they laid down the law, even though years had passed. No mining. I didn't know what else I wanted to do so it was easier to give in to dad and granddad's pushing."

This was the closest they had come to a normal conversation, and Cody shied away from it, afraid she'd mess it up, like May always told her she did. She was awkward enough talking to Rachel, let alone to a man. And Matt seemed content to let silence return.

Cody's jeans and jacket were soon damp from brushing past long dead grass and leafless branches still heavy with dew. In under the trees like they were, the sun wouldn't reach ground until late afternoon. She struggled along as Matt climbed steadily, and was surprised when he passed the spot where Nate and Kelly had fallen. Cody stepped reverently through the area. After the passage of a few days no one coming up the trail would ever know two people had died here. How easily tragedy washed away. How long until even the memory was gone?

"We're not stopping?" It seemed almost sacrilegious to not pause.

"No," Matt answered. "Thought we'd go to the clearing you were at. Retrace your route. See if things look different coming down the trail."

"If I'd known we were going all the way to the clearing I'd have told you to go jump in a lake."

"You want to jump in a lake I'll tell you how to get to Fool's Lake. Good swimming."

"Ha," Cody said trying to find enough breath to talk and hike at the same time. "You aren't the only one with connections to the Forest Service. I know all about Fool's Lake. My grandfather worked in the fire towers one season, and he even signed the log book."

"All the logs are filed at the Ranger Station after each season," Matt said absently. He stopped abruptly and Cody nearly ran into his back. "We're here. What did you do that day?"

Would he think her crazy if she told him she had stood in the quiet woods looking for her grandfather?

"Nothing special. Hung around, sat on a rock."

Wind ran exploratory fingers through empty branches and remnants of rain dripped. Somewhere nearby a squirrel scolded them for trespassing, and as Cody's breathing slowed she could hear the soft whisper of a stream back in the trees.

All sounds that belonged in the woods. No memories of someone now gone.

Pinching the bridge of her nose, she felt lost, the earlier connection from Matt's words abandoning her. Charles was gone, and she didn't believe anything existed after death. She knew logically she was alone. She just felt that more acutely now, since she'd had a brief taste of what it might have been like, had Charles found her sooner. She was wasting time, foolishly dreaming she might find something left behind of a man few remembered.

Matt crossed the clearing, walking away from her, and Cody felt no need to follow. Instead, she found the same boulder she had used before, and sat down again, rubbing her temples, where the seeds of a headache were germinating.

It saddened Cody to think she might end up with just the memory of a few weeks spent in Charles's company. She didn't want to look too closely at the vision looming on the horizon, of her slipping back into the old routine of caring for her mother. Instead she tried to distract herself by watching Matt circling back toward her, eyes fixed on the ground.

"Find anything?"

"Nothing," he said finally.

"What did you expect?" Cody asked, depressed and irritable. "It's not like they made it up this far."

Matt didn't bother responding. Instead he headed back for the trailhead and Cody reluctantly stood.

"I guess this means break time is over?" she called after him.

"Someone who's been sitting on a boulder doesn't need a break."

"I was thinking, not just sitting," Cody said.

Roughly halfway back to where Kelly and Nate had died, Cody stopped to stretch out a sudden cramp in her calf muscle. She watched Matt pause several yards ahead of her, move, stop again, and retrace his steps. Squatting, he fingered through layers of old pine needles, and only then did she see what looked like scuff marks going back into the trees. An animal trail most likely, she thought, joining him as he studied signs so subtle and faint they became invisible if she looked directly at them. As she tried to see what he saw on the damp ground, he straightened and left the trail. Following closely, she stumbled into him when he stopped, and he looked over his shoulder as if wondering where she came from.

"Boot tracks," he said, pointing to the muddy ground.

The tracks headed out toward the main path and even to Cody's inexperienced eyes she could tell they weren't fresh. Filled with the remains of rainwater, the edges softened and crumbling inward, the prints were a mere shadow of the man who had passed.

Cody questioned the wisdom of following this narrow lead deeper into the forest, and wondered if she should point out to Matt the killer might still be around. But he moved forward again, paralleling the faint prints.

"Don't walk on the tracks," he said, slipping out of his backpack.

Unzipping a pocket, he pulled out a digital camera and focused it on the old boot tracks, snapping off several shots.

"We'll see what's up ahead and then I'll radio this in. If we can get a casting of the tracks, we should be able to find out if they match Nate's. If they don't, then a casting might help us match to the shooter."

"Of course if the killer is up ahead you won't have to worry about matching old boot tracks to anything," Cody couldn't help saying.

"If you're scared go sit on your rock."

She was nervous, but there was no way she was going to admit it. Matt bulldozed his way upward and she followed, catching at branches to keep from slipping. Eventually the land leveled, opening to a small rough clearing, neat but cluttered with camping gear. Obviously new, the rawness of freshly cut branches opened up space for a battered one - man tent and a ring of blackened flat rock that had been used for a fire pit.

"Hello? Anybody home?" she called loudly, merely to spite Matt, who didn't react.

Even with nothing to identify the owner, Cody still believed they had found Nate's camp, and Matt must have been thinking along the same lines as he pulled out his radio, keying it open and calling for a team.

"Don't go any closer," he told her after he finished the transmission.

"No kidding," Cody responded in her mother's dripping sarcasm. "Want me to go back out and show them where we left the trail?"

"Sure," Matt said, sounding distracted as he took more pictures.

It was obvious he didn't care where she went, and so she retraced the new path they had broken until she was back at the main trail. It seemed to take a long time for more uniforms to show up, and the sight of them brought back memories of when they had come for Nate and Kelly. Feeling isolated in the group and unexpectedly sad and drained, she pointed the way and left them to their job. Hiking out alone, she paused at the spot where Nate had died, lifting her face to the chill breezes.

Whoever he had been, she wouldn't let him be forgotten.

When Cody reached the gas station she debated whether to walk back to the motel, or to hang around in case Matt still wanted her to do something. While she tried to think what that something might be, Jess pulled up, squeezing the patrol car into an already overfull lot. Cody walked over as Jess got out, arcing her back in a graceful stretch. Her thick black braid sucked in sunlight and reflected it in a deep sheen.

"Cody. Hear you two found something."

"A camp. Matt seems to think it might be Nate's."

"Stands to reason. Anything else come of the hike?"

"Besides sweat?" Cody asked. "Not really."

"Too bad." Jess shut the car door. "Guess I can't put off going up the trail then. Did you see Hailey bouncing her way up there?"

"No. I'm surprised she wasn't shadowing Matt."

"I haven't seen her in a few days. I need to find out what she's been doing. I don't trust her to keep us in the loop. And Matt's been running down so many threads he hasn't had time to baby sit her. You want a lift back to the motel?"

"No thanks. I need to walk after being at Florence's. I don't think the hike was enough to counterbalance cinnamon rolls."

"Fine then. Leave me no more reasons to delay hiking. I'll check in with you later."

Cody walked to the corner of Bank Street where she stood waiting for the crosswalk sign to change. There was a little more traffic today, and it took her a moment to realize it was Saturday. The town seemed to have come out of its slumber for the weekend. As the light changed, she saw a man step off the curb on the other side, and as she neared the center of the road she recognized the mountain man look. The man who had argued with Cell. What had Jess said his name was? Jake. Jake Conrad.

"You," he said when they neared each other in the crosswalk. "I heard you were down here. Got a minute?"

"Not really," Cody said, trying not to back up.

"I'm not going to bite your head off. We can talk right here in the middle of the street if you're nervous."

"Only if you stand back out of reach."

He backed up a few steps. "Far enough or you want me to shout?"

"I guess you're okay." A car came down the street and obligingly went out around them.

"You've messed stuff up for me, telling Jess I was arguing with Cell."

"I suppose you're going to say you weren't arguing?" Cody asked.

"Hell no. I was arguing. I always end up yelling at him. He drives me bat shit."

"There's anger management classes for that kind of stuff you know." Cody rubbed her fingernails against her palms.

"Like I've never heard that before. But that's not why I'm here. I want to know what you saw up there. On the trail."

"What do you mean?"

"Just what I said. What'd you see? What happened?"

"They think we found Nate's camp. That's about--"

"Not today," Jake said. "When you first went up there."

"Nate and Kelly were shot, that's what happened," Cody said, feeling the warmth of unwanted anger moving. "They died, that's what happened. And I don't think I want to talk to you anymore."

"Damn it, I know they died. I don't care about that. Well, I do, but that's not what I'm asking. Ah hell." He pulled off his hat, slapped it against his thigh and clamped it back on. "Look. Kelly and me? We didn't like each other. But not enough I shot him. Believe me, if I killed someone, they wouldn't be found afterwards."

"Is that supposed to be reassuring?" Cody asked. "Because it's not."

"I want to know if Kelly was holding anything. Or if he said anything about me or logging."

"I only spoke to him briefly on my way up the trail. When I came down he was already dead. I didn't see anything. But then I wasn't exactly looking."

Cody turned at the sound of a car engine and saw a forest service Bronco pull up against the curb.

"Shit," Jake said.

Cody silently agreed as Hailey got out.

"I understand there's a situation up the trail," she said. "Fill me in."

"No," Cody said. "I mean, you'll have to go up there to see what's going on. I don't know." Cody clenched her teeth.

She wanted to follow Rachel's advice and start standing up for herself, but every time she tried, she ended up backpedaling.

"Why aren't you under arrest, Conrad?" Hailey said. She stepped closer to him than Cody would ever have dared, planting fists on her narrow hips.

"Maybe because there's nothing to arrest me for," Jake said.

"I disagree. I saw the autopsy reports. I've spent the last couple days following up on some leads from that report. And if I were you I'd be making sure I had money set aside for bail."

"Go to hell," Jake said, and shoved past Hailey.

Cody watched him go, feeling like he'd thrown her to the wolves.

"Is Matt up the trail?" Hailey stared after Jake, sounding distracted.

"Yes." Cody answered quietly, not wanting Hailey's attention to return to her. But Hailey swung back to stare at her anyway.

"So you do know what's going on up there." Her hands planted on her hips again. "I keep telling you this will get solved sooner if you cooperate with me. I'm not the enemy here. I'm trying to keep you safe. But I guess I was wrong in thinking you might want to catch the person who did this."

"Trying to make me feel guilty won't help," Cody said. Hailey had no idea Cody had been manipulated by those emotions all of her life. And that manipulation had been done by an expert.

"Have it your way then," Hailey said, yanking open the Bronco's door. "I've got to get up the trail. I have a job to do. One word of advice. Stay away from Jake Conrad. Jess is going to have to arrest him once I get my new information to her."

Hailey didn't leave Cody time to reply, and Cody wasn't sure what she would have said anyway. She walked toward the motel thinking there were distinct disadvantages to being in a small town. Like running into people you didn't want to see.

Chapter 14

Cody stood in the middle of the motel room staring at the blinking red light on the phone. She took a step toward it but then veered off to drop her wallet and keys on the table. Which would be worse, a call from the whisperer or a call from her mother? Either way her knees were trembling and so she turned her back on the phone and chose instead to look out the window. It was late afternoon and she was hungry, the cinnamon rolls long digested. She could finish the salad she still had in the tiny refrigerator. She could be lazy and while away the rest of the day with her book.

She could retrieve whatever messages were blinking at her. She stood. Took in a deep breath. Crossed the room, and then, reluctantly, picked up the phone. Four messages.

"Cody, this is your mother. I haven't heard from you, and you know very well I worry when you don't report in. For all you know I could be dying. You call me before six this evening."

Cody deleted the message as she glanced at the digital clock next to the bed. Four. Two hours until the call deadline.

The next three calls were hang-ups. Cody deleted them, too, debating briefly about telling Jess. But since there were no messages, there seemed like no reason to go running for help. For all she knew the motel receptionist had dialed the wrong room number. She paced from the window to the bed and back again, ending in front of the phone, an unwanted connection to her mother. She should call.

No she shouldn't.

Impulsively she grabbed her keys and wallet and left the motel. It felt as if the last few days she had done nothing but passively wait for people to come to her with information. Edgy and impatient, she could think of only one person besides Florence who might have stories about Charles. It was a short drive back to city hall and an even shorter walk to the mayor's office.

Kendra stood at the secretary's desk wearing an elegant burgundy skirt and short jacket that made her pale skin glow. "Ms. Marsh. I don't believe we had an appointment, and I'm in the process of leaving."

"One quick question," Cody said. "Where do I find your grandfather?"

"I'm not sure that's a good idea," Kendra said, closing a slim portfolio she had been making notes in. "I doubt he will want to talk to you."

Cody rubbed her fingernails, caught herself doing it and fisted her hands instead. "He's an adult," she said. "He can tell me himself if he doesn't want to talk. I just have a few more questions."

Kendra glanced at her wristwatch. "This time of day he can usually be found at Pulaski's Bar. It's on Third about half way down the block."

"Thank you." Cody turned for the door.

"Ms. Marsh." Kendra followed her to the door and lowered her voice. "My grandfather can get...impatient with people who don't listen to what he says. Please reconsider talking to him."

"Thanks for the warning." The sarcasm in her voice startled her. She faltered and tried again. "No, really, I mean it. I appreciate the warning."

Cody left Kendra, poised on her high heels, portfolio clutched to her breast, a small frown furrowing the perfect makeup. She feared that if she stayed longer Kendra's words would eat away at her tentative courage.

Pulaski's Bar was an anomaly, a building that stood on its own instead of being shouldered up to its neighbors like so many of the false front businesses from the frontier days. It was a new structure made to look old, and wore its veneer of history like a Halloween costume. Cody walked up to the door, trying to ignore her shaking knees and the conviction that this was probably one of the more stupid things she had done.

Inside in the low light, several men lined a counter with drinks in front of them and a television holding their attention. Small tables were scattered strategically, a few surrounded by people, although the bar felt half empty. The place seemed unable to settle on a theme, and held tributes to firefighters, the forest service, and miners. Maybe the theme was the jobs important historically to Wallace. Cody saw a cross cut saw blade over the doorway and an intact and new Pulaski axe over the cash register. Its shape was the only similarity it had to the one she'd dropped in the museum.

Cody moved further into the dim room and saw Sunny coming toward her with a tray full of drinks.

"Wow, this is like, so cool that we keep running into each other!"

"Is there any place in town you don't work?" Cody asked, relieved to see her, as if she now had an ally in the enemy camp.

"I get asked that a lot. But you know, rent is like, so expensive, and I'm saving for school, so I do lots of stuff. Plus tips here are really great. You want a beer or something?"

"No thanks. I'm looking for Keith Naylor and I heard he might be here."

"God, why do you want to talk to that mean old man? I mean, he eats people alive."

Cody's knees shook harder. "You know Sunny, you're right. Maybe this wasn't such a good idea."

"No way. He doesn't even tip."

"Cody Marsh, isn't it? Still asking questions?" Keith spoke behind her.

Cody met Sunny's blue eyes, and saw the same fear she felt. Had he overheard them? She turned around to see the former mayor wearing a practiced smile, and dressed as if for an evening in the city. His concession to a Saturday night in a bar seemed to be the un-cuffed and rolled up sleeves.

"Cell phones are a wondrous thing," he continued. "I received a call from my granddaughter that you were headed this way to speak to me. I thought I made it clear at our last meeting we were done with conversations."

Out of the corner of her eye Cody saw Sunny fade into the dimness of the bar, and couldn't blame her for the desertion.

"You said you didn't want questions about Ethel," Cody said, hoping he wouldn't hear the tremor in her voice. "I'm not really interested in her, other than how she helped my grandfather. But I thought you might be willing to talk some more about Charles."

"I'm meeting with someone." Keith turned away, walking toward tables.

Cody followed him, not sure what he meant by his statement. He hadn't told her no. Maybe all she'd needed to do was make it clear Ethel wasn't a topic she wanted to pursue.

A small table against the far wall held a pitcher partially full of some dark beer, two glasses empty except for foam scum inside, a big bowl of chicken wings, and a plate with a pile of cheese sticks. None of the food looked edible, but Jake was dipping a wing in dressing.

"Conrad, sorry to keep you waiting," Keith said, sitting down and smoothing his slacks. "This is the young woman my granddaughter warned me about."

Keith didn't offer a chair and Cody stood there helplessly, with no idea what etiquette required of her. Did she assume and pull up a chair on her own? Did she wait for an invitation?

"Cody," Jake said. "Guess you survived Hailey's interrogation. I'd offer to shake hands but I'm covered in barbecue sauce. Pull up a chair and have some wings. Want a beer?"

"She not staying," Keith said. "You and I haven't finished our discussion about logging, and she is under the false impression that I desire to talk to her."

Shame flooded Cody, and she could feel the heat of it scorch her cheeks. "I was simply asking if you'd be willing to talk about my grandfather."

"Maybe if you hear this in front of an audience you might pay more attention. You do not understand the dynamics of a small town, how resurrecting long dead rumors impact people. Your digging into old history can have unwelcome consequences for others." He turned over his wrist and looked at his watch. "You may think you are innocently asking about Charles. But you don't seem to realize, in spite of being told, that stories about him inevitably lead to old rumors best left to lie. How many times does something have to be repeated before it sinks in?"

The words were pure May, and Cody felt her insides curling up like a sow bug. She shifted to flee, humiliation and training deeply ingrained. But then she thought of her grandfather, and Rachel's words about standing up for herself.

"I'm assuming locals here allow you to be rude because you used to be mayor," she said, with clear and distinct terror shaking her voice. "But I'm not a local."

"That you most certainly are not," Keith said, pouring beer into his glass. "In spite of your questionable claims to relatives."

"I'm also assuming you don't want to talk to me because you are worried about bringing up rumors of Ethel's affair with your father. I couldn't care less who a madam chose to sleep with. I told you that. But since you keep bringing it up I think I need to research it and find out why you want it kept a dark secret." She slipped her hands into her pockets to hide their shaking.

Keith rose from his chair, and while the anger was clear and deep in his eyes, he continued to smile. Cody didn't want to hear what he had to say, and this time she escaped, hitting the door with both hands, bursting into a full autumn downpour. The rain had come back as if it had never left, as if it had no intention of ever leaving. She took two steps into the deluge, realized her legs weren't going to take her to her car, and backtracked to collapse against the side of the building where the eaves offered slight protection.

The door opened and Cody gripped her arms around herself, convinced Keith came after her. But it was Jake who stepped out with a broad grin on his face.

"Damn, you've got a mouth on you," he said, clapping his hat on. "I had you pegged as a meek dormouse."

"I'm going to be sick," Cody said, sliding down the wall to a squat.

"Wouldn't be the first time someone's fed the birds outside this bar."

"I never talk back to people like that." She covered her eyes with chilled hands.

"Hope it's not your last. Hey, he's a nasty shit and most people are afraid of him. You're not alone."

"Are you?" Cody asked, taking in deep breaths of the wet air. "Afraid of him I mean?"

"Sweetheart, he wants my land. Which means he's buttering me up. At least for now. But you on the other hand, don't have anything he needs. He can be as nasty as he wants."

"Oh, god," Cody said, sinking down even further. "I don't know what came over me."

Jake offered a rough and callused hand, pulling Cody to her feet. "Come on, up you go. Where's your car?"

It was a natural response to take his hand, let him lift her up, and there was a brief second when Cody felt the shock of contact, of kindness offered again, just like Kelly had done. But before she could fully react, a police car stopped at the curb and Jess got out.

"What's going on here, Conrad? Cody, you okay?" She came forward exuding strength, one hand under her jacket at her waist.

"What are you going to do, shoot me?" Jake asked. "Cody needs help up, that's all. She just mouthed off to old Naylor."

"Not smart, Cody," Jess said, before focusing back on Jake. "And no, I'm not going to shoot you, I'm here to bring you in for questioning."

"What the hell for? Don't tell me you're buying into that whole theory of Hailey's that I killed Kelly."

Jess stepped under the eaves, dark eyes scanning Cody. "Sure you're okay?"

"Shaky." Cody stood between the two as if a mediator. Or maybe a barrier. She didn't want to be either and stepped back.

"It will pass," Jess said, and then held out a hand to Jake. "Come on, Jake, I don't have any choice. Let's just go through the motions until we get some answers."

"I already talked to you," Jake said.

"But you didn't explain how you banged up your knuckles so bad."

"What's that got to do with anything?"

"It has to do with the autopsy report and the bruising on Kelly's jaw that occurred less than an hour before his death." Jess's voice had chilled.

Jake raised his hands. "Okay, Kelly and I got into it. That doesn't mean I shot him."

Cody opened her mouth to defend Jake, to say he was kind to her. But she stayed silent, realizing she'd seen him angry, too, and who was she to claim she knew people? She remembered the day Kelly was shot and how he'd been rubbing his jaw as if it hurt. She'd wondered at the time if it was a toothache. Instead, the ache had been caused by a man who had just helped her.

Jess caught the sleeve of Jake's jacket. "You withheld information and lied to me. You saw Kelly right before he was shot. You own a gun of the same caliber and I have a warrant for it. And you have a damn good motive in that the forest service is trying to repossess a home you've had in your family for generations. We've known each other a long time. You've never felt the need to lie to me before. I want to know why you did this time." Anger vibrated under the veneer of professionalism and burned in her eyes.

"Shit!"

"Do I need to pull out the handcuffs?"

Jake slammed a fist into the wall of the bar with such sudden violence that Cody jumped away, heart pounding. Without another word he stalked to the police car and let himself in the back, slamming the door behind him.

"I hate my job," Jess said under her breath. "You going to be okay Cody? Where's your car?"

"Just there," Cody said, pointing. "Do I really think Jake shot Kelly and Nate? He seems okay...well, in spite of his temper."

"Everyone seems okay until you get to know them," Jess said. "As far as Jake goes everything points to him, but it's circumstantial until we get his gun, and everyone assumes he's guilty because of his 'angry hermit' persona. I could see him doing something stupid like punching Kelly. Shooting him in the back is another thing entirely. But what the hell do I know."

Cody thought of Jake's gruff assistance moments earlier. Could he be capable of shooting someone? Well, he was certainly capable of punching someone. She sighed. "I just want this over."

"You and me both. Before I forget, I got something for you." Jess reached into her coat pocket. She pulled out a small shrink-wrapped package and tossed it to Cody. "Pre-pay cell phone. I'm tired of driving around town looking for you."

Before Cody could tell Jess she hated talking on phones and didn't need a cell, Jess had darted through the rain and climbed into the car. Cody watched her pull out into the street, Jake's silhouette in the back window a slumped shadow of defeat, blurred by the rain.

She watched them a moment longer, before realizing Keith could come out at any time. That fear propelled her into the rain toward her car like she was a heat seeking missile. She turned on the car and glanced at the dashboard clock.

Five minutes after six.

Chapter 15

In the car, Cody stared at the cell phone. She could call her mother from here and only be five minutes late instead of driving back to the motel. She struggled for ten minutes figuring out how to use the phone before dialing, and then sat there listening to the ringing. Either May had gone somewhere or she was punishing Cody for calling late. Either way, Cody was in trouble.

She sighed heavily, leaning her head back against the seat. It was dark and the rain was unrelenting. It was time to figure out something for dinner and head back to the motel, one more day eaten away from her allotted time here. She drove down Bank Street, passing people with hoods up or umbrellas open, hunkered against rain, and rushing to get somewhere. She pulled into the tiny parking lot of the gas station, and ran into the convenience store hoping to find something that would pass for a meal. Inside, Cell used one hand to stock a shelf with bags of chips while he texted with the other.

"Hey, Cody," he said, jamming a bag of chips onto the shelf so hard she heard them crinkle in pain and die in a thousand pieces. "Been running up them trails again?"

"I wouldn't say running." Cody stood in front of a warming case staring at egg rolls and corn dogs that looked like they had been there since before Cell was born. "You have anything healthy here to eat?"

"I got some frozen burritos. They've got beans in them, and cheese. You know, your basic protein and dairy."

"And preservatives," Cody said. "I'll take a couple."

"Wicked."

Cody headed back to the motel with her protein, dairy, and preservatives, and a pint of chocolate ice cream for extra dairy. Clutching her bag in one hand and the collar of her fleece in the other, she darted through the semi gloom, rain pelting the pavement, jumping up her jeans and into her shoes. Her room offered sanctuary but as she reached it, the door that stood cracked open wasn't welcoming at all. Cody stood with water cascading through her cropped hair and into her eyes.

Maybe the motel cleaning service had simply forgotten to latch it on their way out. Maybe she hadn't pulled it tight when she left. Whatever the reason, she couldn't stand out here in the wet until she figured it out. But she didn't want to go in, either.

Cody reached out and using only her fingertips, tentatively pushed the door open a few more inches. She saw the shadowed room, saw her things hurled around, saw the mattress skewed off the frame. Her knees turned flaccid, her breath froze, and she backed away. But she was unable to raise her arm in time to block the fist slamming into her face.

Pain blew up in her head, like some sort of M80 on a psychotic Fourth of July. Colors blinded behind closed eyes. Cody slammed into the door frame before ricocheting off to hit concrete. Agony seared upward and she gasped against it. Curling into a ball, she rolled on the rough ground for untold eons until the fires dimmed, the sparks quit shooting, and her lungs inflated instead of crouching fearfully behind her ribs.

Tentatively, she unfolded and managed to get to her hands and knees. She half rose, tasted blood, and stumbled to the doorframe instead. Terror pounded through the pain and she didn't know which way to go.

Disregarding the grocery bag, she stumbled back to the car, locked the doors against the unknown, and pulled onto the street. A car honked. Pain blurred her vision, and her hands shook so hard she had to brace her knee against the wheel to steer.

In yet another parking lot, Cody turned off the car, rain immediately flooding the windshield. A door opened, and she saw the watery image of Matt come out and pause, facing her direction. She shuddered, clutching herself, unable to reach for the door handle, unable to expose herself to the outside. Matt crossed to the car.

"Unlock the door," he said, tapping on the window. "Come on Cody, open up."

Cody flipped the lock button, tucked her hands back under her arms, and squeezed her knees together. She didn't want him to see her shaking.

Matt bent over, rain flattening his hair. "What's wrong?"

Cody turned toward him, teeth chattering and sending waves of pain up her jaw and fresh blood into her mouth. "Someone hit me."

Matt caught her chin and tilted her head to the side. His eyes went cold, his jaw tightened, and so did his fingers. "Who?" The single word was curt.

Cody flinched against his hand on her face, and managed a shrug that sent pain up her neck.

Shifting his grip to her upper arms, Matt carefully lifted her up and out of the car. He fished a cell phone from a pocket and dialed as he helped her to the building door.

"Jess. Get over here." He flipped the cell shut, and supported Cody through the door into a small lobby. A woman in a forest ranger uniform was behind a counter, sorting maps.

"Jess is on her way," he told the woman. "I need her in my office as soon as she gets here."

They headed down a narrow hallway that smelled of old damp carpet. Each step resonated up the side of Cody's head and she cupped her chin with one hand, trying to support the injury.

"Sit," Matt said, pulling forward a chair in a dimly lit office.

Cody sat. Matt flipped a desk lamp on and left the room.

Still cupping her chin, Cody tried looking around without turning her head, seeking distraction from what had happened. The office walls were filled with framed photographs, none of people. Instead there were views of mountains and streams, close-ups of wildflowers, groupings of ferns. So many filled the space that it caused the walls to disappear, pulling the viewer into the woods. The overall effect was peaceful and she soaked it in.

"Here," Matt said, coming back inside. "Hot chocolate. The sugar will help with shock. Any other injuries besides the hook to the jaw?"

Cody shook her head and grimaced as pain flared again. She took the mug from Matt and held the warmth between chilled and damp fingers. There was an odd feeling starting inside, like a small flickering. She stared at the mug trying to decipher the emotion.

"Any nausea? Dizziness?" Matt pulled a chair around from behind the desk and sat in it across from Cody. "Follow my finger," he said, holding his hand up.

"No dizziness," Cody said. "A little queasy." But that didn't account for this slow, almost quiet simmering that was starting inside.

"Normal response to adrenaline and pain," Matt said. He took hold of her chin again and gently lifted it. "You're going to have a hell of a contusion. Doesn't look broken but we need to have a doctor take a look anyway. Any loose teeth?"

"No, but I bit my tongue."

"Bleeding?"

"A little."

"No big deal. Drink that before it gets cold. A little blood won't hurt chocolate."

There was a knock on the door and Jess let herself in. "What's going on?"

"I thought you locked Conrad up," Matt said, standing.

"I questioned him. I let him walk. You know we don't have enough to do anything else yet."

"Someone cold-cocked Cody. Just like Kelly."

"Details," Jess said, her voice suddenly calm and level as if a switch had flipped.

"My motel room door was open." Cody sipped the hot chocolate and the sweetness sent warmth fingering down to her stomach.

"Don't tell me you went in," Matt said.

"I'm not an idiot." The harshness in her voice was new. "I pushed the door open a little, someone came out from behind it, hit me, and took off."

"What did you see?" Jess asked, taking notes.

"Rain. Pavement. Stars."

Matt laughed and Jess glared at him.

"Did you see the person in your room?" she asked, her voice patient.

"No," Cody said. "I saw a blur, a shadow."

"How big?" Matt asked.

"About your size," Cody said and this time it was Jess who choked back something that might have turned into a laugh given time.

"No, wait," Cody said softly, as if the sound of her voice would drown the flash of memory. "I did see something. Color."

"What kind?" Jess asked.

"Green. No, like shades of green."

"Camouflage," Matt said. "Unfortunately there's a lot of that around here. But it's better than nothing."

"Definitely a place to start," Jess said, flipping shut her notebook and standing. "I don't think this warrants an aid car, but get her to the doctor just to be on the safe side. I'm calling this in and getting people to the motel room. Maybe we'll get lucky and find something we can use. Meet me there when you're done."

Matt took Cody's elbow and lifted her to her feet. She winced with the movement.

"Finish that," he said, pointing to the hot chocolate as he pulled a forest service jacket off the back of his chair.

Cody ignored him and set the mug on the table, then followed him out of the station to his Bronco. He opened the door for her and she climbed up to the passenger seat, moving tentatively. Her neck and shoulder were stiffening up.

"I think..." Cody began and then had to pause to consider the odd emotion again. "I think I'm angry. But it feels like more than angry."

"You're pissed off." Matt started the engine. "You have a right to be. And you're not the only one."

His words felt too personal and she deflected them.

"Did you take those pictures in your office?" She wanted diversions from thoughts that kept flashing back to camouflage.

"Yeah."

"They're good. Like being in the woods."

Matt didn't respond and Cody smoothed down her damp hair then tried leaning her head back to ease the pressure. Her jaw felt three times its normal size and she tentatively fingered the swelling as Matt pulled into a small hospital lot. She followed him through sliding glass doors into an empty lobby. He continued past the waiting area, past

a reception desk, and straight back to the exam room.   A
nurse came around a computer console.

"I'm sorry," she said. "You have to sign in first."

"Find me Lorne," Matt said.

"Dr. Lorne is with another patient. He won't see you
until you go through the admitting process anyway."

"Tell him Matt Tanner is here."   Matt turned to Cody.
"Get up there."

Cody obediently stepped onto the ledge at the base of
the exam gurney and listened to crisp paper crinkle as she
boosted herself up and sat. It made her feel like a little kid
waiting for a shot. She resisted the urge to swing her feet,
knowing movement would only hurt. She also resisted the
urge to look at the stirrups at the end of the gurney,
uncomfortable with their implication and irritated with herself
for the embarrassment. She stared at her folded hands.

Matt sat on a rolling stool and flipped one of the stirrups.
"Used to play with these things as a kid."

"Matt," a man came past the curtain, so narrow and
angular he was like the victim of a cartoon steamroller.

"John. I need you to look at an assault for me," Matt
said.

"Nice to see you, too." The doctor pulled a pen light out
of a pocket. "Name?"

"Cody Marsh," she answered.

"Lovely hazel eyes," he said, aiming the light at her.
"Dizziness? Nausea?"

"I've already gone through the foreplay," Matt said,
standing up and pacing.

The doctor met Cody's eyes. "I started out in the forest
service. Matt was my supervisor. I decided the medical field
suited me better. Turn this way please."

"And just who told you what a good paramedic you
were?" Matt asked. "What's the damage?"

"Well, the jaw doesn't appear broken, but she's going to
be sore for a while. Open up Ms. Marsh."

Cody obediently opened, watching the ceiling as the doctor prodded in her mouth with a gloved finger.

"Your tongue will feel swollen for a couple days. No damage to your teeth." He put his hands on her neck, thumbs on her jaw, and gently rolled her head. "Neck stiff?"

Cody started to nod, winced, and answered instead. "And shoulder."

"I imagine you landed on that side when you fell. I'm going to write you up a prescription for pain medication. Stick to soft foods for a few days. Use ice packs, no more than ten minutes at a time. Warm salt water rinses. Any blurred vision, problems swallowing, extreme headache, come back. Expect to be stiff and sore tomorrow including that hip, and worse the next day, and then decreasing pain. Hope you like black and blue because those are the colors you'll be seeing in the mirror for a while. This headache," he added, gesturing to Matt, "will only go away if you ignore it."

"I'll try that," Cody said, gingerly stepping down from the gurney. Now that the doctor had mentioned her hip, she could feel the tenderness there along with stiffness in her elbow. "I think I did more damage hitting the ground."

"Cement's hard," the doctor said, as if discovering a new fact of life.

Matt pulled the curtain back for Cody, waiting as she limped past. "Thanks John."

"Any time Matt." The doctor thumped Matt's shoulder. "It gets dull in between your visits."

Matt led Cody to a pharmacy next to the hospital, and then back to the Bronco and the motel, the whole trip passing in silence. Cody hurt too much for small talk, and by Matt's clearly visible scowl, he wasn't interested in visiting either.

In spite of the rain the motel room door stood wide open. Uniformed police moved in and out, and one stood talking to the desk clerk under a large umbrella.

"Wait in the Bronco where it's dry until I find out what Jess needs," Matt said, parking.

Cody was content to stay, listening to the rain pelt the roof in soothing music. Why was rain so peaceful to listen to and so miserable to be out in? She watched cars go by on the street, trailing rooster tails of mist behind them like earth bound comets. Her jaw throbbed and her tongue felt as thick as the cold congealed oatmeal her mother used to make. As she looked back at the motel she was startled by a sudden flicker of anger. She hadn't come here to get involved in these people's lives. Or their deaths. She had come here to remember her grandfather, but felt like she was being pulled away from him instead.

Distractions.

Just as quickly as the anger flared, it died. Kelly and Nate weren't distractions. Ashamed, she got out of the car, wanting to escape the selfishness.

Wincing with each step, Cody moved through rain that wrapped her in the astringent scent of wet asphalt. At the open doorway she paused, wondering if she dared go inside and get dry clothes. The room was well lit and warmth came out to brush her cheeks. Jess stood next to the bed frame talking to Matt while two officers shifted the mattress.

"Can I come in?" Cody asked.

"Don't touch the door or doorjamb," Jess said. "They're being dusted. Use the plastic sheeting to walk on. You look like hell."

Cody ignored the comment on her appearance. "Can I get my things? Or at least something dry?"

"Look stuff over first," Jess said. "Tell me if anything's missing. Then you can pack up."

"Pack up?"

"I don't want you staying here."

"I guess I can get another room," Cody said.

"No, I don't want you here at all. Between this and the phone call you got, we're going to find you someplace else to stay."

"How about Florence's?" Matt said. "Rachel'd probably appreciate the help and Florence knows you."

"No thanks," Cody said. "I'm not going to be an imposition. There are other motels in town. Besides, if it's too dangerous for me to stay here, wouldn't I be endangering Florence?"

"I don't want you alone," Jess said. "And Rachel's as good as a guard dog. But first things first. Take a look at this stuff. Any idea why someone would have been going through your room?"

"No," Cody said, hating the thought of someone touching what was hers, fingering it, invading her privacy.

Her belongings had been spread out on the box springs of the bed, and she touched them tentatively as if they belonged to a stranger. Everything was exposed for Jess, Matt, and strangers to see. She wanted to scoop up her plain panties, her dirty socks, the brush with short strands of curly red hairs stuck in it, and hide them. She scanned the things she owned, the things that defined her, and paused. Well. Maybe not everything was laid out after all.

"There's a few things missing," she said, feeling that small flicker of anger flare again. If only she knew what to do with the emotion.

"Tell me," Jess said tersely, pulling out her pad and pen.

"I had some pamphlets from the museum about Wallace, miscellaneous things I thought might be interesting. And my camera is gone."

"What kind?" Jess asked.

"A Minolta digital."

"Any pictures on it?"

Cody had to think for a moment. It had been a while since she had downloaded any pictures off the camera and onto her computer at home. Now it was all lost and her stomach filled with lead and sank.

"There were a few of my grandfather," she said, struggling to keep her voice even. "And I'd taken some up at the old clearing on Bounty Trail. The place where my grandfather went as a child."

"What the hell?" Matt said, swinging around. "When did you take those pictures?"

"I don't know," Cody said, confused.

"Maybe the day you passed Kelly and Nate? Maybe during the time someone tore pages out of Kelly's notebook? Maybe when someone was in the trees watching you?"

"Matt," Jess said.

"Why the hell didn't you remember this sooner?" Matt stepped closer and Cody backed away, her insides flinching, curling up, killing her infant anger. In his voice she heard her mother. Quietly, feeling invisible, she gathered a few possessions.

"Ranger Tanner," Jess said, louder. "You're pissed and it's not helping."

"You're damn right I'm pissed," Matt was saying to Jess. "You have any idea how much time I've spent up there in the woods trying to see what we missed, why a friend of mine had to die? And all along she has the answer and didn't remember! How can you not remember something so basic?"

"Because I'm stupid," Cody said, so quietly neither heard her.

"Because she's not a police officer," Jess said. "Because she's been traumatized since before she got here. The death of her grandfather, seeing two men murdered, and now being assaulted. Any one of those is enough to make someone forget something that would seem trivial to a lay person."

Cody shoved things into her bag, picked it up, and walked through the doorway. She knew no one saw her leave. Out in the parking lot, once again in the rain and dark, she stopped, realizing her car was back at the forest ranger station. The familiar numbness that came after every confrontation with her mother rose up, smothering shame and humiliation. She'd have to walk.

She squelched down the sidewalk, moving through pools of light from the street lamps, hearing her grandfather's voice.

"Why do you allow your mother to speak to you like that?"

"Like what?" Cody had been genuinely puzzled.

"She yells at you and demeans you," he responded, putting his hand on her shoulder.

"Only when I've messed up."

Shaking his head, Charles had dropped his hand to his side. "I hope you realize the truth sooner than I did."

Palming wetness out of her eyes, Cody wished her grandfather was there so she could point out to him she'd messed up yet again.

Chapter 16

Cody had only walked a few blocks when a sign caught her eye. The Silver Corner Café. Her stomach rumbled in response, and she realized her protein and dairy dinner was thawing and melting in the rain outside her motel room. She pulled open the door and gratefully left the rain behind.

The Silver Corner was a tiny wedge shaped restaurant consisting of two small tables and a counter with four stools being warmed by four men in frayed plaid jackets and baseball hats. They huddled around their coffee mugs as if life was about to play a cruel joke on them and they didn't want to see it coming. Through a doorway at the other end of the café, Cody could see the dim recesses of a bar, where someone had managed to squeeze in a pool table. She sat down on the cracked red vinyl of a metal chair, listening to rainwater drip to the linoleum. An elderly woman seemed to be the only person working, and she topped off the men's coffee mugs before bringing a menu to Cody.

"Something hot to drink?" Her eyes drifted to Cody's jaw but she made no comment.

"Tea, please."

Cody's hip throbbed and she shifted on the hard chair as she waited for the tea. She wished she'd seen more of the intruder in her room. Something about camouflage bothered her, like a shadow hiding in a corner of her mind. But it was pushed back by the thought of her camera.

Losing pictures of her grandfather made her heart ache as much as her body. If the camera was never found she would have no pictorial record of Charles. She stared intently at her entwined fingers forcing memories to describe him.

He wore bib overalls, or sometimes old jeans, high on the waist, held up by red suspenders. Tennis shoes with extra support for tired ankles. Plaid shirts with a white tee shirt underneath. A battered and stained baseball hat with the logo of the long defunct Rainier beer company. A watch with a broad black plastic band because metal links turned his skin green. Those broad hands, so roughly callused that the fingers had a hard time bending. Those stooped shoulders and bent back, testaments to long, hard years. And his fine soft hair, gray, white at the temples, cut so short it almost ceased to exist. Black framed glasses, so old fashioned they were coming back into vogue. Blue eyes faded to the same color as the washed out fall sky above Wallace.

How long before Cody forgot all the details that made him real? With a photograph she might have been able to look into his eyes and see him alive. It might have pushed away the mental picture she carried, of his body on the too - short gurney.

There had been pictures of the clearing on the camera, too, but those she could replace. She could purchase a cheap disposable camera and go back up Bounty Trail and at least have a record of that place. She could easily stand in the same spot she had before, when her quest had been for nothing more than finding her grandfather. Before Kelly and Nate had changed all that.

There was one thing Cody was sure wasn't on the camera, and that was any sort of picture that pointed to a killer, no matter how much Matt might be hoping for evidence.

The café door banged open and a drenched Matt strode over to the table. "Figured you didn't walk far. What are you doing?"

"I'm going to have dinner. Then I'm going to get my car and go home." Her jaw throbbed with the movement.

"What do you mean, home?"

"I think I've done all I can. So are we through here?" Cody was proud of herself, keeping her voice level and calm, showing none of the humiliation and loneliness flooding her thoughts.

"No we're not through. Can I join you?"

"I don't think so," Cody said.

Matt slaked rain off his face, pulled out a chair and sat. "I owe you an apology," he said abruptly.

Cody waited, not wanting to help him, not wanting an apology, not wanting to have this conversation with him.

"I shouldn't have taken my anger about this case out on you. I shouldn't have yelled at you, and I don't want you running away because of it."

"I don't run away," Cody said, stung. "I've just realized I'm not going to find out much more about my grandfather so there's no reason to stay."

"Yeah, right." Matt backhanded more rain from his face. "I'm disappointed."

"About?"

"I thought you were braver than this. You've held up through everything else, but some jerk yells at you and you disintegrate."

Cody silently agreed with what he said, the part about disintegrating anyway, but she wasn't going to give him the satisfaction of doing so out loud. She simply waited.

"Ah hell," he said. "I'm hungry as well as a fool. Accept my apology and let me sit here and drip with you."

Somewhere inside, an unexpected laugh bubbled its way through the hurt.

"Come on. My treat."

"Okay, okay," Cody said. "Just a meal and then I'm going home."

"Great. Millie, can you make that two?" he said to the waitress, who was headed in their direction with a mug.

Cody put her cold hands between her thighs, looking at the menu without really seeing it. She wasn't quite ready to accept Matt's apology, wondering if he really meant it or if Jess had made him. She felt fragile in his company, as if her protective shell had been breached and she was waiting for the next attack.

Millie brought two heavy stoneware mugs over and Cody clutched the warmth of hers.

Matt picked up his and took a swallow. Grimacing, he pushed the mug away. "That's not coffee."

"Tea." Cody pointed to the tea bag string draped over the edge of the mug.

"Millie, I changed my mind. Can you bring me a beer?"

When the beer arrived, Matt ordered breakfast and Cody asked for soup and a sandwich. When Millie left, Cody sipped tea and watched Matt carefully pour the beer into a tall glass, leaving some liquid in the bottom of the bottle. Studying the remnants, he swished the liquid.

"What are you doing?"

"Wheat beer," he said, tipping the rest into the glass. "The wheat settles, so you leave a bit of ale to work it in and then pour it."

"No, I meant, what are you doing drinking beer when you ordered breakfast?"

"Why not?" asked Matt, raising his eyes to meet hers.

Shrugging, Cody couldn't come up with a reasonable response. "How old is this restaurant?"

"I'm not sure, but not old enough for your grandfather to have come here." Matt put the glass down. "Look, like I said, I'm sorry I yelled at you."

"You were right that I should have thought of the camera," Cody said. "But I don't handle being shouted at very well."

"Who does? Kelly used to laugh when I'd get mad. Said he liked watching me throw things and cuss. Always made me forget about why I was mad. His laughing."

"You get mad often?"

"No, believe it or not. It's just the job."

"If you hate it so much why don't you quit?" Cody asked, swirling the tea as Matt had done his beer, watching it in order to have something to look at.

"I owe my dad. And my grandfather." Matt shrugged. "They always wanted me to follow them. They just assumed I would. Christmas and birthdays I'd ask for a field guide on wildflowers and they'd give me a wilderness survival book. When they died, I hadn't had time to tell them I didn't want to be in law enforcement, and after, it felt like betraying them to consider anything else."

"Why a field guide on flowers?" asked Cody.

Matt gave a rare, brief grin, there and just as quickly gone. "Eventually I realized I wanted to go into the Forest Service, like they did," he said. "But I wanted to be the one to give kids nature talks, to take them out and show them the wilderness. I had dreams of teaching another generation to love the mountains like I did."

"And you can't do that in law enforcement?"

"Hell no. Now I arrest kids instead. Defacing forest service property. Littering. Underage drinking. Domestic violence. Growing pot. All the things you find in the city, only out in the woods. I might as well be a cop in Coeur d'Alene."

Cody wasn't sure what to do with this more personal conversation, and returned to safer territory. "When you were yelling you mentioned something about pages being torn from a notebook. What were you talking about?"

"When we were going through Nate's camp, we found Kelly's notebook. All of us use them, small notebooks to track what we're doing. Kelly had this large, loopy handwriting. He hated the notepads we used, said there wasn't enough room on a page to sign his name. So he kept this green stenographer pad. After a few days it would get this permanent bend in it from being shoved into pockets too small for it. The pad we found had pages ripped out of it."

"So maybe he needed them for grocery lists."

"No, the pages are in chronological order. Kelly kept meticulous notes. Everything's spelled out, up to him and Nate running into you on the trail."

"Maybe nothing worth writing about happened after that." Cody shifted her mug to make room for the chicken tortellini soup and grilled cheese the waitress placed in front of her. "Or maybe he didn't have time to write anything before being shot."

"Then why rip out pages? When would he have had time to do that, and why would he have?" Matt scissored his knife and fork across the sausage links.

"I can think of several reasons. For one, Nate might have needed something to write on." Cody tried a bite of grilled cheese and pain fired up her head. She'd thought it would be soft enough, but it looked like she was going to have to live on soup.

"Then we would have found papers on him. It's not like he had time to do anything with them." With great precision, Matt carefully cut out the yoke of an over-easy egg, picked it up and forked it in whole. "What?" he asked, reaching for more sausage.

"I've never seen anyone eat eggs like that."

"I like the burst of yolk. Are you going to eat that sandwich?" He reached across the table and picked up half.

"So what worries me is the possibility someone was at the camp tearing out paper when you went by."

Something like thousands of ants wearing ice cube boots raced up Cody's back. "What can be done about that?"

"Nothing at the moment. Jess is handling some leads. But after the incident with your room you need to be careful."

"Sounds like another reason for me to go home."

Matt didn't respond. The door behind him opened, and the cold, moisture laden air overran the café's heat. Cody saw a familiar looking man come in, and Matt looked over his shoulder at the sound of voices. The man was followed by Kendra, in a trench style raincoat, shaking out an umbrella. The man nodded to Cody as he passed their table, and she saw the beautiful gentle blue eyes that placed him as the mining engineer who had been talking to Rivers the first day Cody arrived. She heard the scrape of a chair being pulled out behind her.

"Matt," the man said.

"Jim. How's work?"

"Kind of a pain right now. Sorry to hear about Kelly and Nate."

"Yeah, thanks."

Kendra took off her raincoat and hung it near the door. Underneath she had been holding her leather portfolio, and she brought that with her, but instead of passing them she paused next to Matt.

"Ranger Tanner," Kendra said. "May I ask you something?"

"No," Matt said.

"Actually, two things." Kendra continued, ignoring him. "One, has there been any progress in catching my brother's murderer? And two." She looked at Cody as if seeing her for the first time, her eyes sliding over Cody's swelling bruises. "Ms. Marsh has been threatening my grandfather and I'd like to know what we can do about it."

Cody straightened, but Matt shook his head at her.

"Kendra, honey," he said. "If you have a complaint to file go to the police. You know that. And if you want to know about progress, talk to Jess. Or better yet, offer to help."

"I find it…distasteful to deal with Detective Hawking. If you cannot answer my questions I'll have to try Ranger Cutler."

"I'm sure Hailey will be more than willing to talk." Matt pushed his glass of beer back. "You know what Kelly told me a few days before he died? The two of you had an argument about his job didn't you? He was hurt because you wouldn't back off about his choice. He told me he wished you would kick off your heels and go for a hike. Get out into the woods and see why he loved them so much. He even had a trail picked out for you."

"Really?" asked Kendra. "Is that relevant right now?"

"He thought you should go up the Cranky Gulch trail," Matt said.

"How juvenile. Please try to remember that as time passes the chances of catching this person lessens. You may not believe this but I did love my brother." Kendra started to walk away but Matt caught her arm.

"Kelly was a good person," he said. "Your grandfather should have realized that."

"My grandfather can be a hard man." Kendra tugged her arm free and smoothed the sleeve of her suit. "With that said however, he has always known what was best for us. That was Kelly's mistake. Not letting our grandfather help him."

Kendra walked back to where Jim waited, holding out the chair for her.

"There isn't really a Cranky Gulch is there?" Cody asked.

"Sure there is," Matt responded, reaching for the rest of her sandwich.

"Has Kendra always been so friendly?"

"She was okay when she was younger," Matt said. "Before she gave in to family pressures and started moving up the political ladder. Her grandfather was the one who really pushed her, and she's always worshipped the old fart. Or been terrified of him. I'm not sure which. So you're threatening him?"

Cody put her spoon down and pushed the half empty bowl back. "He's worried about me resurrecting old stories about his family. I told him I wasn't interested, but he doesn't believe me. So I told him since he was so worried I'd have to see what he was afraid of. That sound like a threat to you?"

"Not compared to some of the things I've said to him." Matt pulled the bowl over. "Millie makes good soup."

"So could rumors about people long dead really damage her career or hurt their family?"

"Who, Kendra? I don't see how. But I know she's been steeped in family history all her life. Kelly got sick of hearing it and escaped, but she always seemed to suck up everything she was told like it was food for the starving."

"Kind of like you then. Sucking up food like you're starving."

"Funny."

Cody finished her tea, thinking about the similarities between her and Kendra. It sounded as if Kendra was devoted to her grandfather like Cody was to Charles. So why was Kendra afraid of old stories being told again? Cody wanted to repeat her grandfather's tales, hearing them over and over until they sank into her heart and guaranteed her grandfather would always exist. Not hide those stories away and bury them.

"Well," Cody said. "The only thing I've come across about Kendra's family was a book about a mine her great-grandfather used to own. I think it was called the Honey Do. I noticed it because the madam, Ethel was a part owner. Along with...let me think. Oh, Rachel's great-grandfather and someone called Patrick something or other."

"Patrick Cross. Now there was a combination," Matt said. "Brothels, politics, religion, and law enforcement. Can't see why that would bother Keith. Besides, I seem to remember Jim saying someone's hired him to reopen Honey Do. Can't be that big a secret. So have I groveled enough to keep you from going home or do I need to apologize some more?" Matt asked.

"I haven't made up my mind yet. Why doesn't Kendra like Jess?"

"No idea. Jess is one of the few people I trust."

Matt's cell phone beeped and he pulled it out. "Jess. No I'm not yelling anymore. I was telling Cody what a rotten person you are." He listened for a moment. "I can do that. Tell me what Rachel said again? Great. Just what we need."

"What's going on?" Cody asked as he flipped the phone shut.

"Well, we have a problem. Or rather it sounds like you do." He signaled Millie for the bill. "We need to get over to the police department."

"For?"

"Your mother's here."

Chapter 17

"My mother?" Cody gripped the edges of the table.

"She showed up at the museum looking for you, and pissed Rachel off so Rachel took her to the police department. Now Jess sounds stressed. I can take you to your car and you can head over there."

"No. I need to…I don't know. Hide somewhere." She blinked against the heat of tears.

"Hide?" The corners of Matt's mouth turned up as if he was about to laugh, but the reaction died as he studied her face.

"You don't know my mother, Matt. If I see her I'm going to lose everything I've gained the last few days."

"What are you talking about?" Matt pulled out a wallet and handed the waitress a debit card.

Cody could feel her cheeks warming. "This person I am here, it's not…I'm different at home. I'm trying to be someone she won't allow, and it's just so hard. I don't want to be the old Cody anymore, the one before my grandfather, but if she's here…I can't do it." Cody clenched her teeth in spite of the pain, needing to dam the words.

Matt took the receipt, stood, and pulled Cody up by her hand. "I've got to meet your mother."

Cody jerked her hand away and he stepped back, looking startled as she spoke. "I'm not going. I'll go to Florence's. You already suggested I stay there. My mom will never be able to make it up all those steps."

"Hey, come on," Matt said. "Are you that afraid of her?"

"It's not that I'm afraid of her." The words overflowed, flooding out. "It's that I'm afraid of who I become around her. I never realized it until my grandfather showed up. Since he died, like I said, I've been trying to be better."

Matt held the door for her and she stumbled into rain. "I doubt you're the same person you were when she saw you last," he said. "You hadn't seen two men killed."

In the Bronco, Cody hung on to the seatbelt across her chest as if it would keep her rooted. But back at the ranger station she had to let go when Matt opened the door and practically peeled her out.

"It can't be that bad," Matt said, walking her to her car. "Tell you what. I've got a couple calls I have to make and then I'll join you. Jess is there, too, so you'll have friends for support. We won't let her eat you alive."

Cody started up her car, watching him enter the ranger station. He said she would have friends for support. Friends. She rolled the word around inside, analyzing every angle, every letter, trying to decipher the meaning. He was being polite, obviously. But even so, the thought of having Jess and Matt behind her as she faced her mother was like realizing the cliff edge had a sturdy railing. She managed a shaky breath. Did that mean she wanted to see her mother? She pulled out, looking for traffic. Turning right would take her to the police station and May.

She turned left.

The road narrowed as she left Wallace and headed into the canyons toward Burke. Pain took root under her eye and she tried to unclench her jaw. Why was May here? What was she going to do? She couldn't just leave her mother at the police station. It wasn't responsible and it wasn't fair to Jess.

She should turn around and get it over with.

The signs for Black Dog and Frisco flashed by in her headlights, the old abandoned buildings of the Hecla mine ghostly shadows against the night. She barely registered the scenery and slowed only when she reached the outskirts of Burke. She had a half formed idea of showing up at Florence's and hiding there but when she got into town and saw Rivers in a pool of light from an open doorway, she slammed on the brakes and headed for the warmth of the home.

"Cody," Rivers said, picking up firewood. "Come in out of the rain."

Mutely, Cody followed Rivers as she used her shoulder to shove open a rain-swollen door. The window in the door was patched with duct tape and the lock clung to the wood by a single loose screw. Inside the tiny mud room, assorted coats dusted with cobwebs hung from hooks. Chore boots, snow boots, clogs, and sandals were scattered beneath the coats, and newspapers were spread in one corner, catching water from a leak in the roof. The place smelled of age and mildew. River, in contrast, was a bright spot of color in a striped wool cape that looked like it had been made from whatever scraps of yarn were to hand, whether they matched or not.

"Tea?" Rivers asked as they went through to a tiny living room that was cobbled together with odds and ends and didn't appear to have ever seen a piece of brand new furniture. Yet it was clean, cozy, and welcoming.

"Please," Cody said. "Sorry to just show up."

"No worries. I try to never be surprised by what life tosses up." Rivers opened a door on a wood stove and added a chunk of wood. "Though I usually fail at that whole Zen thing."

A cast iron kettle steamed gently on the wood stove and Rivers used a hot pad to lift it and pour water into two heavy mugs. The one she handed Cody had a distinct list to it.

"My niece made these in her pottery class. She needs practice. But they hold water."

"This tea smells wonderful," Cody said, as scents of long hot summer days rose up.

"Let's see. Some oat grass, young nettles. Chamomile. I may have put some licorice root in there. Can't remember. And honey made with lemon balm and spearmint." Rivers sat down on one end of a small lumpy looking couch and curled her feet up under her.

Cody sat gingerly in a rocking chair across from Rivers.

"You have the look of someone running away," Rivers said, sipping her tea.

"I guess I am. My mother's down at the police station."

"Really? How interesting. What did she do?"

"Followed me." Cody took a swallow of the tea and sighed. "I guess I didn't look at this trip as running away until she showed up."

"Oh, I see. She didn't do anything, she's just looking for you. And you don't want to see her."

"How awful is that? She's done so much for me, raising me alone, and I sound like an ungrateful brat."

"Not at all," Rivers said. "You do, however, sound like you have a serious case of the guilts."

The words surprised a short laugh out of Cody, and shocked by an action that felt so disloyal to her mother, she let the simple sound of fire snapping in the stove fall around them.

"How did you get that bruise?" Rivers asked after a few moments.

Cody told her briefly what had happened.

"And so I was at dinner with Matt when he got the call from Jess about my mother."

"Jess is entertaining her then?" Rivers asked, with a broad grin. "That should be interesting."

"Kendra was at the café, too," Cody said. "She doesn't seem to like Jess."

"She doesn't like me, either," Rivers said. "She has a hard time with people who don't fit defined roles. And I suspect her grandfather has planted some bigotry in her, though she probably doesn't realize it. Her grandfather pitched a fit when Jess was hired. He didn't think it suitable that a First Nations woman be in a position to arrest white men."

"That's horrible, teaching that kind of prejudice."

"He's a horrible person." Rivers pulled her long hair over her shoulder and began braiding it, as if her fingers needed something to do.

"He thinks I'm threatening him. That looking for stories about my grandfather will impact him somehow."

"I imagine it could," Rivers said. "There are layers and layers of old stories here, and they overlap just like the flat stones we use to shore up the canyon walls behind our homes. Tell me what you're looking for."

"Any stories about my grandfather that will help me remember him. I'd like to find out who his mother was. I think his real mother may have been Ethel Stevenson." Cody settled back into the rocking chair, resting her mug against her thigh. The heat from the tea seeped through her jeans and eased some of the soreness in her muscles.

"Ah, the madam of Silver Haven. Now I see the connection to the old spider. Keith's father was involved with her for many years. Everyone knew it except the wife of course. Keith wouldn't like people reminded of that. It was a stain on his father's career as mayor, and came up when Keith ran for the position. You should tell Jess about this." Rivers let her neat braid fall from her fingers and reached for her tea.

"Why?"

"He'd be the first person I'd think of for breaking into your room."

"My camera was stolen. They seem to think it's connected to Kelly and Nate's deaths."

"Could be. Could be not. I've been thinking about Nate lately," Rivers said. "We all knew Kelly, so he's the one we're mourning. Who's mourning Nate? Who's missing him, wondering where he is, when he's coming home? Oh, I'm sure Jess is following up on tracing his family. But people here need to remember him, too."

"It's like my camera," Cody said. "With it gone, I have no pictures. How long before I forget what my grandfather looked like? If we don't remember them, they're truly gone."

"Exactly."

"Nate said something that made me think he was looking for his father. When I saw him the first time. He wanted to know when my grandfather had been here, and when I said the 1940's he said it was too early for him, and that his father had been here, too."

"Like I said, layers of old stories." Rivers put her mug on a side table. "Now, tell me why you keep your hair so short. It's such a lovely shade of red."

Cody flushed. "It's frizzy and ugly."

"And that, I imagine, is your mother's voice. Let it grow and decide for yourself."

"My mother," Cody said, feeling the cocoon of comfort disintegrate. "I suppose I need to deal with her."

"I've found that's the best way to move on. Face it, get it over with, leave it behind."

"Easier said than done." Cody stood, putting the tea mug down.

Rivers walked with her to the door and she was amazed that her feet moved forward when her heart dragged like an anchor. She faced the black night and downpour of rain, and rubbed her fingernails with her thumbs. Somehow, over the past few days, her nails had gotten longer and she hadn't noticed them. She needed to cut them away.

"Cody," Rivers said, putting her hand on Cody's shoulder. "You're not who your mother wants you to be. You are the granddaughter of a Wallace man. That gives you iron for backbone. Remember that."

Chapter 18

Cody sat on a bench against a cold wall watching people come and go around her. Ten at night, yet the police station looked as crowded and busy as she assumed an afternoon would be. It would be so simple to approach the receiving area and tell the officer that Jess expected her. She thought of what River had said, and how easy it sounded in her little home. Deal with it, get it over with, leave it behind. It wasn't so easy when her mother was in the same building. A wave of sadness pushed her down, becoming a weight she couldn't get out from under. Where had that brief moment of courage gone? She'd stood up to Keith, she'd been unwillingly involved in murders, she had come so close to friendships and acceptance.

It felt like a sham. She'd thought she was finally discovering who she was, but it was only because May wasn't close by. The moment her mother neared, any courage and independence faded away. Is this what her future was going to be? She thought again of Rivers. Okay, one step at a time. She could do that.

First, face it.

Standing, she worked her way through the crowd, asked for directions, and once again found herself walking down an umbilical cord of a hallway pulling her to her mother. She reached for the door handle as memories washed over her, a flash of past life like those brief moments before death.

Her mother's cool hand on her fevered forehead when she had the flu. Brushing her hair into hated ringlets. Blushing when Cody asked about sex. Brownies when she came home from school. A hall May called her Love Wall, full of framed photographs of Cody growing up. There had been good memories after all. What had happened to them? Ashamed, Cody realized they had been buried under grievances and manipulations and sarcasm. Maybe she and her mother were both to blame. Maybe they could both change.

Maybe. What was it Rivers had said? Second, get it over with. She tried to imagine that iron backbone Rivers had mentioned, and straightened.

Inside the office, Jess sat behind her desk with a polite smile plastered on, fingers laced tightly in front of her. Matt stood leaning against a wall, arms crossed over his chest, and his face tightened into something between horror and fascination.

And May sat in a chair facing the desk. Orthopedic shoes and swollen ankles. Huge purse at her feet. That slightly musty smell of a body with crevices that never get completely clean. A brightly colored caftan not long enough to cover the hairy legs May hadn't been able to reach to shave in years.

Cody couldn't look away from the mother that disgusted her and terrified her.

"Cody, there you are," Jess said, standing quickly. "We were just telling May you should be showing up any time."

"Sorry I'm late. I didn't expect to see you, mom."

"I imagine not," May said. "I did tell you to call me. I was worried about you here on your own, on this foolish trip.

I felt I had to come out here and help you in spite of the risks to my health taking that bus ride."

"Well, it was a wasted trip then. I don't really need any help." Cody's knees were shaking and shame weakened them further.

"I knew you wouldn't call," May said, folding her hands over her belly.

"You told me to call at six but you had to have been on the road by then." Cody rubbed her fingernails.

"Of course I was. I left the message early this morning and then decided I was needed here. It wasn't worth leaving another message telling you I was on my way since I knew you'd just be anxious worrying about me on the bus. Besides, you haven't been very responsible about calling regularly."

Iron backbone, Cody told herself. Iron backbone.

"I've been busy trying to get everything done before my vacation is up."

"You can't accomplish anything on your own. You know that. Every time you try to do something you end up hurt. You know how that breaks my heart, seeing you hurt. Doesn't it matter what you put me through?"

"Cody's doing fine," Matt said. "Let's get you set up in a hotel so you can rest from your trip."

"Who are you again?" May asked.

"Matt Tanner, Forest Ranger." His eyebrows were drawn down as if in irritation.

"Cody, please don't tell me you have a crush again. You know how that always turns out."

"Mom," Cody said, only to have words dry up.

"Crush or not," Matt said, drilling May with a steady green gaze. "It's between Cody and me. And now let's find you a hotel room." He took hold of May's arm, heaved her upward, and handed her the purse.

"You'll have to bring a car to the door," May said. "And Cody will take me. She and I need to have a talk about the realities of the world."

Jess came around the desk. "I think it's best if I escort you, Ms. Marsh."

"I said my daughter will take me." May planted her feet, clutched her purse, and turned into an immovable obelisk.

Cody saw the writing in stone. The weight of unsaid words crushed her.

"I'm sorry, but she can't," Jess said firmly, exuding professionalism. "She has a report I need reviewed for a case she's a witness for. She'll find you in the morning. Shall we?"

"I obviously have no choice. My own daughter won't help me find a place to sleep when I'm so exhausted from my trip I can barely move." May sagged, one hand going to her chest. "I need someplace where I can put my feet up and get a decent meal. You have no idea how hard this trip has been on me. I knew you'd get hurt coming here, Cody. I told you not to do this, didn't I?"

"Yes, mom."

"If you'd listen to me, stay where you are supposed to, I can keep you safe. But you go off chasing the memory of someone who's dead." May paused, sucking air as if it had become a rare commodity. "A man who did nothing to help raise you up, feed you, clothe you."

"Out the door before I forget my manners," Matt said, and with a grunt, tugged May forward. "Jess, plant her someplace. Now."

Jess took over with a grip so firm on May's upper arm that Cody could see indentations, and propelled May out the door.

Matt shut the door behind the two women, but not before Cody saw the expression of profound disappointment on May's face. She gripped the back of the chair her mother had been sitting in.

"What have you done?" she asked Matt.

"Stood up to her for you," he said.

Her breath stuttered across shame. Her mother had slammed her in front of these people who were treating her with kindness. She lost the battle with the tears. "How am I supposed to do this?" Cody asked, as a finger flame of anger toward her mother flickered, caught, grew.

"Do what?"

"I hate this. I hate that I'm her daughter. I hate looking in the mirror and seeing her. Don't you get it? How the hell am I going to ever get past her if every damn person I meet treats me like I need to be protected from her? I need to be able to stand up to her myself. Myself!"

"I'm sorry Cody," Matt said, holding his hands out as if in apology. "She's kind of hard to be around."

"Try living with her!"

"No thanks. Come on, look at it this way. She's gone for the evening and Florence is expecting you. You can dry off, rest, deal with her tomorrow."

"Right. Tomorrow. Well, I'm not going to be here tomorrow. I'm leaving first thing." Cody pushed herself away from the support of the chair.

"What? To where?"

"What the hell does it matter? Who cares?" She headed for the door and Matt sidestepped out of the way.

"Cody, wait, come on."

She didn't respond, slamming the office door behind her so hard she heard something hit the floor. Rage was a cold silence freezing everything inside. She was wet, chilled, exhausted. She'd go to Florence's for the night and in the morning she'd hit the highway soaring over Wallace. She'd fly east, away from home, away from May, away from memories. She'd drive until she found some town where May wouldn't follow her. She could get a job, start over. Maybe change her name. Didn't people do that? Become someone new? If Cody was a failure, she'd find a persona that wasn't.

Or else maybe she'd just keep driving until the fury was gone. The third step, just like Rivers had said. Leave it behind.

Chapter 19

Cody parked her car in the tiny pull off behind Rachel's Jeep. She looked up at the house still resting on its perch, just like the old woman still resting secure in its heart. Warm light from the windows fell down some of the steep stairs, but the rest were hidden in darkness. Cody climbed them hanging tightly to the wet railing with one hand and her bag with the other. Standing under the eaves at the door, she listened to water falling around her as she waited for someone to hear her knock.

Rachel opened the door and light, heat, and the smells of baking pulled Cody in. She felt the ice inside begin to thaw as she followed Rachel into the main room.

"Matt called and said you were on your way. I'm glad you decided to come here instead of finding another motel."

Rachel was barefoot, in low rider gray sweats and a cropped pink tee shirt that said 'Climb Naked, Dance the Rock'. A pearl glowed in the belly button of her flat stomach, and Cody averted her eyes, embarrassed by the exposure. And then embarrassed by her lack of the same ease within her own body.

"Did that hurt?" she asked, pointing to the pearl in an attempt to keep her self-consciousness from being obvious.

"Piercing? Not as much as my tattoo." Rachel lifted the tee shirt further, and turned so Cody could see something like a Celtic knot tattooed in the small of Rachel's back.

"What is that?"

"A rappel knot climbers use. Knot's that are bullet proof, really secure, are called Bombers. A friend used to call me Bomber Butt, so that's why I got the tattoo. There's nothing like climbing. You hang around long enough I'm going to turn you into a rock rat."

Cody seriously doubted that would ever happen.

"Did anyone tell you my mother showed up?"

"Well," Rachel said, hesitating. "Matt said I wasn't to bring her up. Said you were pissed."

"Just a little," Cody said, feeling the thaw spread even more as they entered the kitchen.

"Oh my dear," Florence said, looking up from the table as she lifted chocolate chip cookies onto a cloth to cool. "Your jaw! What happened to you?"

Without warning, the anger was extinguished by tears. Mortified, Cody couldn't stop them. Her hands flew to her mouth, fingers squeezing to deaden grief.

Florence was there, wrapping her arms around Cody, pulling her into a soft, sweet smelling embrace. Cody sank into the unconditional acceptance and was washed away from death, from self-loathing, from shame. She had no idea how long she sobbed there, but the tiny elderly woman wasn't so frail she couldn't hang on for the duration. At some point Rachel's arms came around Florence and Cody, and the three stood in the middle of the kitchen floor like a trinity of tears.

Cody finally straightened, her eyes burning.

"There now," Florence said. "We all need a good cry once in a while. You're all wet, dear. Go get changed and when you come out I'll have tea on. You'd best eat some of these cookies, too, while they're warm and soft. I imagine that bruise makes it painful to chew." She reached up and patted Cody's shoulder. "Go on now, dear. Crying helps, but tea and cookies are even better."

Florence's common sense voice and lack of questions about the tears allowed Cody to regain some composure. She followed Rachel to a tiny spare room and dropped her bag on a twin bed with a heavy quilt and wrought iron frame.

"Come on out when you're done," Rachel said, and gave Cody privacy.

Cody pulled her tee shirt off and shivered as she rummaged for a dry one. She sniffled the remains of tears and wondered if she had ever let loose and cried like that before. She wasn't sure why she had this time, but it felt oddly like release, in spite of the burning eyes and stuffy nose.

Changed and back out in the kitchen, Cody pulled out a chair and sat at the table with the other two women, not sure what to say, feeling like she needed to apologize for losing control. But as she debated what to say, Florence poured tea and passed over a plate of cookies, then settled back and pointed the spatula at Cody's jaw.

"That would never have happened if the bordellos had been allowed to stay open."

Rachel, reaching for a cookie, barely smothered a laugh.

"Why is that?" Cody asked, wondering if Florence's thoughts were as confused as hers.

"During the time bordellos were open, we had law enforcement that knew how to do their job," Florence said. "None of this pussy footin' around reading people their rights. What do you think those old lead lined billy clubs were for?"

"You had me worried there for a second," Rachel said. "I thought you were saying men could work off their frustrations knocking fallen angels around."

"No, no Rachel. You know me better than that. It was the time. The way of life, the way people were. We were treated like ladies, and men took care of their women. If something like this had happened then I'm sure the next day would have found the guilty person dropped down some unused mine shaft. You think any miners around here would have put up with their women being hurt?"

"Granny, you still believe in heroes and myths," Rachel said, pushing her mug back abruptly. "It doesn't work like that anymore."

"More's the pity," Florence said. "Have another cookie, dear. My husband was a real man. Not many of them left anymore. The closest things you'll find these days are the miners. Tough men."

"Not forest rangers?" Matt asked from the doorway.

All three women jumped. Cody twisted in the chair to see him leaning against the doorjamb.

"I came to apologize again, and to see what I needed to do to atone."

"Eat cookies," Florence said, waving the spatula again. "Pull up a chair, dear."

"So you don't think forest rangers are as tough as miners?" Matt asked, sitting down.

"Bunch of wood violets, the lot of them," Florence said.

Matt handed the cookie plate to Cody. "If you can't manage these we're going to have to get you baby food."

"Ha, ha," Cody said. The light banter felt welcoming and all encompassing, like she sat with family, and the feeling was a balm on her weepy spirits.

Rachel reached across Cody and slapped Matt lightly on the side of the head. "Matt dear," she said, sounding like her grandmother. "If you don't stop picking on Cody, I'm going to get one of granny's miners to belt you."

"Children, children," Florence said as she reached into an apron pocket and pulled out an old book.

"What is that?" Rachel asked.

"This is an old journal of mine," Florence said. "I've kept them since I was nine or so."

"I never knew that," Rachel said.

"Of course not, dear. You would have read them. I wasn't always old you know. There are some escapades I'm not sure I want you knowing about."

"I'm going to wait for one of the days when you're out of it and then I'm going to find them and read them all," Rachel said, licking chocolate off her fingers. "I hate secrets."

"No you won't," Florence said calmly. "I've hidden them."

"Well you better tell me where before your mind is completely gone," Rachel said, leaning over to kiss her grandmother on the cheek.

"You're distracting me, dear. Fill the tea kettle again and listen instead of talking."

Matt scooped up another cookie. "No one bakes like you, Florence. Will you marry me?"

"My husband will have something to say about that." Florence's voice was prim but she smiled as she placed the book on the table and rested her gnarled hands on its cover. "You don't know what it's like not being able to remember things anymore. Sometimes it makes me so furious, and sometimes so sad. So many things that shouldn't be forgotten. People now gone that shouldn't be allowed to leave memory. No one is truly dead if there's someone left who remembers them. You understand that, Cody."

No one spoke, and the quiet was filled with crackling flames, an aged house settling, the moaning of wind sent from winter fields on mountains. How long before Kelly and Nate were forgotten? Was Cody the only one who would keep her grandfather alive? She rubbed her fingernails, watching the soothing movement and wondering if memories were worth the pain attached to them.

"And the journal, granny?" Rachel said, her voice a gentle thread pulling Cody back to the present.

"Cody's questions about her grandfather started me wondering if I'd written about him or Ethel when I was young. So I've been reading and it's been quite the journey. I found many stories I'd forgotten. I'm very grateful Cody, that you helped me remember these books, and I'm very grateful I wrote things down."

"Like what?" Rachel asked, drawing her mug close again and taking a sip of tea.

"Oh, let's see. I must have been in my late teens. I had a job at the bakery, and was making my first money. My father had taken up a partnership in the Honey Do. There was talk that she was going to be a good silver producer, maybe even on par with Sunshine or Hecla. She hadn't started producing yet but the owners were selling shares. I thought she sounded worth investing in."

"What happened?" Matt asked. "She obviously didn't pan out like Sunshine or we'd all know about it."

"That's the question, isn't it?" Florence shrugged. "When I went to the assay office, the mine had been closed down. My father never spoke of it again, but I do remember how angry he was. I wrote in my journal because I ended up going to the Sunshine offices to see about buying a share, and met the man I married. Your grandfather, Rachel. He was just coming up from his shift." Florence's eyes filmed with reminiscence.

"Gramps," Rachel said.

"Oh, he was hell bent for leather, that one," Florence laughed and the sound was sweet, like the girl she had once been. "Him and his brothers are always up to one thing or another. My folks don't like him one bit. But oh my, you should see his muscles. He can pick me up like I was nothing. He should be coming off shift any minute, and he'll be happy to see these cookies, I can tell you."

Rachel patted her grandmother's hand. "A Sunshine miner."

"Real men," Florence agreed, with pride in her eyes. "And a mine like no other."

"Definitely no comparison to the Honey Do," Matt said. He watched Florence with an expression of sadness that reflected the sympathy Cody felt. How hard this slip into dementia must be for Florence. And Rachel.

"I read about that mine," Cody said, glancing guiltily at Matt. "I made copies of the page on Honey Do. I think…well, it was some of the papers missing from my room. Sorry, I should have told you earlier."

"Hey," Matt said, raising his hands. "I'm saying nothing here. I've had my ass chewed enough."

"What did the article say?" Rachel asked. Her expression eased, as if relieved by the change in subject, but her eyes never left her grandmother's face.

"Only that the mine was closed because of the difficulty in getting ore out. I think it also said something about someone trying to reopen it."

"I've heard Rivers complaining about a new mining venture," Matt said. He finished the cookie he held and licked his fingers. "And I think Jim Russell is the engineer."

"Probably Keith Naylor opening it," Florence said, as cheerful back in the present as she had been moments ago in the past. "He was the major shareholder and I believe my father and the others relinquished shares to him when the mine closed down."

"He probably kept it," Matt said. "And it wouldn't surprise me that he's trying to reopen it. The way the market and technologies have improved he could make some profit off mineral rights or extraction."

"Is the mine what you were looking for in the journal?" Cody asked, gathering cookie crumbs with her fingertip.

"No, dear. I read the entry about my son's birth, and got to thinking about your questions about Ethel and Charles. I'm wondering what you might find out from the Health Department. You know, that place down by the train museum. Isn't that where you can go nowadays and get copies of old birth certificates?"

"You're right," Rachel said. "But you can get them online, too."

"Would a birth certificate show a biological mother if she didn't want to be known?" Cody asked.

"You don't know that she didn't," Matt said. "You're making an assumption because she didn't keep him or ever tell him she was his mother. That's a good idea, Florence. You could head down there Monday, Cody. Get a copy. Might be something concrete for you."

Cody glanced at Matt, raising an eyebrow. It was a good idea, but she didn't plan on being here by Monday, and he knew that. She would use Rachel's suggestion and look for the birth certificate online, when she ended up wherever she was going. Exhaustion moved through her and she covered a yawn with her hand, wincing as pain flared.

"Alright then, off you go," Florence said, seeing the yawn. "It's almost midnight. Rachel dear, you can spend the night as well. But you, Matt, need to find your own bed."

"Damn." Matt stood. "Fine then. I'll head home all by myself."

"You do that," Rachel said. "Tomorrow's Sunday. If you're lucky we'll invite you over for a late breakfast."

Cody hugged Florence goodnight and stumbled her way to the tiny spare room. She undressed and pulled back the quilt, barely registering what she did. The soft mattress rose around her and she sank into it, burrowing under the covers. Was her mother as comfortable in her hotel room? May would be so furious. Cody closed her burning eyes against the worry, against the vision of May's face, and against her inevitable future.

Chapter 20

Cody woke early, tried dozing, and finally gave up on sleep, easing out from under the blankets and pulling on jeans and a black sweater, wincing as stiff muscles complained and bruises throbbed. At the window she saw the rain had eased and the wind had retreated, trailing its way through tree tops. The early morning sun remained hidden behind flattened, low clouds, leaving deep shadows in the canyons.

As early as it was, Florence was up and standing in front of the kitchen stove in a heavy flannel robe, the hem of a flowered nightgown peeking out at the bottom. "You're up early, dear," Florence said.

"So are you."

"Oh, you need less sleep when you get older. Would you like some tea?"

"Please," Cody said. She took a chair at the table facing the stove so she could watch Florence at work. "Is today going to be a good day?"

"I hope so. I do hate worrying Rachel though. She's all I have left. And she worries too much."

"I suppose with all the traveling Rachel's parents do, they aren't around to help."

"Traveling? Oh no dear. They're dead these eight years now." Florence's eyes teared up and she dabbed at them with the edge of her apron. "My son and his wife were killed driving that awful motor home. My daughter-in-law, Rachel's mother, died instantly and my son lived a day or so longer, but we had to make the decision to remove life support. It was horrible, just horrible."

"I can't even imagine," Cody responded, confused. "Rachel told me they were traveling."

"Well, yes, she tells people that in order to avoid talking about it." Florence joined Cody at the table with mugs for both of them. "Her therapist tells her she needs to open up but she won't."

"No wonder she's so close to you," Cody said, sipping her tea. She put the mug down but continued to hold it, cupping its warmth. "You're all she has left."

"I imagine you would understand better than most. Losing your grandfather so recently. May I ask why you're looking for stories about him?"

"Well, to hang on to him I guess," Cody said, trying to put her feelings into words. "Until he showed up I'd always thought it was just me and my mom. And that's not the happiest relationship." She paused, and then added quietly, "He gave me history, made me feel like I belonged, like I fit in somewhere."

"And so it was hard to let go when he died."

"Very." Cody sat forward. "And who would be left to remember him except for me? I need to know who he was, where he came from. All of that contributes to who I am. Makes me something other than my mother."

Realizing she gripped the edges of the table in her intensity, in her need to make Florence understand, she forcibly relaxed and leaned back in the chair.

"If family is that important, why are you staying here when your mother is in town?" Florence tilted her head, watching Cody.

The pause was longer this time. "Because here, everyone treats me like I'm okay. Rachel and Matt both treat me like a friend."

"You don't have friends?"

"Oh, acquaintances," Cody said, twisting on the chair to find a position that didn't hurt her bruised hip. Or maybe she was just squirming under Florence's gaze. She shifted again.

"I'll tell you this, my girl," Florence said firmly. "Every child needs to find who they are as an individual. You're just a late bloomer."

"On the other hand," Cody said as the heat of self-consciousness washed over her. "One thing I've learned is the importance of family."

"Oh yes indeed." Florence spooned sugar into her mug. "I've always been proud of my family. Why, I don't know how many generations the Blaines and Smithwicks have been around, but Mama can tell you some hair-raising stories about them."

Florence's slides in and out of the present were so subtle and natural that Cody barely had time to grieve for her before the elderly woman was firmly back in the present. It made the conversation poignant and challenging. Cody wasn't sure if she should correct Florence but the flow of conversation didn't allow her enough time to decide.

"Have you written down the stories your grandfather told you, or the things you've learned about him?" Florence asked, spooning more sugar into tea that was beginning to resemble sludge.

"Well, there hasn't been much time to do that," Cody said, moving the sugar bowl away. "But I plan on it."

"It should be a priority, dear, before you forget details. Then years from now you can pull out your stories and he will be just as alive for you."

"Is that why you keep journals?"

"Partly, and with my confusion lately, I'm glad I did. When I pulled them out and read them yesterday, it brought back so many memories. So you just make sure you write down your thoughts."

"My mother keeps journals, too, but the one time I read an entry it wasn't very kind." Cody fidgeted with the tablecloth, rubbing the ivory material between her fingers.

"Which is why you should never read another's journal."

"True," Cody said. "Kind of like eavesdropping."

"Well, I'm not one to give advice, dear, as I have a history of doing the opposite of whatever someone advised me on. But I would suggest you get a place of your own."

Cody nodded, but she wasn't sure if she was agreeing with Florence or just being polite. These people didn't know May as well as she did.

Someone knocked on the front door, and the sound was followed by the dull clunk of boots on the wide plank floors. Both Florence and Cody turned to see Matt duck under the doorway, carrying a box of donuts. His blonde hair was mussed from wind and his nose red from cold.

"I'm hoping if I provide the breakfast you'll make me some of your homemade hot cocoa, Florence."

"Of course I will," Florence replied, with a giggle so sweet Cody turned to her in surprise. "I've been wanting Mama to meet you, but she's having a lie in. Sit down and tell me how your shift was. Did you get to use the jackleg?"

Matt faltered, a slight pause only, before putting down the box and pulling out a chair. His eyebrows were pulled down as if in pain as he reached across the table and took hold of Florence's age spotted hand.

"Promoted to jackleg today," he said. "Drilling's hard work. But the extra pay will be worth it."

The words seemed to be the right ones as Florence blushed and stood. "I'll make that cocoa. Will your wages be enough for you to speak to Papa?"

Matt coughed, looking to Cody and raising his shoulders in question. Cody didn't know what to say. Did you go along with someone's confusion, feed it, or try to reason them back to the right time? Could you reason with someone whose mind was fading? A deep tenderness washed over her, startling her with its unfamiliarity. She watched Florence pull a bottle of vanilla out of the cupboard and pause, staring at it.

"Florence?" Cody asked. "Granny?"

Neither name brought recognition into Florence's eyes. Instead she looked at Cody with fear and confusion, and something like betrayal moved upward into Cody's heart. It was as if someone she had just come to love had run away.

"Mama?" Florence called.

"I'm right here," Rachel said, coming into the kitchen tying the sash on a teal bathrobe.

Matt stood, but Rachel shook her head at him, once and sharply, and her hand came out as if pushing them away.

"There are strangers in our kitchen," Florence said, with a tremor in her voice. "Should I go for Papa?"

"No, dear. They're friends of mine. Let's get you settled by the fire with your books."

Rachel led Florence out to the living room, and in the silence Cody looked to Matt.

"What can we do?" she asked.

Matt shrugged.

"It's best if you leave for a while," Rachel said, as she came back into the kitchen. "Give her a couple hours alone with me."

Rachel's words were brisk, no nonsense, as if she'd said them many times. But Cody saw the tightly clenched hands, the rigid shoulders, the flame of something in Rachel's eyes that could have been fury or fear. Or both.

"We can't help you with anything?" Cody asked, standing awkwardly from the table.

"No. Just go. Quiet helps. And...and I don't like people seeing her like this."

The words had a breath of confession to them, and Cody knew there was nothing to do but honor the request. She picked up her wallet and keys and followed Matt out of the kitchen that no longer felt like home.

"Have you seen Florence like that before?" Cody asked as she pulled the front door shut behind them.

"No," Matt said, staring down the stairs. "But then Rachel protects her. I think people only get invitations when Florence is doing okay. It's like the real Florence has died. I don't know how Rachel does it."

"How can she leave Florence alone when she's like that?" Cody followed carefully, the steep steps slick with dew.

"She can't. Rachel's used up almost all her sick time at the museum and she's talking about having to hire someone full time to be a caregiver for when she's at work. More than likely Rachel's going to have to move back home. I can't see Florence able to be alone at night."

"No," Cody said. "God, no. Can you imagine if she wandered out some night with these stairs?"

"I need to talk to Rachel later. See what we can do to help her out. It's one thing to hear what's happening and something else to see it."

The air was chilly and tangy, with a crispness that numbed Cody's fingers. The most shadowed nooks amid boulders and tree roots held cups of new frost and little daylight reached down over the edges of the ravines.

"Sure is cold." Cody blew on her fingers, her shoes crunching across the gravel as she followed Matt to the cars.

Matt's cell phone rang before he could respond, and he flipped it open. "Yeah?"

Cody went past him and unlocked her car, wondering about the best way to spend the homeless hours until her mother was up. It was too early to call as May was a late sleeper. She waved to Matt, but he held a hand up, holding her in place with the gesture. He flipped shut the cell and brought it up as if to throw it into the street then pulled in a deep breath and jammed the phone in a pocket.

"Matt?"

"That was Hailey," he said, running a hand over his face. "Wants me to come up to Jake's place. You okay on your own?"

"Sure," Cody said. "Think I'll drop in on Rivers."

"You'll have a nicer time than I'm going to. Jake's probably stirring something up. Damn it all to hell!" Matt slammed his hand into the side of the Bronco. "Trouble sticks to him like flies on shit, and shit's something I don't need."

Cody watched him pull out, wheels spinning and spitting gravel at her car. She flinched away, her hand pulling up to protect her face. When she straightened, the Bronco was already rounding a corner heading back toward Wallace.

Why would Hailey want Matt at Jake's place? Something connected to Nate and Kelly, or something totally unrelated? Whatever the reason it didn't concern her. She was in Burke with nothing to do, so hopefully Rivers didn't mind early company.

One of the advantages of tiny towns was that it didn't take long to go from one place to another. A warm yellow light shown from the main room and smoke curled up from the leaning chimney as Cody shouldered through the swollen outer door. She stood in the chilly box of an entryway and knocked on the inner door. It only took a few moments of shivering before Rivers peered out the window then opened the door.

"Cody. Would you like some breakfast?" Rivers held the door wider, wearing a large flannel shirt and red long john bottoms.

"No thanks. I was looking for some company though, if it's not inconvenient."

"Of course not. Come in, we're letting all the heat out. Chilly this morning."

Cody followed Rivers inside and stood clutching her keys, shifting her weight from foot to foot.

"You can sit down you know," Rivers said, pushing up the sleeve of her shirt to stir oatmeal in a pot on the woodstove. "How's your mother?"

"Sleeping, I'm sure. She's always been a night owl so doesn't get up until late. Plus she doesn't sleep well so she's tired all the time. It's hard for her to breathe in bed so she's up and down a lot at night."

"It would probably make a difference if she lost some weight."

Cody shrugged, suddenly aware of her rounded edges and the willowy gracefulness of Rivers.

"Mom says the weight is in our genes."

"Horse pucky," Rivers said.

The casually spoken phrase pulled a laugh up out of Cody, and the unexpectedness of the sound eased tension away. She sank onto one end of the well-used couch. It had a permanent hollow where it was obvious Rivers was most comfortable.

"I spent the night with Rachel and her grandmother. Florence was not doing so good when I left."

"Dementia isn't it? What a horrid thing."

"Yes." Cody fingered the afghan on the back of the couch. "Am I keeping you from anything?"

"No. My niece called from Seattle so that got me up. I have some appointments later this morning though."

"Chaining yourself to trees?"

This time it was Rivers who laughed. "Poor Sunny. Someday I'm going to take her along with me so she can see what I really do. For instance, I have to suffer through a meeting with Kendra and her grandfather at eleven. The only bright spot about that is Jess will be there. She thinks I need a mediator. I'll tell you something though Cody. One of these days I'm going to get Burke cleaned up and the working mines around here up to environmental standards."

"How?"

"One step at a time. It's all I can do."

The phone rang and Rivers followed the sound into the kitchen. Cody held her hands out toward the heat from the wood stove. There was something about this place, or maybe it was Rivers, that made Cody feel content and restful, as if her whole body had just taken a long deep breath.

"That was Jess," Rivers said, frowning. "She's cancelled out on our meeting. Something about Jake's place. A death, or a body. I couldn't quite make it out."

"Jake's place?" The contentment solidified and froze.

"She just got the call," Rivers said. "I wish she had a different job."

"Matt was going up there." Cody stood, digging in her jeans pocket. Where had she put her keys?

"To Jake's? You're sure?"

"Hailey called him earlier. I need to get up there." Cody pinched the bridge of her nose. "What if it's Jake? Or Matt?"

Rivers slipped her hands up the sleeves of the shirt in a self-contained hug. "I'm not sure you want to go into some police activity. You can wait here and Jess will call me back."

"No. Thanks, but what if it has to do with Kelly or Nate?" Cody found her keys and gripped them. "I can't wait. Can you tell me where Jake's place is?" Her words came out fast, with no thought, with hardly any breath.

"Let me throw on some clothes and toss this nasty oatmeal, then I'll go with you. You'll never find Jake's on your own. It's a hell of a place for a hell of a man."

Chapter 21

"Turn here," Rivers said, pointing to a road that cut off before Wallace. "This is Thompson Pass. I'll tell you where to go when we get to the top."

"Is there a town?" Cody wanted to fly, wanted speed to catch her up to Matt. But the rough, narrow road with climbing snakelike turns held her back.

"No. Jake's place is off a couple logging roads. It's bounded on all sides by forest service land, and they'd love to get it back but Jake won't let go of it. Can't say as I blame him. It's been in his family for generations. Plus it's just plain beautiful. I've coveted his place for a long time."

"So no electricity?" Cody tried to look over at Rivers but the rough road demanded her full attention.

"No," Rivers said.

As the road climbed, the pines and tamaracks gave way to an open view high above Wallace. There were no guard rails and barely enough room between mountain and edge for her car.

"Cody, you're so tense it feels like you're going to pull that steering wheel right out of the column," Rivers said, patting Cody's arm. "There's nothing we can do to change whatever is happening. So try some deep breathing."

"Deep breathing. Right. I've never found that to do anything."

"Neither have I but it sounds good." Rivers pointed. "See that break in the trees there on the right? By that corner? That's the first logging road we're going to take. Go slow as the road gets rough from here on out."

"I thought it already was."

"Yeah, but we had pavement. And by the way, scotch works."

"What?" Cody took the corner cautiously, the Subaru bouncing over a washboard of dirt.

"Scotch. Instead of deep breathing. That's what relaxes me. I do yoga, tai chi, but when I'm really stressed, scared, angry, I need a little scotch. A fine one, like a Lagavulin sixteen year old."

"Sounds expensive." The road forced Cody to slow down and a cramp knocked on her calf muscle, as if trying to force her to take her foot off the brake.

"Which is why I try not to stress too often. There, take that turn." Rivers reached out and braced one hand against the dashboard. "God, I hate this road. At least when I'm in a hurry. I'm trying to distract you with all my yammering but I don't think it's working. So tell me where you are with your grandfather."

"I appreciate the yammering, really," Cody said as her knuckles cracked with tension. "With Charles, nowhere, I guess. I need to see if I can find a copy of his birth certificate." The car splashed through a tiny creek slowly eating the road. "I'm not sure what I'll be able to finish with my mom here."

"Your mother. That's right. I'd like to meet her. Do you see that old leaning tamarack? Right beyond it there's a very narrow track. That's Jake's driveway. In the old days his family used horses to get in and out." Rivers was leaning forward now as if her body could propel the car faster.

"Looks like there haven't been any road improvements since then." The tires dipped into more potholes and the steering wheel jerked in her hands.

"Jake likes change about as much as he likes company."

Cody rounded a couple switchbacks and then without warning the road was exposed, as the trees and mountain dropped away on one side to a high expanse of mountaintops and sky. Vertigo washed through Cody like the wind washed up the cliff face. She wanted to slam on the brakes and freeze, but forced herself to inch the car slowly along the narrow track. Cody was vaguely aware of the far reaching vista, but she was too afraid to look away from the road. A faint buzzing in her ears shocked her into realizing she was holding her breath. She sucked in air and inched the car as far from the edge as she could manage.

"I've always loved it up here," Rivers said.

Cody's mouth was dry, her palms sweaty, and she could only hope casual conversation would hide her fear. "Can't see why at the moment. Have you known Jake long?"

"Since he was a teenager. He's too prickly to be called a close friend, but I respect him. I knew his father better."

"What was his father like?" Cody asked, desperate for any distraction from imagining what was happening up ahead.

"Prickly," Rivers said, and laughed, but her laugh sounded as forced as Cody's words.

"Hailey thinks he killed Kelly," Cody said, prodding Rivers into more conversation. "Do you think he could kill someone? I mean, he's only been nice to me."

"Oh, I imagine Jake could do something like that." Rivers turned slightly to face Cody. "But with Jake it would be an accident, in that temper of his. Not cold blooded the way Kelly and Nate were."

"And you're not afraid of Jake?" Cody wondered if she could be so calm if she had a friend with Jake's anger.

"Oh no. You have to look beyond that armor he wears."

It sounded good coming from Rivers, but Cody wondered how idealistic that was. Maybe Jake was capable of more than his friends realized.

They rounded one more corner and the road descended back into woods and solid ground, heading inland to the darker forest canopy where late morning light barely penetrated. But instead of being relieved to leave the cliff, Cody's anxiety ratcheted up as she saw several vehicles parked in a line, including two forest service Broncos. She pulled in and parked behind one.

"Now we follow that footpath," Rivers said, and fumbled open the passenger door.

The short trail cut through trees to a small clearing visible from Cody's car. A cabin with a steeply pitched roof stood in the center of the clearing, and people clustered around its front door. Hailey's blond curls and short stature made her easy to pick out in the crowd. It was just as easy to pick out Jake as he came out of the cabin, shoved through the crowd, and headed in their direction. Cody scanned the crowd for Matt as she shut the car door then rubbed her thumbs across her fingers.

"There's Jess talking to Hailey," Rivers said, buttoning her brightly striped coat against the damp air. There was distinct relief in her voice.

"Jake doesn't seem to like Hailey. The way he lives out here, is he kind of antisocial?" Cody asked, watching him cross the rough ground with the long strides of someone more used to walking land than pavement.

"Rough all the way through," Rivers said. "But most women seem to like him. Well, not counting Hailey I guess. I've decided Jake's a man who attracts three kinds of women. Women who lust, women who dream of redeeming, and women who fear his masculinity."

"Which are you?" Cody asked, knowing she would fall into the fearful group.

"I'm the fourth kind," she said, and her gentle smile with its upturned corners spelled secrets.

"What the hell's going on?" Jake said, nearing them. "This is private property. Not some place for a damn forest ranger picnic. Yet everyone's showing up and not telling me a damn thing."

"Jake," Rivers said, holding out her hands, palms up. "This isn't the time for rough edges."

Hailey separated from the crowd and jogged toward them.

"What am I supposed to have done now?" Jake asked, fists going to hips.

"Jess called," Cody said tentatively. "She said there's a body up here. Jake, where's Matt?"

"Matt? I don't know. He's probably sucked into the crowd with all the trespassers." He looked over his shoulder at Hailey bearing down on them. "Ah shit. Help me out here Rivers. Keep that gnat away from me."

Hailey reached them before Rivers could respond, and kept coming, until she stood, back to Cody and up on tiptoes facing Jake. Her fists were on her hips, too, and if she'd been any closer her breasts would have been brushing Jake's stomach.

"I told you I'd get you," she said, her words coming out staccato. "I told you, and I've done it."

"Back off," Jake said.

"You thought you could get away with murder because no one comes up here," Hailey said, her face flushing. "But I found the body. Me. Doing the job the way it's supposed to be done."

"So you found a body. What's that got to do with me?" Jake said.

"You've been pushing against the law for a long time Jake, and this time I'm pushing back and you can't do anything about it."

Cody caught sight of Matt coming out of the trees and crossed her arms over her chest, gripping her elbows, trying to contain the sudden relief at seeing him. He came up behind Jake and Hailey, nodding only briefly at Cody over Jake's shoulder.

"Hailey," Jake said, losing their stare-down. "You're nuts." He grabbed her around the waist, picked her up, and swung her into Matt.

"Here Tanner, do something with her."

"Jake," Matt said in response, patting Hailey on the shoulder as he moved past her. Even Cody could see the fury resonating through each and every blonde curl as Hailey homed in on Jake again.

"What's this about a body?" Jake asked, as if Hailey had ceased to exist.

"Jess just filled me in," Matt said. He kept his hands loose at his sides, nonthreatening, his voice even. "Hailey found a body in the Honey Do mine east of your place."

"No," Rivers said, and ran to Matt. "Do you know who it is? It's not Jim is it? Please Matt, tell me it's not Jim."

"I saw Jim just a couple days ago," Matt said. "This guy's been there a lot longer."

"Thank the goddess," Rivers said, resting her forehead on Matt's shoulder. "I sent him to Honey Do for a core sample."

Cody looked at the ground, feeling like an interloper as Matt hushed Rivers by rubbing her shoulders. Hailey unexpectedly shoved past Matt, grabbed Jake's wrists, jerked his arms behind him and slapped on handcuffs.

"What the hell?" Jake shouted, twisting around.

"You're under arrest." The ratcheting sound of tightening cuffs was like a parenthesis around Hailey's voice.

"For what?" Jake's voice was more like a growl now, as he circled with Hailey as if locked onto a target.

"Murder." Hailey's eyes were radiant. "And don't you ever, ever touch me again."

"Stay away from me and I won't have to." Jake tossed his hair out of his eyes and lowered his chin as if about to charge.

"Hailey, take the cuffs off," Matt said, holding Jake back with a hand to his chest. "At this point we don't even know if the person was murdered or died of natural causes. All we have is a body that's been out here in the woods for some time. We could be looking at some hiker who had a heart attack."

"And another thing," Jake said, struggling against the cuffs. "The body is in the mine. The mine isn't inside my cabin. So get these cuffs the hell off me and get the hell off my place."

Hailey's smile illuminated her face. She opened her dainty hand, the cuff key resting in her palm. Bringing it to her lips, she kissed the key, watching Jake over her fingers. And then she threw the key high and arcing out into the woods.

"You're getting into Jess's car and spending the night in jail," she said. "Because Matt is wrong. The person was very obviously murdered. And yes, the mine isn't on your property. But considering you're the only one up here, I'd say you're it."

"That's not happening," Jess said. She had come up on them so quietly no one had noticed. "And that was a stupid gesture." She reached behind her to where her handcuff case was fastened to her belt and palmed the key. "All you've done is create paperwork for yourself, explaining how you lost your key. They're universal Hailey."

"You can't release him," Hailey said. "I told you this is a murder and the Forest Service has jurisdiction."

"We don't arrest people simply because they are in the proximity of a crime," Jess said. "And neither does the Forest Service. You know that. This isn't happening."

Jess moved to release Jake, and Hailey jumped forward as if she was about to tackle Jess. Matt caught Hailey's arm, staying her lunge forward as Jess unlocked the cuffs.

"Hailey, get some control," he said. "Let go of this thing with Jake or he'll be within his rights to accuse you of harassment."

"Matt, you know Jake. You can't for an instant think he's the innocent victim here." Hailey made no visible effort to calm down, quivering so tightly it was as if the slightest touch would shatter her into spiraling blonde shards.

"Jake's rarely innocent, I'll give you that," Matt said, smiling as if trying to ease the tension. He dropped his shoulders, bending slightly as if to give their talk more of a conversational feel and Cody recognized the movements as his attempt to diffuse Hailey.

Hailey sucked in a deep breath, her hands fisted tightly on her hips. "So what, just let him go home?"

"Forget him. Concentrate on what you do best, gathering evidence, tallying facts, sifting the story." Matt pulled out a notepad and flipped through some pages. "I'd say, from what we have here, you might want to head back up to the mine with the evidence team. You're the one who's most up to date on new forensics. Make sure nothing's overlooked. We don't want anything compromised in taking the body out."

"Right. You're right. I can do that. I know what to look for." Hailey was already looking beyond Matt, into the woods surrounding the cabin. She started forward, only to have her path blocked by Jake.

"Not on my land, midget." He turned to Matt. "I want all of you out of here. Now."

"I understand." Jess stepped forward, placing a hand on Jake's arm. "Unfortunately this is the only access road. We'll have to have our vehicles here. That's why we were up at your cabin. We were hoping to get permission to cross your place. But I totally get your frustration."

Jake blew out an expressive breath of air and raked fingers through is hair. "Okay Jess. You and your guilt trips. You and your team can cross. But not Hailey. She comes on my land again, she comes near me again, and I'm going for a restraining order and harassment charges."

Rivers laughed, and to Cody the sound was as fresh as birdsong, dissipating everyone's tension. "Oh Jake. I'm sorry, but I just pictured you and Hailey standing in front of a judge with you, the tough mountain man, explaining why you need protection from the little Shirley Temple doll."

"Yeah, yeah," Jake said, his scowl easing, dark eyebrows returning to their normal slant. "Go ahead and laugh."

"All right, here's the plan," Jess said, pulling out a radio. "We'll need the evidence teams, one in the mine, one for the perimeter. I want you, Matt, overseeing the outer work. Hailey-"

But Hailey was already across the clearing and jogging quickly away from them.

"Finally," Jess said. "Dramatics gone. We can get some work done."

Cody shifted, with the intention of telling them goodbye and getting out of the way, but Jess and Matt had pulled out radios and were already talking on them, and Jake left, heading to his cabin. Rivers caught her arm, and tilted her chin toward Cody's car. As Cody nodded her agreement, a sharp snapping sound back in the trees made both of them swing toward the sound.

Jess freed a long sigh, as if all her stress breathed out to join the chilly mountain air, and stumbled back against Rivers before slumping.

Matt tackled Cody, taking her to the ground and onto her injured hip. She rolled away from the pain, but Matt's hand between her shoulder blades kept her pinned while he yanked Rivers down at the same time.

"Jess!" Rivers wouldn't stay down, crawling forward, her voice the sound of heartbreak.

"Don't move!" Matt yelled, grabbing for Rivers.

Cody twisted away from Matt and heard another shot fired, heard the thwack of it hitting a car, heard the sprinkle of glass falling. Terror demanded that she move. She pushed up on fear-slick hands, with the urge to run, to survive, like a tidal wave flooding her thoughts. But she saw Jess lying on her side, knees drawn up where she had crumpled. The front of her uniform shirt darkened, as if night fell over her heart.

"There's so much blood! Help me!" Rivers pulled at Jess's buttons.

Cody's knees were numb and tingling for escape, but she squirmed away from Matt and crept forward.

"Officer down!" Matt yelled into his radio, as he yanked open the Bronco door and pulled out a rifle. "Cody, get your damn head down! Rivers, it's her neck. Direct pressure. Neck, Rivers, neck!"

Rivers still tugged at buttons. Cody reached Jess, catching her collar and pulling it down. A long cut bisected the base of Jess's throat. Blood swelled and flowed and pooled. Jess's eyes were fixed on Rivers but Cody could see her trying to reach for her gun.

"Shot came from the northeast," Matt said to the radio. "I need a medivac chopper now! I need ground teams after the shooter!"

"Matt," Cody said, but what came out sounded more like horror than a word. She couldn't look away from her hands, the freckles disappearing under the darkening flood. "The blood won't stop."

"More pressure," he said, his words as staccato as the gunshots cutting the air to their right. "Just don't cut off her breathing."

Rivers smoothed back Jess's hair. "Jess hates her hair a mess. This beautiful hair and she imprisons it in this braid."

Cody darted a quick glance at Rivers, startled by the calmness of her words. Rivers hunched over Jess, shielding her with odd, unfocused eyes, as if deep in the nightmare.

Blood thickened between Cody's fingers, gluing them. She could feel the rapid flutter of Jess's pulse under her palms, as if she'd captured a fragile moth. She saw the blood soaking into the cuff of her fleece, merging and freshening the dark stain of Nate's death. More blood for her to carry.

Jess raised her hand to cover Cody's. "Get…"

"Get help," Cody said, with a horrible flashback to Nate's last words. Her breath came fast and light and jittery, like a dying leaf in rushing whitewater. "Matt's taking care of that."

"No. Get Rivers away." Jess's voice was a hoarse whisper, a choking that drowned the words.

"I'm not going," Rivers said, bending lower.

"Yeah, you are," Matt said, grabbing Rivers. "You and Cody both. Right now."

"No!" Rivers tried to pull away from Matt but he hung on. "I'm going with her."

"Not going to happen," Matt said. "I need you both out of here now. Medivac will be here any second. They'll airlift Jess to the hospital. Cody will get you there."

A ranger Cody didn't know dropped down next to her. He had a first aid kit already open, trauma dressings in hand.

"Where's Jake?" Rivers asked. "He needs to be here. He'll want to know. He's her friend."

"Someone will find him," Matt said. "Get in the car. Cody, get out of here. Follow that ranger Bronco. Don't stop for anyone, just head for pavement."

More gunfire from the woods made Cody flinch downward as Matt lifted Rivers to her feet and pulled her toward Cody's car. Cody didn't think her muscles worked anymore. There was no way they could support her. But she put a hand on the ground and managed to push upward, pushed against the need to stay low and scuttle for shelter like a spider before the shoe drops.

Matt caught Cody's arm, helping her up and staying between her and the direction of gunshots. He guided her into the driver's seat, reached across her and turned the key.

"George, get that Bronco turned around! I want these two out of here now."

"I'm so cold," Rivers said. "So cold."

Cody thought about turning the heat up, but she shook too hard and had to hang onto the steering wheel for control. She backed up and turned, aiming for the Bronco that was to lead them out, the drying blood gluing her hands to the wheel. But even as her car covered the rough ground, her eyes were on the rearview mirror watching Matt and the other ranger bending to Jess, still and unmoving on her forest bed.

The Bronco ahead of them drove fast, spitting gravel against Cody's car. She hung on, kept her foot on the gas, stayed close, afraid to look at anything but the bumper in front of her. As they came out of the trees, she heard the sound of a helicopter, like a heartbeat of the sky.

"So much blood," Rivers said, and her voice was suddenly thick, as if the words were muted under water.

They hit a pothole so hard Cody lost her grip on the steering wheel. It spun alone for a moment before she caught it.

"I'm going to rip his throat out." Rivers gripped her seatbelt in one hand, pushing against the dashboard with the other.

"Who?" Cody asked, for a moment totally clueless as her mind tried to catch up with what was happening.

"The person who did this to Jess. If she dies, I'm going to kill him."

The peaceful, graceful environmentalist was gone. She'd been possessed by pure fury, a cold darkness that froze words and covered any emotion that might have thawed her dark eyes.

"I hear you," Cody said. "But don't give up on her."

"She can't die," Rivers said, and her voice thinned now, watered with tears. "She's my life partner and doesn't know it yet."

The Bronco turned on to pavement, and brake lights lit up as it swerved to the road edge. Cody pulled up even with it and rolled her window down.

"You should be good from here," the ranger said. "You know how to get to the hospital?"

"Yes," Cody said, knowing Rivers would get her there.

The ranger nodded and cranked the Bronco around, leaving them as fast as he'd deposited them.

"Which way do I go?" Cody asked, pulling out again. "Wallace?"

Rivers was silent, her thumbs running over the drying blood on her hands.

"Rivers. The hospital. Where is it?"

"Oh Cody, what am I supposed to do?"

"Give me directions. Get me there. That's your first step."

The second step was getting Rivers out of the car once they reached the hospital. She clung to Cody, shaking so hard she could barely move forward.

"Come on Rivers, here's the emergency entrance."

Somewhere on River's body an odd chiming sounded, like muffled church bells or gongs.

"Oh, my cell," Rivers said. "Where is it? Is that what I heard?" She patted down her sides as she walked unsteadily toward the glass doors. "Here it is."

Cody watched Rivers pull out the small cell and then stare at it as if she had no idea what to do with it. Gently, Cody took it from her and flipped it open.

"Hello?" She saw the dried blood flaking off her fingers and her stomach turned.

"Cody? That you? It's Matt. Tell me how Rivers is."

"Distraught of course. Confused."

"Have an ER doc check her out. She looked like she was headed into shock."

"I will."

"Your voice sounds shaky."

"I'm okay. Have you found anything?" Cody pushed the automatic door opener with her elbow and supported Rivers into the lobby.

"Not enough." Matt's words were clipped. "I'll check in later."

Cody could hear Hailey's voice in the background as the call ended, but was unable to make out the shouted words. She closed the phone, pocketed it, and aimed Rivers for the admitting desk. First she had to get Rivers taken care of and then she had to get clean.

Chapter 22

If despair had a scent it would be this odd mix of disinfectant and stale sweat in the critical care unit's waiting room. Cody, sitting huddled in a corner, felt smothered. Partly because of the crowded, overly warm and stuffy room. And partly because of watching Kendra and her grandfather working the crowd as they moved slowly closer. Between clasping people's hands, patting shoulders, and distributing hugs, it looked like a political rally.

Rivers sat between Cody and Jim Russell, the mining engineer, wrapped in a heated blanket one of the nurses had given her after she'd been assessed. Jim had his arm around her shoulders, his body turned as if he could shield her.

"We need to call her family," Rivers said. "Her parents are both gone but she has a younger sister. Chloe. Jess is paying her tuition at college. Oh damn, why can't I remember which one?"

"We'll get it taken care of," Jim said.

"What's going on with your job?" Rivers asked, her fingers plucking at the blanket as if looking for the same distraction her words sought.

Jim apparently recognized what Rivers needed. "The environmental checklist is a mess. I seriously doubt I'm going to be able to get any sort of determination of non-significance. The owner is going to be out some serious money if I can't get this to work."

"I might be able to give them some suggestions how to improve the mining practices." Her words sounded rote, and her fingers continued their fearful pulling at blanket threads until Jim covered her hands.

"I'll take you up there when all this is over. But right now I need you to concentrate on one thing."

"What?"

"Holding it together. No famous Rivers Rants. Kendra and Keith are heading for us."

Cody shifted on the hard folding chair. If she walked away before they reached her, would she be abandoning Rivers? But Rivers had Jim to watch over her.

"No, Cody," Rivers said, reaching out elegant fingers that were still shaking. "You're shifting like you're about to run. Please don't."

Cody sank back and the chair bit deeper into her aching hip.

"I'm so sorry," Kendra said, bending over Rivers to enfold her hand in both of hers. "We came as soon as we heard an officer was down, but we had no idea it was Jess."

Keith leaned forward against his cane and smiled at Cody. "Yet another reason why women should not be police officers."

"What does that have to do with anything?" Cody asked as the familiar nausea crept around the unfamiliar courage.

"Women become automatic targets," Keith said. "And when you throw in her Native heritage, you have two bias strikes against her. There are many prejudices in this town."

"No," Rivers said. "There's a lot of prejudices in the old farts who are still alive. The town has nothing to do with it."

"Have you heard any news?" Kendra interrupted, rubbing her hand over her cranberry suit jacket, her fingers working the bone buttons.

"Nothing yet," Jim answered. "Sounds like it's going to be a while."

"Do you mind if we wait?"

The conversation around Cody dried up into a puff of background buzzing as Matt came through the door, his tall frame almost, but not quite, blocking the person behind him. Her relief and sense that he would now take care of things dissipated at the sight of her mother. Her fingernails bit into her hands, and she was trapped.

May scanned the room, supporting herself by hanging on to the back of the nearest chair. When she saw Cody, she made her way forward chair by chair, pausing at each one to breathe heavily and hold her hand to her chest. People were turning. People were staring. Cody was shrinking.

"My god," Kendra said, genuine shock in her voice and her fingers finally still. "Who is that woman in the Hawaiian muumuu?"

"My mother," Cody said on a sigh.

May reached them and held the back of her hand to her forehead as she caught her breath. Her muumuu was the only source of cheerful color in the room and it was as incongruous as a wall of graffiti in a cemetery.

"Cody, you didn't come by the hotel this morning. I was forced to take a taxi to the forest ranger station looking for you, and found out what happened. I don't understand how you could put yourself at risk like that." May's voice rose. "Someone shot at you!"

"Someone was shooting," Cody said. "But I doubt it was at me."

"I need to sit down," May said, turning to Keith. "And you're in my way."

Cody looked at Kendra and saw the same horrified expression that she could feel freezing her own eyes wide.

"It certainly does look like you need to sit," Keith said, moving back slightly. "So Cody is your daughter. I assume she inherited her tendencies toward threatening people from you."

The silence around the pair spread out into the room at large. Cody didn't know what to do to gain control of her mother, or of the conversation. Rachel must have come in behind May. She stood next to Matt, gripping the sleeve of his uniform shirt.

"And you are?" May asked, sinking into a chair that groaned with a loud creak.

"Keith Naylor, former mayor. My granddaughter, Kendra, the current mayor." There was a distinct emphasis on the word, 'my'.

"Never had much use for politicians," May said, wheezing. "Liars and crooks and bastards."

Cody shook her head and felt Rivers place a hand on her back.

"Really," Keith said, the smile finally gone.

"Really. And since you sound like you just insulted my daughter," May said with distinct emphasis on the word 'my', "I think it's time for you to go."

Keith carefully looked May up and down before turning to Kendra. "I believe the press should be here by now. Shall we get your interview taken care of?"

The silence that followed their departure was broken by May and her creaking chair as she settled back and stretched out her swollen feet.

"Well, now that that dirt is scraped off my shoe, I want to know what you've gotten yourself into this time."

Rivers leaned forward to see May around Cody. "Ms. Marsh, I am very, very happy to meet you."

"All fine and well, whoever you are. But I need to find out what's going on. It is very clear to me that Cody is finding nothing but trouble in this town and I am not happy. I've told her for years she's not capable of dealing with things without me and this just proves my point. She leaves home and gets shot at. And why are all these uniforms here and not out catching the person? Doesn't this town care that tourists are shot at? I would think that mayor, or whatever she is, would want to bring business in, not shoot it."

Cody abandoned Rivers. She fumbled her way through the crowd and out into the sterile hallway. The bathroom where she had cleaned up earlier was the only place she could think of where she might find privacy. She didn't know whether to laugh or cry, and there was an unfamiliar sensation building. Was it a tiny seed of pride in her mother?

In the bathroom, Cody ran cold water over her wrists and used her damp hands to smooth down her short curls. She turned her back on her reflection and leaned against the sink. She didn't understand May. Her mother belittled her consistently and constantly, but then turned around and defended her. Why would May care what a stranger thought about Cody, when she so obviously found nothing in Cody to like, love, or respect?

Cody had a sudden flashback to their home, and the hallway of photos. May's Love Wall. Full of pictures of Cody growing up. How could May call it a Love Wall when she raised Cody to believe she was ugly and worthless? It didn't make sense.

The door pushed open and Rachel poked her head in.

"Thought you'd be hiding out in here. Matt says the doctor's coming out."

"Ms. Blaine, there you are."

Keith's voice behind Rachel reverberated with confidence and strength, and Cody backed up. Rachel shook her head and gestured for her to come forward as she turned to greet Keith.

"Didn't know you were looking for me." Rachel stood in the open doorway, blocking Cody's view. "And Kendra. Sorry I didn't see you back there."

"Your odd friend certainly has an interesting mother," Kendra said.

"That's one way to put it." Rachel put her hands on her hips.

Cody heard a rhythmic tapping and it took her a moment to realize it was Keith's wooden cane patiently marking the quiet between their words.

"I wanted to know if you have reached any sort of decision that I will find reasonable," Keith said.

"I've told you," Rachel said, stepping aside so Cody was visible. "The museum stays as it is. The board will listen to me, not you."

"You're making a mistake." Keith's smile was back in place, this time warm and kind, as if he spoke to a small child.

"Maybe, but sure as shit it will be my mistake."

Keith raised his cane and gestured at Cody. "And you need to rein in your mother and choose your friends more carefully. Two killed, one shot, and Rachel not dealing with history as she should."

Kendra sucked air in, either in shock or starting to say something, but Keith glanced at her and she wilted.

"Rein in my mother?" Cody asked, not sure which of the arrows he'd just shot at her hurt the most.

Rachel's laugh held a catch in it as if it masqueraded as something else. "I doubt anyone is brave enough for that."

Cody slipped around Rachel as she squeezed her fingernails into her palms, feeling her pulse thudding with anger and dread. But Keith had just tossed away his son's death, Nate's death, Jess bleeding out, as if they were nothing more than ways to cut people. Plus, he sounded like he was somehow threatening Rachel, and Rachel didn't deserve that, and didn't friends stick up for each other?

"I'm going to the health district for my grandfather's birth certificate." Cody threw the words out before they could sink under her trepidation.

"How nice for you," Keith said, gesturing with his cane for Kendra to follow him.

"It seems there's some question about his parentage," Cody continued. "That maybe the madam of the Silver Haven was actually his mother." She stepped further into the hallway, raising her voice as Keith moved away. "Wasn't she the one your father was supposedly having an affair with? Either I'll prove she wasn't, which should make you happy, or I'll prove she slept around."

"Hardly shocking for a madam of the time," Kendra said, watching her grandfather. She squeezed her perfectly painted lips in, as if imprisoning further words.

Keith lifted his cane in the air in a clear signal he was ending the conversation. "Rachel is learning the drawbacks to digging into the past and you're about to."

When they were far enough down the hall to not overhear, Cody slumped against the wall. "Why does confrontation make me want to barf?"

"Because you haven't done it often enough. That was great. I didn't know you'd found out anything about the madam."

"I haven't. I was just being nasty."

Rachel punched Cody's shoulder lightly. "You go, girl. You'll be like me in no time. Next we're going to have to get you a tattoo."

"Tattoo?"

"Sure. But not a rock climbing tatt like mine. You'll need something strong." Rachel rubbed her eyes as if exhausted. "Let's go find out what's up with Jess."

Cody followed Rachel back to the waiting room where people were standing and holding each other. The doctor, a slender man with short graying hair and wire framed glasses, directed his comments to Matt and the police officers, but the room was so quiet his voice easily carried.

"So at this point we've managed to control the bleeding and stabilize her. We won't know the extent of the soft tissue damage, or the damage to her trachea, for a few hours at least."

"Worst case scenario?" someone called.

"Best case scenario," the doctor replied, "No lasting damage. She could end up with a hoarse voice, or worst case, no voice. But as I said, there's no way to tell at this point."

"Can I be with her?" Rivers asked.

"Only family at this point, I'm sorry," the doctor said.

Matt touched the doctor's arm. "Right now, Rivers is the closest thing to family Jess has. She has more right to be with Jess than any of us here."

"I'll consider the request," the doctor said, tipping his head briefly at Rivers. "Of course all of you are welcome to stay in the waiting area, but she's not going to be alert for several hours."

People milled around after the doctor moved over to the nurse's station. Cody stayed near the doorway watching the doctor confer with a nurse, who then came back into the crowd, spoke to Rivers, and led her away. People moved past Cody, leaving in small worried clusters. She wondered if Jess realized how many people cared about her.

"Cody," Matt said, coming up to her. "Where are you going to be?"

"I don't know, why?" she asked.

"I don't want you going into the woods or wandering around by yourself. We haven't caught the shooter yet and until we do we won't know who he was aiming at or why. With this on top of your assault, you need to be cautious."

Rachel crossed her arms over her chest. "Lay off Matt. You can't seriously think someone tried to shoot Cody. Quit scaring her."

Cody looked from one to the other and wondered what would happen if she bounced up and down like Hailey to remind them she was still there.

"Rachel, all I know is Jess was in Cody's vicinity. So was Rivers, but Cody was the one punched in the jaw recently.

Since I have no idea who the target was, I have no intention of letting Cody wander around until I find out. You want to be her bodyguard the rest of the day, that's fine with me. Just stay out of the woods."

Matt shoved through the waiting room door.

"Right," Rachel said, and picked up a black leather jacket from a chair. "We've been given our marching orders. Care to obey?"

Cody nodded her head, but wasn't sure if she agreed with Rachel or simply gave a response because she didn't know what she meant to do. She rubbed her fingernails and clenched her hands.

"I need to do something with my mother," Cody said. "And then I'm going over to the health department. Florence suggested I look for birth certificates and that's what I'm going to do. You're welcome to come along. Maybe you can entertain my mom."

"No thanks," Rachel said with an exaggerated shudder. "She terrifies me. I'll go home and check on Granny and maybe meet you later."

May was still seated, feet stretched out, hands folded over her belly, watching people like she was at a movie.

"Mom, I'm going to the health department. What are your plans? Do you want me to take you back to your hotel?"

"No. It's past lunch time and I need to eat before my blood sugar gets too low. I saw a deli on the way here. You can drop me off there. After that I believe I may just have a visit with that mayor."

"What for?"

"To have a talk with her about the behavior of that senile old man."

"Mom..." Cody trailed off. How did you ask a parent to not make a fool of themselves, to not make you miserable, to not cause trouble you then had to fix? She sighed. "I'll go get the car."

Outside the sky darkened over the mountain tops, but it still felt too cold for rain. Cody curled her fingers up into the scant protection of her coat sleeves and looked up at the highway above town, remembering how she had planned on joining that exodus of cars today. Wasn't she supposed to be fleeing somewhere? Slipping into that stream of anonymous people on their way to anonymous lives? Hadn't she thought about starting a new life where her mother couldn't find her?

She started up the car. With Jess in the hospital and no idea what the outcome would be, it trivialized all those things that had felt important the day before. Besides, she doubted anyone could escape their lives so easily. Even if she'd managed to gain enough courage to run away, she'd have just taken her failings with her. She needed to find another way to lose them.

There was a wonderful view of the tamaracks and the high canyon walls towering above town, and Cody wondered what it would be like to live here. Could she find a job? Would it forge a bridge to her grandfather's memory if she lived where he had? Maybe the solution to her problems with May was finding a home away from her, rather than trying to run away and disappear completely. But more than likely, her mother would follow her just like she had this time.

May was dropped off at the deli and Cody made a silent apology to Sunny, visible through the glass front of the store. So much had happened and it was barely one in the afternoon. Cody headed toward City Hall, thinking about Jess. She glanced into the back seat where she'd tossed her coat. Would Jess and Nate's blood ever come out? Was Jess going to walk out of that hospital fully recovered? In the short amount of time Cody had been here, she'd developed a healthy respect for Jess. She wanted the police detective to come out with a long life ahead of her.

At the City Hall, Cody found the reader board directing her to the small offices housing the Health Department. Florence's comments about Charles's parentage had raised questions and curiosity that hopefully a birth certificate would cure. At least Cody would be able to fill half an hour or so.

Inside, a middle aged woman with a horribly out of date beehive hairstyle typed on a computer keyboard. Cody told her what she was looking for, and with a few clicks of her mouse she pulled up the information. Then, with a swipe of a debit card, Cody was walking out to the car again, this time carrying a copy of her grandfather's birth certificate. Propping it against the steering wheel, she studied it.

The mother was listed as Alice Mogen, the father as Frank Mogen. Everything was as Charles had said. Disappointed, Cody dropped the paper on the seat next to her. She'd been convinced Florence was right and she would see the madam listed as Charles's mother. Or that something would have mentioned adoption. Of course, now that she thought of it, birth certificates probably didn't mention adoptions, or there would never be stories of people having to search for biological parents. She paused, picking the form up again.

The birth date was wrong. Charles had told her his birthday was July 24th. The birth certificate listed July 18th. Were mistakes like that common on birth certificates? Cody didn't know, and had no idea how to find out. And really, was it that big of a deal to be off by a few days? Maybe it was, if one date was the actual birth and the other was the day his adopted parents celebrated as the day he had come to live with them.

Shaking her head, Cody dropped the paper again, backing out of the parking spot. She was really stretching now, trying to conjure up the slightest thing that might be proof of Florence's theory. But this was the flimsiest evidence possible. She needed something more concrete, and she was sure Rachel would know how to find it. She headed back toward Florence's house.

Cody drove through the dying town of Burke and pulled in behind Rachel's Jeep in time to see her racing down the stairs so fast Cody caught her breath, sure she was about to lose her footing and fall to the rocks. Cody got out of the car as Rachel jumped the last remaining steps to solid ground.

Wild terror danced in Rachel's eyes as she grabbed Cody's shoulders.

"She's gone! Granny is gone!"

Chapter 23

"What?" Cold swept through Cody's veins.

"She was clear, doing better. She wanted a nap. She was asleep when I left. I thought it would be safe to go to the hospital. Now she's gone! Her journals are open on the bed, her clothes are still on the chair. She's out in her nightgown and robe!"

"I'll head up the road, you head down," Cody said. "Call Matt, see if he can get people to help look for her."

"Right, right," Rachel said, fumbling open the Jeep door.

Cody took the corners of the mountain road slowly, afraid of rounding one and finding Florence walking down the middle. As she came into a relative straight stretch, she remembered the cell phone Jess had given her. With one hand she fumbled around between the seats until she felt it. She'd call 911, too, get some police or search and rescue out as well as Matt. She dialed the number but nothing happened, and glancing at it, she saw there was no service. The mountains, of course. Leaving Burke meant she was climbing higher into them. She tossed the useless phone on the seat.

How far could a confused old lady walk? How long had she been missing? Cody kept expecting to see Florence as she crested each rise and rounded each bend but she saw only rocks and trees.

The road ended in an open graveled clearing with a long abandoned power substation at its center and an older model Ford pickup parked near it. The tailgate was down, two boards were in place, and a man, made bulky by camouflage off loaded an all-terrain vehicle. The quad was also painted camouflage, as was the long sheath attached to the side, with the butt of a rifle protruding. Cody drove into the clearing cautiously, seeing no sign of Florence. But as she neared the truck, the man motioned with his hand for her to lower her window.

"Need something?" he asked.

"I'm looking for an elderly woman who wandered from her home in Burke." Cody watched the man come closer to the car. He looked familiar but she couldn't place him.

"Old lady from Burke?" he asked, putting a dirt engrained hand on the window frame. "You mean Florence Blaine."

"Yes." Cody resisted the sudden need to edge away. "Have you seen her?"

"No, just know who she is. Like I know who you are."

"Really." Cody shifted her foot from brake to gas. At least she hadn't shut the car off.

"You know, I just got here. She could have beat me and be up the trail. Come on, I'll give you a ride on the quad. We'll take a quick run, see if she's up there. She's pretty spry."

The words were innocuous. His brown eyes were not, and their intentness gave her chills.

"Thanks, but I doubt she'd go hiking."

"Come on, you can't know that for sure." He stepped closer, slid his hand slowly down the inside of the door, taking hold of the door handle. "You and me, on a ride to adventure. More exciting than visiting old folks homes."

Adrenaline spurted through Cody. She reflexively hit the gas and the car jerked forward, fishtailed in the gravel, and stalled. She twisted the key and got no response.

"Put it in park," he said, coming up beside the car again. "You don't have to run, you could just say no."

Cody slipped the gear shift into park, put her foot on the brake, and twisted the key again. The engine caught as he reached through the window again, this time catching the steering wheel.

"Though 'no' most of the time means 'yes'." He laughed, and Cody caught the whiff of alcohol.

She hit the button for the window and it whined upwards. "Move it or lose it," she said, though her voice shook so bad she wasn't sure the words were clear.

"Big mistake," he said, laughing harder. And then, as the window got high enough to touch his bicep, he pulled his arm out. "Check in Wallace," he yelled through the closed window. "I saw her getting in a car with Cell."

Cody turned the car around and took the twists and turns back to Florence's home shaking like fall leaves in a stiff wind. She hadn't been in any danger. He was just teasing. Seeing if he could frighten her, maybe. But surely he hadn't meant anything. She clenched her teeth to stop their chattering, and realized she wasn't convincing herself. She'd been nervous when she'd first seen the man at the senior center. And now she was scared of him.

At Florence's house, Rachel's Jeep was gone, but Cody kept going and caught up to it at the opposite end of Burke, where Rachel was out talking to a couple who were working on a dry stone wall. Cody honked and pulled up beside the Jeep.

"A guy saw her getting in a car with Cell."

"Damn it, what was he thinking?" Rachel said, slamming her hand on the hood of the Jeep. "Park and get in. We'll go together."

In the Jeep, Cody grabbed the seatbelt as Rachel hit the gas. The floor of the Jeep was still covered in papers and magazines, and Cody tried to shift some aside to avoid stepping on them. She was already sitting on others, and the back seat was hidden under toppled stacks of books.

"I called Matt," Rachel said. "But let's raid the station Cell works at. I just can't believe this."

"Has she done this before?" Cody braced her hand against the dashboard as Rachel took a corner without letting up on the gas.

"No. I don't know what I'm going to do now." Rachel gripped the steering wheel with her callused and scarred hands, leaning forward slightly as if her body could push the car even faster. "If it's getting this bad she's going to need a full time caregiver. How the hell am I supposed to afford that? Sure as shit I'm not putting her on the State, or in some kind of home."

"Maybe she had a reason," Cody said. "Maybe she's clear and just wanted a walk."

"In her nightgown?" Rachel asked. "Get real."

"Sorry." Cody gripped her hands into fists, feeling her fingernails biting.

Rachel blew out air in a sigh that sounded like gale force frustration. "No Cody, I'm sorry. I'm terrified for granny and taking out on you. For god's sake, don't let me do that. It's one thing with your mom, but don't take it from others."

"I understand," Cody said. "I don't take it personal."

"That's wrong." Rachel said. "You should."

Cody was silent, with no words to answer the challenge.

Rachel barely slowed down as they entered Wallace, speeding down Bank Street to the gas station. She jumped out of the car without shutting it off, or shutting her door. Cody reached across and turned off the engine, then followed, keys in hand.

Cell leaned on the counter while Florence sat on it, swinging her slippered feet, drinking SoBe from the bottle and watching as Cell worked his faithful companion, the phone.

"But I don't understand where the cord is, dear."

"See, that's the way cool thing," Cell said, and jumped upright as he saw Rachel. "Hey! I was just calling you."

"Granny, what are you doing?"

"She was hitchin', dude," Cell said.

"You promised you wouldn't tell," Florence said.

"Sorry, man. Forgot how much Rachel, like, scares me." Cell moved back as Rachel reached the counter. "I just asked her if she needed a ride. Being neighborly, you know? I mean, she's an old lady. Old ladies shouldn't have to walk."

"You were hitchhiking?" Rachel's voice dropped, becoming quiet and almost calm.

"Well dear, technically, no. I wasn't standing exposing an ankle or anything. I heard a car coming and I flagged it down. I was a tad scared to be honest. I don't recall leaving the house. I'm afraid I wandered away in one of my less lucid moments. Did I frighten you badly?"

"Not at all," Rachel said. "I'm used to having people I love just disappear."

"Rachel," Cody said, wanting to somehow thaw the ice in Rachel's voice. But Rachel overrode her words, turning to Cell.

"And you didn't think it was strange to find Granny in her nightgown? You didn't consider taking her back home?"

"Is that what she's wearing? I thought it was, like, some kind of old lady dress." Cell pushed tendrils of black hair behind his heavily pierced ears.

"Oh my god!" Rachel pulled at her hair as if to keep her hands from reaching across the counter. "Where's your brain?"

"Hey, chill! What'd you expect me to do? I mean, she's an elder you know? You're supposed to respect your elders!"

"Shit! You should have called me immediately!" Rachel spun away from Cell and shoved through the doors.

"Dude," Cell said. "She's pissed."

"Cell, could you get hold of Matt and let him know we've found Florence? I'll be right back."

"May I try dialing, dear?"

Cody didn't hear Cell's response as she left the two seemingly new best friends behind. Outside the store, Rachel squatted down next to the wall, the palms of her hands pressed against her eyes.

"At least she's safe," Cody said, knowing her words were lame but unable to come up with anything else.

"What am I going to do?" Rachel asked, dropping her hands and staring at the pavement. "She could have been walking down the street thinking she was in her kitchen. What if she'd fallen down those stairs? What if she'd wandered off into the woods instead of sticking to the street? Everything's fucked now. Everything."

"I don't know what to tell you, Rachel. But it seems to me considering all the 'what if's' is just a way to drive yourself insane. She's okay this time, so maybe look at it as a chance to come up with a solution before one of those things happens."

"What kind of solution?" Rachel asked, and her voice was as thick with emotions as a creek bed was with rocks. "She needs full time care and I can't give that to her."

"Aren't there programs where you can be her caregiver and the state pays you?"

"Probably, but I bet they take everything, including the house." Rachel stood slowly. "Look, I'm wiped. Everything with Jess, then Granny. I just can't deal with anything else. I'm going to take her home."

"Probably a good idea for both of you."

It was only as Cody watched the Jeep pull away that she remembered her car was back in Burke.

Chapter 24

Cody sat on the counter in the spot Florence had vacated once she and Rachel left. Cell had insisted Cody make herself comfortable while she waited for Matt, and Cell had filled the time with stories about rock climbing and how many first ascents Rachel had to her name.

"I'm going to do a first ascent someday," he said. "When you do a first ascent you get to name it, and I'm going to name it after my girlfriend."

"Is she a climber, too?" Cody asked, checking to see if Matt's Bronco had pulled up yet.

"A newbie, just learning. I'm going to take her bouldering so she can just, like climb around and get a feel for the rocks. You know, there's a lot of concentrated energy in rocks. It's good for you to be around them."

"Really?" Cody had no idea what he was talking about and didn't want to ask.

"Oh yeah. Sunny, that's my girlfriend, told me all about that."

"Sunny? I know her."

"She's the purest spirit I've met in like, ages, dude." Cell gestured with the phone. "There's Matt."

Cody jumped down from the counter. "Great. Thanks for entertaining me while I waited. And Cell, thanks for picking Florence up. When Rachel calms down she'll realize that was a good thing."

"Like Sunny says, no worries," Cell said. He picked a package of red licorice off the shelf and opened it with his teeth as she left, smiling to herself at his imitation of Sunny.

Cody climbed in the Bronco and as she pulled the seatbelt across, unfamiliar laughter bubbled up.

"What?" Matt asked, as he pulled out.

"Oh dude, I just had a vision of, like, Cell and Sunny's future children."

Matt grinned back at her, and she realized it was the first time she'd seen him without stress and worry etching lines across his face.

"You know though, I think they're a perfect fit for each other," he said. "Young, idealistic, dreamers, feet definitely not on the ground. The new generation of hippies."

"You sound like you're ancient," Cody said. "They're not much younger than you are they?"

"Maybe not in years," Matt said, and the stress was back, as if the moment of lightness had been merely a gasp from someone drowning. "But in experience and cynicism I have them beat."

His drop back into seriousness plummeted Cody down, too.

"You know how upset you got about the camera?" she asked.

"Do I need to apologize again?" Matt glanced at her.

"No, no. But now I'm paranoid about not telling you things. So this probably doesn't mean anything, but it kind of made me a little nervous. Well, maybe a little more than nervous-"

"Cody, spit it out already."

"A few days ago I went to the senior center and this guy came out and asked me if I had any money so he could get a drink. Said something like, he gets sick if he doesn't drink."

"T.J. Culhane. Local drunk."

"Yeah, well, it's not like he said anything threatening, but he made me nervous like I said. And then today, I ran into him again, and this time he was scarier."

"Did he touch you?" Matt's voice changed to its calm, professional pitch.

"No, just the car."

"Can you write up what happened for me? Details, what was said, both instances?"

"Sure," Cody said, relieved that someone else knew, and more relieved that she was taken seriously and not laughed at. She leaned her head back, hit suddenly by fatigue and hunger. "Have you heard any more about Jess?"

"Still no word on permanent damage, but she's more stable. Not enough that they're moving her out of critical care, though."

"It's been such a long day."

"And it's not over yet. Have you had dinner? I'm so hungry I'd even consider something healthy. Though I'd prefer a big greasy double bacon Swiss cheeseburger from the Silver Corner."

"I'm starving." Cody rubbed her stomach as if trying to soothe the hunger pangs.

"The Corner it is. Last time we were there your jaw wasn't working so hot. How's it feeling now?"

"Kind of like a dull faint toothache. That and my hip. But you know, with so much that's happened my aches and pains are nothing."

"It's been a hell of a day, that's for sure," Matt said, pulling onto the side street and parking. "If I fall asleep in my food tell Millie to wake me up for breakfast."

Inside the diner, the four elderly men in plaid coats were sitting at the bar, but this time they were nursing bottles of beer rather than coffee. The place was warm and cozy in the early twilight and Cody followed Matt to the same table they'd sat at before. Matt dropped into a chair, planted his elbows on the cracked linoleum and sank his face in his hands.

"You okay?" Cody asked as she sat across from him.

"Too much going on and each thing needs my undivided attention. Kelly and Nate's murder, Jess getting shot, worry about you, Jake stirring things up, and the body Hailey found. I don't know where to start or how to finish anything."

"And then Florence."

"Florence?" The edges of Matt's voice were instantly sharpened by worry. "What's wrong?"

"Nothing now," Cody said, confused. "I thought you knew. Didn't Rachel call you?"

"No. I was working the shooting and body scenes when Cell called and said you'd been left behind and needed a ride."

"I'm sorry, if I'd known you were working I'd have figured something else out."

"No," Matt said. "I needed an excuse to leave. I'm too wiped to do any good. But tell me about Florence. What's happened?"

"She wandered away from the house. That's why I ran into that guy, when I was out looking for her. Cell found her and gave her a ride to the gas station and she's fine, but Rachel was panicked for a while. She and I were trying to find her, and it was pretty scary. Rachel said she would call you to help search, but she was pretty distraught. I should have realized that and called you myself. Though I probably couldn't have reached you. I tried calling 911 but there wasn't any service."

"Her wandering off isn't good," Matt said. "There're too many nightmare scenarios."

"I know. Rachel doesn't know what she's going to do." Cody picked up the menu.

"I'll see if I can help," Matt said. "I'll call Senior Services and see what kind of resources they have. Knowing Rachel she hasn't talked to anyone. She's not one to ask for help. Always acts like it exposes vulnerabilities someone will take advantage of."

"I know she's worried about finances, but it can't be that expensive to hire a sitter can it?"

Matt lifted a shoulder. "Who knows?" He pushed his menu away and leaned back.

"Have you learned anything about that body?" Cody asked, scanning the menu. "Do you think Hailey will end up being right that it was murder?"

"Oh yeah. It was murder alright. And not for robbery. We found his wallet when we removed him."

"Who was it? Or can you say?" Cody asked.

"No, but I'll give you enough that you can figure it out for yourself. The guy's last name was Johnson."

"Johnson?" Cody looked out the window, watching a car go by. Why was the name familiar? She didn't know that many people here. And then she remembered. "Nate."

"Obviously not Nate, since you can't be murdered twice," Matt said. "But maybe someone Nate was looking for?"

"His father."

"You didn't hear that from me," Matt said. "Not that I'd care if I got fired."

"No?"

"No." He turned his coffee mug right side up in an optimistic gesture that it might get filled at some point. "Well, the assumption is it's Nate's dad, since the wallet has his ID in it. But the official identification won't happen until the autopsy."

Cody watched the waitress slowly making her way to the coffee pot and hoped for Matt's sake that the elderly woman wouldn't forget why she stood there.

"So what does all this mean?" she asked, fingering a corner of the menu. "Are you getting anywhere?"

Matt leaned back in his chair and stretched his legs out into the walkway. "Hell, I don't know. Just when I think pieces are fitting something happens that tosses them all in a heap again. I do have a question for you though. You had any more of those phone calls?"

"Calls?" Cody thought a moment. "With my mother in Wallace there's no need for her to call."

"No, those heavy breathing calls. Someone whispering."

"Just those two times," she said, and shivered. "I'd actually forgotten about them."

"Here's another question," Matt said. "How brave are you?"

"Honestly? I have no idea. It's not like I've been in situations where I've had to be."

"You seemed to be holding it together when you radioed for help with Kelly and Nate." Matt raised his hand to get Millie's attention. "Hey Millie, any chance of coffee before I fossilize?"

"I was pretty scared, Matt." Cody watched Millie wander over, fill the coffee mugs and pull out a pad and pen.

They gave the elderly woman their orders and as Millie headed for the kitchen, Matt dumped four little containers of cream into his mug. "And now? Are you scared now?"

"Here?" Cody asked surprised. "Not hardly."

"I want you to be," Matt said, sitting forward and catching her wrist with one hand. "I want you so scared all you want to do is lock yourself in your room and stay there."

"Okay," she said. "And I should be acting this way because...?"

"Because I think you were the target. I think Jess was hit by mistake."

"Oh come on." Cody tugged her wrist out of his grasp. "Why would anyone want to shoot me? My mother maybe but not me." Her attempt at a joke obviously splatted when Matt's frown cut down into his eyes.

"I want to be wrong," Matt said. "But every time I pick up those pieces I was talking about, the same picture inches out."

"So I suppose you want me to leave again," Cody said, and even she could hear the strong skepticism.

"No. But hide behind your mom."

Laugher escaped Cody and she tried to catch it by covering her mouth.

"Sorry," Matt said, leaning back for Millie to put his burger and fries down. "That was uncalled for. I am serious though about you staying out of sight. Maybe take May on a mining tour off to Mullen or something for a few days."

Cody wasn't sure how to respond, or even what her reaction was. She seriously doubted anything she had done was important enough to make her some sort of target. But she respected Matt's opinion and intelligence. Even if he dipped his french fry in the cocktail sauce that came with her prawns and chips.

She picked up her water glass as the mining engineer she had first seen with Rivers came inside. As always, his startlingly blue eyes made her draw a blank on his name.

"Matt," he said, approaching their table. "The guy at the ranger station told me you were here. Is it okay if I interrupt?"

"No problem," Matt said. "Pull up a chair. The coffee's still fresh if you want a mug."

"I could use some." He sank onto the chair. "Cody, thanks for being there for Rivers today."

"You're welcome. Any news on Jess?"

"No. Rivers will call if there's any change though." He picked up a paper napkin and worked it between his blunt fingers. "And before I forget, Rivers said if I saw you to tell you May wants a call. Your mother, right? Remarkable woman. I've never seen someone shut Keith down so fast."

Had Cody ever received a compliment for her mother before? What did she do with it? If he knew May like she did, would he still admire her actions? The questions rattled around Cody's brain until only one word managed to work its way out.

"Thanks."

"Hey Millie," Matt said. "Another mug here for Jim?"

Cody watched Jim carefully tearing pea-sized pieces of napkin, creating a tiny pile of confetti. Millie put his mug down gently as if the movement might blow away his creation. He paused in the tearing to take a swallow of coffee, and then his fingers went back to work.

"You know about the mine I've been hired on at?"

Matt swallowed a bite of hamburger as he nodded. "Sure. Aren't you working on a geological survey?"

"That, and all the other tests the forest service is demanding." Jim pushed the napkin pieces aside and sat back. "Sorry, didn't mean that to sound like a complaint. I understand the need for all the environmental steps, and this has to be done right. But I have some concerns."

"I don't have much to do with the permitting end of things," Matt said, and forked up one of Cody's prawns. "But what's on your mind?"

"Jake says the forest service wants to revoke his grandfather clause, so they can reclaim his place."

"Jake's a paranoid nutcase," Matt said.

"I got the impression you liked him," Cody said, pushing the rest of the prawns across the table.

"I do," Matt said. "But he's still crazy. He has a prime piece of land, and it's surrounded on all sides by forest service. Part of which is scheduled for logging. He's fighting it because it will impact the watershed where his water supply comes from. He could be right, I don't know. But as far as revoking anything, I seriously doubt that could be done. It's his legally. Why the interest Jim?"

"Anything done with his place, or any logging around it, will influence what happens with the mine. Plus, what happened today also messes with any chance of opening it soon."

"Your mine," Cody said sitting forward. "It's the one where the body was found, right?"

"Well, it's not my mine," Jim said, resuming his work with the napkin. "But yes, that's the one I'm trying to push through opening. Don't get me wrong, this thing with the body is horrible, and Jess getting shot is worse. My work pales with how important your work is, Matt, in finding out what's going on. Besides, even without the delays this will create, I have serious, serious doubts this mine will ever open."

"I looked it up at the office awhile back." Matt dumped another container of cream in his already pale coffee. "Looks like the owner is Keith. Seems like he'd have the money needed to get it open."

"Look," Jim said, glancing over at Cody and then focusing on Matt. "Keith is the owner, you're right. And we all know what kind of man he is. If, as Rivers said, this guy you found was murdered, Keith is the first person I'd be looking at. And it makes sense you'd want to talk to the owner, right? I mean I assume you guys would think the owner might know something."

"Well, yeah, that's usually a first step," Matt said. "I've sent Hailey to interview him."

"That wasn't nice," Cody said, and was rewarded with a smile from Matt before he turned back to Jim.

"So talk to Keith," Jim said. "But don't stop there."

"What do you mean?" Matt asked.

"All I'm saying is, maybe there's an anonymous contributor to the investments in this mine. Maybe there's someone who doesn't want to be connected to the mine visibly. Maybe it's not Keith signing my checks."

"If I start digging and come up with a name it won't have come from you, is that what I'm hearing?" Matt asked.

"Damn straight," Jim said, and then touched the back of Cody's hand lightly with his fingertips. "Sorry."

"No worries," she said, deciding she liked the hopeful sound of Sunny's expression. "I've heard the word before."

Jim stood and placed a couple dollar bills next to his mug.

"Heading back to the hospital?" Matt asked.

Jim nodded and an odd sort of melancholy settled into his blue eyes. "Here comes the rain again."

He stood there a moment, looking out the window onto the street where shadows had lengthened and merged into a dying day.

"Keep digging, Matt," he said quietly, and left the café.

Chapter 25

Cody held the phone between her ear and her shoulder, the handset growing hot as if her mother's words filled it to boiling. Her head throbbed and exhaustion burned her eyes. All she wanted was some way to end a day that seemed like infinity.

After leaving Matt at the café, she had reluctantly returned to Florence's, an interloper in a family drama. Rachel opened the door wearing a baggy sweatshirt that said 'Miners Go Deep' and equally baggy men's boxers. The ragamuffin clothes reminded Cody of an old flannel nightgown she wore when she was sick. Comfort clothes for rough days.

"I think I should find a hotel room," she said, hovering in the doorway as rain splattered the steep roof and used the eaves to give her a shower.

Rachel caught her arm and tugged her into the doorway. "You're letting the heat out."

And that had been the only thing Rachel said, other than to report there was no change in Jess's condition. It was almost ten, and the night was a wet black blanket plastered against the windows. Florence slept soundly in her room, and Rachel had left the door open. Cody glanced in to see a night light glinting off something that moved in the windows. She'd paused for a moment until she'd recognized bells. Rachel had strung bells on all the windows. From her vantage point in the kitchen where she worked at the stove, she would either hear Florence at the windows, or see her if she left the room. Cody continued on to the room she used the night before, finding the bells unaccountably sad.

In the room, Cody slipped off her damp shoes and stood there wondering how best to stay out of the way and not intrude. The phone reminded her that May wanted a call, so she dialed and settled on the bed, hoping for a brief conversation. That was fifteen minutes ago.

"None of your friends impressed me today. Of course it's horrible that poor police woman got shot, but you haven't made good choices about who you spend your time with here. Are you listening?"

"Yes, mom," Cody said. "It's just been a very long day and I'm completely exhausted."

"And that's a direct result of the friends you've chosen. You could do so much better. You should look into those pen pals that are everywhere these days."

"Pen pals?" Cody sank lower on the bed and closed her eyes.

"Pen pals," May reiterated. "On the computer. Like the singles groups they used to have, where people get together and do fun things. The advantage of doing that on the computer is no one has to see what someone looks like. They get to know your personality first. You have a wonderful personality. And you can have those friendships without having to leave your room."

A year ago, a month ago, even two weeks ago, Cody would have taken the underlying meaning in May's words for truth and planted it deep. But now an odd sort of chill iced over that once fertile soil in her soul.

"And you have quite a way with words, mom."

"Thank you," May said. "I'm pleased you realize that. The ability to communicate has always been one of my gifts."

"I'm going to bed," Cody said, giving up. "I'm too wiped out to talk anymore. I'll see you tomorrow."

"What time? You can come by and pick me up for breakfast. You know how my blood sugar is always low in the morning."

"Good night mom," Cody said, promising nothing, giving nothing, apologizing for nothing.

She sagged back against the pillows and rubbed her temples. Scenes played against her mind, images of her life in stark, unforgiving black and white. Everything she had done was a direct result of what her mother wanted. Years trying to please May, millions of words sinking into her heart as if they were sacred gems. That treasure horde was starting to look very tarnished.

Kelly had joked with her, smiled at her, touched her shoulder, and expected nothing in return. Matt and Rachel, Jess and Rivers, all of them spent time in her company and acted like it wasn't that bad. She thought they might be growing into friends. So where was the truth? Did it come from the mother who had raised her, or did it come from strangers who had so recently walked into her life? And if she wasn't who her mother said she was, then who was she?

Her thoughts drifted back to Bounty Trail and the image of Nate and Kelly in death. She doubted the police would ever catch the person. How could they, when there were no witnesses, and no convenient clues left behind? Jake and his temper made him suspect. But the man in camouflage was the only person she'd been scared by. That right there should count for something. Well, unless Keith was included. He was scary in his own intimidating way. Her thoughts circled until they melded into nothing.

Cody must have fallen asleep because when the phone rang, the sound startled her upright and the house held that deep silence that crept into rooms in the wee hours of darkness. She instinctively reached for the phone before realizing it wasn't her house. It quit after the second ring and she stood on shaky knees. The bedside clock said it was three in the morning. No one called at that time unless it was bad news.

An overwhelming fear for Jess cascaded through her so that her heart raced ahead of the avalanche of adrenaline. She stumbled to the door and caught the doorjamb as a light in the kitchen came on and something crashed to the floor.

"Rachel?"

When there was no answer, Cody went down the hall. Rachel stood by the table, one foot on a chair as she tied her boot laces. Pieces of a glass were scattered on the floor around her.

"What is it?" Cody asked.

Rachel reached for a coat hanging on a chair back and tried to pull it on, then glanced at it and realized it was Cody's. She dropped it.

"Where's my coat? I need my coat."

"Rachel," Cody said again, louder. "What's going on?"

"The museum is on fire. I have to go. I don't know how bad it is. I need to get down there, see if I can save anything. Where's my coat?"

"Right here," Cody said, lifting it off a hook by the door. "I'll drive you."

"No!" Rachel caught Cody's arms. "You have to stay here!"

"I think you're too upset to drive."

"I need you to stay with Granny. Thank god you're here. Can you watch her for me?"

"Of course. But are you sure--"

"Yes, yes. I can drive. Where are my keys?"

A frantic search ended when Rachel pulled open the freezer and plucked out frosty keys.

"The freezer?" Cody asked as she opened the door for Rachel.

"Granny," Rachel said. "Who knows why."

Rachel ducked out into the darkness, quickly plummeting down the steps and out of sight. Cody stood in the damp and chilly air until she heard the Jeep start up, and then closed the door and stared at it, wondering what else she could do. She walked to Florence's bedroom door and the night light showed the elderly woman sleeping soundly with the knuckle of her forefinger in her mouth. Cody stepped in to pull the blankets up more snugly and then went back into the kitchen.

Something tickled her cheek as she stood in the middle of the room and she brushed at it. A soft curl wove around her finger and she jerked her hand away. How long had it been since she'd cropped her hair? Obviously too long if the curls were getting visible. She needed to find scissors before her mother started in with her comments on frizzy hair.

Cody filled a tea kettle at the sink and put it on the stove, lighting the burner. Rachel would want something warm when she came back. As the water heated, Cody went back to the bedroom and replaced her nightgown with discarded jeans and the gray tee shirt from the day before. They'd do until she could shower later.

Back in the kitchen, Cody sat at the table, fidgeted, stood, and walked to the sink. There was nothing to see out of the window but her reflection, out of place. She shivered, chilled, as if her blood moved slowly with the night. Her eyes watered with sleep tears and she brushed them away as the kettle whistled. She grabbed it off the burner before it could become frantic and then stood there holding it. Who knew when Rachel would be back? Instead of making tea she carried the kettle through to the living room and placed it on the wood stove where it steamed in a quiet murmur of water.

Rachel had left a scattered pile of papers on an end table, along with a pen and notebook. It looked like she had still been up working when the call came in as a mug of coffee next to the papers was still warm. Cody straightened the pile, picked up a few pages from the floor, and weighted them down with the mug.

She crossed the room and sank onto the edge of an armchair thinking about how much history was here. How many conversations and secret dreams had passed through these rooms? The hushed sleepiness of the place settled around her and she imagined what a stark contrast it must be compared to outside, where a building that was filled with even more history burned.

"I don't know you," Florence said from the doorway.

Cody jumped, sucking in air and almost slipping off the edge of the chair. She stumbled to her feet, seeing the way fear and confusion spread vulnerability across the wrinkles of Florence's face.

"Where's Mama?"

"She's not here," Cody said, and the shakiness in her voice was mirrored in Florence's hands as she held them up, palms out as if to keep Cody back.

"Who are you? What are you doing sitting in Papa's chair?"

"Waiting for them," Cody said quickly. "They asked me to stay here so you wouldn't be alone."

Florence backed away. "I don't know you," she said again.

"It's alright Florence, really," Cody said, and stepped forward.

"Stay away!" Florence's voice rose and she stepped back again, tripping over the door jamb and grabbing the fame.

"Florence, it's okay, really," Cody said, starting forward and then stepping back when Florence reacted by flinching away as if to run.

How did a person calm someone when words didn't make sense? Cody turned away from Florence and walked to the window, hoping she looked non-threatening.

"Sure has been raining a lot lately," she said, watching Florence's reflection as she had watched her own earlier.

Florence wasn't coming closer, but she was no longer backing away, and her hands were at her side, her head tilted slightly as if listening to something Cody couldn't hear.

"And I'm surprised how cold it is already."

"Tamaracks," Florence said, almost as a question.

Cody waited, frozen in place as if movement would break the spell.

"They're gold early this year," Florence continued. "Early winter."

"Think it will be worse than normal?"

"Oh yes. That boy will be cold unless the woman I'm not supposed to talk to gives him a coat."

Cody's heart clenched and she turned away from reflections. "Charles?"

"Charles, yes. Mama says that woman helps him. Papa says she helps all men, and he laughed so loud. Mama smacked him with her stirring spoon."

"Have you talked to Charles?"

"Hello. I said hello. I wanted to ask him why that woman only helps men, but he couldn't talk to me. His mother smacked him and it wasn't a nice smack like Mama did. Do you know nice smacks?"

"I think so."

"I've never had mean smacks. Papa told Mama he wanted to smack the mayor. I don't think that would be a nice smack. Father says the mayor is a right bastard." Florence whispered the last word and looked quickly around the room. "I'm not supposed to say that word."

"I imagine not," Cody said, and smiled at the child Florence had once been. She felt dampness on her cheeks and knew this time it wasn't just sleeplessness watering her eyes. She wiped the tears away quickly, but Florence stepped closer.

"Are you crying, dear? What's the matter?" Her voice was calm and, without warning, in the right place and time.

"Just loss," Cody said quietly.

"We lose so much," Florence agreed, looking out the window where fall aged into winter with the dawn. "So much."

The front door opened, admitting cold air scented with an astringent mix of wet earth and smoke. Rachel shut the door behind her and leaned against it. Soot streaked her skin, striped her face, darkened her hair. Dirt or ash had sunk into the calluses of her hands, and her shirt had marks where she had wiped her fingers.

"Rachel?" Florence asked timidly.

"Yeah, Granny, it's me."

"I've been having a wonderful visit with your mother."

"That's just great." Rachel put a hand over her eyes and slid down the door until she sat on the floor, knees up. "How about going back to bed?"

"Certainly," Florence said, and without another word left them.

Cody watched to make sure Florence went into her room, and then came back to Rachel.

"How bad is it?"

"I doubt anything will be salvageable," Rachel said, and coughed. "God, the smoke was terrible. I don't know what did more damage, the fire, the smoke, or the water from putting it out."

"Do you know what started it?"

"No idea, but the fire marshal was on his way." Rachel dropped her forehead to her knees and wrapped her arms around her legs.

"Do you want some tea? I have water that's hot." Cody shifted, wanting to go to Rachel but afraid of getting too close and intruding.

"Tea," Rachel said, raising her head. "Fu-"

"Rachel!" Florence said loudly from her bedroom. "I don't think so!"

Rachel laughed briefly, and ended it with more coughing. "Shit. Even when she's completely nuts she's still with it enough to not let me use that word. Yeah Cody, I guess I'll take that tea."

"Is there insurance on the museum?"

"For all the good it's going to do. Insurance won't replace things that aren't made anymore, or documented memories from people long dead."

Cody took the kettle from the wood stove and poured water over a tea bag in a heavy mug. She handed it to Rachel, unsettled by her calmness. Rather than appearing like someone who was handling the situation, the calmness seemed like veneer.

Rachel blew across the tea and then sipped it. She rested her head back against the door and looked around the room, studying each thing as if retelling a well-loved story. Cody sank onto the edge of a chair and clasped her hands between her knees.

"I'm going to lose my job now," Rachel said. "No museum, no need for a curator or docent."

"But they'll need someone to salvage stuff, or to start finding things again won't they?" Cody asked.

Rachel shrugged. "No job, no income, no way to take care of Granny." She put a hand down to the floor and heaved upward as if gravity fought her. Once upright she took another sip of tea and then flung the mug across the room where it shattered against the kitchen door jamb.

Cody jumped up. "Rachel," she began.

"What? Please don't tell me we can fix this, that everything will be okay. Just what the hell am I supposed to do now? I can't leave her alone, and now I can't hire someone to stay with her. Think anyone's going to give me a job if I have to bring her to work with me every day? Come on Cody, give me some words of wisdom here because I sure as hell don't have any of my own!"

"You're asking me for words of wisdom?" Cody said, realizing her voice had risen to match Rachel's. "Me, who can't escape her mother, who can't stand up for herself, who can't even talk to people without feeling like a failure? I don't have any! All I was going to say is that you don't have to deal with this alone."

"God, what a cliché." Rachel slumped onto the sofa. "What exactly does that mean, anyway? Yeah, sure, I have friends, but do you think any of them will pay for a caretaker? Or will pay my bills, or give me a job?"

Cody's breath caught on a sudden flicker of anger. "You know, I think I like you better when you keep your mouth shut. Lately when you open it all you do is hurt people's feelings because you're so busy being sorry for yourself. You can't tell me that your friends wouldn't be more than happy to spend an afternoon with Florence. I bet there are plenty of people willing to pitch in until you get on your feet. Maybe you should give your friends some credit."

Rachel stared at Cody, silent, and Cody cringed as she realized what she had done.

"Rachel, I'm sorry…"

"Shit! Don't you dare apologize!" Rachel ran her fingers through her soot streaked hair. "I don't agree with you, and I don't think your rosy opinion of people in this town is accurate. Right now it feels like my only choice is tossing Granny to the state wolves and letting her be put in some home for nuts. And that breaks my heart. But, damn girl, whether I agree with you or not, you're developing some balls."

"I just got angry, and I shouldn't have," Cody said as warmth washed across her cheeks.

"Oh yeah you should have. You didn't solve anything but you said what was on your mind." Rachel pushed up from the couch and palmed her wet cheeks, spreading more soot. "I'm heading for the shower and to try and get a few hours of sleep."

Cody watched Rachel leave the room, her shoulders slumped in either fatigue or depression or both. She bent to pick up the pieces of mug, stacking them carefully in her hand. Rachel was right. She had said exactly what was on her mind, without thinking it through first and without worrying about what someone might feel.

And it had felt good.

Damn good.

Chapter 26

"This isn't breakfast, it's a snack." May tossed her napkin down. "How do you expect me to take care of my blood sugar on this?"

"Four croissants with jam better raise your blood sugar or we'll need to take you to the hospital," Cody said, sitting across the small table from her mother.

She'd managed another couple hours of sleep, dozing off on the couch in the living room, but at the moment she felt like she had been up all night. She rested her chin in her hand, elbow on the table, and poked at the yogurt and strawberries in front of her. She'd left Rachel scrambling eggs for Florence and insisting she didn't need any help. But Cody wanted to get back as soon as possible, to free Rachel to deal with the museum.

"How is that police woman who got shot?" May asked.

"The hospital wouldn't tell me much when I called this morning," Cody said, turning a water glass in circles. "About all they said was that she was more stable. I think I'll need to go up there to get more information."

May pulled her coffee forward and doctored it with half and half and three packets of sugar. "Don't bother. I'll have my packing done by checkout time at eleven. You can pick me up then, and we can get lunch for the drive home."

Cody raised her head. "Excuse me?"

"There's nothing wrong with your hearing," May said. "You pick me up at eleven."

"I'm not going back yet."

May swallowed coffee and pushed the cup back. "I'll be in my room." She stood up, gasped, and caught the back of her chair.

Cody started upward, and then sat back, her insides going very still and serene, as if something had just come home.

"I'm so dizzy," May said, and held a hand to her face.

"Probably all the sugar and caffeine you just had," Cody said, standing and pulling her keys out of her pocket. "You better go lay down. I'm headed over to the museum and then I'll be at Rachel's if you need me."

"I'm not sure I can make it to the elevator," May said.

"If you're that bad off then I'll have the manager call 911 and take you to the hospital."

"Maybe you should," May said, straightening up. Her mouth pursed downward, pushing folds of skin into three chins instead of two. "Since you obviously prefer to go to your new friends who get shot at rather than taking care of the mother who raised you."

Cody's newfound courage faltered at the familiar sting of implied failure as a daughter. She gripped the keys until the ridges bit into her palm.

"And since you're leaving me you should see about getting your hair cut. Those frizzies are getting out of control."

Cody pulled in a deep breath, trying to get the air to reach all the way to her toes and fingers. She managed to ease her grip on the keys, and instead of looking into May's small hazel eyes, she turned away. That small act of breaking eye contact seemed to ease the sense of failure.

"I'm growing my hair out," she said. "I'll check in with you later."

She walked away without looking back, although each step felt like betrayal. She knew she was letting May down, she knew, as a daughter, she should be attending to the dizziness, helping May upstairs, getting her comfortable. But she also knew it was time to, as Rachel had said, grow some balls.

What Rachel hadn't said was how hard it would be, how each increment of separation from her mother would bite into her with teeth that chewed failure. And all she did was walk away for the first time. She doubted this would get easier the more she stood up to May. And that tiny part of her that relished in the strength was like a marshmallow with a sledgehammer hanging over it.

Outside the morning air held more winter than fall, but at least the rain had backed away. The museum was only a couple blocks down Bank Street, and Cody walked in that direction. She would make a quick stop there to see if she could find out anything for Rachel. Then she'd head over to the hospital to hopefully spend some time with Jess before going back to Florence's.

At first glance the museum didn't look that bad. The large front picture window was broken out, and smoke stained the bricks around it. The buildings on either side were also touched with the soot brush. The door was propped open by the old rusty Pulaski axe head, and Cody could hear voices inside the building. She stopped in the doorway, unsure about entering, and watched firefighters sifting through debris.

The long counter that had held so many souvenirs was crushed, and no silver glinted through the burial remains of charred wood. Water dripped from every surface, and the smell of smoke made Cody's eyes water. The stand that had held stapled copies of local stories was gone, and through the entry way that led to the mining displays, Cody could see even more extensive damage. To her untrained eye, the interior looked like a total loss.

Cody heard steps behind her and automatically moved out of the doorway, turning with the intention of apologizing for being in the way. But the apology got stuck in her throat and swallowed back down when she saw Keith, followed as always by Kendra.

"You continue to appear at places that don't concern you."

Cody spoke quickly, allowing herself no time to filter her words. "Since you don't know me, I doubt you have any idea what concerns me."

"We're assuming," Kendra said quickly. "Since you're a tourist."

"I assume nothing," Keith said, directing a look at Kendra that was a mix of condescension and irritation.

Cody knew that sort of look very well and recognized it immediately, as well as the expression of apology and submission that flitted across Kendra's carefully made up face.

One of the firefighters came to the doorway and Cody moved further back to allow him access.

"Mayor Naylor," he said. "I'd offer to shake hands but I'm filthy."

"That's perfectly alright Captain Walters," Kendra replied, her professionalism firmly back in place. "Have you been able to save any of our history?"

"Very little, unfortunately. Metal of course, like the old mining equipment. But anything made of material like the vintage clothing is gone. And of course everything that was paper. All the old journals and books, legal documents, ledgers, we're not finding anything. If you get a salvage team in here they may be able to rescue something."

"Salvage operations can be expensive," Keith said. "I believe, Kendra, it will be simpler to declare the building a loss."

"I believe, Kendra," Cody said, "that insurance might cover any salvage."

"I'm pretty sure they do," Captain Walters said. "Especially in cases of arson."

"Arson?" Kendra asked, catching her grandfather's arm. "Are you sure?"

"We've found the ignition sight, and preliminary samples seem to confirm that. Plus, looking at how hot this fire burned inside, how fast it accelerated, those things lead us toward arson."

"How long until you know for sure?" Kendra asked.

The man shrugged. "We should have a clear decision by this afternoon. But the place will be cordoned off until we're done and the arson and insurance investigations are done."

Keith patted Kendra's hand and then removed it from his arm. "I'll have a talk with the insurance adjustors. I'm sure they will agree to move this along in an expedient fashion."

"Could Rachel help with salvage?" Cody asked, thinking of Rachel's worries about her job.

"Possibly," Kendra said. "But that will be up to the museum board of directors and how they wish to handle her position."

"I'll speak to them, too," Keith said. "I seriously doubt they'll want a suspect in an arson investigation working at the museum."

"Suspect?" Cody asked, looking to the captain. "There's no way she had anything to do with this fire. She was at home when it started."

"Which means nothing," Keith said. "Timers are common in arsons, are they not Captain Walters?"

"Rachel would have no reason to burn the museum," Cody said, before the captain could respond. "She loved her job and needed it."

"We shall see," Keith said, and while his smile was kind, his eyes were not.

Cody watched him escort Kendra, following the fire captain toward the back of the building. Could Keith seriously consider Rachel? Hopefully there were investigators who were as intelligent as Jess, and not as biased as Keith.

Worry for Rachel stayed with Cody until she was at the hospital. There had to be some way she could help Rachel, either with finding another job or keeping the museum one. Although realistically, she doubted there was much she could do in the few days left of her vacation.

Cody wanted to ask about visiting but as she reached the admitting desk she saw Rivers in the waiting room, sitting in the same chair, and wearing the same clothes.

"Has she been here the whole time?" Cody asked a woman behind the desk.

"We've asked her if we can get her anything, we've offered our showers, we've offered a cot, but she just shakes her head and stays there. Her friend, Mr. Russell, has been bringing her food but that's about all she's doing."

Cody crossed the tiled floor and sat down gingerly as if Rivers might dissipate with the slightest breath. After a few moments, Rivers looked up from her folded hands.

"Cody."

"Has there been any change?"

"She's stable. She lost a lot of blood but is improving there, too. Right now she can't talk, and the doctor can't tell me yet if that's going to be permanent or not. Too much swelling and bruising." Her voice caught on the last sentence and piled up around the words as if they were boulders in a creek.

"Can she have visitors?"

"No, but each time the doctor comes out he tells me, maybe."

"Which is why you're not leaving." Cody looked around the sterile waiting room, and imagined sitting here indefinitely.

"I don't want her waking up and being alone." Fatigue and stress etched her face into something paler and harder and it was like Rivers was turning to stone from the inside out.

Cody studied the once elegant environmentalist and wondered how to help her. She didn't have any experience with something like this. If staff had been asking her if they could help, and failing, how could she do any different? She straightened and felt only the slightest twinge in her injured hip. She was healing while Jess and Rivers both were still hurting. It wasn't right.

"Rivers, I'm going to sit here and you are going to take a shower."

"No, I can't leave. And not just because she might wake up. What if the person who shot at her comes back? I mean, the department has a man outside her door, but what if that's not enough?" Rivers gripped her elbows and rocked.

"They know their job. Besides, I'm not asking, I'm telling," Cody said, hoping the nervousness in her voice wasn't apparent. She wasn't used to giving orders. "So stand up and get the shower over with. The sooner you do, the sooner you'll be back at your post. I won't budge until then. If the doctor says she can have visitors while you're gone, I'll get you."

Rivers still hesitated, but she was watching Cody and there was indecision in her dark eyes.

"I said go." Cody made her voice as firm as possible.

Rivers stood. She hesitated, looking around as if she was just waking up.

"Rivers, face it, get it over with, leave it behind."

A slight smile brought the barest warmth to her eyes as Rivers recognized the advice she had given to Cody. But the smile was gone before Cody was sure she'd seen it.

"That suggestion will work for the shower, but nothing else," Rivers said. "I'm facing what was done to Jess. I'm never going to get over it, and I'm certainly not going to leave it behind."

"We've got the police working on that," Cody said, hoping she sounded confident and reassuring.

"Yes, but I've got Jake Conrad."

Chapter 27

Cody held her post while Rivers showered but no doctor appeared. She flipped idly through old magazines until she found one with crossword puzzles. People had started them, and there were varying degrees of completeness, but none had been finished. She didn't know if the fact that visitors weren't here long enough was a good or bad omen. She found a dull pencil between the pages, and started correcting mistakes made by strangers. It made her feel intelligent.

Rivers came back, her long hair wet and glistening as she braided it. Her eyes were more alert, but also more intent, her eyebrows drawn down in a purpose Cody couldn't interpret.

"Feel more human?" Cody asked.

"Somewhat. I called Jake from the nurse's station and asked him to bring me clean clothes on his way here. I hadn't realized what a funk I was sitting in. Thank you for waking me up."

"You'd have done the same for me," Cody said, twisting the pencil between her fingers.

Rivers sat down in her original chair. "Where is your mother?"

"At the hotel waiting for me to check her out and take her home."

"And is that the plan?"

"No," Cody said, and the pencil broke. "I'm not ready to go back and my vacation isn't over."

"But?"

"But," Cody agreed, sighing heavily. "I feel like I'm gaining a spine, but it's sure hard."

"Growth always is," Rivers said. "Which is why so many of us don't. Even me, staying here in my chair."

"Instead of?"

The muscles under the fine planes of her face tightened as Rivers looked down the hallway. "Instead of finishing this."

Cody followed her line of sight and saw Jake coming toward them with a brightly colored bundle under one arm. He wore his trademark beat up Carhartts coat, with a black tee shirt underneath, filthy jeans, and scuffed work boots. He looked like someone who had been tramping roads for days, and the dark stubble seemed like mute witness to those hours.

"Clothes," he said, dropping the bundle and then sitting down on the other side of Rivers. "Cody," he said in acknowledgement.

"Jake," Cody said in return. "Looks like you need a shower as much as Rivers did."

A weary grin spread across his face. "I could use some help with that."

Instant heat seared Cody's cheeks, and Jake laughed. But instead of cringing away, assuming the laugh was at her expense, Cody realized she was smiling back, accepting the action as friendly teasing. It was a moment she wanted to frame and hang in her memory.

"These are interesting," Rivers said, fingering through the clothes. "I haven't worn this bra for years."

"You said clothes," Jake said. "You didn't specify what. I like lace on a woman."

"Right. Tell me what you've learned and then I'll change. And I think I'm hungry," Rivers said, rubbing her stomach.

"About time," Jake said. "I talked to Matt this morning. They found some shell casings but Matt thinks it will be days before any forensic information comes back. He figures the shells came from a 30.06 but he's guessing at this point. And you know how many of those guns live with hunters in Wallace."

"No tracks or anything?" Rivers asked.

"Not that he's saying, but I know Matt and he sure as hell looks like he's not telling me everything. I have some ideas of my own I'm going to follow up on."

"What are you trying to accomplish?" Cody asked. "Don't the police have the skills to take care of this?"

"Of course they do," Jake said. "But so do I."

"I don't care who solves it, Jake or the police," Rivers said. "I've asked Jake to help in case he can get it done sooner. Either way, I want the person who shot Jess."

"For?" Cody asked.

"I'll decide once I know who it is." Rivers didn't smile to lighten the words. Her eyes were black with an intent that, to Cody, looked suspiciously like revenge.

"Do you think you're doing what Jess would want you to?" Cody asked tentatively.

Rivers patted Cody's knee. "Definitely not. But then I've never done what people wanted me to."

A man in the traditional white overcoat of a doctor came into the waiting room and his sudden presence stopped their conversation, reminding them of why they were sitting on hard plastic chairs.

"Rivers, you can see her now," he said simply.

Rivers jumped to her feet, clean clothes tumbling to the floor.

"Wait," the doctor said, holding up a hand. "She's awake but still sedated. Try not to ask her questions. I don't want her stressing her injury trying to talk."

"I understand," Rivers said. "Can I go now?"

"Go," the doctor said, stepping out of the way as Rivers flew by. He smiled politely at Jake and Cody and then followed Rivers down the hall.

"That's good news, right?" Cody asked. "I mean, Jess being awake."

"I assume so," Jake said as he stood up. "What's your game plan?"

"I'm heading back to Rachel's grandmother's in case Rachel needs me to stay with Florence while she deals with the museum fire."

"Heard about that."

"Though I wonder if I should hang around until Rivers is out. To make sure she eats, and to see how Jess is."

"Nah," Jake said, waving a hand. "Now that she's seen Jess she'll function fine."

"Does that mean she'll give up on her revenge quest?"

"No chance in hell. Come on, I'll walk you out."

"Jake, do you really think you can find the person who shot Jess?" Cody asked as they left the hospital.

"Sure. Just can't promise I can do it faster than the police, or Matt." Jake opened Cody's car door for her. "And I'm not doing this just for Rivers, either. Jess is a friend. I take care of my friends."

"Even though Jess threatened to arrest you?" Cody's voice was light, yin against the yang of Jake's intentness.

"Jess threatens to arrest me at least once a month. Usually I deserve it. Doesn't mean she's not someone I care about." Jake pulled the collar of his coat up against the chill air. "And I don't like people I care about getting hurt. I can't afford to lose them as there aren't that many." He laughed, a deep husky sound, as if laughter rusted inside him and didn't get oiled often enough.

"Jess is lucky then." Cody shivered and pulled her jacket close.

"Maybe, but I'd do the same for you because you might end up a friend. If you stick around long enough. Otherwise you're on your own, sweetheart."

"Thanks. I think." Cody hesitated at her car, one hand on the handle. "Jake, did you and Kelly really get in a fight?"

Jake leaned against the car. "It wasn't a fight. Just a couple punches thrown over the logging operation the forest service wants to do around my place."

"What did he do when you hit him?"

"Punched me back, what else?"

Cody tried to picture Kelly and Jake in a fistfight and failed. She could only see Kelly and his engaging smile, and was glad that was her memory of him. "So what happens if the area is logged?"

"I'm going to have a mess. It will cause all kinds of environmental problems with my place, things like erosion and landslides, changing my watershed. I'll be an island in a sea of stumps and slash piles. And during the logging operation I'll have helicopters flying around my house, logging trucks using my road, probably trespassers. It's going to be a nightmare."

"Do you think you can stop it? I mean, the forest service is a huge entity."

"Realistically? Doubt it. But I have to try. The place has been part of my family since it was homesteaded before the towns and mines were here. You're here looking for roots, so you should understand."

Cody tucked her hands up inside the sleeves of her coat, trying to find some warmth. "I like to think I do but I'm not sure you can ever understand someone because no matter how much you try, you're still looking at their story through your eyes." She felt the familiar blush creep over her cheeks. "Sounds corny, I know."

"Nope." Jake tilted his head to one side. "You found what you're looking for? Something to do with your grandfather, right?"

"Funny, but that was so important when I got here, and it still is, but it's kind of got sidelined by everything else that's happening. I have heard a few stories though. Including rumors about his real mother being a madam. That one seems to get Keith fired up."

"I just bet it does," Jake said with a grin. "You checked out the Oasis yet?"

The name sounded familiar and Cody thought about it for a moment, but finally shook her head. "I'm not sure what that is."

"The Mining Museum isn't the only place in town, sweetheart. The Oasis is a museum dedicated to the fallen angels. You know, a kinder label for whores."

Cody winced at the word and Jake's grin broadened. "Hey, a rose is a rose and all that."

"Sure," Cody said. "I understand. I'm just not used to hearing it. Where's the museum?" Cody thought about Rachel, imprisoned at home as a babysitter. Maybe she could afford a quick run into the place and see if they had any resources she could buy and take with her. It would give her something to read while taking over the watchdog role.

Jake gave her directions and after she got in her car, he shut the door for her and touched his temple with a finger in his version of a salute. "Stay out of trouble. And keep letting that damn hair of yours grow."

Cody's hair had been called a lot of things over the years, none complimentary. But as she drove to the Oasis she had to smile. No one had ever talked about it quite like Jake. Usually she was ruthless about keeping it short, and it had become a Sunday routine to trim it back before the days in public view began. But she hadn't cut it here, and in only a week the curls were starting to unwind a little. Instead of stressing about it and seeing it as a symbol of all that was wrong with her, it had suddenly become something she was getting compliments on. She wasn't sure she believed the compliments, but she had to admit it was nice.

The Oasis was in a vintage home in pristine condition. An elderly man greeted her as she entered a large room full of dark antique furniture, mannequins swathed in 19th century dresses trimmed with lace, and framed sepia photos of lounging women, tastefully posed and artfully covered, leaving something to the imagination of those who cared to look.

"Can I help you with anything?" the elderly man asked.

"Please. I'm hoping to find some resources on the madam of the Silver Haven."

"Ah, Ethel. She was quite a forward thinking woman for her time. Her bordello was in competition with the Oasis of course. Would you like to take a tour?" He leaned forward, hands clasped in front of him and with a slightly desperate look on his face.

"I don't have time today," Cody said, hearing the apology in her voice as a counterpart to the disappointment that made the little man sag. "I have to get back home. But I was hoping you might have something I could purchase about Ethel."

"Oh, most certainly. And after the tragedy of the Mining Museum burning, I am very thankful we have a lot of similar material." He picked up a shoebox full of what looked like old postcards, and started flipping through them. "I must say I am quite nervous about our Oasis after the fire. I hear it was thought to be arson."

"That's what I heard, too." Cody watched the arthritic fingers move through the yellowed cardboard and decided the Oasis didn't get much business this time of year.

"Well, I am seriously considering some sort of alarm system. I should have done it years ago but it's never been a worry here before." He paused in his fingering and pulled out a postcard. "Ah, yes, I thought so. Take a look at this while I retrieve a book you might find interesting."

Cody took the postcard as the man left the room. It was in sepia tones like the pictures on the walls, and showed a home with a turret and large bay window made up of small panes of glass. An ornately worded sign hanging over the double doors said, 'Silver Haven, a Heavenly Gentlemen's Club'. And in front of the doors stood a woman, shielding her eyes from a bright sun that must have been behind the photographer. She wore a long skirt, with black boots peeking out underneath, and a snug blouse that showed a trim figure. Her face was in shadow under her hand, but even so the broad smile shown out through the years.

What caught Cody's breath, though, was the boy who stood next to her. Ethel was holding her other hand out to the boy, offering him a brown bag. He was dressed in a shabby coat and trousers that bagged on him, and he was looking up at Ethel, oblivious to the fact that he was being caught for future eyes.

Unexpectedly, tears flooded Cody, and she covered her mouth as if she could contain the grief for something lost. His life, her time with him, all the things that had been and could have been. She had never seen pictures of her grandfather as a child, but all the same, here was physical proof that he had lived.

"Are you alright?" the elderly man had come back into the room, holding a small leather bound book.

"Yes," Cody managed to say. "I just wasn't expecting the photo of Ethel to include my grandfather."

"I'm sorry?"

"The boy in this picture is my grandfather, Charles Mogen."

"Well fancy that. I'd heard stories about a small boy she took under her wing but I never knew the name. I confess when I first saw this picture I assumed the child was her son.

There were always rumors that she had had one, although no one ever came forward."

"Well," Cody said, wiping her eyes. "My grandfather thought she was his real mother but I don't know how it would be proven now."

"How interesting. One never knows what history will reveal. If you ever find out for sure, I would love to hear. In the meantime, I have this book that, while not about Ethel only, does mention her. It's a journal written by a former madam of the Oasis, so as you read, please remember that Ethel was her competition. She wasn't always, shall we say, kind to people. Either way, we sell copies of this as her words reflect a time gone by."

"I'll take it, and the postcard, please."

"Oh, good job." The man beamed as he walked behind a counter and picked up a receipt book. "And you really must come back for a tour someday. We have some fascinating displays."

"I will." Cody picked up the book and slipped the postcard between the pages. "Thanks for your help."

Back in her car she put the book on the passenger seat and turned the key as an unfamiliar beeping startled her. It took her a moment to recognize it as the cell phone Jess had given her. She fumbled around until she found it on the floor of the car, and said hello, fully expecting to hear her mother's voice. Instead there was silence.

"Hello?" Cody said again.

"You've just made a very big mistake." The voice was a whisper, soft and quiet and unidentifiable. And yet Cody was sure it was the same person who had called her at the motel.

"The only mistake I've made," Cody said, knees trembling. "Was answering this phone." She flipped it shut not wanting to hear what else would be murmured so intimately in her ear.

Jess had wanted to know if the person called back, but Jess was in the hospital. So what could she do? She didn't know anyone else in the police department, and if she called there, would they have a clue what she was talking about? She pulled out into the street and drove out of Wallace. It was time to get back to Florence's. She'd see if Rachel knew the phone number of the forest ranger station. She could call Matt.

It was only as she was nearing Burke that she wondered what mistake the caller was referring to. Her presence in the Oasis?

If so, how did they know where she was?

Only Jake knew where she'd been going.

Chapter 28

It was almost noon but the sun didn't have the strength to pull itself up over the mountains and so there was only cold wind in the canyon. Cody climbed the steps to Florence's perch, hoping a fire was going that could dispel the outer cold and the inner chill. But inside, the home, while warm enough, was so quiet it seemed empty.

"Rachel? Florence?" Cody called as she glanced in the kitchen. "I'm sorry I took so long getting back. Anyone around?"

There was no answer, and Cody walked across the creaking wood floor to Florence's bedroom. As she neared she could hear the quiet murmur of the television. Inside, Florence was sitting in a recliner, her feet up, legs covered by a bright afghan, and sound asleep. On a table next to the chair was a pill bottle with the lid off, and alarmed, Cody ran forward and scooped it up. The bottle was empty, the prescription for the sedative Ambien made out to Rachel. Cody sucked in a panicked breath, but as she reached for Florence, she saw her name in large letters on a piece of paper that had been beneath the bottle. Under her name was printed, 'Don't Panic!' Cody unfolded the note.

"Don't worry, there were only a couple of these left. I wanted you to know what I'd given her. I was going to wait for you to get back but the fire marshal called and wants to talk to me about the museum. Keep your fingers crossed for me. I'll pick up something for dinner."

Cody dropped the note back onto the table beside the pill bottle and took a deep breath wondering how long it would take her heart to slow back to normal. Florence was deeply asleep, and she had no idea how long that would last. There was no time on the note, so the pills could have been given to Florence two hours ago or five minutes. But at least for now it looked like Florence wasn't going anywhere.

In the kitchen, Cody rummaged through drawers in a small end table where the phone was until she found a local directory. Thumbing through the government pages took several minutes but eventually she found the number for the ranger station and dialed.

"Wallace Ranger Station."

"Is Ranger Tanner available?" Cody asked.

"No, he's out in the field. Would you like his voice mail?"

No, she didn't want voice mail, she wanted to talk to him in person. But since that obviously wasn't going to happen, Cody agreed, and waited through Matt's voice delivering the standard greeting of not being available and to leave a message.

"I hate voice mail," Cody said at the beep. "But I wanted to let you know I got another hang up call on the cell Jess gave me. I'm at Florence's if you need anything."

If you need anything. Cody snorted as she hung up the phone. What was it about answering machines that made people talk in expected clichés?

How important were these hang up calls? If Matt wasn't around maybe she should call Hailey. She didn't want to talk to the bouncing blond but she didn't want to make another mistake, like she had with the camera. Maybe it was better to be overly cautious. She redialed the station, asked for Hailey, and hoped she'd be able to leave some more clichés on another voice mail.

"Cutler." The voice was terse and professional.

"Hailey? It's Cody Marsh." She could feel the nervousness, the immediate feelings of inferiority starting, and ran a thumb over her fingernails. But then she paused, took an audible breath, and fingered a curl instead.

"Yes?"

"I just tried calling Matt but got his voice mail. I'm not sure if this is important or not, but thought I'd try you since I can't get hold of him."

"Yes?"

Hailey sounded impatient now, and it made Cody feel like an inconvenience that wasn't very intelligent. But then her new baby spine starting to straighten.

"Never mind. Sounds like I'm calling at a bad time." Cody unexpectedly felt a grin spread. Maybe clichés weren't so bad after all.

"Wait!" There was a pause before Hailey spoke again. "I'm swamped with work on this shooting and it's making me tense. What have you got for me?"

Cody filled her in and waited for a response.

"I'm not sure if any of that is relevant or not," Hailey said, and it sounded like the admission was pried out of her. "But I'll record it into my database and make sure Ranger Tanner hears about it as soon as I can get hold of him. I appreciate you calling me."

"You did ask me to keep you informed of anything I told Matt," Cody said, wanting Hailey to hear the unspoken message that she had only called because she couldn't get hold of Matt.

"Actually, what I said was for you to contact me before you called him, since I'm the one who knows what they're doing. I just didn't expect you to do what I asked. That's why I appreciate the call."

The phone disconnected before Cody could respond, and Cody put the phone down carefully, wondering if Hailey had any friends at all. But almost immediately after replacing the phone, it rang, and Cody scooped it up, assuming Hailey had hung up accidentally.

"I don't appreciate being hung up on," she said, feeling childish for wanting to get the first word in with Hailey.

"And I don't appreciate your tone of voice, even if I have no idea what you're talking about," May said. "I didn't hang up on you. Rather, I've been waiting here in the lobby for over an hour."

"I told you I wasn't going home yet," Cody said, frustration flooding her voice.

"That's not a decision for you to make," May said. "You have to learn to think of others. I've checked out, I'm packed. When you get here, pull up to the door so you don't have to carry my suitcases as far. I don't want to have to try and walk all the way across the parking lot, like you made me do before. You know how hard that is on my breathing."

Cody had a sudden clear image of her mother sitting surrounded by her brightly flowered matched set of suitcases in the hotel lobby. She could picture the complacent expression on May's face and the complete expectation of unquestioning obedience. The thought brought a bright flame of anger up into Cody's throat, as if a coal had been smoldering in her heart for too long.

"You have two options Mom," Cody said. She reached a hand up and felt the infant curls, letting them cup her fingertips. "You can ask someone at the desk to get you a bus ticket, or you can see if you can get your room back and wait until I'm ready to leave."

"What are you saying? Everything I've done for you, giving up everything to raise you alone and you dare throw that tone of voice in my face? You dare treat me like this?

Don't you dare leave me sitting here!" May's voice was escalating to a level that always rendered Cody broken and apologetic.

"I'm throwing nothing in your face," Cody said, as tears poured down hers. "I'm simply giving you options since I'm not leaving yet."

"Oh yes you are young lady. This place has never produced anything but people who abandon those who love them. Just like you're doing! You get over here this instant."

"I can't do that." Cody's burst of anger was instantly doused, quenched by understanding. "I'm not abandoning you, mom. I'm not leaving you like dad did. I'm simply staying here until my vacation is over. I think after all I've done for you growing up, you could give me a few more days. Once that's over I'm more than willing to drive you home."

The heavy breathing on the other end of the phone was so labored Cody thought May was having a stroke. Maybe she'd gone too far. She should never have spoken to her mother like that. What had made her think she could stand up to May?

"Mom?" she asked, opening her mouth to apologize, to swear her undying love and devotion, to use all the phrases May had trained her to say.

"Don't you ever mention your father to me," May said, between gasps. "I understand this quest for your grandfather. Though I'm the only family who has ever loved you. Who ever will. I'll give you two more hours. That should be long enough for you to finish whatever you still need to do. Then you come get me and we'll talk about how you speak to me on our way home."

It felt as if Cody's heart had become a large blockage in her chest, stopping words, stopping thought, stopping time. Very gently, she hung the phone up. She leaned forward, gripping her hands between her knees, and tried to breathe. Just breathe. To get one small breath inside. Tears dripped onto her thighs, and she stared at the tiny wet spots on her jeans. How could she be crying when she was dying inside? But no, she wasn't dying. Something roiled and turned under her heart. She stumbled to her feet and barely made it to the bathroom, falling before the toilet and heaving up unsaid words, unhealed hurts, unlived years.

Cody flushed the toilet and leaned back against the wall, drawing her knees up and shivering against a chill that had nothing to do with the hard linoleum floor.

She was still sitting there when she heard the front door open and Rachel call her name. She tried to answer, but the awful taste of failure in her mouth made her cough instead. When Rachel stepped into the open doorway, Cody felt the hot warmth of tears overflow again.

"What is it?" Rachel asked, dropping to a squat in front of Cody. "Oh god, is it Granny?"

Rachel jumped up and ran from the bathroom before Cody could respond, and Cody could only sit there, too swamped with what she had just done.

"Okay, she's sleeping, so it's not that," Rachel said as she came back and filled a glass with water. "Thanks for scaring the shit out of me."

Cody shrugged an apology.

"Drink this and tell me what's going on." Rachel sank down to sit cross legged on the floor.

Cody took the water, rinsed her mouth and spit in the toilet, and then managed a sip. She waited as the coolness seeped a track to her stomach, and when it didn't come back up, tried another swallow.

"Jess okay?" Rachel asked carefully.

Cody nodded.

"Hailey okay?"

Cody nodded again.

"Too bad. Then I'm out of guesses."

"I just hung up on my mom," Cody said, and her throat felt scraped raw.

"You're barfing because you finally did something you should have done a long time ago? You're shittin' me."

Cody shook her head.

Rachel leaned over and glanced into the toilet bowl. "Was it worth it?"

Cody laughed, and the feeling was light, a surprise rainbow. "I told her no, too. And talked back to her. And mentioned my dad."

"Hell, nothing like giving her both barrels. Where is she now?"

"Sitting in her hotel lobby. She's given me two hours to finish what I came here for and then I'm supposed to pick her up and take her home." Cody took another swallow of water, emptying the glass.

"And that's when you hung up on her?"

"Yes."

"Okay." Rachel stood up and offered a hand. "So we have two hours to shake up the world and solve all our problems."

Cody allowed Rachel to help her up. "I'm not picking her up in two hours. What happened at the museum?"

Rachel led the way out of the bathroom and sank onto an armchair as Cody chose to stand in front of the woodstove. She was still shivering and the fire's heat was as soothing as sinking into a hot bath.

"The arson investigator had a lot of questions. Things like where was I last night, and was I the only one who knew the back room held boxes of flammable papers." Rachel rolled her eyes. "Like, what else is a storage room in a museum going to hold?"

"They don't seriously think you started the fire?"

"Well, I'm not arrested, but I get the feeling that's what they want. Oh, and after a conversation with Keith, I'm fired."

"That can't be legal! Firing you as if you're guilty before anything's proven."

"Legal or not it's been done. And I'm relieved. I almost feel happy. It's like the worst that could happen has, so the waiting is over." Rachel lounged back in the chair, long legs stretched out, callused hands dangling over the lace antimacassars.

"But, what are you going to do? This is way worse than me arguing with my mother." Cody hugged herself, the rough skin of her elbows warm from the fire, cupped in the palms of her hands.

"Oh hell, who knows. Work at the Silver Café serving coffee. Millie must be close to petrified wood by now. I can ask Sunny for employment ideas. She's always working."

"I know!" Cody said, stepping closer. "The Senior Center! I bet they'd love to hire someone who knows history, and you could take Florence to work with you. That would solve everything, wouldn't it?"

Rachel tilted her head to one side, studying Cody as she fingered the lace under her hand. "Maybe. That's actually not a bad idea. Doubt they pay as much as the museum though."

"Something's better than nothing."

"Damn straight, Pollyanna." Rachel thumped the arms of the chair for emphasis.

The phone rang and Cody, warm now, sank onto the couch as Rachel answered, not sure if she was annoyed or pleased at being called a label of optimism.

"Hey." There was a pause. "No, not lately anyway. I saw Keith though. Yeppers, down at the museum, when he fired me."

Listening to a one sided conversation felt like eavesdropping, with guilt for doing so filling the pause between each sentence. Cody straightened the lace, rubbed the old braided rug with her shoe, and finally stood up, gesturing toward the kitchen. Rachel shook her head.

"Well, you kind of expected that, didn't you? You're asking me? Sounds like you are but what the hell do I know?

She's right here." Rachel lifted the phone away from her ear. "Matt wants to talk to you."

Cody took the phone as Rachel sat back down, but upright this time, no sense of graceful ease as she watched Cody.

"I got your message about the phone call. You said it was on the cell?" Matt's voice was staccato, and Cody could hear the sound of a car honking in the background.

"Yes."

"I don't think you have to worry about it at this point. But take a look at the cell and see where the call came from."

"You can do that?" Cody asked. "I thought only a land line could give you caller ID."

"Have Rachel show you. Listen, I have to be quick here, I'm on my way to Keith's. Everything's pointing to him, just like I thought from the beginning. I'm following the deputies to his place and sit in on what he has to tell them. Have Rachel tell you what I said earlier, I have to go."

"You're sure, this sudden?" Cody was confused. "I mean, Keith?"

"Either him or Kendra. I'll know before too long. And hey, it may seem sudden to you, but I've been working my tail off on this."

"Sorry, didn't mean to sound like I was questioning your decision."

"You didn't. Oh, and before I forget, your mom called the station. Said you'd be picking her up and heading out today. You weren't going to say goodbye?"

"No, because I'm not going yet," Cody said, liking the sound of defiance in her voice.

"Good. When I get done here, I'll call. If you can lose Rachel maybe we can have dinner or something and I'll let you know how this all pans out."

"Okay," Cody said, this time with no defiance, no confidence, no spine. She sank to the edge of the chair as she hung up.

"What's wrong?" Rachel asked, picking at a callus on a knuckle.

"He said he's on his way to talk to Keith. Sounds like it will all be solved today."

"He thinks Keith killed his grandson? No way."

"That's what it sounds like. He says Keith or Kendra."

"That's even less likely," Rachel said. "Keith's mean enough. But Kendra? Like she'd totter up some trail in her damn heels. But what did he say to make you lose color like that? I thought you were going to barf again."

"He wants to get together for dinner."

"No shit! A date!"

Cody didn't blush so much as incinerate. "No! Nothing like that. He said to go over everything, let me know what's happened."

"Yeah, right," Rachel said. "Notice he didn't invite me along to catch up on stuff. I'm not the one who's caught those pretty green eyes of his."

"Stop it Rachel," Cody said, standing up and heading for the kitchen.

She turned on the cold water at the kitchen sink and let it run over her wrists a moment before filling a glass. She shut off the water, took a drink, took another one, and felt her cheeks cooling, the heat of embarrassment giving way to the paleness of old familiar feelings.

"Seriously Cody," Rachel said at the doorway. "You need to lose this specter of your mom clinging to your back. You think you don't deserve someone like Matt? You think you're not good enough?"

"It's not that," Cody said. "Or not all. I mean, look at me. Short, overweight, frizzy hair, freckles."

"That's your mom's voice. You saying there's something wrong with freckles? And think carefully before you answer, girl."

Cody studied Rachel, tall and lanky, those eyebrows that slanted elf like, and the smattering of freckles over her nose.

"Okay, on you freckles look...I don't know, outdoorsy somehow. On me, they look like I've been walking behind cows."

Rachel laughed so hard she had to grab her stomach and slide down the door jamb.

"That's what kids would tell me growing up," Cody said, feeling close to tears again. "It's not funny."

"The hell it isn't." Rachel snorted. "Okay, Matt aside, we need to celebrate. I mean, this is finally something good happening, right? Keith and all that. Give me a second."

Cody watched the glass of water as Rachel left, to have something to look at she didn't have to see. What was it about people that they felt like they had to be polite all the time, instead of honest? Rachel wouldn't be saying those things if she was honest. And Cody could handle honesty. She could handle the truth about herself. After all, she'd been hearing it for enough years. Her fingers traced the dampness on the side of the water glass. Well, she'd been hearing something from May for years, but who knew what the truth really was? She sure didn't anymore.

"Okay, we're hitting the road. Come on."

Cody followed Rachel into the living room and watched as Rachel opened a closet and started hauling out clanking gear. A beat up back pack, ropes, bits of metal.

"I don't know how to swim," Cody said, looking at a pair of odd thin shoes like someone would wear in a pool.

"Not swimming idiot. Climbing. I called up Sunny and she's going to come baby sit Granny."

"I don't climb, either." Cody backed up.

"Don't you think it's time once and for all to lose that shittin' voice of failure?" Rachel turned on Cody with something very like anger flashing in her eyes. "Don't you ever get tired of being a failure? Of trying everything you can think of to keep people happy and still not succeeding?"

"Of course I get tired of it," Cody said, as answering resentment stirred. "What would you know about it anyway?

I bet you never had to put up with kids spitting on you in school, or co-workers who don't even know you're an employee."

"Oh god, May has so brainwashed you. Listen to that pity me stuff." Rachel yanked on a zipper of the backpack. "You need to hear how much you sound like your mom. Go fill these water bottles for me."

"Quit telling me what I need to do!" Cody said. "And quit bossing me around!" Her hands were fists, her breath coming in short gasps. She'd trusted Rachel. She was starting to think of her as a friend, and now it felt like she'd been betrayed. She put a hand to her chest, and could feel the pounding of her heart all the way through bone and muscle and skin. She couldn't breathe.

The silence stretched between them, Rachel squatting before the backpack staring up at Cody, with some expression Cody couldn't read struggling to mold Rachel's mouth. Why didn't Rachel say something? All Cody could hear was her own breathing. Until it stopped in a moment of understanding so brilliant it stole the remaining air from her lungs.

She could see herself.

Gasping, hand to her chest.

Angry, self-righteous.

She sucked in a deep breath as Rachel collapsed back on her rear end, obviously giving up the battle to not laugh.

"You see it, don't you?" Rachel asked, now mimicking Cody with a hand to her own chest as laughter stole her words so that they were barely recognizable.

"My mom," Cody managed to say.

"Now that you've summoned her, is your head going to start spinning in circles? I mean, you've already spewed."

"Very funny," Cody said, as anger drained.

"Would you please mind going into the kitchen and filling these water bottles for me? If it's not too much of an inconvenience. If you're sure it's no trouble..."

Cody grabbed up four water bottles held together by a metal ring. "Give me those." She turned her back on Rachel, who was still giggling, and returned to the kitchen.

As she was filling the last bottle Rachel came in. "Sunny will be here any minute. I think we're okay to go."

"Not climbing."

"Yes climbing." Rachel stowed the bottles. "Quit worrying, I'll have you home in time for your date. We'll just do an easy route off Bounty Trail. Something you can handle. Think of it as a way to celebrate your new independence. You might even like it. Besides, what else will you do? Sit here all afternoon waiting for Matt? I'm going to do something to take my mind off my problems, and so are you. Climbing helps get your head on straight."

"I've got some stuff from the Oasis to read through. They had a book with Ethel in it."

"Oh?" Rachel's face sobered, the laugh lines smoothing into a frown. "Cody, don't go digging into that stuff anymore. I mean, yeah, Matt may be right and taking care of Keith, but why take chances? Can't you just let it lie and quit pissing Keith off?"

"I'm not doing it to piss Keith off. I'm doing it to find out about my grandfather."

"Yeah, but you just don't get what you're digging up." Rachel slipped an arm through the backpack strap, slinging it from one shoulder. "Come on. Let's leave all this emotional shit here and go climb. It's the only way I know to shut the brain off."

"Think we should wait for Sunny? Or I can stay here with Florence while you go climb." Cody wondered if she sounded too desperate.

"Nice try. The point is for you to try something you'd never do on your own. Besides, she'll be here any second."

Giving up, Cody went into the bedroom and pulled on her fleece, then picked up her wallet. If they fell and died out there someone would be able to identify her. Maybe she should add a note about her mother. The only big woman sitting in the hotel lobby.

"Get out here," Rachel yelled. "You're delaying the friggin' inevitable."

Reluctantly, Cody left the house.

Rachel was stowing gear in the back of the Jeep when Sunny pulled up and Cody walked over to the beat up old Fiat. Sunny got out of the car and tucked a battered Monopoly game under one arm. She was wearing a tight black tee shirt and a necklace that looked like a spiked dog collar.

"Monopoly?" Rachel asked.

"Florence loves it," Sunny said. "We build towns with all the hotels. So Cody, you're going climbing? That's like, so cool. I did the Crazy Gremlin route with the Climb Naked guys yesterday at sunset. What a trippin' experience. It was like communing with rock, you know? No barriers, free style, no gear."

"And no clothes," Cody said dryly.

"Right. Like, nothing between you and earth."

"That's what I'm afraid of. I'm going to die."

Sunny laughed. "Nah, you've got Rachel leading. She's one of the best climbers around here. Just look at her hands. She'll keep you safe. What route you doing?"

"No idea."

"Nothing hard," Rachel said, coming around the back of the Jeep. "And it's got to be short. Cody's got a date for dinner with a certain tall blond ranger."

"Matt? Oh my god, that's like, so cool! He's a hottie." Sunny started up the stairs to the house and then paused with one hand on the rail. "See Cody? No worries."

Chapter 29

Rachel drove back toward Wallace, leaving Burke in the shadows.

"Rivers talked about all the problems Burke has," Cody said, watching the derelict homes drop behind them. "I'm surprised she still lives here."

"Burke gets in your blood," Rachel said, and then grimaced. "And probably poisons it, too. I've wondered sometimes if the pollution contributed to Granny's dementia. I wouldn't live anywhere else though. It's our history, who we are."

"History won't do you any good if you're dead." Cody shifted her feet trying to avoid all the debris on the floor of the Jeep.

"Oh, it's not that bad," Rachel said. "It's just that no one seems to know what to do about it."

They rode in silence a few miles, moving out into sunshine and past the ghosts of old mining sites.

"Matt said you'd fill me in, something he told you on the phone," Cody said as they passed the turn to Thompson Pass and Jake's place.

"Oh, yeah. He said it's positive the body in the mine is Nate's dad, like they thought."

"I didn't think you could autopsy and identify people this fast. Matt said it could take weeks and it's only been a couple days. That doesn't sound right."

"I know, I was thinking the same thing. But that's what he said." Rachel drove with one wrist sagging over the top of the steering wheel and one wrist equally boneless over the gear shift. "So what do you think, Keith or Kendra?"

"No idea. Like you said, Keith is nasty enough. And neither one seemed real upset about losing Kelly. But Kendra? She has about the same amount of courage where Keith is concerned as I do where mom is. Though I think she'd do anything he told her to."

"As you used to," Rachel corrected, smiling slightly. "I'd say you're a lot braver than her, now. Doubt she'd leave Keith sitting in a hotel lobby."

"Don't remind me," Cody said. "I'm still queasy. Of course that could be thinking about climbing."

Rachel laughed as she pulled in behind the old gas station and parked. "Relax. You'll have fun."

"Right. Back to Kelly though, I want to find out who and why almost as much as I want to learn about my grandfather. Kelly should have had a long life, married, had kids, and retired without ever arresting someone. The thought of such a life wasted makes me so sad I don't want to think about it."

"I know," Rachel said. "And not thinking about it means not thinking about Kelly and that's even harder. I think about him all the time."

As they got out of the Jeep and Rachel reached for her backpack, Jake came around the corner of the station, looking as disreputable as ever.

"Thought I heard your Jeep," he said. "The brakes squeal as loud as the door hinges."

"What's your point?" Rachel asked.

Jake shrugged. "None, just stating the obvious. Going climbing?"

"Stating the obvious again," Rachel said.

"If people were meant to climb cliffs we'd have been born with hooves and be called goats." Jake rubbed his knuckles under his chin as if sanding them on the scruffy shadow.

"Like I've never heard that one before."

Jake and Rachel were not breaking eye contact and neither smiled to give humor to their words. Cody looked from one to the other and had a sudden sense of history more recent and personal then the kind Rachel normally dealt with. She wasn't sure what was going on but it felt like each one waited for the other to step onto the trap and grab the cheese.

"I'm going to lock the Jeep and leave my wallet," she said, to remind them there was an audience.

"Sure," Rachel said, and seemed to breathe again.

"Cody, you do know how stupid climbing is, right?" Jake asked.

"I don't know about stupid," Cody said, not wanting to be disloyal to Rachel. "Scary maybe. But I won't know anything about it unless I try it first."

"That's even more stupid. That's like saying you're going to try a head-on collision to see if you want to drive. Where are you going anyway? In case you need rescuing."

"We're not going to need rescuing, Jake," Rachel said, sighing heavily. "We're doing the Crack Horror. Not that the name means anything to you."

"The *what*?" Cody asked.

"Climbers make plays on words for naming routes. Go away Jake," Rachel said. "You're scaring her just because you don't climb. Come on Cody. Let's head up."

"Rachel," Jake called after them as they walked toward the trail head. "You and me have some unfinished stuff."

"And it's going to stay unfinished," Rachel called back.

"You can't avoid me," Jake continued. "I'll just keep following you until you talk."

Rachel didn't respond, and acted as if she hadn't even heard him. Cody glanced over her shoulder and Jake gestured for her to come back. When she shook her head, he waved a hand at her as if giving up and turned away.

Cody and Rachel entered the trees and walked in silence for several yards before Cody couldn't stand it any longer.

"Can I ask what that was about?"

"Jake's an ass."

"I like him, actually," Cody said.

"I do, too," Rachel said. "When he's not being an ass. Which is never."

"So what's unfinished between you?" Cody breathed heavier as the trail steepened and wondered briefly how many times she'd have to do this before it got easier.

"We have completely opposing views about the forest service logging around his place. It's ended up in some loud shouting matches." Rachel held a tamarack branch until Cody caught it.

"So are you for the logging or against it?"

"For it, but I can see Jake's point," Rachel said. "I understand a clear cut is going to affect his place. But he was offered a shit load of money to sell it."

"But it's been in his family for generations. That would be like you being forced to sell Florence's place."

"Yeah, well, shit happens," Rachel said. "And most of the time there's nothing we can do about it. That's life and the only alternative is death."

"Wow, that's kind of hopeless." Cody stared at Rachel, but her friend kept going, oblivious to the shock waves bouncing off her back.

"It's not hopeless Cody, it's realistic. If Jake wants his place he's going to have to deal with the area being logged. He doesn't see that, and has this naïve belief he actually has a say in what happens."

"I'm surprised you'd support logging." Cody stopped a moment to catch her breath, standing with her hands on her hips.

"I'm not Rivers," Rachel said, not noticing Cody had stopped. "One environmentalist in Burke is all we can stomach. Besides, logging that area will open it up to a lot of access."

Cody took a deep breath and started upwards again, lengthening her stride to catch up to Rachel.

"Okay, so a route named Crack Horror is easy? Doesn't sound like it."

"Yeah, well, climbers are as hard to fathom as Jake." Rachel slowed. "I always have a hard time spotting the trail. It's not used often enough to make it really visible." She started walking again.

Cody looked around, realizing they were getting close to her grandfather's cirque.

"Did I tell you about getting a copy of Charles's birth certificate?" Cody asked.

"No. Find anything interesting?" Rachel stopped again, scanning the area.

"The date of birth was a week earlier then what he said his birthday was. And it had Alice listed. So I guess there's no way to prove if Ethel was really his mother." Cody had come to that conclusion privately, but putting the thought into words felt like reaching a decision.

"Probably not," Rachel agreed. "Unless you can find out if Ethel has any descendants. But I think you need to leave this shit alone."

"I don't have many days left," Cody said, ignoring Rachel's opinion. "But maybe the book I got from the Oasis museum will have something."

Rachel stopped. "Here it is."

She left the main trail, stepping into the woods with confidence, even though Cody could barely make out the indentation of a track. She had followed Rachel only a hundred yards when a memory tapped politely on the back door of her mind. But not having spent a lot of time in the woods, it was hard to tell one tree from another.

It wasn't until they broke through the underbrush and entered a roughly scooped out clear area that the internal back door opened.

"I know where we are," Cody said. "This is Nate's camp! Matt and I were here."

Rachel kept walking, barely glancing around. "Yeah, I talked to Nate once or twice."

"I didn't know you knew him."

"I didn't know him. The guy was rude, smelly, and not exactly the talkative type."

"But you knew where he was staying. I got the impression rangers were trying to find him."

"If they were they never asked me." Rachel entered the woods again, leaving Nate's squatting grounds. "Besides, he wasn't hurting anyone hanging out here, so what was the big deal?"

The track got steeper and rockier, and Cody had to let the conversation drop behind her. She needed her breath for walking, not talking. Rachel was like the mountain goat Jake had referred to, stepping from rock to rock, boulder to boulder, as gracefully as she moved from kitchen to living room. Cody went slower, trying to keep her balance, and the distance between them grew. When Rachel finally stopped, Cody realized they were at the base of a long waterfall of tumbled boulders.

"Water break," Rachel said, dropping her pack. "Even when it's cold like it is today, you still need to drink."

"Where exactly are we?" Cody asked, taking a water bottle. "I'm completely turned around."

"Back the way we came, obviously, is Bounty Trail." Rachel swallowed water and capped her bottle. "In front of you is where you are going to do some bouldering. We'll climb up these for a short distance, then cut across to another trail. That one takes us to the Desolation area, where most of the climbing routes are."

"That name sounds familiar." Cody used the back of her hand to wipe her chin where water had dripped.

"Desolation is spider webbed with routes. It's also kind of notorious for aid calls. But before you panic, we're not going that far."

"That's where I remember the name from. When I first met Kelly they'd had a rescue there. And it's where Matt's dad and grandfather died."

"Which is why you aren't starting your climbing career there," Rachel said, repacking her water.

"Where's Burke from here?"

Rachel pointed vaguely. "Out there somewhere. I suck at directions. But what's weird is if we climbed a couple routes on Desolation, the ones around Diamond Gulch, we'd be able to walk to Jake's. Kind of like taking a really, really, tense shortcut."

"Think I'll just drive." Cody handed the bottle back and Rachel stowed it in her pack.

Cody shivered, the chill air seeping through her jacket. She hadn't noticed how cool it was while she was walking, but now she wished she'd brought warmer clothes.

"You'll warm up soon enough," Rachel said. "As long as you're working you'll be fine. Okay, ready for your first boulder?"

"Guess so," Cody said. "But don't laugh when I ask you to boost me."

Rachel pulled on the backpack and turned away. "I don't laugh anymore."

Chapter 30

Cody stood with one hand braced against granite, breathing heavily and sweating in the cold air. A few trees had managed to find purchase years ago, sinking roots into pockets of soil, but for the most part she was surrounded by rock. Behind her was a steep trail she wanted to forget, and was already dreading returning down. In front of her was a literal wall of granite. This wall though, wasn't smooth. Instead it had been folded on itself over eons until it made an old, weathered curtain of cracked and peeling material. Something that looked like it was going to fall down on their heads.

Rachel had opened the pack and had a heap of rope next to her and a stack of clanking metal at her feet. She rearranged it until Cody recognized a harness with a sling that had gear clipped around it so thickly it looked like something you'd use to weight a body when you wanted it to sink and never surface. The one incongruous piece was a bright purple bag stitched with peace signs.

"What's the purse?"

Rachel stepped into the harness, fastened it at her waist and put the sling over her shoulder. "A chalk bag. You use it to keep your hands dry, for traction and grip, you know?"

"No, but I guess I'm going to find out."

"You sure are. Here's your harness."

Cody caught it and held it out. "Where's all my bits of metal?"

"You mean caribiners, quick draws, camelots?"

"Yeah, that stuff." Cody laughed. "You're speaking a foreign language. What are camelots?"

"You stick them in a crack in a rock, like a syringe. They open out until they fill the crack, then you clip the rope onto them to allow the belay person to catch you if you fall."

"I don't want to fall."

"You aren't going to."

Rachel carefully looked over all her gear while Cody wrestled the harness on. Ropes were checked and caribiners were thoroughly examined.

"We'll go slow and easy and if you get nervous we'll stop," Rachel said. "The idea is for you to have fun, try something new. But I want to push you out of your comfort zone so don't give up too easy."

Cody just nodded, too overwhelmed by what she was facing. She'd never done anything remotely like this and really wasn't sure she wanted to.

"Your knees are shaking," Rachel said, jabbing Cody with her elbow.

"It's the cold," Cody said. "You know, I don't have to climb to try something challenging. That trail took me out of my comfort zone."

"Nice try," Rachel said. "Okay, let me show you how to belay."

Belaying was simple in theory. Both of them would be on the rope together, with Rachel at the top, leading, and Cody letting the rope slide through something Rachel called a tuber. It looked like a little pot with two holes at the bottom and a hoop at the top. The idea was that the rope would slide when things went smoothly but if there was an emergency Cody would be able to use the tuber to brake and arrest a fall.

After practicing several times until Cody could manipulate the rope and gear, Rachel pronounced her ready to belay and started the climb.

There was an odd sort of calmness in the midst of Cody's fear. She'd thought climbing would be like hiking, but this was painstakingly slow. Rachel would chalk up, place a piece of gear, clip the rope to a caribiner attached to the gear, then climb ten feet and repeat the process. Cody's job was to remain below Rachel, with the belay rope in place in case Rachel fell. Once Rachel was in place, she would then belay Cody up to where she was. Rachel coached her where to put her feet, how to place her fingers, and how to balance.

Cody's muscles were shocked at being used, but in the exertion, there was a slowing of time. In the middle of open air, suspended on a mountain, there was a sense of space enclosing, shrinking to the small grains of rock sandpaper rough against her fingers, the sound of her fast breathing, of metal scraping and jangling, of the occasional grunt of effort.

It seemed to take a long time to gain any height, but finally Cody made the mistake of looking down.

"Okay, I think I'm done now."

Rachel reached one hand behind her to where the chalk bag swung below the small of her back. "You've just reached your ceiling. Everyone does it the first few times, and usually right around fifty feet. It's kind of like that comfort zone we were talking about. You break through this and the rest won't bother as much."

"So you're not letting me go back down?"

"No. Look to your left and a little up for that face hold."

"What if I refuse?" Cody's hands were trembling and she wanted to hug the rock, plaster herself against something solid.

"Go ahead. It's not like it will do you any good. I mean, you can't get down without me."

"Some friend you are."

Rachel swung up, reaching for a minute rock ledge, and caught it with her fingertips. "You're just pumped. You know, freaked out. That's all."

Cody didn't move.

"Let go of the rock," Rachel said. "Trust the rope. I'm going to belay you up to me.

"No, I don't think so."

"Come on Cody. Just a little further and we'll be at our first crack."

Cody leaned in until her nose was practically rubbing against rock. She couldn't go down. She wouldn't go up. Her calf muscles were starting to quiver with the effort of holding still. Carefully, without looking up, she finger-walked her hand, feeling her way to the rope. But she couldn't bring herself to lose contact with the rock long enough to stretch for it. She clung there, breathing heavily, for several seconds.

"Talk to me about Nate," she said. "What was he like?"

"Smelly, like I said."

Cody tried reaching for the rope again. "You're going to have to do better than that. I need some distraction here."

"So I see," Rachel said, leaning out from the rock to look down at Cody. "Nate seemed like one of those survivalist types. You know, military surplus gear, wanting to be left alone."

"Did you talk to him much?"

"No. And I didn't want to."

Cody still couldn't quite reach the rope and pushed against the granite with her climbing shoes. The friction gave her the tiny bit of extra reach she needed. "I've been thinking about Keith or Kendra being the one who shot Nate and Kelly. I can't see Keith able to get up the trail."

"So?" Rachel pushed with her feet, swinging out and back, for all the world like she was in a school playground. "What are you thinking?"

"That maybe Matt is wrong." Cody grabbed onto the rope, hanging there and exhaling the fear she'd been holding. "Now what?"

"Pull up your left knee and you'll find that foot hold there."

Cody did as instructed and was gratified to find she could move upward a few more inches and wasn't going to spend the rest of her life dangling from a rock.

"Good job," Rachel said. "Hang out while I set the next piece. Then we'll try some crack climbing and then I'll let you go back down."

Cody adjusted her weight and watched Rachel work. She took a deep breath of air so cold and clear it was like sucking in purity. The world was quiet up here, the wind a bare whisper in faraway tree tops, no sounds of water or even a distant hum of traffic. Just the movements of rope and metal against rock, of their breathing.

She was clinging to the side of a mountain. She was trusting her life to a rope and another person. She was pushing herself physically, more than she had ever done. And, the thought came with a sudden expansion inside like an awakening, she was having fun. She was terrified, still shaking, still wanting to be down on solid ground, and yet, she could do this.

"Okay, here's the next hold," Rachel said. "Right hand first, grab on, and up you come."

Another fifteen feet and they were at a long crack in the rock that ran up and slightly to the right.

"We're not doing the whole crack," Rachel said. "You aren't ready for that and we don't have enough time. But we're going to go up a few feet just to give you a taste of jamming your hands in rock."

"I can do it," Cody said.

And fell.

She only dropped a few feet, to the end of the slack rope Rachel had. She fell silently, with no time to cry out, ending it by slamming into the rock face when Rachel arrested her fall.

"Cody! You okay?"

Her forearms were scraped and oozing from where she'd thrown them up to protect her face. Her knee throbbed where it had hit an outcropping. Her heart was pounding so hard she couldn't draw in sufficient air. Adrenaline pulsated in shakes so severe the carabiner in front of her ticked in time against rock. She craned her head back to look up at Rachel, braced in place and gripping the rope.

"It's okay Cody," Rachel said, her voice strong, in control, and calm. "I've got you on belay and you're not going anywhere. The gear did exactly what it was supposed to, arresting your fall. That's why we set pieces so often, so you can't drop too far. Some people climb with more slack, taking more risks, but I'm cautious."

"Rachel?"

"Yeah?"

"You're babbling. Tell me what to do now."

"Get your feet under you, get back in position."

Cody did as she was told, finding the placements she had used earlier. Her breathing was coming back under control, the shakes were easing, and she rested her hand against the cold rock as she gripped the rope with the other.

"Okay, just hang there. I'm coming down to you." Rachel leaned out from the rock face, almost in a seated position, and walked her way backwards.

Cody took a deep breath, and then another one. She flexed her fingers, tilted her head from one side to the other to stretch her neck muscles, and realized that in spite of falling several feet down a mountainside, she was alive and whole and only superficially scraped up.

"How about we save the crack for another day?" Rachel asked as she drew even with Cody.

Cody simply nodded, surprised at how pale Rachel was. And not only was she pale, she was shaking worse than Cody had been moments before.

"You look worse then I feel," Cody said. "It didn't seem that bad. Or am I too much of a novice to realize what just happened?"

Rachel hung there a moment in silence. And then she shook her head slowly, as if in disbelief.

"You don't have to down climb," she finally said. "We're going to rappel."

Rappelling was faster and smoother than going up, once Cody got brave enough to sit back away from the rock. They dropped in rhythm, but silently, as if Rachel was tucked away in her thoughts. Cody concentrated on mimicking what Rachel did, her confidence growing the closer she got to the ground. When she finally had both feet on horizontal earth, had unclipped from the rope, and was out of the harness, she was so grateful she rested both palms on the rock face, as if thanking the mountain.

"For a few minutes there I was actually having fun."

"Until you fell," Rachel said, coiling rope and not meeting Cody's eyes.

"Until I fell," Cody agreed. "And then I was having a blast."

Rachel looked up at that, but still didn't smile, and still looked too pale. "What?"

"Oh, it scared me," Cody said. "Well, it terrified me. But other than those few minutes, I had fun. I can't believe I did it and I can't believe I enjoyed it. But yeah, I had fun."

"Think you'd want to try it again?"

"Not today," Cody said, and laughed. "But some time." She felt euphoric, weightless, as if gravity no longer had any influence over her.

"I'll ask again when the endorphin rush has worn off," Rachel said, zipping up the backpack. "Let's head home."

Cody fell in behind Rachel and they walked out into bars of weak sunlight, angling down from where the sun was sitting almost touching the mountains. The late afternoon was growing colder, and Cody could see her breath. Her knee was stiffening, and the braking motion of going downhill was making it ache with each step.

Rachel kept a steady pace, not pausing to enjoy the setting sun, not tossing conversation back. Cody could see tension in Rachel's shoulders, in the way she hunched under the weight of the backpack. It was as if the fall had been harder on her then on Cody.

"Rachel, you weren't responsible for that you know," Cody said.

Rachel didn't slow down and didn't respond.

"It wasn't your fault," Cody said, trying again.

"How would you know?" Rachel said, swinging suddenly back. "You don't know anything about climbing. How the hell would you know if it was my fault or not?"

"Because I trust you," Cody said, startled by the anger she saw in Rachel's eyes.

"Yeah, well maybe you shouldn't."

Chapter 31

The drive back to Florence's was empty of conversation and Cody listened instead to the rhythmic rub of tire on pavement, the wheezing of the heater trying to warm the Jeep, and the slight intakes of air from Rachel. It was as if she wanted to talk, kept breathing in to form words, and then exhaling back into silence. Cody figured she was trying to find a way to apologize for her abruptness and didn't want an apology. And so she rode in quiet, too.

As they parked and walked up the steps to the house, the cold air bit, grabbed on, and sank its teeth deep into every inch of exposed skin. With the sun well down, the shadows in the bottom of the canyon were like dark robes of winter.

Inside the house, the warmth from the woodstove was as welcoming as Sunny's broad smile.

"So, how was it? Did you try leading? Want to try some free climbing with no gear?"

"It was more fun than I expected," Cody said, shedding her coat and making for the woodstove. "But I doubt I'll ever go without gear."

"Give it time," Sunny replied. "Matt wanted me to call him when you showed up so I did, and he, like, says to get changed for dinner 'cause he's on his way."

Cody's stomach bottomed with the same sense of dropping into a void as when she fell on the climb.

"You know, I think I need to cancel. I should check in on my mom."

"Yes!" Sunny shouted, pumping a fist in the air. "I bet Matt twenty bucks you'd say exactly that!"

Cody turned to hide the warmth in her cheeks, wondering if she was really so predictable.

"How's Granny?" Rachel asked as she dropped the pack and gear next to the closet door.

"Oh, we had so much fun. We built a wild west town with the Monopoly pieces and had a really nice gabfest. She, like, scarfed down the pizza I had delivered, and then fell asleep in the armchair. I had to almost carry her to her room."

"So she was clear, knew who you were?" Rachel asked.

"Oh no," Sunny said. "She thought I was you, then she thought I was her mother, and at one point she was calling me Brandy. No idea who that is."

"Her dog," Rachel said. "She had it when she was a child."

"No wonder she kept telling me to sit." Sunny picked up her purse, a multi-colored rectangle of beads. "See you 'round."

The front door shut behind her and Cody waited while Rachel stared at her with an odd expression somewhere between fear and puzzlement.

"What?" Cody finally asked.

"I don't get you, that's all." Rachel dropped onto the couch and stretched out her legs. "Better go get ready for that hot date."

"You know what Rachel? Sometimes I don't get you, either." Cody tossed her coat on the back of a chair and left.

Lisa Stowe

In her room she took her clothes and threw them across the bed. But there was no reason to change because everything looked the same. Drab. She shoved them on the floor and sat down on the quilt.

She truly didn't understand Rachel. Sometimes she was supportive, sometimes she made Cody forget herself and laugh, and yet sometimes her words cut almost as deep as May's.

Cody stood, dressed, and jammed the rest of her clothes back into the duffel and hefted it up. Who was she fooling? She hadn't known any of these people long enough to think of them as acquaintances let alone friends. Was she so desperate for company? She didn't need friends, and she sure didn't need to go out to dinner with a forest ranger. What she needed was to be alone. She'd never been completely on her own, and maybe if she was she'd figure out what to do with this life of hers.

She dropped her chin, her shoulders slumped, and she drew in a heavy breath. It wasn't Rachel making her grumpy. It was the thought of dinner. Best to just get it over with. She rummaged around through the clothes looking for her wallet before remembering it was in Rachel's Jeep.

Back in the living room, Rachel was slung across the couch, an afghan tossed haphazardly across her legs, and eyes closed. Cody trod quietly across the creaking floorboards and Rachel didn't stir.

Outside, Cody made her way down the steep steps, running her hand reluctantly over the rough wood handrail. She wanted to grip it, to hang on and freeze movement as still as the cold mountain air. Two cars had pulled off the road. One was a Forest Service Bronco and the other a big battered Ford diesel pickup. Cody expected Matt to get out of the Bronco, and was surprised when Hailey jumped out and ran, notebook in hand, to the truck.

Matt got out of the truck and faced Hailey as he shoved hands in his pockets as if restraining them.

He looked different, Cody thought as she neared. Taller, shoulders broader, blond hair and green eyes more defined, like late summer sunlight on mountain water. Maybe it was because he was out of uniform, in jeans and a black shirt, sleeves shoved up and some sort of design above a breast pocket.

Cody left the steps reluctantly as nausea shoved nerves around in her stomach. She realized suddenly that it wasn't Matt who looked different. It was that she looked at him differently. He'd changed from someone safe, a Ranger who was working on a murder, to a man who wanted to have dinner with her. Something that washed away all her newfound confidence and left her exposed.

"You're not listening to me, Tanner," Hailey said.

"You're right," Matt said as Cody slipped past Hailey and pulled open the passenger door of Rachel's Jeep.

Hailey slapped her notebook against her thigh. "I told you what needs to happen here! And what needs to happen now!"

Cody rummaged through the papers on the Jeep floor, searching for her wallet, trying to be invisible.

"And like I told you earlier," Matt said, his voice level. "I think you're wrong. I think you're on a personal vendetta."

Cody found the wallet, shoved some papers back from their bid for escape, and shut the door.

"That thing's a mess," Hailey said, watching Cody a moment before looking back up at Matt. "I want you to do something right for a change."

"Oh, that's going to help," Matt said. "Insulting your superior."

Hailey started to speak, started to bounce up on her toes, and then all movement stopped and the cold air seemed to move into her eyes.

"Never mind," she said, and started for the steps to the house. "I need to speak to Rachel."

Matt and Cody both stared after Hailey as she reached the landing half way up the stairs. She paused for a moment to stare down at them before turning her back and continuing to the front door.

"She's…different," Cody managed.

"She's bizarre," Matt said, and ran a hand through his hair as he sighed heavily. "Let's eat and pretend she doesn't exist."

Cody gestured to the insignia on his shirt, a Celtic design and the words 'Ardbeg'. "What is that?"

"A very fine single malt whisky."

"Rivers like whisky," Cody said once she'd pulled herself up into the truck and buckled her seatbelt. "She said it lowers her stress."

"That it does," Matt said, starting the truck. "Though she likes Lagavulan. I'd settle for either right now. Hell, I'd even take Tullamore Dew, and that's not even scotch."

Silence slipped in after the words, and Cody looked out the passenger window, staring at trees and rocks. What could she talk about except murder? She didn't know Matt. The weather? The climb she went on? She wished for a moment that she was home, cooking dinner, with her mother at the table criticizing what she was doing. Back where life was familiar and safe, if not happy.

"Looks like you fell," Matt said, gesturing at Cody's scraped arms. "Unless someone punched you again."

"A fall. Only a few feet. Rachel stopped it."

Silence fell again. Should she continue on the climbing theme?

"We did part of the Crack Horror. Went through Nate's camp to get there."

"No shit." Matt glanced away from the road, frowning. "I didn't know there was access from that side. Rachel know Nate was there?"

"Sounds like she stumbled across his camp. She only talked to him briefly." She gripped her fingers tightly in her lap.

"Huh. I'll have to try that access. I like the Horror. Did you do any of the crack itself?"

"No. We were almost there when I fell."

Matt laughed, a sound that filled the truck and left no room for nerves. Cody relaxed a little, settled into the seat a bit.

"The third pitch," he said. "I've fallen a few times there myself. And Kelly always fell there. I don't think he ever made it up the crack."

"Kelly was a climber?" Cody braved a quick glance at Matt's profile.

"Oh yeah. Not in Rachel's caliber obviously. His climbing style was kind of like a rugby player in a ballet."

Cody's fingers loosened with audible pops and she flushed, hoping he hadn't heard. "Are we going to the Corner?"

"No. I thought we'd go down to the Pulaski. You've been to the Corner a couple times so I thought you'd like to try something different. And I figured if I offered to cook at my place you'd hit the highway and burn rubber."

The flush warmed and spread. But she knew he was right.

"I've been in the Pulaski," she said.

"I know. I heard. But you were in the bar and the food's not edible there. In the back there's a half way decent diner and they make great Reuben's."

"So what were you going to let me know?"

"Jess has been upgraded and can have brief visits. I thought maybe after dinner you'd want to go by and see her."

"Sure." Cody thought about Jess, her kindness and professionalism. And giving her the cell phone that she rarely remembered to carry. "Oh. That reminds me. I forgot to check the cell phone to see where that whisper call I got came from."

"That's not a problem any more," Matt said. "It's tied in with Keith."

"You still think Keith killed his son?" Cody tried to keep the skepticism out of her voice, not wanting to offend him. "How do you think he made it up the trail?"

"What are you talking about?" Matt turned onto Cedar Street while staring at Cody and bounced over the curb. "Sorry. But what did you say?

"You were talking about Keith on the phone. Like you'd solved everything."

"Not the murder," Matt said. "I'm after Keith for what's happened to you."

"I don't get it." Cody shifted sideways in the seat to look at Matt.

"We're still working on the murders. Kelly and Nate. Nate's dad. And Jess being shot. It's pretty obvious they're all linked. But that's not what I was talking about. I meant your room, you being assaulted, the calls you've been getting."

"But, isn't that because of Kelly and Nate? Weren't you thinking it was something I'd seen? I mean, the camera was taken."

"Hang on. I can't talk about this and drive at the same time." He pulled into the parking lot of the Pulaski Bar and shut the engine off. "Okay. At first I thought everything was connected. Just like you said. But as we worked the scenes, Jess said everything kept pointing back to Keith. Like you, we couldn't figure out why he would kill his grandson. So it didn't make sense until I started separating out the events."

"They're not connected?" Cody tried to make the various threads meet and tie together, but her thoughts were a tangled ball.

"What's been happening to you isn't connected to Kelly and Nate. It's connected to your grandfather. Keith told you how many times not to dig into the past?"

"I don't know. A few. But-"

"Hear me out. Keith didn't want you bringing back old rumors about Ethel. You said you only wanted to learn about Charles. But Keith couldn't risk it."

"Risk what? I'm totally lost here."

"Okay. Let me back up. You go to the museum and meet Rachel. What souvenirs did you buy there?"

"I don't know." Cody thought back trying to remember something that seemed like it had happened to someone else. "Pamphlets with stories about Wallace. The Sunshine mine fire. The 1910 fire. Some histories."

"And shortly after the visit to the museum you start getting whispered phone calls. So do you drop history? No. Not only do you keep digging for Charles, you threaten Keith."

"I didn't threaten him!"

"Okay, maybe Jake exaggerated. Either way you pretty much told Keith you were going to keep looking. And what happens next?"

Cody could only shake her head, hoping the movement might jostle thoughts into place.

"Your room gets ransacked and you get assaulted. And what was stolen from your room?"

"My camera." Cody took in a deep breath of revelation. "And pamphlets."

"Back to history." Matt pulled the keys from the ignition. "Let's get some food. We can finish in there."

"No, wait. Tell me." Cody caught his arm.

"Okay, but I'm starving here." Matt dropped the keys on the dashboard. "Did you talk to Keith about looking for Charles's birth certificate?"

Cody again tried to remember back over the last few days. How could things connected to her grandfather have become so trivial that she was forgetting? Why were things like visits with Rivers, laughing with Rachel, Kelly's smile, so utterly clear?

"I don't think I mentioned the birth certificate. I think I just told him I was going to look closer at Ethel."

"And I think that's all it took." Matt's stomach growled and he absently rubbed it. "Think about camouflage for a minute. Remember T.J. Culhane? At the senior center? And you told me about running into him when you were looking for Florence. Which reminded me that you'd mentioned shades of green when you got assaulted."

"Camouflage," Cody said, as a mental thread became untangled.

"I went over everything with the police, and today T.J. was picked up while driving down Sixth Street on a quad, with a rifle on his back and an open bottle of Rolling Rock in his lap."

"A rifle?" Cody flashed on Jess spinning and sinking, on blood flowing.

"He's not the one who shot Jess," Matt said. "But he was in a pretty damn talkative mood. And once he started talking, the Deputy called me in. Culhane said Keith hired him to steal some old papers. To make those prank phone calls to you, trying to scare you off."

"But why?"

Matt's stomach growled again. "Come on Cody, please can we go get some food?"

Bemused, Cody got out of the truck and followed Matt toward the bar through the deepening twilight. She struggled to separate the things that had happened to her from Kelly and Nate's murder, but it just wasn't making sense.

In the bar, Matt led her back to some tables, flagging a waitress on the way and asking her to bring them at least three different kinds of appetizers. Once they had sat down and accepted glasses of ice water, Matt planted his elbows on the table.

"You've been looking at Ethel because Charles thought she was his mother. Did he ever wonder about his father?"

"No. His dad was a railroad man. His dad is the one who told him to question his parentage."

"So why did you think he meant Charles's mother?"

"Florence thought it. Charles always thought his dad was a secret spy or something. You know, kid dreams."

"Well Florence was partly right, but she's not exactly all there you know. I've been spending most of the day talking to Keith, and would you like to finally know who your family is?"

Cody opened her mouth to say of course she did, that this was the whole reason she had come to Wallace. But the realization of what Matt was going to say froze the words in her throat. She shook her head slowly.

"Ethel was his mother," Matt said, and his voice grew gentler. "And Keith was his half-brother."

"No."

"Keith says he can prove it, although he'd prefer the whole story die. His father was having an affair with Ethel, just like everyone thought. She got pregnant and had the baby, but agreed to adopt it out. Keith's father then had Keith with his wife. Two sons, one legitimate, one not."

Cody gripped the sides of her seat. It had been one thing to consider Ethel as family. A strong woman, independent for her times, taking care of a child she couldn't acknowledge. But to find out Cody was related to someone as nasty as Keith?

"No," she said. "That can't be."

"What?"

"I can't be related to them! I don't want them!"

"Cody, you can't pick your relatives. And they don't define who you are."

"Like I don't know that!" Cody stood up. "All these years dealing with my mother. Then Charles shows up and here's family I can be proud of, someone who loves me. And he dies. So I try to find more family like him, and what do I get?" Hot tears burned across her cheeks. "Keith! I don't need more family to treat me like dirt. I just…I just want to belong someplace where I fit."

"You didn't just get Keith for family," Matt said, and his voice was still calm, and his eyes held sympathy, and she hated it.

"No I didn't. I got Kendra, too."

"I meant Kelly," Matt said. "He was a good person. He was someone to be proud of."

"He's dead, Matt. And you just made it worse. The family I could love consists of two men who are dead."

Cody's throat ached with the weight of loss. She shoved her chair out of the way and ran.

Chapter 32

The night had turned frigid and clear, with a moon so bright it washed out the headlights of passing cars on the highway above Wallace. Cody walked with her hands up the sleeves of her jacket. She was shivering, her cheeks ached with cold, and her nose was running. It was early evening, but places were closing up and there was little traffic. The hotel was brightly lit though.

Cody walked through the entrance and into the warm lobby. She'd half expected to see her mother still sitting there, but the chairs were empty. So instead she approached the desk.

"Can you tell me if May Marsh is still here?"

The desk clerk plunked away on computer keys. "Yes, she decided to keep her room another night. Shall I ring her for you?"

"No, I know the room."

The elevator took her up, and within moments she was knocking on the door and facing her mother with an odd sense of emptiness, as if her emotions had been dropped in the street somewhere along the route here.

May wore her housecoat, a kind of light weight robe she had worn for years. It was getting frayed and faded, but she always said it was too comfortable to replace. She sat back down in an armchair, propped her swollen feet on the bed, and muted the television show she'd been watching. The remains of her dinner piled the table next to her, and she poked at the peel of a baked potato with the fork.

"You didn't come back," she said.

"I told you I wasn't going to," Cody responded, and sat down on the edge of the bed. "You didn't take the bus home."

"Of course not. I knew you'd realize your mistake and come get me."

"I want to ask you something mom." Cody picked at the bedspread.

"Yes? Those so-called friends have shown their true colors haven't they? How many times have I warned you-"

"Stop it mom," Cody said. "Just...stop. You've made it clear over the years that you think I'm worthless. So why didn't you adopt me out? Just get rid of me?"

"What's gotten in to you? What are you talking about?" May dropped her fork on the plate.

"Answer the question. You think I'm stupid, you tell me I'm ugly, you make it clear I'm unlovable. You've had years of telling me over and over what a burden I was to bring up on your own. So why do it? Why the hell didn't you just abort me?"

May's triple chins quivered, and she put a hand over her heart. "Why are you talking like this? How could you ask me something like that? Hand me those tissues."

Cody looked at the box of tissue on the bedside table, within May's reach if she sat upright. Cody would have to stand and take a few steps to pick the box up. She shook her head.

"Why am I talking to you like this?" she repeated. "Why have you talked to me the way you've done my whole life?"

May stretched, wheezing, for the tissue box and pulled one out, dabbing the corners of her eyes.

"By the time your father left us you were almost five. A little old to abort, Cody."

The words were like a sharp pain slicing into Cody's chest. She couldn't breathe and hunched over, gripping her hands between her knees.

"But I would never have done something like that anyway," May continued. "And why would I adopt you out? You're my daughter."

"But you act like you hate me."

"Of course I don't hate you. I've raised you the best I know how, to prepare you for the world. You think I've been cruel? What do you think the world will do? You think anyone out there will be kind to you? You think anyone will be loyal or do what they promise? No!" May was breathing heavier and sat up straighter.

"What are you saying?"

"I'm saying quit feeling sorry for yourself and thank me for making you strong! All I've done is show you what life is really like. You can't trust anyone. The only way you'll be safe from hurt is if I take care of you. Just the two of us, the way it's always been."

Cody couldn't stop the tears. She was being flooded, and the flow was washing out years and unspoken words and misunderstood love. "This is about dad, isn't it?"

"Your father left us," May said harshly. "Left us. With nothing. He said he loved us. But for all he knew we starved to death. He never came back. He left me."

"And what? Did you think I was going to leave you, too? Is that why you brainwashed me into thinking no one else would want me? So I'd stay with you?"

"No!" May struggled to her feet. "No! I've tried to keep you safe! So you wouldn't have to go through the same thing!" She clutched her chest.

"I don't believe you. I think you were afraid to be alone. And you kept me with you by convincing me I was worthless. But I'm not." Cody stood and walked to the door, barely able to see the handle through the tears.

"Where are you going?" May was sweating now, something like fear in her eyes.

"I don't know," Cody said. "But I'm going alone, wherever it is. No family."

"You're leaving?" May's voice rose. "I always knew you'd turn out just like that worthless father of yours!"

Cody walked out without bothering to shut the door, without even being aware of leaving the room. She found herself in the elevator; she found herself in the cold. She walked down the street, letting pools of light from the streetlamps swallow her up and spit her out into darkness. She followed that darkness because in it she couldn't see her reflection in windows, because in it she disappeared.

She was passing the gas station, headed for her only connection to Charles, when headlights swept across her, blinding her. She heard the engine cut out and the slam of a door as she rounded the station, taking the now familiar route.

"Cody." Matt caught her arm. "I've been looking for you."

She had no words to answer him, but he wouldn't let go of her.

"It's too dark, and getting too cold, for you to hike up there. I get that you don't want to talk to me, but at least let me take you back to Rachel's."

Cody watched the shadowed dance of tree branches pushed by a frigid breeze creeping slowly through the woods. "It's not you, Matt," she finally said. "It's me. Lost, overwhelmed, sad, I don't know what I'm feeling except for the anger. That's pretty clear. And I think I'm as mad at myself as I am at my mother."

"So be angry," Matt said, tugging on her coat sleeve. "But how about you do it inside the truck where it's warm?"

She let him lead her back to his truck, and wordlessly sank into the seat, lifting her face to the heat blowing from the vents. She shivered, and her teeth chattered as if speaking the words she couldn't give voice to.

"Here," Matt said, getting in and gesturing to a cup holder. "I got you hot chocolate. Figured you'd be half frozen."

"I think I understand my mom," Cody said, accepting the warm cardboard cup. She sipped at the sweetness and felt heat seep down to her stomach.

"Okay," Matt said, "Is that a good thing?"

Cody shrugged. "She looks at me and sees my father. She thinks I'm going to leave her like he did."

"If you're smart you will," Matt said. "You want me to take you to see Jess, or to Florence's?"

"Florence's," Cody said, feeling as drained as her hot chocolate cup.

"Look," Matt said after a few moments of silence. "I'm sorry I dumped the stuff about Keith on you. I should have figured you'd be upset by it. I was just thinking it meant you'd have relatives, connections to your grandfather. I didn't stop to think about the quality of those relatives."

"It's okay," Cody said automatically.

"No, it's not," Matt said. "But at least we're cleaning up part of this mess. Keith will face charges for what he's done, and maybe we'll finally be rid of him. And you won't be a target anymore with T.J. locked up."

"I never thought I was," Cody said.

"I knew you were, I just wasn't sure who was aiming. At first I thought it was connected to Nate and Kelly, like I said earlier. If I'd been more aware of what was going on, I would have solved this long before you got punched in the jaw. So I'm sorry about that, too."

"Quit apologizing," Cody said. "I'm finding that really annoying. I don't think I'll apologize for anything ever again."

"Well, then I'm sorry dinner didn't work out, too."

"Knock it off."

"And I'm sorry I didn't get a chance to tell you I was sorry about...sorry, I lost my train of thought."

Cody shook her head and tried to hang onto the self-pity, but somehow a laugh worked its way out. She let it escape, and then sighed.

"I think I've been clinging to my mom as much as I have to my grandfather, for different reasons. I don't have anyone to blame but myself for staying with her as long as I have. And I think I've done that so when things go wrong I can point to her as the reason."

"What are you going to do about it?" Matt asked as they neared the pull off to Florence's.

"No idea," Cody said. "I was thinking earlier I needed a place of my own, away from her."

"That's a start. It gets old doing nothing but trying to keep family happy."

Cody shrugged, as if pushing away his words. "I need to figure out who I really am, not who mom tells me I am, and I don't know how to do that."

"No one does, Cody. We're all products of what people expect of us. I sure as hell wouldn't be in law enforcement if I hadn't been trying to please my family."

"So you're saying there's no way to be happy?"

"We figure out how to find little spaces of happiness. We learn how to get by, how to be content with what we've got. We try to hang on to a few dreams, maybe hope for something more. But that's about it."

"I don't know if that's sad or cynical," Cody said as Matt parked. "Is that the dome light of my car on?"

"No, I think it's Rachel's," Matt said.

Cody got out of the truck and walked around to the Jeep. The front passenger door hung open, and as she reached up to shut it, she glanced inside.

"Wow. Rachel's cleaned it."

"She's early," Matt said. "She usually only does that in the spring."

Cody shut the door and the dome light blinked off. She waited a second for her eyes to adjust to the moonlight, and then started for the steps. "Coming up?"

"Yeah, I suppose I can for a minute. Maybe Florence will feed me."

"I'm not apologizing for you not getting dinner," Cody said.

"Maybe not, but you agreed to have a meal with me, so you still owe me."

Cody climbed the frosty stairs feeling light, as if she'd shed her mother's pounds. Maybe she didn't need family in order to be part of something. Maybe having a few friends would be enough.

Chapter 33

Rachel sat cross legged in the middle of the living room floor. Scattered around her were cardboard boxes, gaping open and spilling papers in total disarray. Florence sat in the armchair nearest Rachel, with a paper tucked into her green blouse, like it was a napkin.

"How was dinner?" Rachel asked, not looking up from the box she was elbow deep in.

Cody glanced at Matt. "Fine."

"Yeah," Matt said. "Except that I'm starving."

"Men are as bottomless as the mines around here," Florence said. "Would you like me to fix you a sandwich?"

"Yes," Matt said. "Maybe a couple?"

Florence laughed, waving her hand at him as if erasing his words. She used the arm of the chair to lever herself up slowly, and worked her way to the kitchen, leaning heavily on furniture.

"She okay?" Cody asked.

"Why wouldn't she be?" Rachel said.

"She looks tired." Cody watched Florence pause at the kitchen door, and then enter the room, trailing her hand along the jamb.

"I gave her a sedative," Rachel said. "She was pretty upset just before you got here. I couldn't reason with her at all."

"So what are you working on?" Matt asked, walking to Rachel so he could look over her shoulder.

"Hailey said my car was a mess, and it got me wondering if anything from the museum was in there. I used to bring work home a lot. So I hauled all the papers up here, and that reminded me of the boxes I'd brought home to look for Cody's grandfather."

"That's great," Cody said in surprise. "Then not everything was lost at the museum."

Rachel looked up at Cody, smiled, opened the wood stove, and shoved in a handful of papers.

"What the hell?" Matt looked from the flames to Rachel. "What are you doing?"

"Burning paper, what's it look like?" Rachel smiled again. "Should have done it a long time ago."

"Rachel," Cody said, "You love history. And you're burning it?"

"Love history?" Rachel asked, gathering up another lap full of papers. "I suppose I do. But what Keith wants, Keith gets."

Matt bent down and grabbed papers from Rachel's hand. "Knock it off. You can't burn this stuff! It's irreplaceable."

Rachel unfolded and stood easily, then walked out of the room.

"What's gotten into her?" Cody asked.

Matt shook his head, but didn't say anything. Instead he was riffling through the pages in his hands.

"Matt?"

Florence chose that moment to come back into the living room. She was walking carefully, holding out a plate with a book on it. "I think I got carried away with your food," she said. "It's heavier then I expected. But I hope you like the sandwich." She held out the plate and book.

"Thanks Florence," Matt said, reaching for the plate. "I could use a napkin."

"Well," Florence said, looking around. "Napkins?"

"How about the one you're using? I won't need it very long."

"Oh! Certainly, dear." Florence handed Matt the paper in her blouse.

He added it to the pile in his hand, scanned it, then ran a hand over his face and Cody saw the papers tremble.

"Matt?"

He shook his head, not responding.

"You got here too soon, Matt," Rachel said as she came back into the room. "I thought dinner would take longer."

"What's going on?" Cody asked. She looked from Matt, grabbing the back of the chair as if for support, to Rachel, who was standing in the doorway with an expression of profound sadness pulling her face into lines someone her age shouldn't have.

When neither answered, Cody stepped between them, taking the pages from Matt. He didn't try to hang on to them, and as they left his fingers, he turned away from Cody.

The pages were from a green stenographer's notebook, and they had been torn out roughly, leaving fragmented sentences at the tops. The writing was large and slanted, flowing at a steep angle over the paper.

"…Nathaniel Johnson, missing since July, called son (BF), from area. BF camping off Bounty, Rachel's helping him search. BF believes father at Thompson Pass, something to do with mine. Rachel's taking Crack Horror over to pass, will meet there. Taking BF to station, fill out missing person report, we'll assist, take him to meet Rachel at mine."

"Nate wasn't missing," Cody said slowly, trying to make sense of the words. "He didn't have a son. And who's BF?"

"Bigfoot," Matt said, the word flat, as pale as his face. "It's what Kelly called Nate, before we knew his name. When people were telling us they were running into a wild man in the woods. Nate was named after his dad, Nathaniel."

"But, wait, this doesn't make sense," Cody looked at the pages, water stained, imprints of dirt from fingers and shoes. Her own, she suddenly realized, stepping on papers on the floor of Rachel's Jeep. "These are Kelly's?"

"Kelly's," Matt said.

"But, how did you end up with them Rachel?"

Rachel leaned against the kitchen door jamb. "I took them from Kelly's notebook."

"Why would you do that?" Cody struggled to find some way to keep the pieces from falling together in the way they were headed.

"The question isn't 'why', but 'when'," Matt said. "Kelly's notes place you in Nate's camp the day they were shot. They were headed down the trail to the station, and you were going to do the Horror. The route that drops a climber off near Jake's."

"Rachel?" Cody swung around to stare at her friend. "You were up Bounty that day and never said anything? Did you see anyone? Did you see what happened?"

"I saw you go past on your way to your grandfather's clearing," Rachel said. "Of course we hadn't met yet."

"Thank god you didn't go down with them," Cody said. "You could have been shot, too! But why didn't you tell Matt or Jess all this?"

"Because it places her at the scene," Matt said. "Because it gives her opportunity."

"What are you saying?" Cody's heart was racing so fast it was like she was back at the Horror, like she was falling again, only this time with no one to catch her.

"I'm saying Rachel followed them down the trail and shot her friend in the back."

"No." Cody shook her head as if that would make the word strong enough to be truth.

"It's not something I wanted to do," Rachel said. "I've wanted you both to know since it happened, to understand. But it's been so hard to find the right time to tell you."

"To understand what Rachel?" Matt's voice was getting stronger, coming back to life. "That you're a murderer? That you shot and killed two men? Are you the one who shot Jess, too?"

"I'm not a murderer!" Rachel hit the door jamb with a fist. "If I was, Cody would have died on the climb today! You realize how easy it would have been to just let go when she fell?"

Cody flashed on how shaken Rachel had been. As if the fall had scared her more than it had Cody. "You thought about it, though, didn't you?" she asked, clutching the pages.

"Of course I did," Rachel said. "It would have solved everything. Climbing accidents happen all the time. And you would never have had to know what I did. But I couldn't do it. You're a friend."

"You were able to shoot one," Matt said.

"Oh, Matt dear, Rachel has always been good with guns," Florence said, and the cheerful voice startled all three of them. Florence sat in her chair, folding one of the lace antimacassars carefully. "She hunts with her father, and he always insists on gun safety. He should be home any time now."

"He's not coming home, Granny!" Rachel wheeled away from the doorway. "He's dead!"

"Of course, dear," Florence said calmly, and reached for another doily.

"You see?" Rachel swung back to Cody. "Thoughts are melting through her brain like ice cream. There's nothing I can do except keep her safe and comfortable until her brain forgets to tell her to breathe. She's gotten worse just since you arrived. She needs round the clock care."

"We talked about that," Cody said. "But Kelly? And Nate? I can't...you killed them? Just shot them and left them?"

"Did he know?" Matt asked. "Kelly? Did he know at the end that a friend, someone he trusted, was about to kill him?"

"No!" Rachel paced a tight circle in front of the door. "Look, you don't understand. I didn't want to shoot him. I had no choice with Nate. I was hoping to catch Nate alone, but Kelly was so damn friendly with everyone! He just kept visiting with Nate, walking him down the trail. I couldn't let Nate go to the mine."

"I should have listened to Hailey," Matt said, straightening. "She said from the beginning it was either you or Jake. But I was too busy chasing Keith down. I screwed up." He reached into his jeans pocket and pulled out a cell phone.

"Don't Matt," Rachel said. "Listen to me! You and Cody are my closest friends. Once you hear what's going on you'll help me. I can make you understand if you just listen a minute!"

"No Rachel," Matt said. "Kelly was my friend, and a good man, and he's dead because of you and I'm calling the sheriff."

"Don't make me do this again!" Rachel shouted, tears in her eyes and thick in her voice.

"Rachel, calm down," Cody said, reaching out to touch Rachel's arm. "Please. Let's figure out what needs to happen."

"What needs to happen is that she goes to jail," Matt said, dialing.

"No, no, no!" Rachel shouldered away from Cody, dipped down, and came up with a rifle that had been in the corner, leaning against the door jamb.

Everything in Cody's body shriveled, froze.

"This is Ranger Tanner. I'm in Burke, at-"

The rifle barrel rose, Matt held up a hand and stepped back, and Cody lunged forward as Rachel fired.

Cody's palm hit the cold metal, shoving the barrel back. But she wasn't quick enough. Florence's scream was an echo to the shot, and Rachel dropped the rifle, running to her.

"Aw, shit." Matt's voice was airy and breathless and as Cody turned, he toppled, taking the side table with him.

"Not again, not again," she repeated, so low she wasn't sure if she said the words or thought them.

Blood was rapidly flowing across Matt's knee, soaking into the braided rug. He tried to sit up, reaching for the wound, but as Cody dropped beside him, his green eyes rolled to white and he collapsed on his side.

"Direct pressure," Cody whispered, remembering him yelling the words at her when Jess was shot.

She pressed one hand against the knee, and with the other, swept the floor for his cell phone.

"Granny, it's okay," Rachel said. "It's okay. Those loud noises happen all the time, you remember?"

"Loud noises," Florence repeated.

Cody found the cell phone under Matt's hip, by following the sound of squawking.

"No, Cody, don't," Rachel said, scrambling across the floor.

"I need an aid car!" Cody yelled into the cell phone.

Rachel grabbed the phone and threw it across the room. "Cody, I said don't."

"Or what Rachel?" Cody had both hands pressed against Matt's knee now, but there was no slowing the flow.

"Please," Rachel said. "You don't understand."

"No, I don't," Cody said. "So either shoot me or get the hell out of here."

"Granny needs to be taken care of," Rachel said frantically, kneeling next to Cody. "I've gotten myself in serious trouble because of that. I'm going to lose everything!"

Pressure on Matt's knee wasn't helping. Cody's hands were dark red all the way to her wrists, and yet the blood ran hot and fast. His leg was at an odd angle and his breathing was slowing. She glanced at Rachel, saw the tears streaming, and shoved Rachel over, leaving bloody handprints on Rachel's shoulders.

She lunged to her feet, swinging around. She couldn't see the cell phone anywhere, but Florence, sitting in her chair with lace in her lap, held up the land line and smiled with a sweet gentleness.

"Do you need a phone, dear?"

"Granny!" Rachel shouted. "No!"

Cody reached Florence first and grabbed up the phone, dialing 911 as Rachel struggled to her feet.

"911, what's your emergency?"

"A man has been shot. He's unconscious and bleeding badly."

"What's your location?"

Cody felt weight in her stomach as the realization that she didn't know the address bottomed like a boulder.

"I'm in Burke, at Florence Blaine's. I don't know the address."

"Well, I do," Florence said primly. "Mama made me memorize it."

She rattled off the house number and street and Cody repeated it into the phone. The dispatcher told her to remain on the line and asked her if she was safe, but even as the question was forming, Cody tossed the phone to Florence and ran back to Matt.

She pushed against his knee just like she had pressed against Jess's wound. She could feel tears of panic burning, and shook her head. There wasn't time to cry, or to let fear in. She sank her hands into Matt's blood and started counting each time his chest rose. Counting felt like a promise that the next number would follow, the next breath would enter.

"My goodness it's getting cold outside," Florence said in a conversational tone that was a surreal contrast to the growing sound of sirens. "Rachel is so bad about remembering to shut doors."

Cody glanced up.

Rachel was gone, out into the dark mountain night.

Chapter 34

The hospital room was overly warm and stuffy and Cody sat, listening to the beeping of machines and wondering how long she was obligated to stay before she could escape.

May was propped up by pillows, elevated by the bed, breathing with the aid of oxygen, and yet still wheezing. Her eyes were fixed on the television as her fingers marched across the remote swallowed in her hand. She was refusing to concede Cody's presence.

A nurse came in, dark graying hair in a ponytail and round wire framed glasses low on her nose. She nodded to Cody, checked monitors, IV's, and readouts, and then pushed a button.

"Time for a blood pressure reading, Ms. Marsh."

"Do you know how lucky I was that my heart attack wasn't more severe, Beth?" May asked the nurse.

"Yes," Beth said. "You told me about it the last time I was here."

"I was so lucky I was able to get to the phone," May continued. "My daughter just walked out on me, even though I could barely breathe. If I'd had a more severe attack, I would have died right there on the hotel room floor, and no one would have known until time for maid service the next day! I certainly wouldn't have been found by my daughter because she left me to go visit with her so-called friends. Just left me."

Cody sat forward in order to rub the small of her back, where a deep ache had settled from kneeling over Matt.

"It appears your breathing is better mom," Cody said. "You're talking fine."

"My daughter doesn't know anything about medical issues," May said to the nurse. "She can't tell when someone needs oxygen, and she didn't even recognize the signs of my heart attack." May flipped to a channel where the only sound was in Spanish.

"It does seem like we can try going without oxygen though," the nurse said in a cheery voice. "I'll have the doctor come in and talk to you about it. And tomorrow morning we've scheduled you an appointment with a nutritionist. As you said, this attack was very mild. So let's see if we can't get you a bit healthier so we can avoid anything worse."

Cody couldn't help it. A laugh bubbled up and out, flowing like liquid sound. How long had it been since she had laughed? Too long. And how long since she had laughed in front of her mother? Never.

"I didn't say it was mild. And I certainly don't think it is something to laugh about. Do you see anything humorous here?" May asked the nurse.

"Now that's a dangerous question," Cody said, and laughed again as the nurse turned her face away from May, hiding an answering smile. "I hope the nutritionist gets hazard pay."

"I can only hope, Beth, that you have no children."

"Four boys," the nurse said. "Well, men now. Plus four siblings."

"Speaking of nutrition," May said. "When am I going to get something to eat? It's almost midnight and I was told I would get some dinner after being admitted."

Cody stood up and arched her spine, then twisted side to side in an effort to stretch out the backache. She nodded to the nurse and headed for the door.

"You were given dinner at eight," Beth said.

"That was a sandwich, not a dinner," May replied.

Cody let the door swing shut on the nurse's answer, and headed down the hallway. Four doors down, she glanced in the partial opening and saw Rivers sitting in a chair. Her legs were curled up underneath a brilliantly colored skirt in shades of emerald and turquoise. The fringe that hung almost to the floor held tiny beads that caught the low light in the room and twinkled when Rivers raised her hand to wave Cody in.

Jess was also propped up in bed with a tray across her lap holding papers. She was tapping a pen on them and talking on the phone. Her throat was heavily bandaged and her voice was a gruff whisper.

"I know it's midnight. I know I'm in the hospital. But that doesn't mean my brain has shut off. Quit dicking around and get Search and Rescue called out. By dawn they can be in place to search Desolation."

"Rachel?" Cody asked, all laughter gone.

"Jess refuses to admit she's on medical leave," Rivers said. "Everyone is out looking for Rachel. There's even police at her house, with Sunny, in case Rachel comes back for Florence. Jess thinks that's what she'll do, but she wants the areas searched around Jake's place and Nate's camp just in case."

Cody could only nod. Thinking about Rachel hurt.

"That's a beautiful skirt," she said instead.

"It's the one I wear belly dancing," Rivers said. "I swear, Jake is having way too much fun going through my clothes."

Jess hung up the phone and dropped her pen. "What's the news on Matt?" she asked, and winced as if the whisper cut.

"He's still in surgery," Cody said. "It sounds like his knee will have to be rebuilt. He's going to have pins and some kind of bar, like an internal brace put in. I don't understand it all."

"The doctor told me if you hadn't deflected the shot, the rifle would have blown his leg off at such close range," Jess said.

Cody shrugged, staring at the floor, trying to ignore the building ache in her throat. "They don't know how long it will be before he can walk again."

"But he's alive," Jess said, and even whispered the words were firm.

Cody nodded, but couldn't manage anything else. The ache had grown to such pressure that tears built up around it. She covered her mouth with her hands, holding her breath as if that could stop the hurt and betrayal and fear from the last several hours.

"Oh, Cody," Rivers said, standing and wrapping her arms around Cody.

The sobs spilled, grew, spilled again in shaking silence. Hot tears burned against her closed eyes, soaked her face, ran between her fingers and down her wrists. Rivers held her tight, held her up, held her until she could breathe again.

"Rachel..." Cody began, and could get no further past fresh tears that surged upward through the distress.

"Rachel was your friend," Rivers said. "She did horrible things, but she didn't let you fall did she?"

Cody shook her head.

"And she didn't shoot you either, did she?"

Cody managed another shake.

"When you were on the phone she could have picked up that rifle and shot you instead of running, couldn't she?"

This time Cody was able to nod.

"Then remember that."

"That's bullshit," Jess said in her whisper. "Rachel killed people. Get mad Cody. You deserve better friends then that."

"She has us," River said, rubbing Cody's shoulders. "And we're not going anywhere."

"Well, I'm sure as hell not," Jess said. "Since they won't even let me pee alone."

The words had their intended effect, making Cody smile a little, giving her a light moment to take a deep breath and try to regain some composure.

"So you don't know when Matt will be out of surgery?" Rivers asked, offering Cody a change of subject as if it were a gift.

"No," Cody said, wiping her eyes with tissue Jess offered.

"Well, you can stay here with us," Jess said. "I could use someone other than Rivers to talk to."

Rivers dropped down on the side of the bed and leaned forward to kiss Jess on the forehead. "You know you love me," she said.

"I know no such thing," Jess replied, but she didn't resist when Rivers entwined their fingers.

Cody sat down in the chair Rivers had been using and fatigue was a weight that pinned her there. Her emotions were so shattered they had become miniscule granules washed away by her tears.

There was nothing left except numbness, and she closed her eyes in gratitude.

Chapter 35

The hospital filled with sounds as nurses made their rounds with breakfast trays. Cody found the growing bustle soothing as she walked down the hallway toward the critical care unit. Matt was out of surgery and even though he wasn't conscious, Jess had badgered the doctors into allowing Cody to sit with him. She entered the room quietly, as if any noise might penetrate the drugs in his system and wake him.

The doctor was cautiously optimistic that the surgery had gone well. Barring infection, or rejection of all the new parts in his body, he was expected to walk again. After physical therapy, of course. And the doctor had made it clear there would be a lot of physical therapy.

But for right now, his leg was encased and elevated, and he was hooked up to more equipment then Cody had ever seen in one room. May would be jealous.

She sat down as a low hum kicked on and the blood pressure cuff around Matt's arm swelled like some kind of blue leech. She watched the numbers climb on the monitor, and listened to the soft hiss as the air escaped, the numbers paused, and machines went back to their ticking. She didn't expect him to wake, especially with the slow morphine drip turned on, but she badly wanted him to. If he'd at least open his eyes, she might have proof the doctor knew what he was talking about.

An elderly man came into the room, wearing a tag that identified him as a volunteer. He carried a small basket that held a woodland fern in a bed of moss.

"This was delivered for your friend," he said. "I'll just put it here by the window, shall I? This envelope came with it, but it has your name on it. The nurses told me where to find you."

Cody took the thick envelope and held it long after the volunteer had left. Practically everyone she knew was here at the hospital. Even Jake, who'd shown up as soon as visiting hours officially started, with muffins and donuts. She rubbed her thumb over the envelope, and then picked up the phone and quietly asked Rivers to join her.

"What is it?" Rivers asked as she came inside.

Cody handed her the envelope, and waited while Rivers studied it.

"Well, let's see what she has to say, shall we?" Rivers finally said, as she opened the envelope and began to read out loud.

"A year ago I was reorganizing the storage room at the museum, and found an account about the opening of the Honey Do mine. It caught my interest because my great grandfather was listed as one of the owners. The mine didn't pan out and was closed and it appeared the mayor, also one of the owners, bought out the others.

"The more I researched the mine, the more I realized that it had been closed simply because of its location. Not because the ore was no good. I realized that with modern advances, it might be able to be reopened and turned into a good producer.

"And I needed money. You know what's going on with Granny, Cody. My wages at the museum sure as hell weren't going to keep her out of the nuthouse. So I climbed in bed with the devil. I signed over Granny's house as collateral to buy the mine from Keith. The house my family had lived in for generations. My history."

Rivers paused and took a sip of water from a plastic cup by Matt's bed. Cody walked to the window and stared out at the returning rain, muting even the glow of the tamaracks, and wondered where Rachel was. It seemed easier somehow to hear Rachel's words with her back to Rivers and the letter.

"Things would have been fine if it hadn't been for two problems." Rivers resumed reading out loud. "One was the environmental stuff connected to reopening the mine. I didn't know ahead of time how hard it would be, or how much money it was going to take to just get the thing up and running. I had to hire Jim Russell to handle that end of things for me, and his wages took even more money. I'd wiped out my savings and wasn't anywhere close to getting any kind of return. I couldn't make the payments to Keith anymore. Several months ago he told me he was going to foreclose, take the house. He didn't care what that would do to Granny. He didn't care that he was taking away her home and she wouldn't understand. That's when I realized he'd sold me the mine so he'd have a hold over me, could manipulate me, could control history."

"So I started working the mine myself, secretly. I would spend as much time there as I could, drilling, and even blasting a couple times when Jake wasn't around. Because the mine, as I'm sure you've figured out, is the one by his place. The ore I was getting wasn't near what I could have been doing with it open legally and being worked by experienced miners, but I was seeing some money coming in. I thought I'd be able to keep Keith away from Granny.

"Until the second problem. A man showed up one day. Looking for the mine. He had a map, said he was the grandson of Patrick Cross, one of the original owners, that he by rights, still owned a share. I told him the mayor had bought out the partners, but this man didn't believe it. He was going to contest it, he was going to have everything frozen until ownership could be established. We got in a fight when he came into the mine. I grabbed a Pulaski, and swung. To be honest Cody, I don't know whether I was trying to kill him or just scare him, but I swung that axe as hard as I could and practically cut his head off. I swung that axe so hard the handle snapped clean through. Think about it, Cody. You touched it, that first day you came to the museum when you knocked all that crap over."

Cody pressed a fist against her mouth, swallowing against the urge to gag and leaned her forehead against the cold glass of the window.

"It was the most horrible thing I'd ever done. I couldn't sleep, couldn't eat, stayed away from the mine for days trying to figure out what to do. The therapist I was seeing for depression gave me that prescription, thinking it was stress about Granny. And that's when I realized I had to put my problems aside because saving the house and taking care of Granny had to be my priorities. It was all I had.

"I thought it would be safe to hide his body far back in the mine, in some of the old workings, since the mine wasn't opening and it was just me in there. I thought everything would be fine. Until Jake started nosing around wanting to know what I was doing. And until Nate showed up looking for his dad. I should have tossed the guy down a mineshaft but I just couldn't bring myself to do that, to just throw away someone."

Rivers snorted. "She can kill people but not put them down a mineshaft?"

Cody heard the anger behind her voice, and understood what Rivers was saying even though she had no response. She simply watched the rain wishing she had never accepted the letter.

"So, yes I shot Jess. I think she was figuring everything out. She was coming by the museum a lot, asking questions.

And I kept seeing her questioning Jake. And that damn bouncing bitch, Hailey, wouldn't leave me alone. When she saw the pages from Kelly's notebook in my Jeep, I pretty much decided everything was going to come out. But I thought if I explained it all to you and Matt, you'd help me.

"I was losing everything, can you see that? Keith kept calling me wanting more money. The mine wasn't opening, the costs were climbing, Granny was getting worse. I couldn't even leave her alone anymore. And then the shittin' museum burned down. And no, that wasn't me. I needed that job. But once it burned, I didn't even have that anymore. I couldn't provide care for Granny, I was going to have to look in her eyes and tell her I'd lost her home. And I couldn't keep her safe anymore. I'd killed Nate's dad to hang onto the mine. I killed Nate to keep him from finding out about his dad. I killed a friend because he was in the wrong place at the wrong time. All to care for Granny, to let her live out the rest of her life in the home she'd grown up in, to hang onto our lives.

"I was so stupid. What I should have done was killed Keith.

"So I'm going back to the mine. There are a lot of ways to have an accident in an old mine. I know if I'm gone there won't be any financial support for Granny and the state will have to step in. God how I don't want that to happen. But I don't know what else to do, and we're going to lose the house now for sure. I'm begging you, Cody, to take care of Granny. I don't want her knowing what I've done, and I sure as hell don't want her visiting me in jail. So I'm ending this my way, and trusting you, as my friend, to watch over her for me.

"And oh yeah, I'd suggest Jess take a good look at Keith. I think he's the one who burned the museum. Think about it. Not only did one fire destroy all the stuff you were looking for, but it also destroyed stuff about the mine. Or so he thinks. But, shit, you know me and papers. Scattered everywhere. I hate to say it, but I'm beginning to think Nate's dad may have been right. Which means you and Kendra might be co-owners of my mine. So maybe you can have some financial help with Granny's care.

"I hope so anyway.

"I also hope you'll remember me as a friend."

The blood pressure cuff started inflating again, and Cody watched it tighten around Matt's bicep. She stood and walked to the edge of the bed, placing her hand lightly on his chest. She saw the heart monitor tracking him, she heard the machines working. But she needed tactile proof under her fingers, that he breathed, that he was alive.

Remember Rachel as a friend?

After she'd killed people?

After she'd shot Matt?

Anger stirred, and took root deep inside.

Remember Rachel as a friend?

Not a chance in hell.

Chapter 36

Spring had come to the high places, but down in the canyons, pockets of winter hung on with the tenacity of Burke residents. The Presbyterian Church was filling but this time Cody wasn't sitting outside in her car, afraid to go in. This time she was walking beside Jake as he pushed Matt's wheelchair up a ramp to the door. Matt had a cardboard box on his lap, and as they entered the church he asked an usher to hold it for him.

The church was only about a quarter full, but then, this was the memorial service for Nate and his father, not Kelly. This time only the people who knew the Johnson family had come. A young woman stood at the front of the sanctuary, talking to the minister. She was short, lean, and muscled, but not as stocky as Nate. Her hair was the same color though, and in the same long dreadlocks, and when she turned Cody realized that she was Nate's twin sister, Nellie, the one who had organized the memorial service.

Cell approached the young woman, talking to her with his hands as much as his voice, and the sight of him reminded Cody of a question.

"Jake, what were you and Cell fighting about?"

"Which time?"

"When I was in the gas station and you came in."

"Hell, I think that one was because he'd conned me into paying him in advance for a job. He was supposed to split up a couple cords of firewood for me. But I'd paid him something like two weeks before and he still hadn't shown."

"Can't believe you paid him before the work was done," Matt said.

"No shit." Jake lined the wheelchair up at the end of one of the aisles. "I'm a soft touch, what can I say."

Matt snorted rudely.

Cody hesitated a moment before reaching out to catch Jake's sleeve. She wanted another answer but was afraid the question would offend him.

"That last prank phone call I got…well, it sounded like the person knew I'd gone to the Oasis."

"Yeah?" Jake said.

"Well, you were the only one that knew I was going there." Cody said the words fast before she could lose her courage.

Jake stared at her a moment, and then laughed, the sound incongruous over the muted voices in the church. "I ran into Rachel and she asked where you were. She probably told Keith. But you thought I did it, didn't you?"

"No! Of course not!" Cody could feel heat rising in her cheeks.

Matt shifted in the wheelchair so he could look back at Jake. "Yes she did."

Both men were grinning as Jake side-stepped down the narrow aisle to sit in the pew. He patted the wooden seat. "Sit down Cody. It's not like you're the first person to think I'm a villain."

"If I did, it was only for a second." Cody sat down at the end of the pew next to the wheelchair and between the two men, and changed the subject to avoid any more embarrassment. "Do you think Kendra will come?" She smoothed her black dress over her knees, secretly relishing in the softness of the silk and the quiet music of tiny bells along the hem. Rivers had given it to her, along with an emerald green scarf, telling her she needed to wear something other than jeans and tee shirts.

"No," Matt said. "She's probably visiting her grandfather in jail. I heard she's resigning as mayor."

"She is," Cody said. "She told me this morning when we were talking about the mine."

"What's up with it?" Jake asked, running a hand through his disheveled hair as if trying to straighten it. Rivers had had a long battle outside the church convincing Jake to leave his hat behind.

"The lawyers are having a good time," Cody said. "But it looks like Keith's father never legally bought out the others. It kind of sounds like he just waited around for them all to die or move away, and then assumed ownership."

"So who will the owners be?" Matt asked.

Cody shifted in the pew, uncomfortable with the answer. "Kendra, Nellie, me, and Florence."

"Not Rachel?" Jake asked.

"There's no body," Matt said. "Search and Rescue found her climbing gear, her rappel rope going down into one of the shafts, with no knots. Meaning if she rappelled, she committed suicide. But like I said, they haven't found a body down there in the dark yet, and searching for it's pretty dangerous."

"She's not down there," Jake said. "I'm willing to bet she took off and staged the gear."

"Either way, doubt we'll see her again," Matt said, rubbing his thigh.

"Time for a pain pill?" Cody asked.

"Not yet. I'm trying to get off them."

Jake shifted on the pew and rubbed a hand over his stubble. "I owe you both an apology." He said the words abruptly, staccato, as if to get them out before he swallowed them back.

"For what?" Matt asked.

"Rivers told me to find who shot Jess. If I'd been able to figure out Rachel, maybe I could have kept you from getting shot. Or Cody from going through what she did."

"No apology needed," Matt said. "I didn't see it either, and it was my job."

Cody put her hand on Jake's arm. "No apologies for me, either. But can I ask you something else?"

"Shoot," Jake said, and then winced at his word choice.

"Remember stopping me on the street that day? You wanted to know if Kelly had been holding anything. What were you expecting?"

"An environmental impact statement in favor of the logging. He was supposed to have picked it up that day. I was hoping maybe he'd dropped it or something up on the trail. So I could find it and burn it."

"Like that would make it go away," Matt said, shaking his head.

Rivers and Jess came down the aisle and joined them as organ music signaled the beginning of the service. The minister talked briefly about the tragedy of losing someone too young, and as with Kelly's service, the words rang flat and rote. He finished by asking people to share their memories, and Cody remembered Rivers doing that for Kelly, reminding them who he had been. Ignoring her shaking knees, she stood and addressed Nellie.

"I didn't know your brother, and I'm not going to pretend I did, but I want you to hear one thing about him. When he was dying his last words were telling me to get away. I think most people would have been thinking of themselves, but he wasn't. And that simple act tells me he was someone I would have been very grateful to have had as a friend. I'm sorry I never got the chance."

Cody sank back onto the pew, gripping her hands. She'd never talked in front of a crowd like that and her cheeks were hot with the feeling of exposure. But Matt reached over and covered her fingers with his.

"Nicely done," he said.

The memorial service wound through more speeches, and then through a digital viewing of photographs of Nate. Cody found it incredibly sad to watch images of him throughout his life, this man she'd never known and never would. When the viewing was over, people dribbled downstairs in small groups, to a room where cake and coffee was served.

Cody, Matt, Jake, Rivers, and Jess sat around a table with a white plastic cloth, holding paper cups of coffee and tea. On the table was the cardboard box Matt had been carrying.

"Think you'll be able to pin the fire on Keith?" Matt asked Jess.

She shrugged, and then winced, one hand coming up to the raw flesh of newly formed scar tissue. "I think if we press T.J. Culhane some more he might just remember being hired to light a match."

"Jess has something for you, Cody," Rivers said, and her beautiful smile seemed to lift them all up and away from thoughts of death.

"Took some finagling," Jess said, looking very smug. "Technically this is evidence until T.J.'s trial is over. But I managed to convince people it needed to be returned since you're headed out tomorrow."

Jess dug into the pocket of her black slacks, and pulled out Cody's camera. "Didn't you say there was a picture of your grandfather on there?"

Cody took the camera carefully. "Thank you Jess. This means a lot to me."

"Turn it on," Rivers said. "Show us this man who brought you to us."

Cody pushed the power button, but nothing happened. "The battery must be dead," she said, saddened that she wasn't able to show them the grandfather who had loved her. "I'll have to get more batteries. But I have a postcard of him as a child, with Ethel. I'll bring it next time I see you."

"Wonderful," Rivers said.

"I have something here for you, too, Cody," Matt said. "Actually something for both you and Rivers."

"Me?" Rivers asked, surprised. "What did I do?"

"Besides being a pain in my ass?" Jake asked.

"Not me," Rivers said. "And hey, you need to treat me nicer because I think I've got Jim convinced to help you with your logging problem. No guarantees, but with his assistance you might have a chance."

"Bureaucrats," Jake said.

Cody put her hand on Jake's shoulder. "The alternative is a clear cut. So restrain yourself and be a good boy."

Matt took a rectangular box out of the bigger one, and pushed it across the table. "For all the stress you've been put through Rivers. And for being there for Cody."

Rivers opened the end of the box, peeked inside, and then hugged the box to her chest with a gleeful expression in her dark eyes. "Scotch."

"Not just scotch," Matt corrected. "Macallan eighteen year old. And you better make sure I'm invited when you open it."

"You're on pain meds," Jake said. "I'll have to take your place."

"You don't know the difference between expensive scotch and Coors," Matt said.

"No," replied Jake. "But alcohol is alcohol."

"And that's just plain blasphemy," Matt said, reaching back into his box. "And in a church at that. Cody, remember Charles's story about Fool's Lake?"

"The spring that rangers sent fishermen to," Cody said.

"Right. You told me Charles had signed the logbook that used to be up there. I had a hell of a time finding it, but here it is."

Matt lifted out an oversized leather book, heavily stained with hard use. The papers made brittle crackling noises as Matt carefully opened it to a flagged page and turned the book toward Cody.

People had signed in using every scrap of space on the pages, and every imaginable writing implement, including crayon. But in spite of the overlapping words, Cody spotted her grandfather's handwriting immediately. She tried to read it, but tears blurred the words and so she pushed the book back to Matt, who read the message out loud.

"After sending fishermen up, decided it was time to visit. Haven't been in years, but hope to come back. Just found out I have a granddaughter. Going to find her and bring her here, show her why Wallace gets in your blood and in your heart. Not all memories are good ones, but by god, this is home, and I hope she comes to love this place. It's her legacy, her history, and hopefully our future as family."

Cody wiped her eyes, wanting to thank Matt but finding no words strong enough to hold all the emotion she carried.

"I can't give you the book," Matt said, closing it up carefully. "But I'll have a copy made before you leave."

Cody could only nod her thanks, but she hoped he understood.

"What are your plans, Cody?" Jake asked. "Back to your old life?"

"Well, not exactly," she said slowly, not meeting anyone's eyes. "I've used up my leave of absence, and I need to go home and make sure mom is doing okay on her own. But I'm kicking around the idea of coming back with Charles's motor home. Staying in it until I can figure out what I want to do."

"Got some reasons to come back here?" Jake asked, and reached behind Cody to punch Matt on the shoulder.

"I've applied to be Florence's caregiver," Cody said, blushing. "I don't know yet if she'll be able to remain in the house, but I thought whatever happens might be easier if someone she knew was with her. Sunny offered, but she's only got so many hours in the day."

"That's a fantastic idea," Jess whispered. "I can help you."

"I'd appreciate it," Cody said. "And I thought...maybe I might try to finish what my grandfather started. Finding my dad. I'm not sure if I really want to but I think I should try."

"That should make May really happy," Rivers said.

"Yes, well, that thought was added incentive to come back here. More distance, you know?" Cody rubbed her thumbs over her fingernails, feeling the gloss of clear polish from the manicure Rivers had insisted on treating her to.

"I'm going to be making some changes, too," Matt said, twisting his coffee cup back and forth.

"Yeah, like what, moving into a motor home?" Jake asked, and this time it was Rivers who punched him.

Matt shook his head. "No. I've put my resignation in."

"But the doctors say you can go back to work," Jess said.

"Not because of the knee," Matt said. "Because I screwed up big time. I let my dislike of Hailey get in the way of listening to what she said. If I'd done my job, I wouldn't have been so fixated on Keith and I wouldn't have ended up shot, and Cody wouldn't have had to go through what she did."

"Hailey is pretty difficult to like," Jess said. "None of us listened to her. First she was fixated on Jake and then when she started going on and on about Rachel, waving that stupid flowered notebook around, I figured she'd just shifted her obsessions."

"Right," Matt said. "But that's no excuse for me, as her supervisor, blowing her off like I did. She's annoying as hell, but she's good at what she does. Better than me."

"What are you going to do?" Rivers asked.

"I've applied for a different position at the ranger station. Public liaison. You know, directions to hiking trails, questions about local flora and fauna, where the nearest outhouse is. Complaints from Jake about logging."

The laughter around the table eased the sadness that followed change.

"You might want to think about working with me," Rivers said. "I've decided it's time to take on cleaning up the environmental mess in Burke."

"I'll think about it," Matt said. "But don't expect me to chain myself to trees."

The conversation stalled for a moment, until Jake slapped his palms on the table.

"I'm out of here," he said. "People overload."

"Tactful as always," Jess said. "But we need to be going, too."

"Right," Rivers said. "I need to get home for a phone call. I have a niece out in Montana who's thinking about coming to stay with me for a while."

"Cody, let us know when you're back," Jess said, standing. "Don't forget you promised to let me treat you to a tattoo."

"And I want to take you bouldering with the Climb Naked guys." Rivers shook a finger at Jake. "And before you ask, no you can't go."

"I've written it down," Cody said as Matt choked on his coffee. "Plus going out for dinner with Sunny."

"Sure," Matt said. "Dinner with Sunny when I still haven't gotten mine."

"Life's unfair," Rivers said as she and Jess stood.

Cody stood as well, to hug Jess and Rivers goodbye, and then after a second of hesitation, Jake. He clasped her so tight her ribs cracked, and then squeezed her shoulder.

"Jake," Cody said, then hesitated.

"Yeah?"

"I never seriously doubted you."

"Don't worry about it," he said, and then gave her another rib-cracking hug.

"That's for Kelly," he said. "Friends that could have been."

Cody nodded, again with no words to voice what she felt. But Jake wasn't the type who needed words. He nodded back, slapped his hat on and left, followed by Jess and Rivers. Cody watched until the door shut behind them, and then sat down again.

"I think it is time for a pain pill after all," Matt said, kneading his thigh again.

"Good thing you're not driving."

"Cody, about that dinner you owe me."

"Yes?" Cody asked.

"How about a sleepover instead?"

Acknowledgements

This story is dedicated to those who planted the seeds:

My father, who lived with the paternity question and died with no answer. My siblings who grew up with the question and allowed me to create my own answers.

My husband. I write only for you.

My son, who stood behind me and said, "I'd put a comma in there," and was right. Keep being my inspiration. Arthur again, and Rowan, for letting me borrow the Crack Horror. Congratulations on bagging a first ascent at age thirteen.

Sabrina, a wilderness poet and an incredibly strong woman, who loves my writing, even when I don't. Thanks for sharing the woods, the trails, and the mountains, and for talking me out of tossing pages.

Sue, for forty years and counting of loyalty and unwavering friendship. Let's see what trouble we can get into in the next forty years. Jenni, for reading multiple versions, and sharing your wisdom and friendship.

For everyone in Kris's sandbox, you'll recognize compilations of names, and to any television trivia buffs out there, see if you can figure it out.

Special thanks to author Susan Schreyer for lots of coffee and hand-holding, and to Monika Younger for her artistic intuition.

For Wallace and Burke

Thanks to the past and present residents of Wallace and Burke, Idaho. For being a story and dream throughout my life, for meaning so much to my father, for giving him good memories, and for being patient with all the fictional changes I made in order to answer his question. People and places in this story evolved in my imagination to become unique and in no way are meant to represent the real Wallace or Burke, or real people. I took the liberty of moving the Ranger Station only to make it easier for the characters to get around. I also did some damage to the Mining Museum, but in reality it's just fine and a fascinating place to visit. Hopefully locals will understand the changes were made to fit what the story needed and not because the real thing needs changing. Wallace is still the center of the universe.

About the Author

Lisa Stowe writes and edits in the Pacific Northwest woods where her family has given her the nickname of 'bear magnet'. After living off-grid in the past, she has now joined the 21st Century and can be found telling stories on her blog, www.thestoryriver.com, or on her website at www.lisastowe.com.

53295617R00188

Made in the USA
Lexington, KY
29 September 2019